THE CHRISTIE AFFAIR

Nina de Gramont lives with her husband and daughter in coastal North Carolina, where she teaches Creative Writing at the University of North Carolina Wilmington. Her interest in writing about Agatha Christie began in 2015 when she first learned about the famous author's eleven-day disappearance. Christie's refusal to ever speak about this episode particularly intrigued Nina, who loves the fact that someone who unravelled mysteries for a living managed to keep her own intact. *The Christie Affair* is her fourth novel.

'This story is all about murder and lies and love and discovery. I loved it so much. I could not put it down. I read it in one sitting'
Reese Witherspoon

'A completely fascinating and fabulous piece of storytelling. I paced myself as I did not wish to miss one detail of its clever and twisty plot. Bravo to the skill and imagination of the author'
Elizabeth Buchan, author of *Two Women in Rome*

'A delightful puzzle of a book, so cleverly constructed but with real heart and soul. The ingenious yet playful mystery keeps you turning the pages right till the end, but the real treasure of the book is the poignant tragedy buried deep in its core. Such a moving and satisfying read'
Mary Paulson-Ellis, author of *The Other Mrs Walker* and *Emily Noble's Disgrace*

'*The Christie Affair* is a pitch-perfect hat-trick of a novel, delivering a fascinating glimpse into history, with the sensational and unexplained disappearance of Agatha Christie, a layered and completely satisfying murder mystery, and a moving, emotional rendering of love, loss, revenge and redemption – all with effortlessly stunning prose. I loved every page, and will be recommending this to everyone I know!'
Paula McLain, author of *The Paris Wife*

'I loved this novel. A clever re-imagining of what happened in the days when Christie disappeared as well as a stunning murder mystery which will keep the reader guessing. *The Christie Affair* is stylish, compelling and multilayered, exploring the themes of love, loss, revenge and sacrifice, tugging at our emotions as the truth is revealed. An original and captivating read that has stayed inside my head'
Jenny Quintana, author of *The Missing Girl* and *The Hiding Place*

'Nina de Gramont's skilful storytelling is exceeded only by her tenderness for her characters, and I was swept up, turning the pages and savouring them, too. This is a cracking good read'
Therese Anne Fowler, author of *A Good Neighbourhood*

Nina de Gramont

THE CHRISTIE AFFAIR

PAN BOOKS

First published 2022 by Mantle

This paperback edition first published 2022 by Pan Books
an imprint of Pan Macmillan
The Smithson, 6 Briset Street, London EC1M 5NR
EU representative: Macmillan Publishers Ireland Ltd, 1st Floor,
The Liffey Trust Centre, 117–126 Sheriff Street Upper,
Dublin 1, D01 YC43
Associated companies throughout the world
www.panmacmillan.com

ISBN 978-1-5290-5419-4

1 3 5 7 9 8 6 4 2

A CIP catalogue record for this book is available from the British Library.

Typeset in Goudy Oldstyle by Palimpsest Book Production Ltd, Falkirk, Stirlingshire
Printed and bound by CPI Group (UK) Ltd, Croydon, CR0 4YY

Visit **www.panmacmillan.com** to read more about all our books
and to buy them. You will also find features, author interviews and
news of any author events, and you can sign up for e-newsletters
so that you're always first to hear about our new releases.

For Liza Jane Hanson

Part One

Here Lies Sister Mary

A LONG TIME ago, in another country, I nearly killed a woman.

It's a particular feeling, the urge to murder. First comes rage, greater than any you've ever imagined. It takes over your body so completely it's like a divine force, grabbing hold of your will, your limbs, your psyche. It conveys a strength you never knew you possessed. Your hands, harmless until now, rise up to squeeze another person's life away. There's a joy to it. In retrospect, it's frightening, but in the moment, it feels sweet, the way justice feels sweet.

Agatha Christie had a fascination with murder. But she was a tender-hearted person. She never wanted to kill anyone. Not for a moment. Not even me.

'Call me Agatha,' she always said, reaching out a slender hand. But I never would, not in those early days, no matter how many weekends I spent at one of her homes, no matter how many private moments we shared. The familiarity didn't feel proper, though propriety was already waning in the years after the Great War. Agatha was upper crust and elegant, but perfectly willing to dispense with manners and social mores. Whereas I had worked too hard to learn those manners and mores to ever abandon them easily.

3

I liked her. Back then I refused to think highly of her writing. But I always admitted to admiring her as a person. I still admire her. Recently, when I confided this to one of my sisters, she asked me if I had regrets about what I'd done, and how much pain it had caused.

'Of course I do,' I told her, without hesitation. Anyone who says *I have no regrets* is either a psychopath or a liar. I am neither of those things, simply adept at keeping secrets. In this way the first Mrs Christie and the second are very much alike. We both know you can't tell your own story without exposing someone else's. Her whole life, Agatha refused to answer any questions about the eleven days she went missing, and it wasn't only because she needed to protect herself.

I would have refused to answer, too, if anyone had thought to ask.

The Disappearance

One Day Before
Thursday, 2 December 1926

I TOLD ARCHIE it was the wrong time to leave his wife but I didn't mean it. As far as I was concerned, this game had gone on far too long. It was time for me to play the winning hand. But he liked things to be his own idea, so I protested.

'She's too fragile,' I said. Agatha was still reeling from her mother's death.

'Clarissa died months ago,' Archie said. 'And no matter when I tell her it will be beastly.' *Fragile* was the last word anyone would use to describe Archie. He sat at the great mahogany desk in his London office, all pomp and power. 'There's no making everybody happy,' he said. 'Somebody has got to be unhappy and I'm tired of it being me.'

I faced him, perched on the leather chair usually reserved for financiers and businessmen. 'Darling,' I said. My voice would never achieve the genteel tones of Agatha's, but by then I had at least managed to wash away the East End. 'She needs more time to recover.'

'She's a grown woman.'

'A person never stops needing her mother.'

'You're too indulgent, Nan. Too kind.'

I smiled as if this were true. The things Archie hated most in the world were illness, weakness, sadness. He had no patience for recuperation. As his mistress, I always maintained a cheerful demeanour. Light and airy. The perfect contrast to his not-quite-fooled and grief-stricken wife.

His face softened. A smile twitched the corner of his mouth. As the French like to say, 'Happy people have no history.' Archie never enquired after my past. He only wanted me now, beaming and willing. He ran a hand over his hair, smoothing what was already perfectly neat. I noticed a bit of grey at the temples. It made him looked distinguished. There may have been a mercenary element to my relationship with Archie but that didn't mean I couldn't enjoy him. He was tall, handsome and in love with me.

He stood up and crossed the room to kneel before my chair.

'Archie,' I said, pretending to scold, 'what if someone comes in?'

'No one will come in.' He put his arms round my waist and laid his head in my lap. I wore a pleated skirt, a button-up blouse, a loose cardigan and stockings. Fake pearls and a smart new hat. I stroked Archie's head but gently pushed it away as he pressed his face against me.

'Not here,' I said, but without urgency. Cheerful, cheerful, cheerful. A girl who'd never been sick or sad a day in her life.

Archie kissed me. He tasted like pipe smoke. I closed my hands on the lapel of his jacket and didn't object when he cupped his hand around my breast. Tonight he would be going home to his wife. If the course I'd planned so carefully were to continue, it was best to send him to her thinking of me. A sponge soaked in quinine sulphate – procured by my married younger sister – stood guard inside me, protecting against pregnancy. Never once had I encountered Archie without preparing myself in this way, but for the moment my precautions proved unnecessary. He pulled my skirt modestly back into place, smoothing over the pleats, then stood and walked back round his desk.

Almost the moment he returned to his chair, in walked Agatha. She rapped lightly on the door and at the same time pushed it open. Her sensible heels made the barest sound on the carpet. At thirty-six, she was much taller than me and nearly ten years older. Her auburn hair had faded towards brown.

'Agatha,' Archie said sharply, 'you might have knocked.'

'Oh, Archie. This isn't a dressing room.' Then she turned to me and said, 'Miss O'Dea. I wasn't expecting to see you here.'

Archie's strategy had always been to hide me in plain sight. I was regularly invited to parties and even weekends at their home. Six months ago, he would at least have made an excuse for my presence in his office. *Stan's loaned Nan to do some short-hand*, he might have said. Stan was my employer at the Imperial British Rubber Company. He was a friend of Archie's but never loaned anybody anything.

This time Archie didn't offer up a single word to explain me, perched where I didn't belong. Agatha's brows arched as she realized her husband couldn't be bothered with the usual subter-fuge. She gathered her composure by addressing me.

'Look at us,' she said, pointing to her outfit and then mine. 'We're twins.'

It was an effort not to touch my face. I was blushing furiously. What if she had come in two minutes earlier? Would she have pretended ignorance despite all evidence, just as doggedly as she did now?

'Yes,' I said. 'Yes, it's true, we are.'

That season nearly every woman in London was a twin, the same clothes, the same shoulder-length hair. But Agatha's suit was authentic Chanel, and her pearls were not fake. She didn't register these discrepancies with any disdain, if at all. She wasn't that sort of person, a virtue that backfired when it came to me. Never once did Agatha object to the daughter of a clerk, a mere secretary, entering her social circles. 'She's friends with Stan's daughter,' Archie had told her. 'Excellent golfer.' And that was all the explanation she ever required.

In photographs from this time, Agatha looks much darker, less pretty than she really was. Her eyes were sparkling and blue. She had a girlish sprinkling of freckles across her nose and a face that moved quickly from one expression to the next. Finally, Archie stood to greet her, taking her hand as though she were a business associate. And I decided – the way someone who's doing something cruel can decide – it's all to the good: she deserves better than Archie, this pretty and ambitious woman. She deserves someone who'll collect her in his arms with un-abashed adoration and be faithful to her. As guilt crept in to discourage me, I reminded myself that Agatha was born on her feet, and that's how she'd always land.

She told Archie, likely for the second or third time, that she'd had a meeting with Donald Fraser, her new literary agent. 'Since I'm in town, I thought we might go to luncheon. Before your weekend away.'

'I can't today.' Archie gestured unconvincingly towards his empty desk. 'I've a mountain of work to get through.'

'Ah,' said Agatha. 'You sure? I've booked a table at Simpson's.'

'I'm certain,' he said. 'I'm afraid you've come by for nothing.'

'Would you like to come with me, Miss O'Dea? A girls' luncheon?'

I couldn't bear seeing her rejected twice. 'Oh, yes. That would be lovely.'

Archie coughed, irritated. Another man might have been nervous, faced with this meeting, wife and lover. But he'd moved past caring. He wanted his marriage over and if that came about from Agatha walking in on us, so be it. While his wife and I lunched he would keep an appointment at Garrard and Company to buy the most beautiful ring, my first real diamond.

'You must tell me about your new literary agent,' I said, getting to my feet. 'What an exciting career you have, Mrs Christie.' This was not flattery. Agatha's career was leagues more interesting to me than Archie's work in finance, though she wasn't well known at this time, not in the way she would come to be. A rising star not quite risen. I envied her.

Agatha put her arm though mine. I accepted the gesture with ease. Nothing came more naturally to me than intimacy with other women. I had three sisters. Agatha's face set into a smile that managed to be both dreamy and determined. Archie sometimes complained about the weight she'd gained over the past seven years, since Teddy had arrived, but her arm felt thin and delicate. I let her lead me through the offices and out onto the busy London street. My cheeks turned pink from the cold. Agatha released my arm abruptly and brought a hand to her forehead, steadying herself.

'Are you all right, Mrs Christie?'

'Agatha,' she said, her voice sharper than it had been in Archie's office. 'Please call me Agatha.'

I nodded. And then proceeded to do what I did every time she made this request – for the bulk of our time that afternoon, I didn't call her anything at all.

9

Have you ever known a woman who went on to become famous? Looking back, you can see things in memory, can't you? About the way she held herself. The determination with which she spoke. To her dying day Agatha claimed not to be an ambitious person. She thought she kept her intensity secret, but I could see it in the way her eyes swept over a room. The way she examined everyone who crossed her line of vision, imagining a backstory she could sum up in a single sentence. Unlike Archie, Agatha always wanted to know about your past. If you didn't care to reveal it, she'd create something of her own and convince herself it was true.

At Simpson's Agatha and I were escorted upstairs to the ladies' dining room. When we were seated, she removed her hat so I did too, though many other ladies wore theirs. She fluffed her pretty hair back into place. The gesture seemed less one of vanity than a way to comfort herself. She might have asked me what I'd been doing in Archie's office. But she knew I'd have a lie at the ready and didn't want to hear it.

Instead she said, 'Your mother's still living, isn't she, Miss O'Dea?'

'Yes, both my parents.'

She stared at me frankly. Assessing me. One is allowed to say it in retrospect. I was pretty. Slim, young, athletic. At the same time, I was no Helen of Troy. If I had been, my relationship with Archie might have been less alarming. The modesty of my charms indicated he might very well be in love.

'How's Teddy?' I asked.

'She's fine.'

'And the writing?'

'It's fine.' She waved her hand as if nothing mattered less. 'It's all a parlour trick. Shiny objects and red herrings.' A look

10

crossed her face, as if she couldn't help but smile when thinking of it, so I knew, despite her dismissal, she was proud of her work.

An enormous bang erupted as a white-coated waiter dropped his tray of empty dishes. I couldn't help but jump. At the table next to us, a man dining with his wife covered his head with his arms in a reflex. Not so long ago loud crashes in London meant something far more ominous than shattered dishware and, of course, so many of our men had seen the worst of it.

Agatha took a sip of tea and said, 'How I miss the calm before the war. Do you think we'll ever recover, Miss O'Dea?'

'I don't see how we can.'

'I suppose you were too young to do any nursing,' she said.

I nodded. During the war it was mostly matronly types who tended the soldiers, by design, to avert the bloom of unsuitable romances. Agatha had been assigned to a hospital dispensary in Torquay. It was where she learned so much about poison.

'My sister Megs became a nurse,' I said. 'After the war, as her profession. In fact, she works now at a hospital in Torquay.'

Agatha did not ask more about this. She wouldn't know someone like my sister. Instead she asked, 'Did you lose anyone close to you?'

'A boy I used to know. In Ireland.'

'Was he killed?'

'Let's just say he never came home. Not really.'

'Archie was in the Flying Corps. Of course, you know that. I suppose it was different for those in the air.'

Didn't that sum up the whole world? Always the poor ones carrying the world's scars. Agatha liked to quote William Blake: 'Some are born to sweet delight, some are born to endless night.' In my mind, even at that moment – lunching at Simpson's while her husband shopped for my engagement ring – I considered Agatha the former and myself the latter.

An expression kept rising to Agatha's face that I could see her actively pushing away. As if she wanted to say something, but couldn't bring herself to. She had brought me to luncheon, I'm sure of it, to confront me. Perhaps to ask for mercy. But it's easy to postpone the most unpleasant conversations, especially if confrontation is not in your nature.

To do so, and because she meant it, Agatha said, 'What rubbish, war. Any war. It's a terrible thing for a man to endure. If I had a son, I'd do whatever I could to keep him away from it – whatever the cause, even if England was at stake.'

'I think I'll do the same. If I ever have a son.'

Our meat was carved tableside and I chose a piece that was rarer than I liked. I suppose I was trying to impress Agatha. The richer the people, the bloodier they liked their steak. As I sawed into the meat the red oozing made my stomach turn.

'Do you still think of the Irish boy?' Agatha asked me.

'Only every day of my life.'

'Is that why you never married?'

Never married. As if I never would. 'I suppose it is.'

'Well,' she said, 'you're still young. And who knows? Perhaps he'll turn up one day, recovered.'

'I doubt that very much.'

'There was a time during the war that I thought Archie and I would never be able to marry. But we did and we've been so happy. We have, you know. Been happy.'

'I'm sure that's true.' Clipped and stern. Talk of the war had steeled me. A person who has nothing might be excused for taking one thing – a husband – from a person who has everything.

The waiter returned and asked if we wanted a cheese course.

We both declined. Agatha put down her fork with her meat half eaten. If her manners had been less perfect, she would have pushed her plate away. 'I must start eating less. I'm too fat, Archie says.'

'You look just fine,' I said, to soothe her and because it was true. 'You look beautiful.'

Agatha laughed, a little meanly, derision towards herself, not me, and I softened again. It gave me no pleasure to cause anyone pain. The death of her mother was dreadfully timed, too close to Archie's leaving. I'd never planned on that. Agatha's father had died when she was eleven, so in addition to the loss of her mother she now found herself in her family's oldest generation at far too young an age.

We walked outside together after Agatha insisted on paying the bill. On the street she turned to me and reached out, curling her forefinger and thumb around my chin.

'Do you have plans for this weekend, Miss O'Dea?' Her tone insinuated she knew perfectly well what my plans were.

'No,' I said. 'But I'm taking a holiday next week. At the Belle-fort Hotel in Harrogate.' Immediately, I wondered why I'd told her. I hadn't even told Archie. But something about sharing a woman's husband makes you feel close to her. Sometimes even closer than to him.

'Treating yourself,' she said, as if the concept did not appeal to her sensible nature. 'Lovely for you.'

I was thankful she didn't ask how I could afford such an extravagance. She let go of my chin. Her eyes held something I couldn't quite read.

'Well, goodbye, then,' she said. 'Enjoy your holiday.'

She turned and walked a few steps, paused, then walked back to me. 'You don't love him,' she said. Her face had utterly changed. From contained and still to wide-eyed and tremulous. 'It would be bad enough if you did. But since you don't, please leave him to the person who does.'

All my edges disappeared. I felt ghostly in my refusal to respond, like I might dissipate, the pieces of me floating off and away into the air. Agatha didn't touch me again. Instead she held my face in her gaze, examining my response – blood leaving my cheeks, the guilty refusal to move or breathe.

'Mrs Christie.' It was all I could manage to say. She was demanding a confession I did not have permission to make.

'Miss O'Dea.' Clipped, final. Returning to her usual self. Her name on my lips had prefaced a denial. My name on hers was a stern dismissal.

I stood in front of the restaurant and watched her walk away. In my memory she vanishes into a great cloud of fog but that can't be right. It was broad daylight – crisp and clear. More likely she simply walked around a corner, or into a crowd.

I was due to return to work but instead I headed towards Archie's office. My secretarial job no longer meant much to me as Archie covered more and more of my expenses. I knew he would be worried about my lunching with Agatha, and if he really did tell her he was leaving tonight, she might level the charge that I didn't love him. So it was important to leave him feeling as though I did.

On my way I passed a bookshop that displayed a mountain of copies of a pink children's book, a little teddy bear clutching the string of a balloon and flying off into the air. *Winnie the Pooh*. It looked so whimsical, I went in and bought a copy for Archie to give to Teddy. For a moment I considered giving it to her myself, as a Christmas gift. By then her parents might be living apart. Perhaps Teddy would spend Christmas with her father and me. Cosy, the three of us, exchanging gifts beneath a Christmas tree. Sometimes one did hear of children living with their father, after a divorce. And Archie always claimed Teddy loved him better. Though that was like Archie, wasn't it, not only to say such a thing but also to believe it.

When I returned to Archie's office I gave him the book to give to Teddy himself. He locked the door and drew me into his lap, unbuttoning my skirt and pulling it up around my waist.

'It won't be like this much longer,' he breathed into my ear, shuddering, though I did believe he liked it like this. Didn't all men?

I stepped off him and smoothed my skirt. My hat was still on my head, it had barely budged.

'How did she seem?' he asked, returning to his desk.

'Sad.' If she ever told him she'd confronted me, I'd deny it. 'And worried.'

'You mustn't go soft on her,' he said. 'It's kinder to plunge the knife quickly.'

'I'm sure you're right.'

I blew him a kiss and headed towards the door, hoping none of my protestations had made a dent in his resolve. My conversation with Agatha made his leaving her all the more urgent. I unlocked the latch.

'Nan,' Archie said, before I could step through the doorway. 'Next time you see me I'll be a free man.'

'Not at all,' I told him. 'You'll belong to me.'

He smiled, and I knew there was nothing for me to worry about, at least in terms of Archie breaking the news to Agatha. The man had a mission. Once he decided to do something, he did it with the coldness required of a pilot releasing bombs to cause death and havoc below. All the while sailing through the sky, untouchable.

The Disappearance

One Day Before
Thursday, 2 December 1926

I N THE HISTORY of the world there's been one story a man tells his mistress: he doesn't love his wife, perhaps never loved her at all; there's been no sex for years, not a whisper of it; his marriage is absent passion, absent affection, absent joy – a barren and miserable place; he stays for the children, or for money, or for propriety; it's a matter of convenience; the new lover is his only respite.

How many times has this story been true? Not many, is my guess. I know it wasn't true of the Christies.

That evening Archie made his usual commute from London to Sunningdale. The couple had named their home Styles after the manor in Agatha's first novel. It was a lovely Victorian house with substantial gardens. When Archie came through the front door Agatha was waiting for him, dressed for dinner. He never told me what she was wearing but I know it was a chiffon dress the shade of seafoam. I imagine the cut emphasized the swell of her bosom, but Archie only said she seemed so distracted he decided to wait till morning to tell her he was leaving. 'Emotions do run higher at night, don't they?' he said.

Agatha, who knew the news was coming, resolved to do silent battle. Usually her little terrier Peter never left her side but tonight she had sent the dog to bed with Teddy so he wouldn't be an annoyance. She tried to exude the cheerful countenance her husband required.

I've sometimes thought Agatha invented Hercule Poirot as an antidote to Archie. There was never an emotional cue Poirot missed, nor a wayward emotion for which he didn't feel sympathy. Poirot could absorb and assess a person's sadness, then forgive it. Whereas Archie simply wanted to say *Cheer up* and have the order followed.

Having decided to postpone the inevitable scene, Archie sat down to a quiet dinner with his wife, the two of them seated at opposite ends of the long dining table. When I asked what they'd discussed, he said, 'Just small talk.'

'How did she seem?'

'Sullen.' Archie spoke the word as if it were a great personal affront. 'She seemed self-indulgently morose.'

After dinner Agatha asked him to adjourn to the sitting room for a glass of brandy. He declined and went upstairs to see Teddy. Honoria, who doubled as Agatha's personal secretary and Teddy's nanny, was in the middle of putting her to bed.

The little dog dashed out the door as soon as Archie stepped inside and Teddy let out a wail of protest. 'Mother promised Peter would stay with me tonight!'

Luckily Archie had my gift, *Winnie the Pooh*, to offer as consolation. Once Teddy had torn away the wrapping excitedly, he told me, he read her the first chapter. She begged him to go on reading, so that by the time he retired, Agatha – never knowing this was her last chance to recover him – was already asleep. 'Like the dead,' Archie added.

But the following Saturday, when I arrived at Styles to return Archie's car from Godalming, I saw *Winnie the Pooh* on a table in the vestibule, still in its brown paper wrapping. And at Simpson's, Agatha had had the vague and scarcely animated look of an insomniac, feeling her way through the day after too many sleepless nights. She loved her husband. After twelve years of marriage, she loved him blindly and hopefully, as if in her thirty-six years of life she'd learned nothing about the world.

I know she wouldn't have gone to sleep before Archie came to bed. Here's what I think really happened:

Agatha was there to greet Archie when he arrived home. That much would have been true. The colour in her cheeks was high and determined. She'd resolved to win him back not with anger and threats but with the sheer force of her adoration, and so had dressed carefully. I know exactly what she wore because on Saturday morning it still lay crumpled in a heap on their bedroom floor, the maid having been too upset to collect and launder it. When I saw it there I kneeled and picked it up, holding it against me as if trying it on. It was much too long, seafoam chiffon flowing past my feet. It smelled of Yardley perfume, Old English Lavender, light and pretty.

A silly garment to wear in the middle of winter but still. How lovely she would have looked, there to greet him. Freckles sprinkled across her nose and across her breasts, high and visible. Perhaps she had a drink in her hand, not for herself (she almost never drank) but to hand to him; his favourite Scotch.

'A.C.,' she said, stepping close to him, placing one hand on his chest, letting him trade his winter coat for the drink. Since their wedding night they'd called each other that, A.C.

'Here.' Archie did not return the endearment. Along with his coat he handed her the wrapped children's book. 'It's for Teddy.' He didn't tell her I was the one who'd bought it, but she likely suspected. Archie wasn't one for books – he hadn't even read the novels she'd written, not since the first was published. Agatha slid the package unopened onto the table.

In the sitting room she poured water for herself. She was good at waiting things out. She'd waited years to marry Archie, then she waited out the war for them to live together. She sent her first book to a publisher and waited two years before they accepted it – so that by the time she received word that it would be published, she'd almost forgotten she'd written a book. She signed a miserable contract with Bodley Head for her first five novels, realized her mistake almost immediately, then waited it out instead of accepting their many offers to renegotiate. Now she was free and had moved on to a far superior publisher. A person *had* to put her mind to something and hope for the best. A person had to be willing to bide her time.

The house was too cold. Goosebumps rose on her bare arms, propelling her to stand closer to Archie. He had a hale and impenetrable mien, radiating warmth, not of the personal kind, but actual heat.

'Where's Teddy?' he asked.

'Upstairs with Honoria. Having a bath before bed.'

He nodded, inhaling the lavender. A man does like it when a woman tries, especially when she's foreign to him, as his wife had become the moment he'd decided to tell her he was leaving. Agatha had instructed the cook to prepare his favourite meal, Beef Wellington, a good winter dinner. She lit candles. Just the two of them and a bottle of good French wine. Agatha poured herself a glass to be companionable but didn't take so much as a sip. She sat, not all the way across the table, as Archie told me, but just beside him. He, left-handed, she, right-handed, their elbows bumped against each other with the intimacy of people who'd passed so many hours, living in the same home, sleeping in the same bed. Archie was only human, and worse than that, only a man. A kind of melancholy overtook him. It wasn't true that he'd never loved her at all. In fact, his determination to marry me brought to mind the last time he'd felt such urgency, which was to marry Agatha, even though the war was raging, they had no money, and both their families – especially his mother – insisted they wait. Now in the candlelight she looked much as she had on their wedding night. Their anniversary, Christmas Eve, approached. It was impossible not to dwell on memories like that, this time of year.

He finished his meal and did not stop in the nursery to bid Teddy goodnight. It was late, after all, and she would already be sleeping.

I know it was Archie who removed his wife's dress and left it crumpled on the floor. He liked a naked woman while he was fully clothed. And this was his last chance with this particular woman. Alone in their bedroom, his wife shivered with relief and joy as much as the cold. The maid had lit the fire in their bedroom. In the dim and flickering light, Agatha looked vulnerable with adoration.

Marriage. The way two lives intertwine. It's a stubborn thing, difficult to let go. Archie was not an unfeeling man and on this last night with his wife, after so many months of damming his feelings towards her, he let the floodgates open one final time.

'Agatha,' he said to her, over and over again. I suspect he also said, *I love you*. So that she would have returned the words, tears running down her cheeks as though she'd won him back for good. Not realizing, as they stayed up late, the sheets increasingly tangled as they made love again and again – that for this one night she was the mistress, never again to be his wife.

The Disappearance

Last Day Seen
Friday, 3 December 1926

AGATHA OPENED HER eyes to find herself alone. Archie had risen before dawn, leaving their night behind him as only a man can. He bathed, washing away the scent of his wife, whatever emotions he had for her already abandoned in the bedroom. Whereas Agatha stirred, the irregular discovery of her nakedness beneath the sheets immediately reminding her of all that had happened. She smiled victoriously and stretched. Archie was hers again. She had won him back.

Humming to herself, she dressed in what she would have slept in, a long silk nightdress. Before she went downstairs she added a flannel dressing gown. A quick glance in the mirror showed all she needed was quick fingers through her fading red hair. Even she, critical of herself, could see that she looked lovely. Flushed with happiness. *Happiness.* The aspect Archie admired most. Today his first glimpse of her radiant self would fill him with love, visible love. She hurried downstairs to catch him before he left for the office.

Imagine her dismay as she reached the bottom of the stairs to find Archie, dressed, his weekend valise packed, his attitude hardened.

'Surely you're not still going on your weekend?' Her face

paled, the flush left. All the delight and joy vanished before Archie could see it.

'Agatha.' His voice was full of warning. A scold. As if she were a child who had misbehaved.

'Agatha,' she echoed. Her voice rose, high pitched, spiralling up the stairs. Perhaps it travelled through the door of the nursery where Teddy lay – asleep or awake; neither parent had gone in to check on her. '*Agatha*,' she said again. 'You sound as if *I'm* the one doing something wrong. As if *I'm* the one causing trouble. I say it's you. It's *you*. Archie. Archie. Archie.'

He sighed and glanced towards the kitchen, where the cook was preparing breakfast. Honoria would bring Teddy down any moment. He didn't want anyone to overhear Agatha, whose hysteria would only grow once he'd said what there was no longer any way to avoid. He had a plan and nothing would derail it. My engagement ring sat in his valise, its hefty price tag paid in full.

'Come here,' he said, maintaining the tone of a father scolding an unruly child. 'We can talk in my study.' He stepped forward and grabbed her by the elbow.

Agatha didn't have an office of her own. She wrote her books wherever she found herself, so long as she had a table and a typewriter. Really, she didn't even think of herself as an author. Her primary occupation and identity was Married Lady. That's who she was. Married. To Archie. Who would she be if that were no longer the case?

She took a seat on the silk sofa in Archie's study. Peter trotted in and jumped up beside her. Archie didn't like dogs on the furniture but he had more important matters to address so he held his tongue and pulled the door closed with a click.

Agatha once told me that upon her first heartbreak, thrown

over by a boy she'd adored, she'd run to her mother with quivering lips. Clarissa Miller had handed her daughter a handkerchief with one hand and raised the other with forefinger pointed, moving it up and down to mark her syllables. 'Don't you dare cry. I forbid it.' Obedient by nature and wanting nothing more than to please her mother, Agatha had shuddered once, swallowing the tears as they threatened to fall.

But there hadn't only been heartbreaks. In her youth she had been gay and lively, turning down one marriage proposal after another. In fact, when Archie pressed his hand upon her she was already engaged to another young man, Tommy, who was diffident and kind, and never – she felt sure of it – would have brought her to this moment, struggling to follow her mother's erstwhile advice.

Archie didn't sit beside her on the sofa, but settled into a wingback chair close enough for her to be able to reach for him. It was a natural gesture after the night they'd spent together and she gave into it, holding out her arms.

'Agatha,' came the hard reply, and then the words she'd been dreading for months. 'There's no easy way to say this.'

'Then don't say it,' she pleaded, dropping her pathetic, outstretched arms and pulling Peter into her lap, stroking the dog to calm herself. 'Please just don't say it at all.'

'I'm only telling you what you must already know. I love Nan O'Dea and I'm going to marry her.'

'No. I won't have that. It can't be. You love *me*.' The memories of last night hovered so clear, so close, it might still have been happening. Unlike Archie she hadn't bathed. His scent clung to her, drowning out the lavender perfume. 'I'm your wife.'

'A divorce,' Archie said. It was easier to just burst out with the word as a simple statement of fact. An end goal so obvious it needed no context, not even a complete sentence. What a triumph over emotion. Archie felt nothing, not even worry about his wife collapsing in front of him, only a commitment to the word. Divorce.

Agatha sat, silent. Her hand ran faster and faster over the terrier's soft fur, her expression unchanging. Archie, unwisely emboldened, began to talk. He admitted our relationship had been going on for nearly two years.

'You needn't have told her that,' I said later, though I knew he hated to be chastised.

'You're right,' he admitted. 'I was fooled by her silence. It was the last thing I expected. It was almost as if she couldn't hear me.'

Turning too quickly to detail, he instructed Agatha to file for the divorce. 'It will have to be adultery,' he said. In those days that was the principle claim the courts allowed. 'I've spoken to Brunskill . . .'

'Brunskill!' Mr Brunskill was Archie's solicitor, an addled, moustached man. A new outrage, that he should know this assault lay in wait for her.

'Yes. Brunskill says you can just say, unnamed third party. The important thing is to keep Nan's name out of all this.'

Agatha's fervent petting of Peter halted abruptly. '*That* is the important thing?'

Archie should have realized his mistake but instead he pressed on. 'This might be in the papers,' he said, 'because of your books. Your name. A bit known, these days.'

She stood up, Peter falling to the floor with a reproachful yelp. Usually solicitous of the dog, she barely seemed to notice.

Archie remained seated. As he told me later, 'There's never any point trying to reason with a woman once she's become unhinged.'

Agatha's husband was in love with someone else. A life-changing transgression stated simply as the time of day. Now she was meant to receive this information with calm and dignity. Archie had broken rules with passion as his excuse and she was asked to rationally pick up the pieces. She was to take measures to protect her rival's reputation. It was more than she could bear. She clenched her fists and let out a scream, loud and full of rage.

'Agatha,' said Archie. 'Please. The servants will hear you, and the child.'

'The child. The child! Don't you talk to me about the child.' Because he refused to stand, she had to bend from the waist to pummel him, fists balled up, raining down upon his suited chest. The blows caused Archie no pain. He told me he had to watch himself to keep from laughing.

'How cruel you are,' I said, but let the words fall lightly, as if cruelty bothered me not one whit.

Poor Agatha. She had woken from her fondest dream into her worst nightmare. And nothing she said or did could wrest any emotion from her husband.

Finally, Archie stood. He grabbed her wrists to stop the blows. 'Enough of this,' he said. 'I'm leaving. After work, I'll be going to the Owens' for the weekend. We can sort the rest next week.'

'I suppose she'll be there too?'

'No,' Archie said, because it was the reply he thought would cause the least reaction, and lying had become second nature to him since he first got tangled up with me.

'She *will* be there,' Agatha said. 'I know she will. A house party, a couples' weekend. Only you won't be with your wife, you'll be with her, that harlot. That nasty little harlot.'

A common mistake wives make as they watch their husbands

27

go. The road back to Archie's affections was not paved with insults to me. He was that most impenetrable of creatures, an infatuated man. The darkest scowl crossed his face and he tightened his grip.

'You mustn't talk about Nan that way.'

'You,' she said. 'Telling me what I shouldn't do. *You* shouldn't go away with a woman who's not your wife. *You* shouldn't be leaving me now, when I need you most. I will talk about Nan any way I like.'

'Calm down, Agatha.'

She kicked him in the shins. As she only wore slippers it barely made him flinch. How maddening her own ineffectual strength must have been. She twisted her wrists out of his grasp so furiously that when he let go she fell backwards. Archie noted welts already beginning to form as Agatha stroked each wrist in turn, but he wasn't able to regret it, so firm was his conviction that she had brought this on herself. He had one goal and one goal only and that was to be rid of her.

The night before, Archie had succumbed to nostalgia and carnal longing. But today he returned to his mission. Like any good zealot he would not allow himself to be dissuaded. With long-legged strides he crossed the study to return to the front hallway. He picked up his valise and walked out to his car, the second-hand Delage Agatha had bought for him with money from her new contract. It was rather a grand car and Archie preened in its presence, as if its ownership were something he'd achieved entirely on his own. It had an electric starter motor, no cranking was necessary, and he could just hop in and escape. How galling it must have been, as she flung herself through the doorway, seeing him drive away in that extravagant gift.

'Archie!' she cried, running down the long drive. 'Archie!'

Dust flew up from the tyres, a cloud in front of her. Archie didn't even turn to glance through the back windscreen. His shoulders were set, firm and determined. He was gone from her, unreachable in every possible way.

'Unreachable' is the same word Honoria used later, to describe Agatha. It was Honoria's job to wake Teddy and ready her for school, and after she'd risen, she heard loud voices from inside Mr Christie's study: a marital squabble and a bad one at that. So she went to the nursery, where Teddy sat in a corner, already awake and playing with her dolls. That was the sort of child Teddy was, a seven-year-old who could climb out of bed and set to amusing herself, troubling no one.

'Hello there, Teddy.'

'Good morning.' Teddy pushed dark hair out of her eyes. She was not surprised to see Honoria. Often Teddy awoke to find both parents already gone for the day. Before she was five her parents had left her an entire year, to travel round the world. Agatha herself had been raised largely by a beloved servant she called 'Nursie'. To Agatha, it was a perfectly reasonable way to bring up a child.

'Come,' Honoria said, reaching out her hand. 'Let's find you some breakfast. Then it's dressed and off to school.'

Teddy got to her feet and slipped her hand into Honoria's. The two of them reached the top of the stairs just as Archie was escaping Agatha's histrionics in his study. Teddy reached out, as if to wave in greeting, but Archie didn't see her. He closed the door behind him. It only stood closed a moment before Agatha emerged, the air around her so thick with urgency that for a moment Honoria thought she'd been attacked. She stepped forward as Agatha flung the door open and ran outside. Teddy grabbed the edge of Honoria's cardigan, keeping her there with her, and Honoria hugged the child to her ample hip, patting her in comfort, as Agatha cried, 'Archie! Archie!'

Honoria waited inside, politely pretending none of this was happening. She heard the car drive away, but Agatha didn't return. So she shepherded Teddy downstairs and into the kitchen. Then she went back into the front hall. Styles boasted great windows at the front and back of the house. Through the former, Honoria could see Agatha standing in her dressing gown and slippers, her hair moving in the slight wind, the dust around her settling in the flat morning light. Honoria had never seen a person stand so still and yet emanate so kinetic a sense of disarray.

'Agatha?' Honoria said, stepping outside. The two women were intimate enough to put aside the formality of employee and grand lady. Honoria reached out and touched her shoulder. 'Agatha, are you all right?'

Agatha stood as if she couldn't hear, looking after the long-gone car in disbelief. When Honoria spoke again, she didn't answer. Honoria didn't feel right going back into the house, leaving her alone, but it felt so odd, the two of them. One fully clothed and ready for the day, one still as a statue, dressed as an invalid with a long road to recovery.

The spell didn't last too long. Agatha roused herself and headed into Archie's study, where she sat down to write a letter to her husband. It may have been a plea. It may have been a declaration of war. Nobody would ever know, except for Archie, who read it once then threw it in the fire.

I wonder now if Agatha had a plan. A writer, after all, she would have carefully considered every line of prose she wrote and every possibility to spring from her next movement. When I picture her at her desk, I don't see a woman in a fugue state or on the verge of amnesia. I see the kind of determination you only recognize if you've felt it yourself. Determination borne of desperation transformed into purpose. Soon afterwards, when I learned of her disappearance, I wasn't the least surprised. I understood.

I had disappeared once, too.

Here Lies Sister Mary

PERHAPS YOU'RE FINDING it difficult to feel kindly towards a homewrecker like me. But I don't require your affection. I only ask you to see me on a wintry day in Ireland, riding in a borrowed milk wagon. I was nineteen years old.

A sorrowful Irishman – old by my standards at the time – held the reins of two shaggy horses who pulled the cart. My coat wasn't warm enough for the damp chill. If Finbarr had driven me instead of his father, I could have cuddled beside him for extra warmth. But Finbarr never would have driven me where we were headed. Mr Mahoney, though, was not entirely without kindness. Every now and then he would let one hand go of the reins and pat my shoulder. It may have made him feel better but it did nothing for me. Empty milk bottles clanged as we rode over rutted dirt roads. If the bottles had been full, I expect the milk would have frozen by the time we reached the convent. It was a long road to Sunday's Corner from Ballycotton.

'I won't be here long,' I said, allowing my father's brogue into the rhythm of my words, as if anything could endear me to Mr Mahoney. 'Finbarr will come for me as soon as he recovers.'

'*If* he recovers.' His eyes were grim and looking anywhere but at me. Which would be worse? I wondered. His only son dying?

Or recovering and claiming me and the shame I'd brought? As far as Mr Mahoney was concerned the best outcome would be Finbarr getting well, then forgetting he'd ever laid eyes on me. For now what he wanted was me safely locked and stored away so he could get home and see his son alive at least one more time.

'He *will* recover,' I said, fierce with believing the impossible as only the very young can be. Beneath my coat the dress I wore held a faint spattering of blood from Finbarr's coughing.

'You sound like an Irish girl,' he said. 'Not a bad idea to keep that up. The English aren't so popular these days, around here.'

I nodded but I only understand his words in retrospect. If he had said *Sinn Fein* aloud, it would have meant nothing to me. I wouldn't have been able to say what IRA stood for. My Ireland was the ocean, the shore birds, the sheep. Green hills and Finbarr. Nothing to do with any government, its or my own.

'You're a lucky girl,' Mr Mahoney said. 'Not so long ago the only place for you would have been the workhouse. But these nuns look out for mothers and babies.'

I thought it would be better if the workhouse was the only place for me. Surely Mr Mahoney would never have the heart to deliver me to a place meant for criminals, so he'd have to let me stay with his family. As it was, I'd spent my last penny on the journey to his door. I suppose I went along with him voluntarily, but that doesn't seem the right word when you've nowhere else to go.

Finally we arrived at the convent in Sunday's Corner. Mr Mahoney jumped from the wagon and offered a broad, calloused hand to help me down. The convent was beautiful. With red bricks and turrets it loomed and rambled, looking like a cross between a university and a castle, both places I never expected to see inside. On the grass out front stood a statue of a winged angel, hands clenched at her side rather than raised in prayer. Over the convent's door, in a vaulted nook where a window should have been, stood another statue made of plaster – a nun wearing a blue-and-white habit, her palms at her sides, face out, as if offering sanctuary to all who entered.

My parents had never been religious. 'Sunday's for resting,' my father used to say, explaining why he didn't go to Mass. My mother was Protestant. I'd mostly only been to church with my Aunt Rosie and Uncle Jack.

'That must be the Virgin Mary,' I murmured.

Mr Mahoney let out a joyless chuff of a laugh, a sound that derided how little I knew about everything in the world. I'd come to Ireland hoping to live in his modest, dirt-floored house. Mr Mahoney had deep circles under his faded eyes but I could tell they'd once been just like Finbarr's. I looked at him, willing him to see me and change his mind.

'The Sisters will take good care of you.' He may have believed this was true. His voice was gentle, almost regretful. Perhaps he'd go a little way down the road then turn around to come back for me before I could even unpack. 'We'll send word to you about Finbarr. I promise that.'

He lurched my suitcase from the back of the wagon – my mother's suitcase; I'd stolen it from her before I left. She would have given it to me if I'd asked. Better yet, she would have begged me to stay, or run away with me herself. 'How could you ever have thought otherwise?' she would ask me, too late. 'I would have done anything, fought anyone, including your father, to keep from losing another daughter.'

If I'd known in that moment what I do now, I would have trudged off on my own two feet, away from the convent. I would have walked down its long drive, over the hills, and swum across the freezing Irish Sea back to England.

Inside the nuns traded my clothes for a drab, shapeless dress that wouldn't need replacing no matter how big my belly grew, and a pair of ill-fitting clogs. A young, sweet-faced nun took my suitcase. She smiled warmly and promised, 'We'll take good care of this for you.' I never saw it again. An older nun sat me down and cut my hair so that it barely covered my ears. I'd only ever worn it long and worried what Finbarr would think when he came to get me.

I didn't follow Mr Mahoney's advice and speak with an Irish brogue. Once the nuns had explained the rules of my new home, I barely spoke at all, not for weeks.

A young person can't know her life, what it will be or how it will unfold. When you grow older, you gain a sense that hardships occupy particular moments in time, which, by and by, will pass. But when you're young, a single moment seems like the whole world. It feels permanent. Years hence I would go on to live a bigger life. I would travel all over the world. But that winter I was scarcely more than a child. I knew exactly two places: London and County Cork and only tiny pockets of both. I knew I was young but I didn't understand *how* young, or that youth was a fleeting condition. I knew the war had ended but I didn't yet believe it. The Great War had seemed not so much an event as a place, unmovable as England but nowhere near as destructible. In London my father's favourite pub had been blown to rubble, kegs of ale rolling out onto the street as more bombs fell. For the rest of his life my father would say the world lost its innocence during the Great War.

The first task I was given at the convent – my hair shorn, my own clothes taken away – was tending the nuns' graveyard. With two other girls, both of them heavily pregnant, I went out to sweep and rake, and clean the headstones of lichen. The cold air might have tasted like freedom if not for the iron bars extending around the perimeter, as far as I could see. To the right was a high stone wall. Thin sounds carried over it, which I didn't realize were the voices of small children, brought out for a breath of air before their supper. Visible through the iron bars lay the road that led away from the convent; no sign of Mr Mahoney returning for me with a change of heart. Neither of the other girls spoke to me. We weren't supposed to speak at all, or even know each other's names.

The nuns' headstones were thick crosses, each one etched with the words *Here Lies Sister Mary*. As if only one woman had died but she somehow needed fifty graves. I ran my coarse cloth over the stones, dipping my fingers into the carved grey words. And I knew in that moment. The world had never been innocent.

But I had been innocent.

Let's go back a little further. Before the war, this time. See me at thirteen – skinny and nimble as a cricket – the first time my parents sent me to spend a summer at my Aunt Rosie's and Uncle Jack's farm.

'Nan likes to run,' my father said, formulating the plan. 'She wasn't meant for the city, was she.' He worked as a clerk at the Porphyrion Fire Insurance Company, and often said these same words – not meant for the city – about himself. It pained him to stoop long hours over a desk for little money. I always suspected

Da would have regretted leaving Ireland, if that wouldn't have meant regretting us. His wife was English and that meant his family was too. Except, apparently, for me.

My sisters Megs (elder) and Louisa (younger) were proper girly girls, interested in clothes and hair and cooking. Or at least that's what they pretended to be interested in. My sister Colleen (eldest) only cared about books and school. I liked books, too, but I also liked kicking a football with the neighbourhood boys. Sometimes after dark my father would come and find me with them, sweaty and filthy in an empty lot.

'If she were a boy, she could be a champion,' he boasted.

'She's too old for that now,' my mother complained, but my father took pity.

'Those other three are yours,' he said to Mum, 'but this one's my Irish girl.'

My father had grown up on a farm just outside the fishing village of Ballycotton. Since I'd been born he'd gone back to visit once or twice when his brother paid the way. But there'd never been enough money for us all to travel there. The thought of my going at all, let alone for a whole summer, was thrilling. I knew it was a modest house but much roomier than our London flat, which only had two bedrooms, one for my parents and one for us four girls. Uncle Jack had done well with the farm. His wife Rosie inherited a small amount of money when her father died, and they'd added solid wood floors and lined the walls of the sitting room with bookshelves. They kept the grass near the house cut short for lawn tennis. ('Tennis,' my father scoffed, when he told us. 'Now that's an idea above his station.')

The landscape existed in my mind, the most vivid green. Rolling hills and low stone walls – uninterrupted miles for me to kick a football through the meadows with my little cousin Seamus. I clasped my hands together and fell to my knees beside my mother, imploring her to let me go, only partly joking about the fervour.

My mother laughed. 'It's just I'll miss you,' she said, and I jumped to my feet and threw my arms around her. She had a dear, freckly face and wide green eyes. Sometimes I regret losing my East End accent because it's meant losing the sound of her.

'I'll miss you, too,' I admitted.

'It won't be a holiday,' my father warned. 'Jack'll pay your passage but you'll be doing plenty of chores to pay him back.'

Most of the chores would be outdoors, with horses and sheep, a joy to me. I was grateful that my uncle would hire a girl to do them.

And so we come to the Irish boy. Finbarr Mahoney was a fisherman's son. Two years before we met, he came upon a wizened farmer at the village docks, about to drop a puppy – the runt of a litter of border collies – into the freezing sea.

'Here,' Finbarr said, hoisting a bucket of mackerel. 'I'll trade you.'

Nobody would have known there was anything urgent in the transaction. Finbarr had the lightest, smiling air about him. As if everything – even life and death – was easy. He hoisted the puppy under his chin and handed over the bucket, knowing he'd have to pay his father back for the fish.

'The man was about to throw the puppy away,' Finbarr's father scolded. 'Do you really think he expected to be paid for it?'

Finbarr named the dog Alby, first bottle feeding then training him. Uncle Jack was glad to hire Finbarr to bicycle over to the farm on his days off the boat, to help move sheep from one pasture to the other. Jack said Alby was the best herding dog in County Cork.

'It's because of the boy,' Aunt Rosie said. 'He's got a way with creatures, hasn't he. He could turn a goat into a champion herder. You can't tell me another handler would have the same results with that dog.'

My uncle's collie was a passable herder but nothing to Alby. I thought that dog – small, slight and graceful – was the most beautiful thing I'd ever seen. I thought Finbarr – hair black and silky, gleaming nearly blue in the summer sun – was the second most beautiful. He had a way with creatures, as Aunt Rosie had said, and after all, what was I? Finbarr was a few years older than me. When he rode by, he'd pretend to tip the hat he wasn't wearing. I have never liked people who constantly smile, as if they think everything's funny. But Finbarr smiled differently, not out of amusement, but happiness. As if he liked the world and enjoyed being in it.

'It seems a wonderful thing,' I said to my Aunt Rosie that evening, while we did the washing up, 'to always be happy.'

Right away she knew who I was speaking of. 'He's been like that his whole life,' Aunt Rosie said, with deep fondness. 'Sunny. Proves rich or poor doesn't matter, if you ask me. Some people are just born happy. I think that's the luckiest thing. If you're sunny inside, you never have to worry about the weather.'

One evening after supper, Finbarr bicycled over to the house when Seamus and I were playing tennis. I'd learned to play in my first week and now won every game. 'I don't know where you get the energy after a full day of work,' Uncle Jack had said to us, shaking his head in fond admiration.

'Where's Alby?' Seamus called to Finbarr. He was ten then and as dazzled by the dog as I was.

'I left him at home. I thought you'd be playing tennis. He'll chase the balls and spoil the game.'

My uncle's collie, Brutus, lay under the porch, tired after a day of herding, uninterested in playing.

'You can play with Nan,' Seamus said, handing over his racket. 'Win one for me, will you?' His red curls drooped from the failed attempt to best me.

I bounced the ball on my racket, recognizing it as showing off but not able to help myself. Finbarr smiled as usual, blue eyes turned grey by fading evening sunlight. 'Ready, then?' I hit the ball over the net before he could answer. We goofed like that a bit, sending the ball back and forth to each other. Then we played in earnest. I won two games before Alby came crashing over the hills. Running straight for Finbarr, then changing course, leaping to snatch the ball from the air.

We threw our rackets down and chased him. There were other balls but it seemed the natural thing to do. Laughter filling the sky. Uncle Jack and Aunt Rosie came out to the porch to laugh along with us. Finally Finbarr stopped running, stood stock still and yelled, 'Alby, stop.'

The dog halted so immediately, so precisely, it was clear Finbarr had this power all along.

'Out,' Finbarr commanded, and Alby spat the ball onto the grass. Finbarr approached him with measured steps, scooped the ball up and held it in the air. 'Nan,' he said, 'make a wish.'

'I wish I could stay in Ireland forever.'

He threw the ball, a long arc, and Alby went rushing for it, catching it mid-air, paws miles above the ground.

'Granted,' Finbarr said, and turned to me. Magical enough to make it so.

A few days later, he came by the house after helping Uncle Jack. I had finished mucking out the stables and lay on the hill in a pocket of clover, still reeking of manure, reading *A Room with a View*. Brutus lay beside me, resting his head on my stomach.

'Your uncle will need a new dog before long,' Finbarr said. Alby stood at his side, ears perked. 'You can tell they're getting old when they're tired at the end of the day.'

'Doesn't Alby get tired sometimes?' I shaded my eyes to see him.

'Never.' Finbarr said it with a confidence so firm it had to be wishful.

'Well, Brutus will never get old,' I said, also wishful, patting the dog's narrow, tawny head. From somewhere nearby a skylark chirruped, continuous and complaining. Of course, there were birds in London but I'd never noticed them much. Since coming to Ireland I'd learned the sky was its own separate universe, just above our heads, teeming with its own brand of singing life.

'I brought you something.' Finbarr held out a four-leaf clover. I reached for it without sitting up and straight away the fourth leaf fluttered away. He'd been holding it there with his finger.

'Fake luck.' I flicked it away with a laugh, still delighted.

Finbarr flopped down beside me. He never minded being contradicted, just like he never minded me winning game after game of tennis. He never minded anything.

'I hope I don't smell like fish,' he said.

I thought about lying and saying no. Instead I said, 'Well, I smell of sheep and horse shite, so we're a good match.'

'I smell of those things too.' He wove his fingers together, arched his arms over behind his head and made a pillow of his hands. 'You like to read, do you?'

'Yes.'

'I could read that book when you're done.' He stared straight up at the sky, not at my book. 'Then we can talk about it.'

'Do you like to read?'

'No. But I could start.'

'This one's mostly about a girl.'

'I don't mind reading about girls.'

I turned my head and stared at him, and he tilted his head towards me. Long black eyelashes framed eyes of layered blue. Soon Uncle Jack would come up over the hill and he wouldn't like to see us, lying side by side, even though we were a good two feet apart.

'I think I'd like to be a writer,' I said. It was nothing I'd ever thought of before. I liked to read but had never tried my hand at stories or poems.

'You'd be a grand writer,' Finbarr said. 'You'd be grand at anything.'

He put a strand of grass between his teeth and turned his eyes back to the sky. Legs crossed at the ankles. Alby tugged at his trouser legs, dissatisfied with a full day of running, or else eager to get home for the evening meal.

'Nan O'Dea,' my aunt called from the house. 'You get up this minute, please, and wash for supper.'

I knew the sternness in her voice was over me and Finbarr lying down together, not my need to wash. We jumped to our

feet, both of us with mussed hair, sun from a day working outdoors rosying our cheeks.

'Stay for supper, Finbarr?' Aunt Rosie called, forgiving him,
as no one could ever help but do.

'I'd love to, Mrs O'Dea.'

With as much energy as the younger of the two dogs, we raced
each other to the house. Finbarr won. He jumped on the porch
with both feet, raising his arms up in the air. Victory.

Sometimes you fall in love with a place, dramatic and urgent as
falling in love with any person. I started begging to return to
Ireland almost the moment I arrived back in London. My sisters
belonged to my mother and England, but Ireland was where I
belonged. I had an ancestral memory of those green hills. The
place lived in my bones so they ached when I was away from it.
At that age, when I thought of Finbarr, it was as another part of
the landscape.

'I'll only send you back if you promise never to stay,' my
mother said. 'I don't want any of my girls living far from home.
Not even you, Colleen.'

Those last words were spoken in a loving tone but Colleen
didn't answer. She sat sprawled at the kitchen table, her green
eyes fixed on the pages of a book by Filson Young about the
Titanic. Her wild blonde hair spilled onto the table, curtaining
her face. The rest of us had brown hair and brown eyes like our
father.

Mum laughed and shook her head. 'The roof could fall in
around that one and she wouldn't notice.'

Louisa, the most practical of all of us, pushed her hand
against Colleen's shoulder. Colleen sat up, blinking, as if just

woken. 'She's already living off far from home,' Louisa said, tapping the pages of the book.

Oh, let me pause for a moment here. Colleen, seventeen years old, with her life ahead of her. All of us together and hopeful for the future, in the tiny, rundown kitchen that was the heart of our home. Our mother still able to believe her four girls would transition seamlessly from providing her a house full of children to one full of grandchildren.

My father stamped in, breaking the merriment as he sometimes did, carrying his heavy day with him. 'That Jones boy was hanging about outside waiting for you,' he said to Colleen.

She put her book aside and lifted her heavy hair to knot it on top of her head. Years later I'd read a poem by William Butler Yeats and chafed at the lines, '*only God, my dear, / Could love you for yourself alone / And not your yellow hair.*' It brought my sister to mind, and how boys who didn't know a thing about her loved her in an instant. My mother worked a few days a week at a haberdasher's, Buttons and Bits. One time Colleen covered a shift for her, and the owner forbade her from ever working there again because she drew too many boys, leaning on the counter with no interest in buying anything. Colleen's hair was like a siren, screaming out to the city streets, drawing attention, and not from God. I hated that poem.

Every night when we sisters settled into our beds in the room we shared, Colleen would tell us stories, sometimes recounting the book she was reading and sometimes making up her own. There were mornings all four of us woke with a stoop in our back, our stomachs aching from having laughed so hard the night before. I would have loved Colleen if she had no hair at all. So would Megs and Louisa. And my mother.

'That Jones boy can wait all he likes,' Colleen said. 'I never said I'd see him.'

'There must be something you do,' my father said, shaking off his coat. 'To lead those blokes on.'

Colleen let out a quick, outraged laugh. Just yesterday Derek Jones and two other boys had dogged Colleen and me on our way to the Whitechapel Library. 'You're spoiling our walk,' she'd finally told them, sharp and firm, and they drifted off with longing glances over their shoulders. Colleen wore a knitted woollen hat and pulled it down over her ears. Much as she liked to disappear into books, when she returned to the world, she was direct and no nonsense. 'Lucky me with such admirers, eh, Nan?' she'd said.

'Hush with that,' Mum said to our father. 'She does nothing but live in the same world with them. Do you want me shaving her head? Leave the girl be.'

Colleen snapped up her book and disappeared into our room while the rest of us worked on dinner. Mum patted my back because I was nearest, and it always soothed her to touch one of her children. Perhaps she was thinking what she must have already known. Sometimes living in the same world with them was all it took.

The next summer, Finbarr came to the farm for tennis almost every night. He trained Alby to lie absolutely still, no matter what happened. I think Alby would have expended less energy running ten miles than it took to fight his every instinct and stay frozen in the face of that bouncing tennis ball. But stay frozen he did, never jumping to his feet until Finbarr gave him the command.

'Ready. Ball,' Finbarr would say, and finally the dog could catapult into the air.

In the autumn, back home at my family's dinner table in London, I listed the tricks Alby could do.

'Finbarr tells him to sidestep one way and then another. He tells him to stand still until he gets the command to move.'

'Not so impressive for that breed,' my father said, from the looks of him remembering the dogs of his youth.

'I'm not done. Alby can do all the usual tricks – sit, sit pretty, cover. Uncle Jack says he's the best herding dog he's ever seen.' This would mean he'd be the best my father ever saw. 'And Finbarr taught him to catch a football and balance it on his nose. He taught him to jump on a horse's back and sit pretty.'

'You make it sound as if Finbarr's the clever one,' said Megs. 'I'd say it's the dog.'

'They're both clever.' But I knew Finbarr could do the same with any dog. He had a gift.

'Perhaps I'll go next summer, too,' Megs said.

'Give your sister some competition for this clever Mahoney boy,' my father said.

My sisters and I had a particular look we exchanged when my father said something ridiculous. We would never fight among ourselves over a boy.

Mum ended the conversation by saying what she always did, speaking to me but looking at Colleen. 'Don't you go marrying that Ballycotton boy. I don't want to have grandchildren I only see but once a year.'

'Why do you always look at me first?' Colleen objected. 'I'd be the last one ever to leave you, Mum.' She stood up and collected our plates, stopping to give Mum a kiss on the cheek.

That night in our room Colleen said, 'What if I go with you next summer, to get out of the city? Do you think I'd like it?'

Colleen and I slept in one bed, by the window, Louisa and Megs in another, pressed against the wall. I sat up and said, 'Oh, you'd love it.' I started to spill into my usual paeans for Ireland and she clapped a hand over my mouth.

'Yes, I know,' she said. 'It's sheer heaven. But even heaven's not for everyone.'

'Heaven may not be. But Ireland is.'

The following summer I was fifteen. Uncle Jack's farm was going strong, but not strong enough to pay passage for two of us.

'I wonder if Colleen should have a turn,' Mum said, when Da got Jack's letter. She was tying a bow at her collar, trying to look smart on her way to work at Buttons and Bits.

'Oh, I'd never take Ireland away from Nan,' Colleen said quickly, before I even had a chance to turn pale with loss.

'Just as well,' Da said. 'I want this one here where I can see her.' He tapped her chin fondly but the way Colleen bit her lip I could tell she knew he was only half joking.

The exchange occurred so fast I only realize in the telling of it the debt I owed my sister. Travelling back to Ireland on my own. I must have had my share of doubts and forebodings, during this time in my life, as we do in all times of our lives, even childhood. But what I remember is a beautiful ignorance of everything the future held. Ignorance of the looming war, and how it would permeate all our days to come. Reality wasn't the newspaper making my uncle's face crease with worry. Reality was the way the ocean carried through the air I breathed. Reality was the clean white sheets we hung on the clothes line to dry in the sun, so that by the time they got to our beds a hint of brine stayed with them, filling our dreams with waves, rocks and seals. Reality was the black-haired, blue-eyed boy and his dog, travelling over green hills to see me.

'Nan,' Aunt Rosie called. It was morning. I had just come downstairs and was tying my apron on to help her with the boxty. 'Finbarr Mahoney's out front. He's wanting you to ride with him.'

'May I go?'

'Sure you may.' As much as my mother hated the idea of my one day moving to Ireland, her sister-in-law loved it. 'Jack's got errands in town so there's no work with him today. You can ride Angela. Let Finbarr take Jack's horse. Be home in time to help me with supper. And take Seamus with you.'

The three of us rode half a mile down the road, towards the shore. Alby trotted beside us. Finbarr drew his horse to a stop and pulled tuppence from his pocket. He sailed the coin over to Seamus. It was a good toss but Seamus missed it. He had to struggle down from his horse to collect it off the road.

'There's a good lad,' Finbarr said. 'Go off on your own, will you? We'll meet you here in a few hours.'

Seamus tossed the coin back to Finbarr. He was only twelve but knew he'd been sent along as my chaperone. 'I think I'll be staying,' my cousin said, and climbed back on his horse.

Finbarr laughed. He clucked and his horse took off, galloping towards Ballywilling Beach. I understood I was meant to follow, the two of us outrunning my cousin, but Seamus was a stalwart sort and he saw through this plan. He had also been practically born in the saddle and was a much better rider than Finbarr, who'd never had his own horse, or me, who'd only learned to ride two years ago. So, as Aunt Rosie envisioned, it was the three of us, riding in a group, sandpipers and plovers rising into the sky to get out of our way. Clouds overhead moved aside to let the sun through. I would have betrayed my mother in an instant, taking myself and future children away from London, across the sea, to live on these shores forever.

'The tide's out,' Finbarr said, as my horse came to walk abreast of his. 'We can pick across the tide pools from one beach to the next.'

Horse hooves clipped over tiny pebbles and dipped into the salty water. Alby splashed through the waves, porpoising through the deeper shallows. We climbed off the horses and Finbarr showed me some whistles he'd been working on as commands. Seamus stayed on his horse, a polite distance, eyes on us.

'Here,' Finbarr said, trying to teach me to whistle. He cupped his hand around my chin, pushing my lips into a pucker.

I tried to release the same sharp-noted whistle that had made Alby run forward, then backtrack in a wide circle. But the saddest little bit of breath came out.

'Try with your fingers,' Finbarr said. He put both forefingers into his mouth and let out a noise so loud it made me jump. Alby raced forward and came to a sitting stop at our feet. Finbarr took a small rubber ball from his pocket and cocked his arm to throw it.

'Make a wish,' he said.

'I wish this day would never end.'

The ball and the dog flew.

'Granted,' Finbarr said, when Alby caught it.

Alby trotted back to us and spat the ball at our feet. I kneeled to embrace him. 'Thank you, Alby. You're beautiful. You're perfect.'

'Just like you.' Finbarr kneeled beside me and pushed my hair behind my ears.

'None of that,' Seamus called. His voice hadn't changed yet.

'Thank you for joining me, Nan,' Finbarr said, when we'd

returned the horses to the barn. 'There's always work to be done but I hope we can go for another ride together before the summer's end.'

'I hope so too.'

August came and with it the war. Finbarr appeared at our farm. That's how I'd come to think of it. Not just Jack's, Rosie's and Seamus's farm. Mine too.

From the window in the kitchen I could see Finbarr walking over the hill, Alby at his heels. The boy and dog with matching strides, at once purposeful and carefree. There was no conscription; Finbarr joined the British Forces with his parents' blessing because that's what patriotism meant in those days, to a certain kind of person. *Britons never, never, never shall be slaves* and *Come and do your bit*. My Uncle Jack would join, too, once the efforts were underway. But we didn't know that yet. For now war was a young man's business.

'Go on out,' Aunt Rosie said, when she caught me watching through the window. This time she didn't send Seamus with me. She knew what Finbarr had come to say. We make special dispensations for soldiers, even when it comes to girls.

'I'm sorry to leave,' Finbarr said. His voice was sombre but the lightness hadn't left him. None of this was real. War was nothing but a ruined summer. 'This wasn't how I imagined things would go.'

Tears clouded my eyes. At first this embarrassed me but Finbarr reached out and took my hand.

'Are you frightened?' I asked.

'Sure, I think I am. Though I don't quite know what to be frightened of. I can't hardly imagine what it'll be like.' The world around us stood green and untroubled. 'Do you know what I *can* imagine? After it all. The war won't take long. Six months tops and it'll all be over. And you'll come to Ireland to stay, and we'll have a farm of our own, and I'll train dogs, and you'll write books.'

My face broke open into a smile that nearly cracked my body in two. He hadn't said the word, married, I was too young for that, but everything else he'd said spelled it out, didn't it? I could marry Finbarr. I could marry Ireland. My future was sealed, just one quick war to get out of the way.

'Will you pray for me?' Finbarr asked.

My father had left his religion when he left Ireland. I had never prayed in my life, not even when I went to church with Rosie and Jack, but I promised I would.

'May I have a picture of you?' he said, another soldierly request.

'I don't have one here.' My parents had exactly one picture of me, with my three sisters, taken and framed years ago. 'But I'll get one made. I'll send it to you. I promise.'

Finbarr gathered me in his arms and held me a long while. He didn't rock or sway or move. He just stood, his arms tight, our bodies together. I wished we could stay inside that stillness. No moving forward into the future, nor ever leaving that precise spot. Finbarr's lips rested in the curve of my neck. I could feel Aunt Rosie watching from the window but I didn't care, not even when Finbarr finally pulled away and kissed me a long time, until Rosie knocked on the window loud enough for us to hear and pull apart.

'You're my girl,' he said, holding me by the shoulders. 'Isn't that the truth, Nan?'

'Yes,' I said. 'It is.'

He pulled a Claddagh from his pocket and slipped it onto my

right ring finger, crown pointing towards me. I was taken. There was a tiny emerald in the crown, no bigger than a crumb from a slice of soda bread. Terrible to admit, the main emotion I felt was joy, crackling through my body. How many girls that summer felt the same callow happiness, a boy admitting his love and bestowing a ring before walking off to war? We didn't know what it meant. None of us did.

The Disappearance

Last Day Seen
Friday, 3 December 1926

S OMETIMES A LIFE is so entirely disrupted, on such a large and ungraspable scale, all one can do is face the ruined day. After Archie drove away, Agatha tried to pull herself together. Briefly, she placed her hands on the keys of her typewriter then gave up at once. Nothing she wrote would be any good. Nothing she did would be any good until she could sort things out with Archie – until she could rectify this mess. She would find a way to do this today and then she would write tomorrow.

Despite what was widely reported only days later, Agatha never contemplated suicide. This was not in her nature. In fact, the idea affronted her. When hearing of someone else's suicide, she always felt enraged. Wasteful and cowardly. As long as there was life there was hope.

Hope. She could crank up her beloved Morris Cowley and follow Archie to London. She could march into his office and grab him by the lapel and insist he see the necessity of working things out. She could shake his love for her back into him. He would remember she was flesh of his flesh. He would not go away for the weekend with his mistress but end things with her, and return home where he belonged.

All of that would involve a scene. Agatha had not been

raised to cause scenes, or to display emotions in public. She was raised to keep busy, so she bundled up in her fur coat and accompanied Honoria and Teddy on their walk to school. 'Here,' she said to Teddy, handing the little girl her hoop and stick. 'You can spin this along the way.'

Teddy obliged till the end of drive, then tossed the hoop on the grass to skip ahead. Peter followed her. He was a wonderfully companionable dog; there was never any question of a leash. Agatha reclaimed the hoop and rolled it herself as they walked along the dirt road.

'My mother didn't believe in schooling for a girl,' Agatha said to Honoria. 'She thought it was best to let my mind develop naturally.'

Honoria knew this perfectly well but listened attentively as if hearing it for the first time. A person in despair likes to visit the past. Agatha's past had included her beloved Nursie, and a governess here and there. She'd spent occasional months in proper schools in Torquay, and overseas when she was older. And she'd gone to finishing school; one couldn't do without that. Honoria nodded, as if finishing school would have been an option for her.

'But mostly I ran wild in Torquay, all over the grounds at Ashfield.' She stared after Teddy, a pretty child whose brown hair seemed to grow richer and darker by the day. Agatha's eyes glazed over with the past, as she remembered how she used to roll her hoop in the gardens at home, through the dark ilex, past the elms, around the big beech tree, making up imaginary friends to keep her company. Did Teddy have the same goings-on in her private thoughts? Did she entertain herself with endless stories and invented companions? Or was she only concerned with the tangible world, the real friends that would preclude a need for pretending?

'Oh, Honoria,' Agatha said. The hoop calmed her but slowed them down. It was child-size and she had to stoop to make it work. Teddy ran ahead down the road, in sight but out of earshot. Agatha gave up, tossing it to the side to collect on their way home.

'You'll have to face it, Agatha.' Honoria was weary of the way Agatha believed the game was still on, when so clearly it had already been won by someone else. 'I know it's hard but face it you must. He's gone for good.'

'I simply can't believe that.' Agatha would never speak of intimate things between herself and her husband so she didn't tell Honoria about the night before. Instead she rattled off a list of examples, friends she knew whose husbands had had a lark with some other woman but then got over it and returned home. She thought again of waiting out her contract with Bodley Head so that she could settle handsomely at William Collins. The strategy had worked with her career and now it would work with her marriage. All one needed to get through these things was patience and a plan.

Honoria listened but it sounded to her like desperation. She could tell by the way Agatha wrung her hands, she knew it was desperation too. Sometimes hard truths needed to be stated plainly.

'Colonel Christie won't get over it,' Honoria insisted. 'I'm sorry to say so, but it's no use painting the lily. I see it in his face. And why would you want to stay married to a man who prefers that little tart? Better to face facts. He's gone from you.'

'Gone from me,' Agatha echoed. Her cheeks stung from the chilly air.

Her mother had warned her only last summer – the summer that turned out to be her last – not to spend too much time in

Torquay, away from her husband. 'If a woman spends too much time away from her husband, she loses him,' her mother had said. 'Especially a husband like Archie.'

And indeed at that time Archie was already deeply embroiled with me, and somewhere inside her Agatha knew it, and all the same she *refused* to know it – refused to see she could lose her mother and her husband in so brief a span of time. So she had squeezed her mother's frail hand and ignored the death rattle in her voice, and promised, 'There's no man more loyal that Archie. He's faithful to his core. You can bet your life on that.'

Perhaps her mother *had* bet her life on it. And lost.

By this time Teddy, always bold and impatient, had gained a considerable distance ahead of Agatha and Honoria. Sunningdale, in Berkshire abutting Surrey, was an easy distance to London by train. The houses were far apart from each other and private, with lovely gardens. The roads weren't paved, and dust flew up when the occasional carriage or bicycle or automobile went by. The two women were not hoverers by nature and were happy to let Teddy meander ahead. They didn't worry when she crested the hill and disappeared.

As Honoria and Agatha caught sight of her again, a good way down the road, they could also make out the figure of a man, kneeling on the ground, talking to her.

'Do you know him?' Agatha asked Honoria. For all she knew this was someone they ran into regularly, part of their daily routine.

'No. I don't believe I do.'

Both women shielded their eyes from the sun with their hands. Strangers always seemed to take to Teddy. Once on the beach at Torquay a woman had scooped her up and hugged her.

Agatha could see the man patting Peter's scruff with both

hands in a way that made her feel he must be the right sort. Then the man stood. He was tall – taller than Archie – and young. Seeing the women, he raised his hand to his forehead in a salute. Instead of heading towards them or away from them on the road he stepped into the hedgerow.

'How peculiar.' Agatha watched the spot where he'd stood, as if he'd been a mirage she could make reappear by squinting into the sun.

'Teddy,' Honoria called. 'Stay where you are now, you hear me?'

By the time they reached her the man was nowhere in sight. Teddy waited, shifting from one foot to another. 'It's too cold to stand still,' she said. In her mittened hands she held a little figure, carved from wood recently; Agatha caught the scent of sawdust as Teddy held it up to show her.

'How lovely,' Agatha said, though her brow furrowed in consternation. 'Is it a dog?'

'It is,' Teddy said. 'Mr Sonny gave it to me.'

'Is that who you were talking to? Mr Sonny?'

'Yes. He said I could call this dog Sonny, too, if I like.'

'Well, then you shall.' Agatha took the little girl's hand.

'He says in America all dogs are named Sonny.'

'That hardly seems likely, does it? Was he American?'

'I don't know.'

'We'd better get a move on,' said Honoria, 'if we're to get to school on time.'

'I think I'll go home,' Agatha said. 'See what I can get done.'

'You won't go anywhere?' Honoria cautioned, meaning, you won't go to Archie. 'Promise?'

'Promise.'

Agatha stood in the road as Honoria and Teddy walked on.

She watched them until they disappeared, Teddy with a jolly skip in her step, holding the hand-whittled dog high in her hand. Agatha found herself racked with inordinate worry and regret. She should have taken the dog herself, put it in her pocket, to make sure it wouldn't be lost.

Perhaps Archie will come home, she thought. Perhaps during the day he'd remember all that passed between them last night – and all these last years – and return to his senses. Become, once more, the man who'd pressed so urgently for her hand in marriage. When dinnertime came round, he would march through the door, suitcase in hand, no use for it now, as he'd decided to come home to stay.

You may well wonder if you can believe what I tell you about things that occurred when I myself was not present. But this is as reliable an account as you can ever hope to receive. Think for a moment. Don't you know about events that pertain to you, but which you didn't witness? Don't you find yourself, sometimes, recounting them? There's plenty we remember that we never saw with our own eyes, or lived with our own bodies. It's a simple matter of weaving together what we know, what we've been told and what we imagine. Not unlike the way a detective pieces together the answers to a crime.

For example, Inspector Frank Chilton, who's not yet important to this story but who will soon become so. The two of us have stayed in touch, written letters to each other about the different ways we remember this time, recreating for each other what little we didn't already know. And then there's everything Archie and Agatha have told me. And what I know about both of them.

Some reports of this day, the one which would turn into the night Agatha disappeared, claim Agatha paid a visit to Archie's mother. But Peg – who meted out admonishments in her thick Irish brogue – was the last person Agatha would have wanted to see. Peg had never been on Agatha's side, not a single time. Like my father, Peg hailed from County Cork. Her answer to all ills was a dismissive admonition: *You must get over it.* Why visit someone who'd tell Agatha what she already knew? There was no choice but to get over her mother's death and the defection of her husband. Agatha was brought up to get on with things, to keep her head and never make a fuss.

But that evening, the clock's chimes persisted, one after the other, and her husband didn't return. How she lost her head. How the fuss rose up inside her.

Agatha locked herself in Archie's study, feeling torn to pieces over the battle between what she wanted to happen (Archie striding through the door) and what was proving to be true (Archie somewhere else, gathering me in his arms instead of her).

No, no, no, no.

Who hasn't heard that word, ringing through the body, rebelling against events unfolding contrary to our dearest, most desperate wishes? No matter what happened in Agatha's novels her characters always reacted with admirably low affect. 'It's a bad knock,' one of them might say, upon discovering their loved one's murder. In my experience loss is seldom taken so lightly, even by those who pride themselves on cool heads and unquavering lips. When something unendingly dear to you is taken away, with no hope of return, wails can't help but ensue.

Somewhere in the midst of her sorrow Agatha stopped to make an inventory. The things she couldn't live without. Her car – the wonderful car she'd bought all on her own. The typewriter that had made it happen. Her child and her dog. What if she did lose Archie? Given all the pain he was causing her, might Nan in fact be taking her biggest problem off her hands?

No. That wouldn't do. It couldn't be borne. Archie was hers. Her own husband. She would never give him up, *never*.

'The only person who can really hurt you in life,' she would write, many years later, 'is a husband.'

Agatha's wails recommenced. Honoria, the cook, the butler and Anna, the new parlourmaid – all of them lived at Styles with the Christies but not one reported hearing these wails. Still, I know they occurred. She must have stifled them somehow. Her sleeve. A pillow from one of the chairs.

This was not a bad knock. This was a demolition. Agatha's pretty face grew puffy, her blue eyes narrowed to slits. Peter covered her face with kisses in an attempt to console her. She pushed him away then grabbed him tightly to her chest. Tears wet his wiry fur. The sobs that could be contained but not halted ravaged her throat. *No, no, no, no.* This *mustn't* be her life. This *mustn't* be how events unfolded.

She tried to muster up the resolve her mother would have demanded, but it was not to be achieved, any more than Archie's return. The night stood stubborn and dark outside the windows. Agatha gave herself over to utter collapse – falling into red-faced, sobbing, wounded pieces.

By now Archie and I were fully ensconced in our weekend away with Noel and Ursula Owen at their cottage in Godalming. After a lovely dinner we'd adjourned to the drawing room for brandy. Earlier, upon his arrival, Archie had taken me aside to announce he'd ended his marriage.

'We'd best lie low for a bit,' I said. 'After this weekend. We should stay out of each other's way, to give you a chance to sort out the details, let the dust settle.' If Archie hadn't left Agatha as promised, I would have fabricated a trip to my sister Megs so he wouldn't question my upcoming absence.

'Don't you know I'll go mad without you?' The kiss that followed was furtive and triumphant, but I could tell he accepted my reasoning. I'd have the next week, at least, to myself.

Noel Owen was a ruddy-faced man who'd inherited a good-sized fortune from a titled relative. He had the air of someone who'd rather be outdoors shooting doves, and he always spoke loudly, as if his voice had to carry a great distance over the sound of popping rifles. He and Ursula claimed to be fond of Agatha but this did not intrude upon their willingness to accept me as a fourth in golf and as a guest at weekend house parties.

Ursula and I sat together on a lilac settee, talking about an article she'd read recently about a new term in psychology called Lucid Dreaming.

'The idea,' she said, 'is that in a dream a person might be able to control events. And I thought how much better I'd like it if there were such a thing as Lucid Living. Much better to control what happens in life than what happens in your dreams.'

She laughed and so did I, though it brought me back to summers in Ireland, which always hit me with a kick in the gut. Those days when the whole world had seemed like lucid living, and I could summon a boy cresting the hill to visit me as if out of thin air.

Noel poured me another brandy, then grabbed my hand and

bellowed to Archie, 'Can't you give her any better jewellery than that, Mr Christie?'

I wanted to snatch my hand away but instead I smiled, letting him examine the ring. From this company's point of view it must have looked inexpensive and insignificant, like something a child might wear, turning the skin beneath it faintly green.

'It's sentimental,' I said.

Noel did not let go. Ursula's smile looked waxen. She was bespectacled and too thin but, as far as I could tell, her husband adored her almost as heartily as he seemed to adore Archie.

'She'll have something better than that soon enough,' Archie said. He stood smartly, holding his snifter, elbow resting on the mantle. He had the something better in his suitcase, and planned to present it to me before the weekend was out. He smiled at me over the rim of his glass. He wasn't one to worry over past romance and had never asked me a word about the Claddagh. In his presence I always wore it with the crown pointed away from me.

A little while later, Archie and I stood upstairs in the hallway between our rooms. If he fretted at all about his wife's wellbeing, his countenance did not betray it. He kissed me, fierce and anticipatory, before the brief subterfuge of retiring to his own room. It would not do for the Owens' servants to find his bed undisturbed in the morning.

At the bookshop the day before, along with *Winnie the Pooh*, I had bought a copy of a new novel by the American author F. Scott Fitzgerald: *The Great Gatsby*. I read a chapter while waiting for Archie to sneak back across the hall. I've said already, haven't I, that at the time I didn't think much of Agatha's novels, though, unlike Archie, I had at least read them. I fancied myself more high minded. E. M. Forster and John

Galsworthy were my favourites, though lately I'd also taken a liking to American writers like Hemingway and Gertrude Stein. And Fitzgerald. As I turned the pages of his novel, I thought he was on to something very fine indeed.

When Archie crept into my room – stealthy, as if the household didn't know full well what we were up to – I put aside my book to do what he liked best, taking off my clothes while he lay on the bed, still in his suit and even his shoes, watching me.

'Take your hair down,' he said, his voice hoarse.

I did as I was told, wondering if we'd continue like this – the commands, the straddling, his thrusts through unzipped trousers – once we were married. If a part of me hated him – despised him, even – that only abetted the performance he most enjoyed. His smooth hands ran down my sides and I closed my eyes, shutting out the consequences, the devastated wife, and even my own motives, to enjoy what pleasure there was, in completing the task at hand.

The Disappearance

Last Day Seen
Friday, 3 December 1926

A<small>T HER NEW</small> home in Ascot, not far from Sunningdale, Miss Annabelle Oliver – aged seventy-seven – was experiencing lady troubles.

It had been going on for some days. It was what her mother used to call heat from the bladder. Not the sort of thing one likes to talk about, even to a doctor. Doctors were men, after all. It would be better if she took care of it on her own. Drinking lots of water was the thing to cure it. That had always worked in the past. There was no telephone at the house she'd inherited when her brother died. He hadn't believed in them and neither did she.

It was a clock that woke her up with unfamiliar chimes. Gongs, ten of them, sounding through the house that was much too big for just one person. Miss Oliver's eyes flickered open. Her face felt rather hot but she had the distinct feeling she ought to be somewhere. A party, that was it. She got out of bed and dressed, disappointed with the clothes she found. High of neck and dark of colour. Why, you would think they belonged to an old lady.

She walked outside expecting to find a carriage waiting for her. Instead there was only a car, a black Bentley, sitting unused and forlorn in the drive. Very well. She preferred horses to engines but was used to doing things for herself. It was not entirely appropriate for a young lady to arrive at a party alone but if she didn't show up, her hosts might worry. She rolled up her sleeves, cranked up the car and sat herself behind the wheel to drive off into the night.

The car, like the house, had belonged to her brother. Miss Oliver didn't remember that at the moment. She did remember how to drive, and so she did, away from her house, lurching down the dark roads in no particular direction, only her phantom destination.

Goodness, it was hot. She lifted the back of her hand to her brow. It was almost pleasing, the pulse of heat, skin on skin, proof that she was alive and heading somewhere exciting, where many loved ones awaited. She only had one light hand on the wheel and the car swerved a bit to the left, one wheel skittering on pebbles and brush. She grasped the wheel and righted herself on the road, peering through the windscreen at the road ahead of her.

An awful pain seared, sharp enough to snap her into a moment of clarity. The car lurched and she slammed on the brakes, smacking her head into the windscreen.

Now there was a new pain, and blood trickling into her eyes. She pushed the door open and stepped out of the car. Terribly cold. Head clearing. And terribly lonesome – a dark country road in the dead of night. For a moment Miss Oliver could understand. She was not a young girl on the way to a party, but a confused old woman who had driven miles from home and then off the road. The car sat there, looking whole and well. Not even needing a push. If she could just crank it back up, she could turn around and drive on home to her own bed.

'What was I thinking?' Miss Oliver said, crossing her wrists and pressing her hands to her chest. 'I might have been killed.'

Oh, it was hot. The fog descended upon her again. She took off her wool coat and threw it upon the driver's seat.

'I must get to the party,' she said. 'My hostess will be so worried if I'm late.'

She walked off into the night, leaving her car by the side of the road, not heading back towards home, but straight into the brush and brambles. Nettles scraped across her wrists. Still she kept walking, even when her feet began to sink into murky water, icy enough to feel like something was biting her about the ankles.

'I might lie down a bit,' she said to no one, and sank to the ground, feeling not at all well, and rather cold, and wondering where on earth her coat had gone.

The Disappearance

Day One
Saturday, 4 December 1926

THE SUN HAD been up for hours when a maid knocked on Archie's door. I lay in bed across the hall reading *The Great Gatsby*. This, I thought, turning another page, is the kind of book I would write, if I were an author. Not detective stories.

Despite the thickness of the walls I could hear the maid's voice clearly. 'Colonel Christie,' she said, 'there's a telephone call for you. The lady says it's urgent.'

The rush of air that followed indicated Archie used too much force opening the door. Then I heard his sure-footed steps, following the maid down the hall. I could guess the words going through his mind. No doubt he thought – as I did – that the call must be from Agatha, in the midst of unbearable torment, longing for him to come home and calling it urgent. I shivered under the covers, glad I wouldn't be the one to hear her tears and pleas.

I closed my book and rose to dress. At least Agatha hadn't shown up on the Owens' doorstep. There's no telling what someone will do, in a true state of bereavement. Especially a woman.

The Owens kept their telephone in their sitting room. When I got downstairs Archie was just emerging, wearing a dressing gown, a broad scowl on his face.

'Was it Agatha?' I whispered.

'It was Honoria,' he said, tightening the sash around his trim waist. 'She claims Agatha has gone missing.'

'Oh dear,' I said. 'I hope she's all right.'

'I'm certain it's just histrionics. A ruse to get me back to Styles. I'm ashamed of Honoria, that she'd go along with it.'

'But Archie.' I reached out my hand to touch his elbow. 'Shouldn't you find out? Make sure everything's all right? There's Teddy to think of.'

He frowned at my misstep, sounding like an admonishing wife instead of a mistress. I stepped closer and placed my hand on his chest. 'Indulge her,' I said. 'She's hurt. Badly hurt.'

Archie's face softened. He nodded. I felt a pang of humiliation on Agatha's behalf. That kindness from her husband should be directed by me. He jogged up the stairs and I went to join the Owens in the dining room to take breakfast. I'd already finished my jam and toast when Archie bustled in, fully dressed and holding his pocket watch. I looked on impatiently while he poured himself a cup of coffee. It seemed important that he hurry off home and make sure all was well.

The door bells chimed. After a few moments a maid came in looking puzzled. 'So sorry to interrupt,' she said, 'but there's a policeman here.'

Noel got to his feet. 'I'll see what this is about.'

The maid said, 'He's asking for Colonel Christie.'

'Well, then,' Noel said, with the confidence of a man who rules the police, and not the other way around. 'I suppose you'd best show him in.'

'I'm on my way out,' Archie said. 'I'll see what he wants as I go.'

He nodded to me and I took this as instruction to stay where I was. The men went into the hall and when Ursula followed them I decided I might as well, too. By the time I reached the foyer Archie had gone rather pale.

Noel was scolding the police officer. 'This is preposterous, Thomas,' he said. 'Surely you can trust the man to see to his business on his own.'

'A lady's missing,' the policeman said. He was young – still spotty across his chin – and the effort it took to contradict Noel Owen was evident in the quaver of his voice. 'I've been told to bring Colonel Christie back to Sunningdale.'

'I'm sure it's all a mix-up.' Archie recovered himself, willing colour back to his cheeks. 'I'm happy to go home and clear it up, obviously that's what's needed, but if I could just drive my own car, so I don't have to send someone round for it . . .'

'Sorry, sir.' The officer looked pained to say it. He wasn't looking forward to a drive with Archie. 'I do have my orders.'

'I'll drive your car to Styles,' I said.

Everyone turned towards me at once. The police officer raised his brows. I could see his eyes dart about the hall, searching for a husband to go with me. A husband who didn't already belong to someone else.

Archie had taught me to drive on the country roads through Berkshire and Surrey, but this was the first time I'd done it alone. The novelty of driving solo chased other thoughts from my head. I was not especially worried about Agatha, not yet. I sympathized with her impulse to run away, and I also believed that, one way or another, the world protected people like her. I drove slowly and arrived to see the young police officer from Godalming heading home, no doubt relieved to be rid of Archie from his passenger seat.

By the time I arrived at Styles, the local constable's car was parked in front of the house, so I drove around the back and walked inside through the servants' entrance. In those days, doors were seldom locked anywhere outside London. Since the war had ended there was very little to fear. I tiptoed through the house into the front hall where I saw the new parlourmaid, Anna, her ear pressed to the sitting-room door. Archie must have been in there with the police. The book I'd bought Teddy lay on a little table by the stairs, still wrapped in its package. I retrieved it and tucked it under my arm.

Anna turned towards me. She was a plump, pretty, freckled girl who blushed easily. Archie claimed she flirted with him, and I had no patience for such girls, who preyed on husbands – or even available men – simply to better their own circumstances. I regarded her sternly as she stepped back from the door, blushing at being caught eavesdropping.

'Oh, Miss O'Dea,' she said. There were people, at the time, who regularly came and went from Styles and I was one of them. 'I didn't know you'd come round. Is there anything I can get you?'

'No thank you,' I said. 'I have a gift for Teddy. Is she nearby?'

'I believe Teddy's upstairs in the nursery. Would you like me to take it to her?'

'May I take it myself? You do look busy.' I said this in a way that promised I wouldn't say a word about her eavesdropping, so long as she didn't stand between me and the nursery.

'Yes, that would be fine.' Anna gestured towards the stairs.

I made my quick detour into Archie's and Agatha's room and observed her dress still on the floor. Then I went to the nursery. The door was slightly ajar. Teddy sat cross-legged, playing with toy soldiers and a little wooden dog. At the sight of me she jumped to her feet, ran to the doorway and threw her arms round my waist.

'Miss O'Dea!' she said, the delighted sort of greeting only a child can perform.

I returned the hug, happy to find her alone, without Honoria hovering. Teddy was small for her age, with delicate bones. She raised her little face up towards me. Her cheeks were pale and she had violet marks under her eyes, as if she hadn't slept well.

'Look at you, you little beauty.' I took her chin in my thumb and forefinger, the way Agatha had mine the other day. 'Everything all right?'

'Everything's fine.' Teddy sighed in the tentative way of a child who knows things are amiss but doesn't want to say so.

'I brought you a present.'

She stepped back to expend some effort untwining the string. When she'd managed to unwrap the book she tossed the brown paper to the floor. At her age I would have found a proper place to discard the wrappings but this was the life Teddy lived. Not aristocratic, but posh enough that clothes and rubbish were simply flung aside for someone else to clear away. Once I became her stepmother I'd encourage her to be the sort of person who folded her clothes and put them away, who attended to her own discarded wrappings. But for now it wasn't my place to say a word.

'Oh,' Teddy said, smiling at the cheerful pink cover. 'What a funny little bear.'

I sat myself down on the round woven rug and leaned against the wall. Teddy climbed into my lap. Her hair tickled my chin and I leaned my cheek against the crown of her head as I read. It was a lovely book, inexplicably touching, Christopher Robin wandering off to find the Hundred Acre Wood.

71

'But don't you ever wander off like that,' I said to Teddy. 'Your mum and dad would miss you terribly.'

'I won't.' Her mouth opened into a great yawn as she added, 'Thank you for this book, Miss O'Dea. I do like it.'

Teddy read one page to me herself, then I continued reading it aloud even as I could feel Teddy's breath slowing down, her little head tilting forward. I hoped the evenness of my voice and the sweetness of the prose might help her continue with the sleep she so dearly needed. And before long I found my eyelids fluttering closed, my head resting on the top of hers as I fell asleep, too.

'How dare you.'

Honoria spoke in a furious hiss, designed to wake me while allowing the child to sleep. Peter trotted into the room, tail wagging, and for the first time I felt alarm. Agatha took the dog with her almost everywhere.

Teddy stirred sleepily and Honoria scooped her up and laid her on her cot. Then she gestured furiously with her head. I kissed Teddy on the forehead, then followed Honoria into the hallway.

Just at that moment Archie crested the stairs. 'Good Lord,' he said to me. 'This won't do, Nan. We can't have your name wrapped up in all this.' It was something he'd said repeatedly, about the divorce. Now that police were afoot it seemed to have become doubly important – getting me out of the way.

'Wrapped up in all this what?' I asked. 'Where is Agatha? Is she all right?'

'Of course she's not all right,' Honoria said. 'This is all owing to you, Nan O'Dea. Don't pretend it's not.'

'That will do, Honoria,' Archie said.

She refused to retreat, crossing her arms defiantly. Archie took me by the elbow and led me downstairs to his study, where he closed the doors behind us. The room was cold. Someone had allowed the fire to go out.

'Agatha drove off late last night and nobody's seen her since.' He didn't look at my face as he told me the rest. Her Morris Cowley had been discovered in the wee hours of this morning, at the lip of the chalk pit below Newlands Corner. Off the road, its lights shining until the battery ran out. The bonnet of the car rested in the shrubbery. In the back seat were a fur coat, a packed suitcase and a driving licence. There were frustratingly few clues and it was disturbing to think that she might have wandered into the cold night without her coat.

'Honoria says her typewriter is gone.' Archie lay his hands flat on his desk, where Agatha sometimes wrote during the day while he was at work. His hands looked as though they were trying to absorb her last moment of industry, as if her work above all else would hold a clue to her whereabouts.

Despite the chill, a fine layer of sweat formed on Archie's brow. He mopped it with his handkerchief. When he returned the cloth to his pocket, he drew out a folded letter. After staring at it for a moment, he ripped it into bits and threw it on the fire.

'What was that?' I asked. 'Was that from Agatha?'

'This is all some damnable stunt,' Archie said. 'To punish me. To punish *you*. To get your name into the papers.'

'That doesn't sound like her.'

'That's the point, isn't it? She's not herself. This whole bloody business has made her not like herself.'

Me. I was the whole bloody business. I didn't know what to say. Certainly this was no time for the smiles he always craved.

Archie clapped his hands, as though he had a task to complete but first had a few things to get out of the way. In the corner of the room, on the floor, I saw light glint off a band of gold, Agatha's wedding ring. I pointed to it and Archie bent, reddening, to scoop it up and bury it in his suit pocket.

'The important thing,' he said, 'is for you to get out of here fast as possible.'

I stood, unsure of what to do. In a way this was perfect – an added excuse to be out of touch over the next several days. At the same time it was unnerving, what seemed like Archie's momentary defection. That wouldn't do, not at all.

'Nan, are you listening? You mustn't be here. It doesn't look right.' He reached out and drew me to him. When I pressed my head against his chest, I could hear his heart, knocking away at an alarming clip. For a woman, a damaged reputation could bring about all manner of horror, in those days. But I knew it wasn't concern for me that was making his heart erratic.

'Agatha,' he whispered into my hair as he held me tight, 'where are you?'

On the ten-minute walk to the Sunningdale station, the bitter cold stung my face. Unlike Agatha I did not own a fur coat. I wondered how she managed now, wherever she was, having left her warmest garment in her car. What if I wandered by Newlands Corner and helped myself to it? The thought made me laugh and frown at the same time, pulling my wool coat close around me.

With luck Agatha would turn up by the end of the day. At this very moment police were searching through the brush all around Sunningdale, but certainly she wouldn't be found there;

she would return, perfectly hale and well, under her own steam. It wasn't for me to worry about. My knuckles burned with the cold. I blew into my hands. They smelled like Teddy's soap and I wondered what they'd tell her about Agatha's whereabouts. If anything happened to Agatha – anything permanent – I would become the little girl's full-time mother. That was if Archie wasn't too traumatized to go ahead with our plans, and didn't blame me for whatever happened to his wife. A certain kind of man does tend to blame a woman.

But if he didn't, I could take over. I could be the one walking Teddy to school in the morning and stealing into Archie's study while he was at work to scribble down stories. Even Honoria would have to change her tone, wouldn't she, if she wanted to stay on at Styles.

I shook these thoughts away. I didn't want any harm to come to Agatha. I wanted her to be found, whole and healthy. But there was nothing I could do to help and I needed to turn to my own affairs. I needed to focus on the week ahead, leaving the Christie family behind for just a little while, before coming back to join it forever.

The Disappearance

Day One
Saturday, 4 December 1926

WHEREVER YOU MAY be sitting, reading these pages, however much time has passed, you will know that Agatha Christie did not stay missing. You know she didn't die in December of 1926. She survived to a ripe old age and wrote many more novels and stories. At least one book a year – 'Christie for Christmas,' her publisher used to say, banking on those December profits. Agatha moved past Archie and her shattered marriage, not only to become the bestselling author of all time, but also to find a love much better suited to her, the way a woman with a little life under her belt will, once she's clear-eyed about her past and can see what's best for her future.

Nobody could know any of that when the police fetched her car back to the road. There was plenty of petrol in the tank, the engine seemed to be in fine working order. No signs of any trouble. No explanation readily discernible. A little ways away another group of policemen, perhaps six of them, stood on the edge of the Silent Pool. Over the years more than one corpse had been dredged from those spring-fed waters.

One of the policemen said, 'We'll have to drag it if she doesn't turn up by morning.'

At Styles the police gave Archie a brief rundown about what

little they'd discovered, and what they planned next. Archie imagined nets cast into the Silent Pool. He envisioned them returning to shore, his wife's body snarled in their threads, and covered his face with such sincere horror for a moment that the police stopped suspecting him of having done something criminal.

In the nursery Teddy said bedtime prayers as usual, Agatha's absence regular enough, Archie's agitation far removed. Outside, night had fallen but still policemen spread out, along with volunteers from the town, scouring and searching all over the countryside. Bodies of water glimmered ominously. By now everyone in Berkshire and Surrey was developing a theory about where Agatha might have gone, what might have happened. Not one of them anywhere close to the truth.

I didn't have a telephone in my flat but there was a call box on the corner. In the evening I walked out to it, pressed the A button, deposited my pennies, and waited for Archie to answer.

'How are you?' I asked, speaking in a low voice, as if the passers-by might hear. 'Is there any word?'

'No.' If I hadn't known it was him, I'm not sure I would have recognized his voice. There was a tremor, an uncertainty that seemed wholly out of character. 'The police are involved, Nan. They are highly involved.'

'Well, that's good, isn't it? They're serious about finding her.'

'Frightfully serious. They mean to find her as quickly as possible. She'll be mortified when she finds out about all this fuss.'

I nodded, imagining it, the crack in her dignity. It did seem alarming that she wouldn't rush back immediately to prevent exactly that. I could tell from Archie's voice, it terrified him. He'd take more comfort if the police had dismissed the whole thing as nonsense.

'I've been searching through her papers,' he said. 'There's a story about you, I think.'

'Is there?'

'Yes. I'm quite sure it's you. An adulteress. The main character pushes her over a cliff in the end.'

I drew in a breath that was half inhale, half laugh. Perhaps Agatha really had gone mad. Though one could argue her wanting to kill me was perfectly reasonable.

'Perhaps I should be looking over my shoulder.' I made my voice sound light, but Archie had already moved on to other worries.

'Oh, Nan. Why did I have to be so callous with her? You were right. I should have waited.'

'No,' I said. 'There never would have been a right time.' It was disconcerting to hear him so distraught, his voice strangled by what seemed to be real grief. 'She'll turn up. She's just upset. The moment she realizes what a fuss has started she'll run right home.'

But cheering up didn't seem to be what Archie wanted. I could hear someone come into the room and he told me he needed to ring off. Quickly, I asked what he'd told Teddy about Agatha's whereabouts.

'I said she went to Ashfield to see after her mother's things.'

'Might she really be there?'

'The Torquay police have already looked into it. She's not there. She's not anywhere.'

I didn't know how to reply.

'Look,' he said, his voice hardening. 'Better if we don't

78

communicate till this is all sorted out. We don't want your name in all this.'

'No,' I agreed, 'we don't.'

He rang off without saying goodbye.

I placed the earpiece back on its rung and opened the door to the box, stepping out onto the street. The sky had gone dark, streaked with the last colours of a sunset I'd managed to miss. My breath tumbled out, visible in the frigid air, and I didn't realize until I'd walked halfway home that I'd been examining the face of every woman, to see if it was Agatha.

She would be all right. I felt sure of it. She was far more practical than I. And it wasn't as though she were a desperate young girl, with no resources or place to go. The whole world stood with its arms out, holding a net to catch her once she fell. She might be distraught but I knew she would never commit suicide. Nor would she endure discomfort, the way I did, walking a while instead of returning straight home, past the point of shivering, without gloves, teeth beginning to chatter.

When you don't see someone, standing right before your eyes, when you don't know where she is, you imagine all manner of horror befalling her. By now the number of people were increasing – their minds picturing Agatha struggling through the brush. Running off into the wood, stumbling into a freezing cold lake.

I shook my head. She had taken my chin in her hand. She had chastened me. *You don't love him.* As her Inspector Poirot liked to say, 'One must respect the psychology.'

Agatha was a rational, practical, contained Englishwoman. How fond her novels were of categorizing people. A woman does this, an American does that, Italians are just like this. Perhaps she felt comfortable with these generalities because she fit her own so splendidly. Stiff upper lip, a fine English lady.

Now she had abandoned her natural character, thanks to me. At the same time, what she did best was spin stories. Plot. And all of this had the air of a plot, a way to remind Archie how much she meant to him. Indeed how much he loved her. Worry tends to give way to such emotion, doesn't it?

I gave into the cold and went home. My flat was tidy, like a barracks. No decorations, no photographs, no mementos. My quilt was the same colour as the walls, not quite white, not quite ivory. The landlord had rented it to me on the condition that I entertain no men. My neighbour, Mrs Kettering, an ancient widow, was supposed to keep an eye out for misbehaviour, but she liked me, and hadn't revealed the rare occasions Archie had come to my door. You'd think he might have noticed, even from standing on the threshold: this was no home, but a station, for someone on a quest, who doesn't have time to adorn the present day, only to plan for the future.

I packed for my trip to Harrogate, my mind unwelcomely focused on Agatha. I folded a pair of knickers and thought: she's gone off to a posh hotel to nurse her wounds, not even realizing anybody's worried. But that didn't explain the abandoned car. So I thought: she left the car so we *would* worry, which would serve us right, and then she'd gone off to a posh hotel to laugh at us, or to wait for Archie to find her, his worry rekindling his love. But what were the chances she'd pull something like that off without help? Honoria – the most likely accomplice – seemed as worried as the rest of us.

'Agatha's an emotional sort,' Archie once said to me. 'Don't let the manners fool you.'

An emotional sort. As if there's any other kind of human. Show me an unemotional sort and I'll show you someone dangerous. How can emotion be avoided, when life careens in its unexpected directions? During the war Agatha had written to her new husband, exhortations for his safety like incantations upon the page, fountain pen flying over paper. Now, in Sunningdale, it wasn't Archie in danger but Agatha. Archie realizing he was rather an emotional sort himself – not allowed to join the search. He paced the floors of the house, fit to climb the walls. He regretted tossing her letter upon the fire so hastily. What clues might she have hidden in those words that could have been useful to the search? How dear the evidence of her being alive and vital and forming sentences, so recently, heat and heart upon the page.

I took the Claddagh off my finger and put it back on, crown pointing towards me. The last time I saw Finbarr, years ago by now, was when he came to find me in London, after our child was lost to us. He'd gathered me up in his arms and cried, soaking the hair at the crown of my head.

'Was she beautiful?' he asked, when I told him I'd had his baby.

'Yes,' I said, past the point of weeping, my hands clutching his collar. 'More beautiful than you can imagine.'

The memory of our child's beauty had no healing power. None of it was Finbarr's fault and still I sent him away. With Ireland embroiled in its war for independence, he left Great Britain for Australia, where nobody would expect him to fight for any country, and he could work training herding dogs. He had wanted me to go with him but I refused. Just this past September I had written to him at the last address I knew, to tell him about Archie, the marriage I believed was impending, and my reasons for stealing another woman's husband. I owed him that much, but I never heard back. Perhaps the words I wrote repulsed him, written by a woman he'd never imagined I could become. Or perhaps he'd simply moved again, to America, or back to Ireland. Beyond it all. A place I could never reach.

It was too soon for Agatha to move beyond anything. I packed my warmest clothes, boots and hats and gloves, so I could go for walks while I was in the country. Perhaps if I found a deserted road, I would even run. I tried to picture Agatha, running beside me, the two of us invisible to the outside world and finally equals.

I folded a skirt and thought: she headed to Godalming so she could confront Archie and me, make a great scene in front of the Owens. In her unaccustomed Sturm and Drang she'd driven off the road, then left her car and wandered out into the frigid night. First thing tomorrow morning I'd hear the news, her body had been found frozen in the hedgerow, or in the nets they used to drag the Silent Pool.

I folded a cardigan, a gift from Archie, the softest cashmere I owned, and thought: right now, Teddy might be playing upstairs at Styles. She might be reading *Winnie the Pooh*. Not knowing Agatha had gone.

Do you ever think about the Irish boy?

Only every day of my life.

I wrapped a pair of walking shoes in a scarf. She'd boarded a ship to America and now sat snug in a first-class cabin. The whole world and a new future ahead of her. Me having provided the impetus she needed to escape.

I snapped my suitcase shut. That was that. No more thoughts of my lover's wife, or even Finbarr, could intrude. Whatever happened next, in its aftermath my life with Archie would begin. I had one week to myself before then. I planned to immerse myself fully.

Here Lies Sister Mary

I MIGHT HAVE STAYED in Ireland during the war if Colleen hadn't died. As soon as I received word I knew the exact moment it had happened. I'd been walking with Brutus up from the barn, my hair loose, clapping my hands together to rid them of saddle soap. Daylight was waning while mist descended as companion to the coming dusk. And a chill came over me out of nowhere, like I'd been plunged into icy water. 'Someone walked over my grave,' my mother used to say.

When I received the telegram days later, nothing could keep me from home.

'It doesn't say how,' I sobbed to Aunt Rosie, holding up the wired letter, a few lines, pennies saved. 'She's only nineteen. Why doesn't it say how?' And, of course, I thought, if she'd come to Ireland instead of me, she would have been safe.

Rosie thumped my back in comfort, looking solemnly at Uncle Jack. It had to be grave indeed, for someone so young to die of something that couldn't be told in a telegram.

'You ought to stay here with us,' Aunt Rosie said. 'There's nothing you can do to fix this. And you'll be safer here than in London.'

Perhaps I would not have rushed back to England if only I'd

83

been told how Colleen had died. But it was the kind of news, posing the kind of question, that prevented sitting still. The only thing I could bear was being on the move. On the boat from Dublin I stood on deck gripping the handrail, refusing to smile at soldiers. 'Come now, lass,' an old woman hissed at me. 'It's your duty to send them off with happy memories.'

All I could think about was getting home to Colleen. I knew this was illogical, and yet I felt determined to see my sister. At the same time I had this sense, a vision, that as I headed to England she was on another boat heading to Ireland, both of us on the choppy Irish Sea, travelling in opposite directions, sailing past each other without so much as a wave.

When I arrived home my mother was in bed. She sat up and hugged me close but wouldn't say a word.

'What happened?' I asked my father.

He took me by the shoulders, his fingers digging in in a way that made him foreign to me.

'She ran wild,' he said.

'Colleen? Wild?' I'd never heard something so absurd.

'I won't have my girls running wild. None of you, do you hear, Nan?' He let go of me. His face looked changed and would be forevermore. As if someone else had stepped into his body, taken it over. I felt a tug of fear that once I knew Colleen's story, the same would happen to me.

Megs came and took me by the elbow, her dark eyes and pointed features much like my own; she was the exact same height as me. Colleen had been the tall one. Megs and I walked through London in the summer fog, from the East End to Waterloo Bridge. 'Walking's the thing for grief,' Megs said.

These were my mother's words. 'Walking's the thing for grief,' she had told us. And Colleen had looked up from her book and said, '*Solvitur ambulando.*' At Mum's blank expression Colleen translated the Latin: 'It is solved by walking.' And Mum laughed and said, 'My clever girl.'

Now, faced with the worst grief of her life, our mother didn't walk. She was unable to move. Louisa, too, had taken to her bed and refused to leave. Colleen's death could not be solved by anything.

But Megs and I walked just the same. 'Da won't let us have a funeral,' she told me.

'Why ever not?'

By the time we reached the bridge, I knew the story. Colleen had been pregnant. The fellow had gone off to war and never answered her letters.

'Who was he?' All I could think of was the boys she'd turned away, without ever seeming remotely tempted.

'He told her he was a philosophy student,' Megs said. 'She met him at the library. Perhaps he was a cad or perhaps he was killed in the war. Either way, when Da found out about the baby, he turned Colleen out of the house.' Her face was pale, dark eyes lustreless. Hating to tell me there was something we could do – we girls – that would rob us of our father's love. I'm not sure I ever saw my father smile again after Colleen died, but it may be that I just stopped looking at him. When he hardened himself against one daughter he hardened the rest of us against him. His wife, too.

Under a dull sun on Waterloo Bridge I stood arm in arm with the one older sister I had left. ' "It was only love," ' Megs told me. 'That's what Colleen said. Da said it was a sin and a disgrace. She said, "No, Da. It was only love." '

'How could he?' I never thought, *How could Colleen?* I knew about love by now. It was easy to imagine taking the same path as Colleen. But my father's? I closed my eyes and tried to picture the young man clever enough to enchant my smart and beautiful sister, then callous enough to abandon her. He must have been killed, I decided.

Megs kept her anger focused on our father. 'I suppose he figured he had one to spare.' Her voice sounded empty and resigned. How many of us would Da go through before there wasn't one to spare?

Megs and I let go each of other and leaned forward, staring down into the water. Colleen had walked here, taking the South Bank route, I knew that's how she would go, and still nothing had been solved. Megs and I had walked the same way and still our sister was gone forever. As I look back now, with my view from the future, I see two young, brown-haired girls, small in the scope of things, and all around them machines of war, galvanizing themselves from every corner of the globe to encroach upon their world. But in that moment Megs and I didn't see it. Never in living memory had a war touched English soil and it still seemed impossible, the way it wouldn't years later, when the second one came along.

All I had at the time was the view from behind my own eyes. A foggy summer day in the city. Megs and I, exhausted from our walk, and from our loss, leaned against each other. I wished I could cry but my insides were leaden with the same flat, hollow ring of Megs's voice. If I'd had flowers, I would have tossed them, to flutter down into the water, the same spot where Colleen had flung herself into the Thames.

Years later I would see a film, *Brigadoon*, and it would remind me how I held Ballycotton in my head during the war: protected, perfect, untouchable. Safe from the ravages of time and progress. Hiding in the clouds, waiting for my return.

In London the world was empty of its young men. My mother finally got out of bed and took me to have my portrait made. I was surprised when she walked into the kitchen, dressed for the day.

'Put on your best dress,' she told me. 'We're going to have a picture made in Forest Hill, to send to your Irish soldier.' She finger-curled my hair and gave me Vaseline for my lips and eyelashes.

On the bus my mother blinked and blinked, unaccustomed to the natural light that poured through the windows. She'd stayed inside so long. 'Oh, Mum,' I said.

'Never you mind.' She grabbed onto my hand. 'We're going to take care of you, Nan. My darling girl. And you mustn't be crying. He doesn't want to see tears in his picture, I'll tell you that.'

I thought Finbarr wouldn't mind seeing tears. I'd never known him to mind anything. Still, I smiled dutifully at the camera, sitting on the photographer's stool, sincere in my happiness as I imagined looking at Finbarr's cheerful face. Some days later I went on my own to collect it. It was a pretty picture, so much prettier than I was in real life, I worried he'd be disappointed when he saw me again. My smile showed off the good luck of my straight, white teeth. In the letter I sent along with the picture, I wrote in tiny, crowded print. Paper was scarce during the war and I wanted to tell him the truth about everything. Over the next four years I wrote to him regularly and dutifully. I wrote about what had happened to Colleen and how

I couldn't look at my father anymore, nor he at any of us. I wrote simple things about school and my friends. I wrote how the war had reached us in London with the Zeppelin bombing, and how Megs wanted to work as a nurse but Da wouldn't let her and in this case Mum agreed. I admitted I knew his danger was much greater but I was terrified of the aerial attacks. 'Nothing could be crueller than attacking from the sky.' As my pencil moved carefully, sparingly over the page, I held in my head the same Finbarr from peacetime. In my mind, his smile broke open as easily as ever. He wrote back, saying he hoped to get enough leave, and save enough money, to come to London. He kept the picture of me tucked into his sleeve during battle and tacked beside his bunk at night. I imagined the edges frayed and worn. He'd touch my cheek before sleeping and tell me goodnight. I wished I had a picture of him.

Two men had failed my sister. First the philosophy student and then our father. But I knew Finbarr would never fail me. He would crouch in the trenches with my smiling face tucked into his sleeve, and he would think about the day on Ballywilling Beach. He'd remember our goodbye kiss and put his fingers to his lips.

'I love you, Nan,' Finbarr wrote. The letters were a celebration on the page. I'd never heard him say it aloud. 'Wait for me.'

As if I'd ever do anything else.

Four years of war. Four sisters turned to three. I wrote a poem about Colleen that won a contest, a five-shilling prize. It was printed in the newspaper but my father refused to read it. One morning after he went to work, Mum called Megs, Louisa and me into her bedroom.

'Look here,' she said, opening her bottom drawer and pulling out a tea tin. She twisted off the lid to show us where she'd been squirrelling away the money she earned at Buttons and Bits. I'd been working there myself, a day or two a week, and knew it would take considerable time to amass what Mum was showing us. 'None of you will go the way of Colleen, do you hear?' Her voice sounded as stern as I'd ever heard her. 'If ever you're in trouble, come to me. We'll take this money and run away.' She showed us she'd put her mother's wedding ring in the tin along with the bills and coins. 'We'll go to America or Australia and say you're a war widow. And then we'll come back and say you got married there, and he ran off, or widowed you. Your father be damned. You promise me, now. I can't lose another of you.'

We promised, all three of us. I handed over the five shillings for my poem, to add to her cache.

When news of the Hundred Days Offensive began, I worried myself sick, especially when letters from Finbarr ceased with no warning. 'There might not be any post coming from the front,' my mother tried to soothe. 'Let's not fret till there's cause.'

There was plenty of cause. Bad news arrived for girl after girl, mother after mother, father after father. By now I was nineteen but I think in my heart I may have been much younger. The world quaked around us. One minute my mother would be her old self, brisk and loving. Then she would fade away, pale and still, staring out the window.

'What are you watching for, Mum?'

'Nothing,' she'd say, and go back to some busy work. But I knew what she was watching for. Colleen, heading towards home, a small child's hand in hers. Love and reason have never been well acquainted.

On Armistice Day I had never seen so many people in one place as there were on the streets of London. With Megs, Louisa and our friend Emily Hastings, I went out into the celebrating throng. What noise and joy. We couldn't stand shoulder to shoulder, everybody moved sideways.

Megs, Louisa, Emily and I tried to hold hands as we made our way through the streets but it was impossible. It should have been frightening, being trapped in the midst of so thick a crowd, but the happiness was even thicker. You can't imagine the joy and goodwill. If you tripped, a hundred hands reached out to catch you. If you sneezed, a thousand people said 'God Bless You'. A soldier caught Megs's arm as she tripped over the curb, then tipped his hat and revelled on with his mates. I searched the crowd, as if there were any reason for Finbarr to be held within it, as if – being lucky enough that he loved me – I could be lucky enough to summon him before my eyes.

Somewhere out in the masses, Agatha Christie was walking too. During this stretch of time, a lonely married lady with her husband off to war, she'd occupied herself by taking a course in shorthand. When Armistice was announced right in the middle of class, everyone stumbled out into the celebrations, marvelling at the crowd just as we did. Englishwomen – Englishwomen! – dancing in the street. For all I knew, Agatha and I were shoulder to shoulder, either once or many times during that heady day.

I'm not sure when Megs and I were jostled apart, but somewhere I lost hold of her fingers, a laughing matter and not a frightening one. We'd all catch up eventually. I made it as far as

Trafalgar Square. A delivery truck rumbled up Northumberland Avenue with soldiers draped over every inch of it, so I couldn't make out the advertisements written on its side. Just as the truck came to a halt, not able to go a single bit further because of the crowds, a soldier jumped off the bonnet and landed up ahead of me, his peaked army cap covering cropped black hair.

It was such a swift and light-hearted movement. Seconds earlier the world had been only the throng, no individuals, just one great mass of human life. I had barely existed myself except as a part of it. Now, though, even though a good fifty bodies jammed into the space between us, there were only two people in all of London. Finbarr and me. Facing each other with joyful eyes. Oh, as if I'd conjured him up. *Make a wish, Nan.* The sort of miracle that convinces us life on earth has meaning. His black hair shone blue in the London grey as it had on his own emerald island.

'Is it you?' he shouted. He held a bottle of champagne in one hand. 'Am I drunk? Am I dreaming?'

'It's me.' My voice rasped with the shouting of it.

'Step aside,' Finbarr commanded the crowd. 'That's my girl. I see my girl.'

Could the Red Sea refuse Moses? Could the throng refuse this handsome, blue-eyed soldier, home from victory safe and sound?

In his khaki uniform and army boots, Finbarr made his way through the cleared path and swept me up in his arms. When the crowd closed back in, he hoisted me onto his shoulder, and I saw multitudes spreading all over London, as if an ocean of people had washed into the city, flowing through its undammed streets. All of them beaming, the sky above us free of danger.

'You didn't tell me you were coming to London,' I shouted down to him, and he slid me off his shoulder and into his arms.

'I only found out day before yesterday,' he said. 'There was no time. Anyway, I knew I'd find you.' As if London were Bally-cotton and he only had to wander the docks, asking fishermen where Nan O'Dea lived. 'It's like a miracle, isn't it,' he said. 'You're like a miracle, same as ever.' His voice had changed. Deeper, raspier, as if something had broken inside his throat, which indeed it had. In that moment I owed it to the shouting but would learn later it was a permanent alteration, brought on by mustard gas.

He kissed me, deeply, and I kissed him back. Everyone around us cheered. Celebrating not just the end of the war but our re-union. Nan and Finbarr, together as we should have been had the world never cut us apart. Victory was ours. The world had been righted. Now we could return to our happy old selves.

We moved sideways through the crowd, hand in hand, and I feared we'd be cleft apart as Megs and I had. I could scarcely see which direction we were headed in or which shops we passed. When Finbarr pulled me into the lobby of a grand hotel, it was like falling into a bubble of quiet emptiness. There were no guests anywhere, and nobody stood behind the front desk. Everyone who should have been here had abandoned their posts to celebrate in the streets. The lobby was unbearably grand – a pocket of silent extravagance I could never imagine affording. Welcoming us. Beside imposing stone columns, great potted palms reached their velvet fronds towards the ceiling. The marble floors felt cold through the soles of our shoes. If we'd whispered, it would have echoed.

So we didn't whisper. Finbarr still had hold of my hand, and we rushed up the wide, grand staircase. At the door to each room Finbarr turned the knob, until one fell open for us, and we stepped inside with a sharp slam, a bubble inside the bubble.

Here was a talent of Finbarr's I hadn't yet discovered but would come to know well: finding places to hide amidst any manner of excitement or turmoil.

A little while later there would be the barest bit of time to talk, hastily, as we dressed. Finbarr suggested marrying before he returned to Ireland but I couldn't leave before I had my mother's blessing. He would promise to send money for my passage to Ireland. The next day I would meet him at the train station to kiss him goodbye. We agreed we'd be married inside mere months. Even if my mother forbade it, I'd give her a kiss and a thousand apologies and say my farewells. No hurry. The war was over. We had all the time in the world.

But first. Just us. How many couples faced each other in that same moment, all across the world? An entire generation with only moments to reclaim their lost youth. In our stolen hotel room there was no time to spare for words. All Finbarr said was, 'I have to be back with my regiment before sundown.' So we took a long moment to inhale the sight of each other, and the nearness. The aloneness and the quiet. He offered me the champagne bottle and I took a swig, warm bubbles burning my nose, I'd never had so much as a sip of champagne before that moment.

We gathered each other up and fell into a wide bed the likes of which we'd never known. But the only luxury we revelled in was the two of us, unchaperoned and unfettered and together at last after all this time.

In any moment during that afternoon did I recall my sister Colleen as a cautionary tale? I did not. There was no comparing her disappeared man to the one present and before my eyes. This was Finbarr. I knew he would never forsake or abandon me. He would never break a promise, or say an untrue word.

And he never did.

The Disappearance

Day Two
Sunday, 5 December 1926

MISSING PERSONS NOTICE sent to police stations throughout England:

> Missing from her home, Styles, Sunningdale, Berkshire, Mrs Agatha Mary Clarissa Christie. Age 36, height 5 feet 7 inches; hair red, shingled part grey; complexion fair, build slight; dressed in grey stockinette skirt, green jumper, grey and dark grey cardigan and small velour hat; wearing a platinum ring with one pearl; no wedding ring; black handbag with purse containing perhaps 5 or 10 pounds. Left home by car at 9.45 p.m. Friday saying that she was going for a drive.

Inspector Frank Chilton rode in the third-class smoking carriage from Brixham to Harrogate. He was glad to make the trip. It had been a mistake to move back to his mother's seaside cottage during the chill winter months, when the wrong breeze from offshore could climb into your bones, stirring up the cold from those nights in the trenches, the cold that still lived there and always would.

'They want police officers searching in every country,' Sam

Lippincott had told him. 'I'm shorthanded since you left, and as Jim is off on his honeymoon.'

Within an hour of receiving Lippincott's telegram, Chilton had bicycled over to the Cooke estate to borrow their telephone. 'Every inch of England scoured, as if the Queen herself were missing,' said Lippincott, his voice crackling through the wires. The words were scornful but his tone was jolly. Chilton's old police chief was happy to have an excuse to summon his friend back to Yorkshire so soon. 'Out of retirement with you. You can pass the lady's photograph around and take a motor through the countryside. You'll never have an easier job than searching for someone who's surely someplace else.'

'Nor a more frustrating one.' But Chilton had already decided to join in the probably fruitless search. Busy work was better than no work at all. He'd left his position with the Leeds police three weeks earlier, to be closer to his mother. He hadn't yet found new employment and his old outfit was short of inspectors. Now this lady author was missing – famous enough for every police force in England to be in on the hunt, spread out over the entire country – but not so famous that Chilton had ever heard of her. Yorkshire headquarters already had men searching Huddersfield and Leeds. They didn't have a man to spare for Harrogate and Ripley. Except the one who'd only just left.

'We'll put you up at the Bellefort,' Lippincott had said. 'My cousin and his wife own the place, you know. They say they'll be glad to give you a room free of charge.'

Chilton certainly did know about Lippincott's cousin. Simon Leech had married a girl from Antigua. Isabelle Leech was a lovely person, possessed of the rare combination of flawless manners and her own strong mind. But the marriage had scandalized the family and also jeopardized Simon's hotel and spa.

It was one thing to have a dark-skinned woman working the front desk, another to discover she was married to the hotel's English owner. No doubt in addition to needing an extra man searching for Mrs Christie, Lippincott's cousin needed more guests. Empty rooms tended to breed empty rooms. The cousins were as close as brothers and this was a chance to help both the hotel and Chilton. As for the missing lady, nobody really expected her to turn up in Yorkshire. But Chilton would search all the same. He wasn't the sort to shirk, even when assigned a hopeless task.

'It can be a working holiday for you,' Lippincott said, clearly pleased to be able to offer such a thing. 'Won't get a better offer than that any time soon, will you?' Chilton and Lippincott had been in the same regiment during the war and fought together all the way to the end. Lippincott was one of the ones who had come out all right. Not too all right – any man with a heart would be altered by battle in some way – but fine enough to do his job, love his family, hear a door slam without jumping through the roof.

On the train north, Chilton stared out the window at the passing wych elms and hedgerows, the landscape nearly empty of people, wind whipping, everyone hunkering indoors. He was as likely to find Agatha Christie wandering beside the train tracks as anywhere.

Chilton's left arm had gone limp since taking shrapnel in the shoulder. His good hand shook as he lit his cigarette. You might think detective work wouldn't suit a man whose one working arm still trembled from war memories. You'd be right. Which is why Lippincott calling him out of retirement after less than a month was likely a way of giving him a parting gift, rather than expecting a crime to be solved.

'Have a soak while you're at it,' Lippincott had said, once all was agreed upon, proving Chilton's suspicions. Harrogate was famous for its natural hot baths, a luxury Chilton hadn't even considered partaking in when he lived nearby. 'It'll do you good.'

Smoke from Chilton's exhale rose to mingle with the other passengers'. If a fool's errand was all he was good for, at least it was something more than wandering the beach by his mother's house, an old man at forty. For much of his life Chilton had two brothers. Now he had none. The youngest, Malcolm, had died at Gallipoli. The second youngest, Michael, died in the labyrinth at the Battle of Arras, where Chilton had fought beside him. From that day forward, for the sake of their mother, Chilton had committed to staying alive, even as the stench of rotting bodies followed him from the trenches and refused to ever leave.

Once their mother was gone, though, Chilton would be free and clear. Perhaps then he'd follow the lead of this Christie woman, who from the sound of it had committed suicide. The place they'd find her was at the bottom of a lake. Chances were they'd have found her corpse closer to home by the time he arrived at the hotel. He'd spend one night there and turn around, back towards home.

Suicide. The word had a way of hounding Chilton. A hard thing for a woman to do, when she had a child. But then, from what Lippincott had said – and the fact that police all over England were being mobilized for the search – the Christies were of the breed who had enough people to look after the child so that she might not even notice her mother was gone. Chilton's mother had been there for her sons every bedtime, every meal, every skinned knee of their childhood.

The train whistle blew for a stop. There *were* some pleasures left in this life, things he would miss when he left it. Chilton did like the sound of a train whistle. A time away, train travel was. A chance to gather your thoughts or have no thoughts at all. Nobody would be looking for him and nobody would find him either, here on a train. Perhaps that's what this Agatha Christie was doing. It's what he would do, if he wanted to get away from the world. Board a train and ride it all over England. Never get off at any stop. Everything you needed, from privies to dining cars to shelter from the rain and a place to rest your head. If he wanted to escape, to disappear, he'd simply ride on and on to nowhere. Which was, now that he thought about it, very close to what he was doing – searching for someone in a place she surely wouldn't be found.

After a while, Chilton fell asleep with his head lolled back, mouth slightly open, cigarette still burning in his hand. The woman across the aisle, old enough to be his mother, hadn't wanted to ride in the smoking carriage, but there were no seats left in the non-smoking one. She looked at the sleeping man kindly. He had that particular look about him, so many did now-adays. And he was a handsome fellow, if you looked beyond the edges, a little squidgy and rumpled, but a good strong chin. Nice broad hands. She reached across the aisle and took the cigarette from his fingertips, sneaking one small puff before grinding it out in the ashtray.

In Surrey and Berkshire, a hundred policemen continued to search through the brush and hedges in the damp cold. They walked through the villages handing out circulars. Archie was shown a copy of the Missing Persons notice and he registered the description like a blow to his heart. *Slight. Fair.* In their youth he had seen her in ballrooms. Peach silk and pale freckles. Twirling and smiling. Once at a house party, on a gallop around a field with their hosts, she hadn't bothered with a riding outfit and had simply worn a pink dress. Her hairpieces – all women wore them in those days – flew off her head and into the wind. The long curls that had looked fetching when attached to her now seemed as ghastly as any discarded body part. Agatha slid from her side saddle to retrieve them. Archie held tight to his reins, participating in this ride out of duty rather than pleasure. His father – a judge in the Indian Civil Service – had died after a fall from a horse, the blow to his head turning into a brain infection. To watch Agatha you'd never know riding could result in injury or death. Just mirth. What a sight she'd been, holding her skirts in one hand, scooping up the errant hair in the other, roaring with laughter all the while, yet controlled enough to accomplish the task at hand, then hoist herself back onto her horse. What a good sport. What a delight.

Archie thought: I can't imagine Nan handling such a situation – hair flying right off her head – with the same mirthful gales of laughter. Does she even know how to ride a horse? Different manner of upbringing altogether.

In truth it was hard for Archie to imagine me at all, at this time. What he thought about was his wife. The things he once loved about her. Slight and fair. Is that what she looked like? Somehow he had forgotten to notice.

He had noticed when they first met, at a ball in Chudleigh. A week later he had ridden a motorbike all the way to Torquay to see her. He knew she was engaged to some other bloke but that hardly seemed an obstacle. When Archie made up his mind to have something, he had it. Agatha would have registered this trait with a writer's eye. Attaching it to him in quick strokes.

She wasn't interested in romances; she placed them in her books because that was the fashion. She especially disliked romances in detective novels. They were a distraction.

Oh, what a distraction she had been, to Archie, at one time. With her vanishing it all came back to him, as if the corporeal had left and all these memories – all these feelings – had erupted exactly as she herself departed the plane. Now what distracted him was the inability to see her. As if the sight of her would solve everything – certainly the way Deputy Chief Constable Thompson and his minions looked at Archie, as if they might see blood dripping from his hands. He calculated who knew about him and Nan, versus who suspected. The Owens. That pair he could trust to remain discreet. Then there was Honoria, who would have told the cook, who would have told her husband, who also happened to be the butler. Perhaps the new maid didn't know but the rest of the staff did and even now the police were interviewing them, one by one.

'A nervous breakdown,' Archie had told Deputy Chief Constable Thompson, at once, before the officer got the chance to pose a single question. He saw Thompson's eyes narrow, clearly finding the outburst suspicious, but Archie couldn't help himself. 'She's been suffering terribly from nerves.' As if the rephrasing could abate the hole he was digging himself.

'I see,' said Thompson. He had a full, protruding chest of the sort particularly athletic men develop when they get on in years. An impressive grey moustache and an eternally scolding countenance. *Give me no nonsense*, Thompson's bearing seemed to say, *and I'll spare you further ruin.* 'Had she consulted a doctor?'

'Goodness, no,' Archie said. 'Neither of us believes in that sort of thing. Fresh air and a firm bearing, that's what restores a person's mind.'

Thompson nodded. Approving of the philosophy, if not the man.

Honoria watched this exchange, arms wrapped round herself as if to keep all she knew inside. Agatha had written two letters – one to Archie, which nobody else ever saw, and one to Honoria, saying, 'I'm off to Torquay for the weekend.' Honoria had handed hers over to the police, but hadn't yet mentioned Friday morning's fuss; or Archie's affair. Fond as she was of Agatha, if her employer never returned, that would leave Archie in charge of her livelihood. The man was a cad but certainly (likely?) not a murderer. Honoria hoped to stay on at Styles, tending Teddy, even if the lady of the house never returned. And weren't the letters proof that Agatha had planned all this, that she had in fact *left* rather than *vanished*? Nobody would have batted an eyelash over her absence, or checked to see if she really was in Torquay (she was not) if it hadn't been for that abandoned car: ominous evidence of something terribly amiss. Telegraphing that whatever Agatha's destination, she surely had not arrived there.

When I stole away to Ireland, I left no letter for my parents. My mother found her tea tin, empty of every last penny she'd hidden. That was all the information she needed. I imagine her holding it to her bosom, lamenting the part of her plan I'd omitted – bringing her along with me.

When I went missing, just after the war, there weren't a hundred policemen to be found in England. They'd all gone off as soldiers and took their time returning to duty. And I hadn't been an author, or a wife. Just a disgraced girl from a family that barely scraped by, the kind who went missing every day. There weren't enough police in the world to set out looking for all of us.

But for Agatha Christie: thousands of men – policeman and locals; hounds; even aeroplanes; combing every inch of every forest. Spread out, even after dark, carrying torches. Searching and searching. The great mass of them in Surrey and Berkshire but inspectors dispatched all over the country. As if the sheer force of her anguish had made her, inexplicably, the most important person on earth.

The Disappearance

Day Three
Monday, 6 December 1926

S PECIAL CABLE TO the *New York Times*:

Mrs Agatha Christie, Novelist, Disappears
in Strange Way from Her Home in England

LONDON, 5 Dec. – Mrs Agatha Clarissa Christie, the novelist, daughter of the late Frederick Miller of New York and wife of Colonel Archibald Christie, has vanished from her home at Sunningdale, in Berkshire, under mysterious circumstances, and a hundred policemen have searched for her in vain during the weekend.

Late on Friday night Agatha packed an attaché case with clothing and went out alone in a two-seater automobile, leaving a note for her secretary saying she would not return that night.

At eight o'clock yesterday morning the novelist's car was found abandoned near Guildford on the edge of a chalk pit, the front wheels actually overhanging the edge. The car evidently had run away and only a thick hedge growth prevented it from plunging into the pit. In the car were found articles of clothing and an attaché case containing papers.

All available policemen were mobilized and have conducted an exhaustive search for miles around but no trace of Agatha has been found.

Colonel Christie states that his wife has been suffering from a nervous breakdown. A friend describes Agatha as particularly happy in her home life and devoted to her only child.

The grounds of Styles had been bustling with police officers throughout the weekend. Now the reporters arrived. Fleeing from their persistent questions, Anna, the new parlourmaid, broke down and told one of the handsomer policemen that Archie and Agatha had had a terrible row on the morning of the day she'd disappeared.

'She didn't seem herself after,' Anna said, tearfully. 'And what woman would? He spoke so cruelly to her.'

The officer patted her shoulder clumsily. She stepped closer to him and he put his arm around her. 'There, there,' he said. 'Men are dogs, aren't they?'

She lifted her fetching, tear-stained face. 'You seem nice.'

'I think I am,' he said, as if deciding just in that moment.

After a rather pleasant interlude (they would be married the following February) Anna and the officer headed back to Berkshire Police Headquarters to deliver the new information to Deputy Chief Constable Thompson. He frowned that such news would only come to light after a full weekend of intensive searching. Bad enough the press had to get hold of the disappearance. Now this.

'You think the colonel killed the old girl?' asked the young officer.

Thompson snorted. Young people think anyone a minute older than them is old, don't they? This poor fellow didn't know;

thirty-six would be upon him before he could blink. Thompson had a daughter Agatha's age, born the same year and month. How he hated the thought of anything happening to her.

'Can't know yet, can we?' Thompson said.

'But constable—' Anna, flush with the situation's drama, spoke in almost a whisper.

'If you've got something to say, might as well be loud enough to hear.' Thompson didn't mean to snap but he did hate a mutterer.

'I think there might be a lady involved. A different lady.'

She hadn't raised her voice one whit but Thompson heard her loud and clear. His face darkened. If his daughter's husband were ever to do anything of the kind, Thompson would wring his neck. He got to his feet. 'I'd better get back to Styles and have a chat with Colonel Christie.'

'Oh,' Anna said, 'he's left. Gone off to London. Says he's going to get the Scotland Yard involved.'

'The Scotland Yard!' As if they were for hire at the snap of a rich man's fingers. Worse, as if the Berkshire Police couldn't handle it themselves. Thompson had already known Archie Christie was arrogant. Now he knew he was an arrogant cad. Nothing put a cloud of suspicion over a man like a strumpet on the side. Thompson feared more than ever for Agatha Christie's life.

Archie was as yet unaware that his dalliance had been revealed. All he knew was the Berkshire and Surrey police were useless, not turning up so much as a strand of Agatha's hair. He was glad enough they didn't seem to know about his extramarital relations but then what did that say about their investigative prowess? Archie had his solicitor arrange a meeting with the Scotland Yard, but that proved another dead end.

'Sorry, colonel.' The young inspector – so thin he looked as if taking nourishment would be an exhausting business – gave a shake of his head. He might not have been on the job long but marital spats and women who stormed off because of them were beneath his purview. 'If the local police ask for our help, then we're all hands on deck. Until then?' He raised his hands in the air, indicating that they were not on deck in the slightest.

Archie hated to betray emotion but he was afraid he did. A hand, raised to his brow, shading his eyes. He pulled it away at once, horrified the inspector might think he was crying. Archie thought – the way he wouldn't have otherwise – of his last night with his wife. Why had he indulged himself so? Mightn't she have taken it better if he'd left well enough alone? Or what if he'd never been enticed by Nan in the first place, when he saw her from a distance on the golf course, best swing he'd ever seen from a woman? That same afternoon there she was again, drinking a gin and tonic on the patio. He had strode over as if he had every right to her, and she had blinked through the sunlight as she offered her hand, looking both demure and knowing, a smile twitching the corner of her lips. As if she knew everything that was about to happen. *How do you do, Colonel Christie.* Her voice was so low, so beautifully modulated, he couldn't believe when she said she was Stan's secretary.

What a mistake. What a bleeding, terrible mistake. Nan had used her acquired manners to befriend her employer's daughter and gain entry to the country club. He ought to have let her remain their guest, never becoming his own. Agatha didn't need to acquire manners, she was born with them. She was from Archie's world. A.C. and A.C. They fit. In the midst of this family emergency, Nan seemed a foreigner, someone who'd elbowed her way in. Troublesome at worst, irrelevant at best.

Out on the street, Archie blinked into city daylight. Crowds bustling about as he stood on the pavement, undecided. Across the street, a tallish woman with a particular stride caught his eye. He knew it wasn't his wife but all the same found himself crossing. The woman wore a dark fur coat. Surely Agatha had one just like it. She turned down one street, then another, then rounded a corner. When he turned the same direction, she was gone. As if she had melted into thin air.

Nonsense. She'd probably just gone into one of the buildings. With no one to chase, Archie reclaimed his car and navigated the streets to my flat. He sat parked on the street, staring up at my window. No sign of life. It could be I had gone to work. Work! In the midst of all this mess. What a luxury it would be, to pretend to business as usual. Perhaps he should go straight to his office. Perhaps if he behaved as though everything were normal, it would become so. Agatha would return – breeze right in without knocking, as she had last week, fashionable and cheery and trying too hard. This time she'd find him alone. He'd gather her in his arms and give her a proper kiss. *Of course I'd love to have luncheon with my beautiful wife*.

How had he missed it, what she'd been on the brink of? Or was it that he'd seen it but simply hadn't cared? Once upon a time, he'd been so protective of Agatha, so jealous, he couldn't bear seeing even a waiter talk to her. He'd told her he never wanted to have a son, because he never wanted to see her doting on another man. Her doting belonged to him and him alone.

He got out of the car. Hands in his pockets. Staring up at my window as though waiting for a sign. If he saw any movement, he'd run up and knock. And if I opened the door, he knew – despite all his very real feelings, and the desire to find his wife and change the course he'd so rashly set her upon – he would gather me up in his arms and lose all this terrible commotion for a while. He deserved that. No matter what, a man deserved that, to forget his troubles. Until Agatha came home nothing could change what he'd done, and if he'd known that night at the Owens' was the last time he'd make love to me, well, then, surely he'd have savoured it a bit more. The way he had with Agatha.

A pretty young woman bustled by in a worn winter coat. She scowled at Archie as if she'd read every one of his thoughts. He looked away from her, up towards my window, watching for any passing shadow.

Nothing. Did he know I didn't love him? No. Archie wasn't the sort of man to know such a thing.

He turned and walked to his car, brim of his hat pointed towards the pavement. The thought of Agatha, dead somewhere, or injured and alone, was too much to bear. How lucky he'd felt, in the old days, when she turned her light on him. How long it had been since he'd felt lucky, rather than simply believing the world should belong to him, without ever requiring so much as a thank-you.

That night, home at Styles, Archie did something he had never done in all the seven years since she'd arrived. He put Teddy to bed.

'What's wrong, Father?' It was more disruption than treat to have him sitting on her bed, wearing his shirtsleeves, eyes glassy with whisky and remorse. Peter nestled in beside her; the dog was always a comfort. She closed her hand into his wiry fur.

'Nothing's wrong, darling,' Archie said, stroking her forehead with the particular fervour of a distant parent who may have lost everything but his child. 'I just want to say goodnight to my little girl. Is there anything wrong with that?'

'No.' Teddy had her covers pulled just under her chin, blinking through the darkness, wishing he would go away and take the strangeness with him. A child does not like to feel responsible for an adult's emotional state. If he hadn't been so bleary, an uncomfortable volatility brewing, she might have asked him to read more *Winnie the Pooh*. Honoria had already finished it once but she wanted to start over and reading herself was a painstaking business.

'Is Mother coming back?'

'Of course she is,' he said, too sharp. 'Mother always comes back, doesn't she?'

'I meant tonight.'

'Sorry. No. No, I don't think tonight.' There were no machinations to keep Teddy from knowing, the fuss kicked up around her was a search for her missing mother. Only straight denials of the truth. Not a ruse that could be maintained for long, when all of England was searching.

'Well, then.' He kissed her forehead. 'Sleep well, Teddy.'

She closed her eyes tightly, pretending the kiss had put her straight to sleep.

For me the same day began far away from all that clamour. The previous night I had arrived at the Bellefort Hotel and Spa, low key and cosy, the perfect place for anyone who needed to lie low for a bit. The woman at the front desk – West Indian, from the look and sound of her – greeted me warmly.

'I am Mrs Leech,' she said, with her lovely Caribbean lilt.

'You just be sure to let me know if there's anything you need. Anything at all.'

She handed me a fountain pen to sign the registry. I paused for a moment. I'd made the reservation under the name Mrs O'Dea. It wouldn't have been proper for a young unmarried woman to stay on her own at a hotel. Now I found myself adding another name. 'Mrs Genevieve O'Dea,' I wrote, a painful scrape forming in my throat. Genevieve was the name I'd given my lost child. Perhaps I ought to have written Genevieve Mahoney, if only to have seen it written one time.

'Thank you, Mrs Leech,' I said. 'Would it be possible to take dinner in my room?'

'Of course it would,' she said. 'I'll send up a lovely tray for you.'

A woman who'd been approaching the stairs wearing a hotel dressing gown – likely just returning from a spa treatment – bustled over to the front desk. 'Dinner in room!' she said to Mrs Leech. 'Why, that's just the thing, isn't it? We'll do the same, if you please.'

'Yes, Mrs Marston.'

The woman, Mrs Marston, turned to me. She was about Agatha's age – perhaps a year or two older – with a round, jolly face. Roses in her cheeks. 'We're on our honeymoon, Mr Marston and I,' she told me, looking right into my face without – I suspected – really registering me. 'Have to keep our energy up, you know!'

Mrs Leech and I exchanged a quick glance to share our aversion to thinking further on that matter.

Morning came quickly and I knew I couldn't stay in my room forever, so I headed down to breakfast. The Bellefort was a comfortable establishment but not a particularly posh one. It wouldn't have done for a setting in one of Agatha's novels. But

E. M. Forster would have liked it – the chairs comfortable to sink into but worn about the arms. I made my way to the dining room, took a seat and asked the grandmotherly waitress for extra cream.

'Mind if I join you?' an American girl asked.

I looked up. She was my age or thereabouts, with bobbed blonde hair and an intent, intelligent face. There were other seats available at empty tables but instead of pointing this out I nodded. She sat across from me and smiled.

'My name's Lizzie Clarke,' she said, louder than was necessary, typical American. 'I'm here with my husband. He's still asleep, the slugabed. The hot waters are knocking it right out of him.' She laughed, again too loudly.

I glanced around the room to see if the other diners seemed bothered. Lizzie took this as a request to fill me in on our fellow guests. She pointed out a fantastically pretty woman, young enough to have been a child during the war, with hair so blonde it was nearly white.

'Her name's Mrs Race,' Lizzie said.

Mrs Race sat alone, staring out the window forlornly.

'How pretty she is,' I said, warmly enough for Lizzie herself to take it as a compliment. 'She can't be here on her own. Can she?'

'Oh no. She's got a husband with her. They're on honeymoon.'

'I met another woman here on honeymoon.'

'Yes,' Lizzie said. 'I've met that one too. Much more pleased about it than the one over there.'

I glanced again at the young bride. The poor thing's lower lip trembled.

Lizzie said, 'She and her new husband seem to do nothing but argue. So the old honeymooners are jolly, and the young ones are not. Pity anyone shouldn't be jolly on their honeymoon. Isn't it?'

I smiled. 'You like people-watching, do you?'

'It's my favourite hobby,' Lizzie admitted, with a self-deprecating laugh that made me feel fond of her.

Who should enter just then but the older honeymooners, Mr and Mrs Marston. They sat on the far side of the dining room and I indulged in a bit of people-watching myself. Mrs Marston had dark hair, just a few strands of grey and a broad, ample back. I stared over her shoulder, directly at her husband. Mr Marston was a jowly, red-faced fellow who didn't seem to notice me, he had eyes only for his new wife. How sweet.

'Say,' Lizzie said, when we'd finished eating, 'are you heading to the baths? Would you like a walk before? We could get good and chilly so the hot water will feel that much better.'

Lizzie was already on her feet. I pushed my chair back. We left the dining room together, then went to our rooms to collect warm clothes before meeting outside to venture down the frigid road, cold grey skies settling in around us. It was a good idea to get ourselves nice and cold before a soak back at the Bellefort Hotel, and cold we would get, despite our coats, hat and gloves.

'What's your husband like?' I asked as we walked. If she could be direct, so could I.

'He's lovely,' she said. 'I recommend American men. They're different from British. More emotional and expressive.' Away from the gaze of our fellow guests she slipped her arm through mine as if we were old friends.

'It's nice,' I said, 'that you speak so kindly of him. Not all women do, of their husbands. They complain about them and malign them, and then they're surprised when they run off with someone else.'

Lizzie laughed. She stopped and lit a cigarette, shading the flame of her match with gloved hands. 'If the husband deserves his wife's complaints, the person he runs off with will complain about him one day. Probably about the very same things. True?'

I patted my hat back into place. I'd taken pains to look respectable and put together. A proper married lady on holiday. Composed, running away from nothing, simply taking a little time for myself.

Lizzie's gaze turned away from me, focused down the road. A young man came into view, walking towards us. He was tall, with a graceful step. Even at this distance, more than a hundred feet, he was clearly fixated, coming directly towards us as if he had something urgent to relay.

'He doesn't look quite right,' Lizzie murmured.

I didn't look at her, but remained focused on the man. My impression was precisely the opposite to Lizzie's. He looked quite right to me. Almost nothing in my life required the sudden control and presence of mind to keep my voice neutral when I spoke. 'Funnily enough, I happen to know him. Would you mind excusing us a moment?'

'Not at all.' She gave a pretty little shiver. 'I'm about ready for some hot water. Perhaps I'll see you in the baths?'

'Perhaps.' But I had already started moving in the opposite direction.

'Remember not to trust strangers too quickly.'

'Thank you.' I spoke without looking back at her. 'Thank you for the reminder.'

My feet moved swiftly, like they used to when I was young.

Carrying me towards the man. It was like hurrying towards the best part of the past. A shift had occurred in the atmosphere. Skies opening up to bestow a gift when I least deserved one.

He wore an Aran jumper and a pea coat, open and unbuttoned, despite the cold. Black hair fell across his brow. The smile had been stamped out of his eyes, but they were still the loveliest layered blue. My heels were chunky, fine for walking, but ill-suited to the run I couldn't help but break into. I couldn't get to him fast enough. My coat blew open, too. If I ran into his arms, I knew he would pick me up and spin me around, but for some reason I stopped just short of them. Looking at him, making sure this was real, felt more important than embracing him.

'Finbarr,' I said. 'Upon my word.'

'Hello, Nan.' He reached out and took my hand. Brought my palm to his lips, three beats of a kiss. 'I've missed you.'

In Berkshire and Surrey, they searched as though for a dead woman. The Silent Pool, the brush, ditches. Hounds bayed, noses to the ground. If Agatha Christie were found near her home, it would be because she'd died there, by her own hand or someone else's.

Elsewhere in England authorities searched for a live person in hiding. There were police officers from Land's End to Cold Stream, showing Agatha's photograph to hotel guests and proprietors. *Have you seen this lady?* Chilton was one of many going through these motions. He'd been charged to search for her, so searching was how he planned to conduct himself. On his arrival the day before, he'd acted an ordinary guest, checking in and eating dinner in the dining room with the sparse assortment of guests. Simon Leech's wife had ushered him to a table and sat him opposite a pretty young lady with abundant dark hair whom Mrs Leech introduced as Miss Cornelia Armstrong.

'Surely you're not here all on your own,' Chilton said to Miss Armstrong, before he could stop himself.

Miss Armstrong smiled as if she found his incredulousness a compliment. 'Why, surely I *am*,' she said, with no small note of good-natured reproach. 'It's 1926, or haven't you heard? Men went to war at my age. Surely I can manage a spa.'

Chilton smiled, and the proprietor patted the table as if pleased the conversation was off to a rousing start. 'Be sure to tell all your friends which is the best hotel in Harrogate,' Mrs Leech trilled, before bustling off with an industrious smile. The rest of Chilton's evening passed agreeably, as he learned more about suffrage from Miss Armstrong than he had ever known before.

On Monday morning, first thing after breakfast, Chilton caught a ride into town with Mr Leech. Leeds Police Headquarters was much as he'd left it. Lippincott always kept his door open. He waved Chilton into his office.

'Quite a time to take your retirement, just as the crime of the century's been committed.'

They laughed, having agreed this was no crime at all. Just a lady with a tiny bit of renown, missing when nothing else was occurring in the world, creating a Silly Season in winter. The papers were going wild. Lippincott gave Chilton some police bulletins and a photograph of Agatha from her publisher, the same one being placed in countless hands across England.

'If she's not dead, she'll be frightfully embarrassed at all this fuss,' Chilton said. Looking at Agatha's photograph – wistful and lovely – he regretted his laughter. It was a stark business, suicide, but he understood that when you had to go, you had to go. Surely she'd had her reasons.

Lippincott revealed his more-cynical-but-less-tragic theory. 'What she'll do is sell a lot of books,' he said. 'A handful of English readers knew her name on Friday. If she doesn't turn up by the end of the week, she'll be a global sensation.'

'Publicity stunt, you think?'

'Some sort of stunt. But that's why I wanted you back, Chilton. I knew you'd treat it like it was real, either way. And we must take it seriously. No one yet knows where this woman's gone. She might as well be here as anywhere.'

Chilton saluted in agreement, half in jest, but it made them both grim for an instant. They'd seen a lot together, the two of them, when saluting was an everyday business.

'Look here, though, Chilton,' Lippincott said. 'Thanks to my cousin I can put you up at no expense. And I've got a police auto for you to use to conduct your searching. You retired too early for us to give you a fancy watch, or anything of that sort. So take this as a bit of a holiday, won't you? Search for Agatha Christie but take the waters too. Enjoy the hotel. Eat well. Have a massage, for goodness' sake.'

Chilton could not begin to imagine submitting himself to a massage. 'Do you know I lived in Yorkshire for seven years and never put so much as a toe in the baths?'

'Well, then,' Lippincott said, even though Chilton was sure the same was true for him. Lippincott might wish his dear cousin's establishment well but was unlikely to ever frequent it. 'High time.'

For me the cold of the day had disappeared, along with the clear blue sky. All I could see was Finbarr. He put a gentle hand on my elbow and steered me away, looking over his shoulder to see if Lizzie Clarke was still there.

'You needn't worry about her,' I said, but he didn't seem to hear me. He led me off the road, through a hedgerow, into a stand of silver birch trees.

'Finbarr,' I said. When we were young in Ireland this sort of detour might have been playful, testing how game I could be. 'What are you doing?'

'I might ask the same of you.' His raspy, post-war voice sobered me.

'I'm on holiday. How on earth did you find me?'

'Never mind that. The important thing is what happens next. You and me, leaving this plot of yours behind, and going home to Ballycotton.'

'Ballycotton is not my home.' I pulled my arm out of his grip. At first sight of him my brain had gone to atoms. Now those atoms started to swirl and sharpen, forming a clearer picture. 'It never was and it never will be.'

'It was and it will be again. My father died, Nan.' From the way he said it I gathered that his mother had died too, perhaps a good while ago. 'I've saved enough money to buy a small place, where I can raise and train dogs. We can go home. You and me.'

I pictured the home he meant, and the road to Sunday's Corner. I knew I should say I was sorry for his parents' death. But I wasn't sorry and never would be.

'Nan,' Finbarr said. 'You can't go through with this. It's wrongheaded, and wrong, besides. You belong with me, not with a man already married.'

So he *had* received the letter I'd sent him. And this was his answer. It had been a mistake to write to him, a moment of weakness.

'It's too late,' I said, hoping my voice sounded more sad than reproachful. 'You're too late.'

He put his hand around my wrist, firm but gentle, and pulled me further into the wood. My hat had started to fall and he pulled it back onto my head, down over my ears, which must have been burning red from high dudgeon, and the chill. Finbarr didn't want me to be cold. After the Armistice celebrations, when we had lain together in London, in the midst of a passion that had been building for years, he'd paused to adjust the pillow beneath my head.

This was the third time I'd seen him since that day. The first was in Ballycotton, when he lay delirious with influenza. The second was nearly a year later, after I had left Ireland forever, and finally he came to find me in London. He had pleaded with me to go away with him to Australia. But I didn't.

The Finbarr who'd made love to me on the day of the Armistice celebration had seemed his old self. Or it could be that was just what I'd wanted to see – a blissful, fleeting illusion. By the time he came back for me, neither of us were ourselves. I was wrecked by loss. And he was just wrecked. Twenty pounds lighter. No trace of the joyful air that had been his salient trait. His voice, ruined by the mustard gas, didn't sound a bit like the boy I remembered.

('Sometimes,' Agatha Christie wrote, years later, 'one cannot help a tide of rage coming over one when one thinks of war.')

'No,' I'd told him then. 'I can't go away with you. I can't go anywhere.'

Now, six years later, in Harrogate, Finbarr and I might not have returned to our original selves. But we could at least face each other calmly. I could look at him and feel no recrimination. None of this had ever been his fault.

'What we need,' he said, gathering my hands up in his, 'is to get away from here. We can start over. You and me.'

'Oh, Finbarr,' I said. 'That's not what I need. Not at all.'

I pulled away from him. There was a considerable amount of brush to crash through, to get back to the road. The winter sky opened wide above me and I hugged myself tightly. *Breathe in, breathe out.* That's how I'd get through these next days. One breath followed by another.

Finbarr was just behind me. He put his hand on my shoulder and I shrugged it off. The last time I'd seen him, my insides were melted to grey. There was still so much to be reckoned with. And then there was the change in him. A few days from this moment Inspector Chilton would say something to me about going to war. How the world seemed one way beforehand. Then, afterwards, you had seen the Big Sadness and you couldn't ever unsee it. Finbarr had not a single line on his face. He owned the same tall, spare and agile form. But the sun had left him. Like the rasp in his voice had replaced the old clarity, the Big Sadness had replaced his joy. If it hadn't made him seem like a ship that had lost its anchor, it might have made me love him even more. I had seen a measure of that sadness myself.

He reached out and pulled me back into his arms. Three beats. Then he let me go, turned and trudged off down the road, the same way he'd come. Perhaps he thought I'd follow him but I didn't. I just stood watching him go. He knew I was still there because while I was still in earshot he raised one arm, without looking back, and called, 'You'll see me again soon, Nan. Very soon.'

More than an hour later, just before entering the baths with Lizzie Clarke, I asked myself the logical question Finbarr hadn't answered: how had he known to find me in Harrogate?

'Are you all right?' asked Lizzie, as I settled beside her in the hot water.

I nodded, a gesture that didn't say *yes* so much as *I'll tell you later*. I was wearing the knee-length bathing dress I usually took to the beach, with matching shorts underneath. Although Lizzie was in water up to her chin I could tell her outfit was considerably more daring, not least because it was the colour of a ripe tomato. All the women wore caps, our hair completely covered; it was a kind of uniform, no matter how different our bathing costumes were.

Steam settled around me and my brain felt suddenly light. Perhaps I had managed to conjure Finbarr. Lucid living. Or perhaps the very opposite, and I'd imagined his being here. I almost wanted to ask Lizzie for confirmation: *Did a black-haired man walk down the road towards us? Did you leave me alone with him? Did you say he didn't look quite right?* Would it be better or worse if it hadn't really happened at all, me back in Finbarr's arms?

The natural baths at the Bellefort were beneath the hotel in what felt like steamy caves. Low stone ceilings, so even the smaller of us had to bend our heads until we were neck deep. One needn't be staying at the hotel to use them, for a small fee, but on this day it was mostly our fellow guests bathing with us. Sitting across from us, immersed up to her chin, was the older of the newlywed brides, Mrs Marston. She observed Lizzie and me cheerily through the steam. We stared frankly back at her, but she wasn't the sort to examine others. There was something shallow about her gaze. I supposed that if she were asked about Lizzie and me later, she wouldn't be able to name a single trait

– hair colour, eye colour, nothing. Only our sex and approximate age. We existed as an audience for what she had to tell us.

'How are you two dears?' Mrs Marston asked, with a warmth that sounded genuine.

'We're just fine,' Lizzie said, with her direct American syllables.

'We met last night,' I said, before Lizzie could announce my name. I could tell Mrs Marston had no recollection of this. 'I'm told congratulations are in order?'

The woman laughed, large brown eyes twinkling. 'Indeed,' she said. 'Six days of married life and counting. It's bliss, I tell you. Bliss.'

'How wonderful for you,' Lizzie said. 'And where did you two lovebirds meet?'

'Oh,' Mrs Marston said. 'We've known each other a long while, Mr Marston and I. Star-crossed, you might say. Pain and drama, ladies. Mark my words. It makes it all the better, when the stars finally align.'

'I can't say I agree.' Lizzie kept her eyes firmly on Mrs Marston. 'My husband and I had our share of pain and drama. I could have done without all that. Well and truly.'

'Well, then you know,' Mrs Marston said, casting off the disagreement.

I thought of Agatha, all of her current pain and drama, and hoped she might one day be happier than she'd ever been, by virtue of the pain I was causing her now. I refused to consider Agatha's death as a possibility. We were connected, Agatha and I. If anything happened to her, I would feel it in my bones, the same way I had when Colleen died.

Mrs Marston settled more fully in the water, letting it cover her chin, bright eyes sparkling away as if to prove her happiness.

Then she lowered her head closer to the water and said, 'I was rather dismayed to find out this hotel was owned by a coloured person. Don't know if we would have booked it had we known.'

'Mrs Leech?' said Lizzie. 'She seems perfectly nice to me.' Her voice was clipped and firm, putting an end to that.

To her credit, or else an inability to broach dissent, Mrs Marston obliged by changing the subject. 'Do you have any children?' she asked Lizzie.

'We had one,' Lizzie said. 'He died shortly after he was born.'

'Oh, my dear,' Mrs Marston said, all motherly comfort. 'But you're young. You'll have another? And then another, and another. Won't you?'

'I hope so.' Lizzie's expression was hard to read. 'But that doesn't mean I'll ever forget the first.'

'Of course not,' Mrs Marston said. 'Truth be told I'm hoping it's not too late for me. To have a child. Stranger things have happened. And that's all I've ever wanted, really. A baby. Well. A baby and Mr Marston.'

I stood and grabbed a hotel dressing gown to cover my bathing dress. 'I feel a bit light-headed,' I said. 'Perhaps I'll see you at tea.'

Mrs Marston said to Lizzie, as if I had already left, 'A morose one, your friend. She needs to find a husband, that's all, isn't it?'

'Who says I haven't found a husband?' I pulled the belt of my dressing gown tight, my voice too baldly irritated.

'Now, now,' Mrs Marston said, as if she were used to being in charge. 'Keep your head, dear, I was only japing.' As if to prove it, she let out a merry laugh, trilling through the cavern, reverberating; the least happy sound I could imagine.

Here Lies Sister Mary

ALL OVER THE world girls waited to hear from soldiers they'd never see again, but I was lucky to love a man who kept his promises. Finbarr folded a pound note into the first letter he sent.

He wrote, *I thought I'd grown dead inside till I saw you standing there in the square.*

He wrote, *It wasn't just Armistice that swept me away.*

He wrote, *We should have waited for our wedding night, it's true, but I know in my heart there never will be a more perfect moment. And our wedding night will come, Nan, never you doubt it.*

And then his second letter arrived, empty of money. It only said, *I love you* and *I'm afraid I've come down with a fever.*

I didn't feel too well myself.

My father received word from Ireland. Uncle Jack survived the war – remaining unscathed in battle. But he came home from the front with influenza and gave it to his wife and child. Aunt Rosie recovered. Uncle Jack did not. Nor did Seamus. It had seemed such a mercy that my sweet cousin was too young to fight in the war. And now he was dead all the same. It seemed

123

the tides of this war would never stop lapping our shores. I wept for my lost second family, my beloved farm standing empty. My mother comforted me, not able to stop herself from pressing her palm against my forehead.

When Emily Hastings got sick, Megs, Louisa and I were forbidden to visit her. 'It'll be a miracle if it passes you girls by,' my mother said at dinner, wiping tears away. 'Did you know Andrew Pennington died just yesterday? All these young people. Boys who came home safe from the war, only to be killed by the flu.'

The giant and kindly crowd that swept Finbarr and me together had been teeming with invisible sickness. My mother gave up her job at Buttons and Bits and insisted I do the same.

'No you don't,' my father said, when he caught me trying to leave our flat. 'It's not safe to be out and about just now.'

'Megs thinks we already had it last spring,' I said. All three of us girls had come down with mild fevers and recovered quickly.

'Thinking is different to knowing,' he snapped. 'And knowing's what I'd need before letting you into danger.'

For years there had been little warmth between us. But in that moment I could see in his face the loss of his eldest child, and his brother, and the nephew he'd scarcely known. Da had aged a hundred years since I'd last allowed myself to really look at him. So I hugged him tightly. I thought of Finbarr's letter. Would there be anyone left in Ballycotton who'd know to write to me if he died? We didn't have a telephone. Certainly the Mahoneys didn't, there was hardly even electricity in Ballycotton.

'You look green around the gills, Nan,' my mother said that evening. She checked my temperature again. She couldn't keep her hands away from our faces. 'You'd better rest. I'll bring you a plate.'

I sequestered myself in my room, both hands spread across my belly. I didn't have the flu. I had something else. My mother's fear of influenza had replaced, at least temporarily, her fear of pregnancy. It made her blind to what really ailed me. She couldn't know that for this brief span of time, whenever she touched me or held me, she touched and held her grandchild, too.

Colleen had been my age, almost to the day, when she tossed herself into the Thames. I wouldn't ever let that happen to my mother again. I didn't tell Megs and Louisa I was pregnant because I didn't want them fearing what would become of me. And I wouldn't give my father a chance to thunder me away. I'd get myself across the Irish Sea and marry Finbarr. Even if he were dying, it was better to be a soldier's widow than a soldier's fool. The small detail of 'I do's' and a priest's blessing would render the difference between heroine and pariah. All I had to do was get myself from my island to Finbarr's.

The only place my mother went these days was the grocer's. As soon as she was out of the door, I went to her room and pulled out the tea tin she'd shown us. Between the money she'd secreted away and the pound note Finbarr had sent me, I'd have just enough to get to Ballycotton. I shook my grandmother's ring into my hands and considered slipping it onto my finger. Instead, I put it back in the tin. I didn't need to disguise myself as a married woman. I'd be the real thing soon enough.

The last of my money went to the fisherman who carried me in his mule-pulled cart from the train station to the Mahoneys' white clay cottage in the village. Masts from the harbour dinged and gulls swooped and sang. I knew Alby was not allowed inside but slept underneath the house, and was disappointed he didn't bound out to greet me. But perhaps that meant Finbarr had recovered and was off making a good wage herding.

Mrs Mahoney opened the door. I'd met her before, at Sunday church services. But then she'd been smiling. She was a tiny woman, with shoulders so bony I could see the sharp 'V' of them through her cardigan.

'You can't see him,' she said, before I could even remind her who I was. 'It's not safe for you.' Still, she stepped aside to let me in, then lit the stove to make a cup of tea. It was cold in the house and I wanted to pull my chair closer to the fire, but I didn't want to insult her. The floor beneath my feet was dirt. At another time the sight of boats through the window might have been cheerful but just then they looked to me like everything in the world Finbarr didn't want. Noticing my gaze, Mrs Mahoney stood up, went to the window and drew the shutters closed.

'I'm Jack O'Dea's niece,' I said.

'I know who you are.'

I could tell she wanted to say something about Seamus and Jack. Perhaps offer condolences. Perhaps blame them – Finbarr would have gone over there, wouldn't he, before they'd fallen ill. She slid the cup of tea in front of me without offering milk or sugar.

My eyes roamed the small kitchen. There were two doors – the one I'd come in, from the outside, and the one leading to the rest of the house, firmly closed.

'Is Finbarr here?' I asked his mother. 'Is he all right?'

'He's here and he's not all right and he doesn't need you upsetting him.' She sat down to her own tea. From the way she refused to let her eyes rest on me longer than a few seconds I could tell it was an effort to refrain from kindness. Did she know?

126

About me? Or was her coldness due to worrying over her only child?

'Is it the flu?'

'It is and you mustn't catch it. We must get you out of this house straight away. I've been tending him day and night; I could be carrying it myself. I'm sure I am.'

'If I could just see Finbarr—'

'You can't.'

'I could stand in the doorway.'

'Are you deaf, girl? I said no.'

'Nan,' I said. 'My name's Nan. Finbarr wants to see me. I know he does.'

She looked away, towards the shuttered window. She had black hair like Finbarr's, streaked through with grey. Like his would be one day. I'd thought her rosy cheeks were caused by the cold but up close I saw there were little broken blood vessels along her cheekbones. Careworn. She would have been beautiful once. Finbarr told me she wished she'd had a hundred children. Now here I was offering her one more.

'Where's Alby?' I asked.

'Traded off for provisions during the war.'

Would they have written to tell him? Or had Finbarr arrived home and found Alby gone? I imagined him whistling around the house till his father finally gathered the strength to admit what had been done. Finbarr would have worked extra hours at every farm near Ballycotton, first to earn my passage home and then to buy his dog back.

I reached into my bag and pulled out one of Finbarr's letters. 'Look,' I said, holding it towards her. 'He wants to marry me. He sent me money to come here. So we could be married.' I pointed to the words on the page. 'He promised.'

She stared at me, unmoved. I shook the letter under her eyes. A horrible feeling, when something you think holds power turns out to be useless.

'And don't you know,' said Mrs Mahoney, 'that's what a man says, to get a woman to do what he wants. The trick is in saying no. That's how you get a man to marry you. Before. Not after.'

How did she know? It must have been my urgency that gave me away. I was as thin as I'd ever been. Still, there was no use arguing. 'He wrote this after,' I said simply, then put my head down on the table. I was so tired. And suddenly horribly, horribly hungry.

'Don't you cry,' she said.

As if it hadn't occurred to me until I heard the words, that's exactly what I did. Great, guttural sobs, filling the small house. For a moment I felt embarrassed, but then I thought, if Finbarr heard me, perhaps he'd will himself out from wherever he was, and come into the kitchen. He'd tell his mother the truth. He'd insist on marrying me that very day. But no matter how I sobbed, he didn't appear, and his mother didn't soften. I cried until I fell asleep, my head resting on my arms.

'At least let me give her something to eat,' Mrs Mahoney said to her husband, willing to expose softness when she believed I couldn't hear.

I opened my eyes to see Finbarr's parents, standing by the door that led to the rest of the house as if they meant to guard it from me. If he'd inherited his joyful air from either of them, it was gone from both now. Still they had made him, these two people, they had made Finbarr and raised him in this small, dirt-floored house. *I love you* and *thank you* rose in my throat, but I choked the words back. They wouldn't want to hear them from me.

'Let me give her a glass of milk and some bread,' his mother said. 'And there's stew left over from last night. The poor girl, in the way she is, she must be famished.'

I lifted my head, feeling the creases in my face. My eyes felt swollen from sleep and crying. *The poor girl.* I recognized Mrs Mahoney's new sympathy as a bad sign. If she no longer needed to steel herself towards me, my fate was no longer in her hands. Somebody else had taken over.

Mr Mahoney sat in the chair beside me. He wore an oilskin coat and smelled of fish and salt air. His wife set to bustling, making me a plate.

'If you'd just let me see him for one moment,' I said. 'All I ask is one moment.' And then it would all be clear to everyone. They'd never seen us together. They couldn't know. If they did, they would understand.

Mr Mahoney put his hand on my arm. Slim, like his wife, but much taller, with a full, ruddy face, hard bitten by years on the sea. When he spoke it was with the brogue that still sounded like music to me.

'Listen,' he said to me. 'Nan, is it?'

I refused to nod. Shouldn't he know by now it was Nan? Of course he knew.

'I know you'd like to speak with Finbarr. But he's not in a way for that now. He can scarcely lift his head from the pillow.'

'I don't mind.'

They looked at me, the two of them, like I'd lain with every soldier home from the war and landed on their doorstep to trap their son's eternal soul.

'You don't understand,' Mr Mahoney said. 'The poor boy, he might not live to see tomorrow morning.'

'Please,' I said.

They looked at each other.

'You promise you won't touch him?' said Mrs Mahoney. 'We don't need you getting sick too. You've more to think of than just yourself now.'

Perhaps she cared about me and my baby after all. It was impossible to think of being anywhere near Finbarr without touching him but I nodded.

The door swung open with a creak to reveal a dark room hanging heavy with despair, the curtains drawn. My nostrils filled with a sad, pungent odour, like mushrooms and sweat. The figure on the bed barely made a rise in the covers.

I walked to the side of the bed and kneeled down to see his face. 'Finbarr,' I whispered. 'It's me. I've come to you.' I reached out my hand to stroke his hair off the feverish head but his mother was behind me now and caught it before I could touch him. Finbarr's eyes, open, did not land on me, or focus. Though I hadn't touched him I could feel heat emanating from his body, almost as warm as the stove. A stale, awful scent like he'd soiled himself settled around us. He moved and a damp cloth that may have been cooling his forehead fell to the dirt floor. It was crusted with blood and so were his ears. His lips had turned an odd dark blue and they didn't move or say my name. He didn't see me. I struggled to tear my hand out of his mother's so I could touch him. Surprisingly strong, she increased her grip.

'If you let me stay,' I whispered, 'I could take care of him for you.'

'And where would the sense in that be?' Mr Mahoney put his arm around my shoulders. He pressed me to my feet, turned me around and gently pushed me out of the room.

They fed me dinner and made me a pallet by the stove in the kitchen. When I was sure they'd be sleeping, I crept into Finbarr's room and lay down beside him. 'Dogs and books,' I whispered, the words scratching my throat with despair. 'We'll get Alby back and it will be dogs and books and you and me and the baby.'

His body moved and for a moment I thought he'd answer, but instead he coughed; shaking, dry coughs that didn't bring him to consciousness. I froze, worried his mother would hear and run into the room, but she didn't. Finbarr's body quieted. I stayed beside him, awake all night, so before dawn I could be found on my pallet, a good girl.

'Might I say goodbye to him?' I said, before we left.

'You must think of what's best for the baby, dear,' his mother admonished.

I nodded, not yet realizing that as far as the world was concerned, what was best for the baby could mean something entirely different from what was best for me.

The Disappearance

Day Three
Monday, 6 December 1926

P ERHAPS IT'S ONLY hindsight, rearranging memory. But it seems to me that evening at the Bellefort Hotel, when I first saw Inspector Frank Chilton, I knew he was searching for Agatha. Not that I knew his name yet – that discovery was moments away. He stood at the front desk, talking to Mrs Isabelle Leech, our Caribbean proprietress. My senses were heightened from being held in Finbarr's arms. I might have turned and headed back to my room to avoid Chilton, if he hadn't glanced my way. Once he spotted me, a retreat would only garner suspicion. I kept my eyes down and tried to head past him to the dining room.

'Pardon me,' Chilton said. 'Miss.'

'Mrs,' I corrected him, then smiled too stiffly. I could feel the edge of my lips stretch unnaturally. 'Mrs O'Dea.' After escaping the baths I had walked to another hotel to clear my head, and bought a new shawl at their gift shop, as well as some paper and a fountain pen. Perhaps I'd write a story while I was here, or a poem. I pulled the shawl close around me, and its price tag tumbled from the dark threads.

Chilton reached out and touched it. 'Is that what you're worth, then?'

It was the sort of jest I loathed, but something in his face made me relax. He looked embarrassed at making such an easy joke. He looked mild, even kind. It was bad luck to have a police inspector at the hotel, but I saw at once it was good luck that it happened to be this one.

'Here you go,' said Mrs Leech, passing me a pair of shears. 'Inspector Chilton's here looking for a lady gone missing from Berkshire.'

'Goodness,' I said. 'Missing from Berkshire and you're searching for her in Yorkshire?'

'All of England's in on this hunt,' he explained. 'Inspectors and police officers dispatched to every county.'

This news set my teeth on edge. I smiled to conceal it and said, 'My, my. She must be ever so important.'

Chilton intercepted the shears and cut the tag off for me. 'If I could trouble you just a moment, Mrs O'Dea.' He placed the snipped price tag in my hand. His fingers were chapped and tobacco stained, his clothing rumpled. He held out a photograph with his right hand. His left dangled at his side. 'This is the lady. Have you seen her?'

'May I?'

He nodded and I eased the photograph out of his hand. Agatha stared back at me, hair swept off her face, head tilted, wearing pearls and a suit jacket. I thought of my mother, wresting herself out of her grief over Colleen to help me have the little picture made for Finbarr, to send to him at the front. I had worn my best dress, no jewellery at all, nowhere near so glamorous.

'Pretty,' I said. 'But no, I haven't seen her in Yorkshire.' Hopefully he'd remember my precise words, if any connection between the two of us were drawn later. 'I do hope she'll be all right.' I handed the photograph back to him.

'Ah well,' Chilton said, as if he hadn't expected any other reply. 'Thank you for looking.'

As I entered the dining room, I saw that Mrs Race – the beautiful blonde bride – was now joined by her handsome, scowling husband. The two of them sat by a window, too absorbed in their silent unhappiness to notice my probably obtrusive stare.

My new friend Lizzie Clarke waved me to her table, and her husband stood to offer me a chair. He was a lanky fellow, charmingly inelegant, in the way Americans can be, with dark eyes and a sweet, earnest expression.

'Donny Clarke,' he introduced himself.

'Hello, Mr Clarke.'

'Please,' he said. 'Call me Donny. Thanks so much for entertaining Lizzie this morning. Fun to make a fast friend on vacation.'

I'd scarcely unfolded my napkin before I heard merry, unmistakable laughter as Mrs Marston entered the room with her husband. She looked quite a bit different to how she'd looked when I'd last seen her at the baths. Her hair was curled, and she wore a smart jacket and faux pearls.

'Well, look who it is,' Mrs Marston said, stopping by our table. 'The chummy young ladies.'

Her husband, Mr Marston, stood by her side. He was decades older than she, a weathered, ruddy-faced man in his sixties. He placed a hand at the back of Donny's chair, his smile the indulgent sort a certain kind of man likes to bestow upon young ladies. I turned my eyes back to our table. Lizzie stared back at him more frankly.

'How do you do, Mr Marston,' Lizzie said. 'I trust married life is treating you well?'

'Sure it is,' he said, thickly Irish. A change came over his face and he seemed suddenly eager to return to his table. 'Are you ready to eat now, Mrs Marston?'

She trilled with delight at the sound of her married name. Mr Marston put his wide, meaty hand at the small of her back and guided her hastily to an empty table.

'You all right, Lizzie?' I asked. She nodded emphatically.

The waitress came to take our order. We had a choice of fish pie, roast beef, or chicken stew and we all chose the roast beef. The room had great, tall windows and I found myself staring through them, one at a time, expecting Finbarr to be standing on the other side, watching me. The sun had long since set; even if he'd been there, he wouldn't be visible. Where was he spending the night? Would he have a hot meal, or any meal at all? Just this morning it had been years since he'd last held me. Now it was merely hours.

I glanced over at the Marstons, busily unfolding their napkins. Mrs Marston appeared as cheerful as ever. Her husband was harder to read.

'Don't bother yourself with those two,' Lizzie said. 'There's much better people-watching over there.' She jutted her chin at the beautiful young couple. Mr Race looked peeved and arrogant, Mrs Race stubbornly tearful.

Almost as if Lizzie had known exactly what was about to happen, a commotion erupted.

'I don't care,' Mrs Race cried, loud enough for every diner to not only hear but also fall silent. She jumped to her feet nimbly, throwing down her napkin. 'I don't care how much the wedding cost or what people will say. I can't go on. I simply can't!'

'See here,' her husband said, in a whisper that was no less audible but far more chilling than his wife's outburst. 'Sit down and stop making a scene.'

The young bride turned as though to storm out of the room. Her husband reached out to grab her wrist. Before I had a chance to worry about damage to those slim, delicate bones, she picked up her foot and stomped on his foot, hard enough to make him let go.

'What will you do?' she asked. 'Hit me? In front of all these people?'

There was a scuffle as most of the men in the room – including Donny and Inspector Chilton – rose to their feet and approached their table, ready to intervene. Lizzie stood, too, and stepped towards the scuffle for a better look. Her bravery impressed me but I remained seated, my view of the scene obscured by the crowd of concerned onlookers.

The door to the dining room flew open and in marched the owner of the hotel. 'Look here,' Simon Leech said. 'That's quite enough of that.'

'This is nobody's business but our own,' Mr Race announced to the room at large.

'In that case, best not to have rows in public.' The last thing Mr Leech needed was trouble at his struggling hotel. He kept his voice stern but kind. 'Let me buy you a bottle of champagne. You're newlyweds, after all. It's a time for celebration, not arguing.'

I looked over at Mrs Marston, who was still twisted round in her chair, away from her husband, so as to watch the spectacle. A look of consternation crossed her face, as if she – also newly wedded – deserved a bottle of champagne, too. Mr Marston rose to his feet, but his purpose was not to request equal treatment. He had his hands to his throat, and he sputtered wildly as if he wanted to gasp but couldn't.

'Darling,' his wife cried, turning back towards him. 'Oh, my darling. Help him, please, somebody help him!'

Mr Marston fell to the floor. His eyes bulged, his hands clasped his throat and his feet kicked like a freshly landed fish. Almost everyone – the hotel staff as well as the guests – headed over to the scene of distress.

It was young Mrs Race who reached him first. 'Stand back,' she commanded, seeming a different person to the one who'd just done battle with her husband. 'I'm a nurse.' She loosened Mr Marston's tie and shirt collar, then took his pulse. She had his head pulled into her lap and I thought there was something grotesque about that pretty young girl balancing his wide, red, froggish face so close to her body.

By now Lizzie had returned to her seat. She and I did not move from our table. We sat, quietly watching everything unfold. Lizzie took a sip of wine and said, 'Too many cooks.'

'If you ask me, it's too late,' I said. The violence in Mr Marston's body had come to rest. His eyes stared glassily at the ceiling.

The doctor who performed massages had gone for the day, but there was another one, a guest staying in room 403. Someone ran to fetch him. All poor Mrs Marston could do was crouch beside her husband, staring in shock at the scene before her. The doctor arrived in a state of half-dress. He was a youngish but prematurely white-haired man who looked elegant and purposeful despite his indecent state.

'It's no use,' the doctor said, after a swift examination. He looked around the room, addressing all of us with an appropriately solemn expression. Then with practised fingers he pulled Mr Marston's eyelids closed.

The sound that emanated from Mrs Marston was altogether unholy. She clutched at her throat as her husband had done earlier and, for a moment, I thought she might also fall to her death.

'Come now,' said Inspector Chilton, stepping forward. He put his arms around her shoulders. She accepted his embrace, her scream giving way to sobs. Chilton led her across the room to another table and seated her with her back to her deceased husband.

'A hefty dose of brandy will do for her,' the doctor said. 'And perhaps a sheet for him, while we wait for the coroner to arrive. Best go ahead and call the authorities.'

'Oh, you've no idea,' Mrs Marston was sobbing. 'How long we waited, what we've been through, what we've given up. Oh, my poor, dear darling. It can't be. Just like that? It can't. Where will I go? What will I do?'

She pushed herself up from the table and rushed back to her husband, throwing herself upon him and weeping. The force of her ministrations startled the body enough for his eyes to pop back open. Mrs Marston gasped, a pathetic and hopeful moment, then commenced to weep again as she realized he hadn't come back to life, and she lost him for the second time.

'I believe I'll take this plate to my room,' I said to Lizzie and Donny. I'd barely taken a bite.

'Yes,' Lizzie said. 'We'll talk later. Will you be all right?'

'I believe I will. And you?'

She nodded but her eyes brimmed. It was a shocking thing we'd witnessed.

As I passed the grandfather clock in the front hall, I saw Mr and Mrs Race by the stairs, no longer scowling or arguing. The tragedy seemed to have subdued them. Her head was lowered and though his hand was on her arm, it did not seem to be an aggressive grip. Their foreheads pressed together. Perhaps he was apologizing, or even comforting her. I paused a moment, and when neither of them looked towards me I continued on.

My room had a wide four-poster bed and a little writing desk. I sat down at the latter and used it for my dinner table. It was in front of a window, and again I looked out into the darkness, as if for all the world I was fourteen years old and back in Ireland, knowing Finbarr might arrive any moment for lawn tennis.

The death I'd witnessed had not spoiled my appetite, not for food and not for love. I cleaned my plate, having learned during the war never to waste food. Sleep was another matter. The bed was comfortable. Eventually, the ruckus downstairs quieted. I lay very still, trying to clear my mind, unable to close my eyes, staring up at the canopy. I must have fallen asleep eventually, because by the time sunlight poured through the curtains I'd forgotten to close, I was awakened by a scream.

The Disappearance

Day Four
Tuesday, 7 December 1926

I DONNED MY DRESSING gown and peered into the hall. Several other faces dotted the corridor, all belonging to women. I could hear the doctor's voice inside a room not far from mine, presumably the origin of the scream, trying to calm someone down. Mrs Leech, I surmised. The door directly across the hall from me opened with an urgent, audible whoosh, bespeaking great confidence. There stood Miss Cornelia Armstrong, the young lady travelling on her own.

'That was Mrs Marston's room,' she announced, for the whole hotel to hear. Miss Armstrong was barely nineteen, with impeccable posture and thick black hair spilling down her back in astonishing quantity. She had a way of lifting her chin as she spoke, daring the listener to contradict her.

'Oh dear,' I said.

'I'm going to see what's happened.'

There was no stopping her. Miss Armstrong marched down the hall towards Mrs Marston's room. She had her dressing gown loosely belted and showing more of her décolletage than likely she intended. When she returned, her face was pale, and her voice shook as she reported: 'Mrs Marston is dead. I saw the doctor pull the sheet over her face.'

By now more guests had gathered in the hall, including a painfully thin spinster who covered her mouth with one slim, freckled hand and gasped, 'How dreadful.'

'I suspect she died of a broken heart,' Miss Armstrong announced to the bleary-eyed gatherers with an air of diagnostic expertise. She had delicate white skin and eyes almost as black as her hair. 'They'd been star-crossed, you know, Mrs and Mrs Marston. Before they married.'

I wanted to say I was thankful I shouldn't have to hear that phrase – *star-crossed* – ever again in my life. I wanted to say that if it were possible for a broken heart to kill, I'd have been dead long ago. Instead, I closed my door without another word. Given the situation, the usual manners did not apply.

Chilton was downstairs using the telephone to call Lippincott. He heard the scream but, muffled as it was, did not pay it particular notice. Perhaps one of the ladies had come upon a spider.

'Will you be sparing a man to investigate?' he asked Lippincott, referring to Mr Marston's death.

'There's no man to spare, that's why you're here in the first place. Probably nothing to it. A heart attack, is my guess.'

Of course, this was likely right. Why would anyone want to harm the old Irishman?

Just as Chilton rang off, Mrs Leech came rushing down the stairs, looking most discombobulated.

'Mrs Leech?'

She held up her hand, too weepy to answer, and rushed to the kitchen where her husband was overseeing breakfast preparations. After a moment, the doctor came downstairs, no more fully dressed than he'd been the previous night, sweat gathered on his brow despite the season. Chilton gave him a handkerchief. The two had chatted last night while they shared a cigarette and waited for the coroner to collect poor Mr Marston, and had already established battles in common.

The doctor mopped his brow. 'Damn it all,' he said. 'I'm supposed to be on holiday.'

'What's happened now?' Chilton asked.

'Another death. The wife. Mrs Marston. What a honeymoon they're having, eh?'

'Gads. Well. Perhaps now they're having the ultimate honeymoon. Reunited in the hereafter.' Chilton didn't believe this for a moment but he had an inkling the Marstons would have liked the idea. They had that look about them, a smug religiosity, like happiness was owed, in this life and whatever followed. He hadn't had a chance to chat with Marston before the old man keeled over, but even though plenty of older men had signed up to do their bit, Chilton could tell Marston hadn't been one of them.

Because jocularity could be soothing under the most dire circumstances, Chilton thought about saying something such as, *Who'd you think would want to off that pair?* Certainly the odds of the first death being suspicious was elevated now the man's wife was dead.

'Any ideas about the cause?'

'Not a mark on her, at least at a glance, nor anything else disturbed. Young for it to be heart failure, though she'd certainly had a shock.'

'Did she take anything? Last night?'

The doctor bristled. 'I gave her a simple sleeping draught. Perfectly harmless.'

'Of course,' Chilton said. 'Damn shame.'

'Indeed. I might be cutting this holiday short. Hardly seems right. Or restful, for that matter.'

Chilton nodded and took his leave. He felt a little guilty for having disliked the Marstons at first sight. For now he'd take care of his primary order of business, searching for Agatha Christie. He'd canvas the hotels, keep an eye out on the roads. Carefully doing his duty.

After the unfortunate ruckus I skipped breakfast, instead bundling up in my warmest clothes. As I passed the front desk, Mrs Leech greeted me with frantic cheer. 'Off for a walk, are you? Lovely day for it, cold air will do you good. Terrible about the Marstons, him dying of a heart attack and her of a broken heart.'

'Has the coroner made his conclusions already?'

'Well, then, what else could it be? So sad, so sad, but could have happened anywhere! Nothing to do with us!'

I gathered more than one guest had already checked out, the hot baths not seeming much of a cure in the wake of two sudden deaths: the last thing their hotel needed.

Walking down the dusty road, I thought of my conversation with Ursula Owen at Godalming on the night of Agatha's disappearance, about Lucid Dreaming. And how Lucid Living would be a lovely corollary. As a girl, I'd had that very ability – to think of Finbarr and suddenly he'd appear. On this day in Harrogate, for the first time since the Armistice celebration, I knew I'd regained the power. Nothing else supernatural was afoot. I felt confident the ghosts of the Marstons were well and truly departed. But I knew that if I walked in the same direction Lizzie and I had done yesterday, Finbarr would appear.

Sure enough, when I rounded the corner I'd envisioned, there he was: hands in his pockets, breath gusting out before him, cheeks rosy. This time I didn't run to him but walked, and kept walking, as he held out his arms, straight into them.

'Are you all right?' I asked. 'Are you eating? Sleeping?'

'Yes,' he said into my ear. His hand at my back was steady, no tremor. 'Are you?'

'Me?' I pulled away from him. 'I'm staying in a hotel. Luxury. Food. Roof and hearth fires. Where are you staying?'

'Where there's a roof and a hearth. You're not to worry about us, Nan.'

'Us?'

Someone walked over my grave. I had the most illogical, most glorious vision: Finbarr beside a wide hearth with a crackling fire, holding our child in his lap.

Chilton drove over rutted roads in the car Lippincott had provided. He slowed down as he passed a couple – young, if not tenderly so, the man old enough to have been in the war and with the look of someone who had been (Chilton could tell at a glance from almost any distance). Sometimes, it seemed he himself still lived in the tunnels at Arras, under the shaking ceilings; with the rubble falling and the claustrophobia – and the knowledge that if you followed your instinct and broke free, you'd find yourself in an onslaught of enemy fire. Then you'd find yourself dead, riddled with machine-gun bullets. If only Chilton had known at the time how he'd come to long for that outcome.

This young man must still want to be alive, judging by the way he held the girl by the elbows – with such fervour Chilton slowed down to make sure the embrace was a willing one. Both were so caught up in each other's faces that they didn't seem to notice the car, or Chilton's scrutiny. The girl was small and dark haired, her face so full of emotion that she might not be British. French, perhaps. Whatever her nationality, it was clear she wasn't in peril – at least from the fellow who held on to her. From her own emotions, well, that was another matter.

Chilton changed gears and motored on, the girl's face still in his mind. He had met her. Yes, she was staying at the Bellefort Hotel; he'd shown her the picture of Agatha Christie and she'd examined it dutifully. No wonder he hadn't immediately recognized her. She had seemed perfectly contained in that moment – a good English lady after all. Mrs O'Dea, she'd said. The young man wasn't her husband, and he wasn't a guest at the hotel, he was sure of both. What secret lives people did lead.

Chilton's reveries took him on one wrong turn, then another, down a particularly dim country road. He pulled over to take out the map Mrs Leech had given him. As he turned off the motor, he noticed a house, shut up for winter, the windows boarded, but with smoke rising from the chimney in a steady swirl. He stepped out of the car. The air smelled like firewood and mulched leaves. As he got closer to the house he saw there was an automobile parked beside it. Somebody had meant to hide it, from the looks of the way it was left towards the back, with low elm branches obscuring it from the road. Dragged there, not grown. The car was large and black. Chilton couldn't tell the make of it, he wasn't much for cars. The front stoop of the house was caked with frozen dust. No footprints. Chilton put his ear to the door, which was made of thick wood – a modest but well-built country house, sturdy and generous with space and materials. Lovely gables. From inside he heard a clattering. It took a moment to identify it as typewriter keys. A cheerful, industrious sound, clackety clack clack clack. He used the heavy brass knocker and felt almost sorry when the noise abruptly stopped, followed by irritated footsteps. He stepped back as the door flung open.

The woman was on the tall side, with red hair and lively eyes. Her face rearranged itself the moment she saw him, from expectation to dismay to the kind of courteous mask people use to protect themselves from the truth. She wore a man's clothes: trousers and a thick jumper over a collared shirt. Then, just barely visible, pearls.

'How do you do,' she said, in smooth, posh tones. Her hair fell to her shoulders in loose waves. She brushed both sides self-consciously behind her ears, then held out a hand as if he'd been invited for tea.

Chilton took her hand. She was prettier than the picture he'd left on the passenger seat of the automobile. Fairer and more youthful, with the kind of movement in her face – even as she tried to appear unmovable – that no picture can properly capture. Eyes not dark, as they'd seemed, but bright blue, flecked with green. At the same time, unmistakably the same woman.

'Mrs Agatha Christie,' Chilton said. 'My goodness. We've been looking for you.'

Part Two

The Disappearance

Day One
Saturday, 4 December 1926

A GATHA DROVE AWAY from Styles just past midnight, hardly caring if she ever saw it again. The house was unlucky, she'd felt it from the first day she'd set foot inside. Archie had been the one who'd wanted to buy it, so he could be nearer to his golf club. Damn golf. Damn Archie. Clearly there was no reasoning with him. Perhaps she'd have better luck with me.

She had left the house earlier at 9.45 p.m. for a short while. The reports were correct on that account. Agatha headed out, driving for a while to clear her mind, then she turned round and came home, letting herself inside while the household slept. The house felt dark and quiet and empty. Bad luck clung to the ceilings like billows of smoke. Her skin was too small to contain the rage and sorrow and anxiety, she wanted to claw at herself to escape it. She wanted to burst, splattering herself and all her misery over the walls. She yanked off her wedding ring and threw it as hard as she could at the wall, so that it dinged the paint and then fell to the floor, spinning several times before wobbling to rest. Let it be swept up with the dust tomorrow.

It wouldn't do. It couldn't be borne. If she were a drinker, she would have polished off a bottle of something, but she wasn't, so she gathered up her typewriter and some things to carry her over for a few days. She would go to Ashfield to get her mind straight. But once she had loaded her things into the car and climbed behind the wheel, she changed her mind. She would not politely allow that monstrous little hussy to upend her life entirely. Not without a fight. Instead of slinking away to her childhood home to brood she would drive directly to Godalming and march into the Owens' cottage and cause an unbearable scene. So what if it was past midnight? So what if she woke every last person in the house? It wouldn't endear her to Archie but what did that matter? She'd already thrown herself on his mercy and found he had none. But his mistress might be a different story.

Agatha regretted the genteel approach she'd taken with me on the pavement in front of Simpson's. Now she imagined grabbing me by the shoulders, perhaps with a measured shake, and demanding I give up her husband. If that didn't work, she'd fall to her knees and beg. She'd let all the anguish pour out, visible and audible. '*Angoisse*,' her mother would have said; she'd liked to use French when discussing emotion, on the rare occasions she determined emotion must be discussed. But Agatha would not allow any mollifying translation. Imagining it, she thought, Nan might take pity. The girl was a slut, not a monster.

It was difficult to see beyond the windscreen, between the darkness and her eyes, puffed to slits from crying. Otherwise she might have seen him earlier, the man who walked down the middle of the road, trying to flag her down, his long arms waving in and out over his head in an 'X' formation. As it was, she nearly ran him down to his death. It felt to her like the last moment, when she swerved to miss him, realizing – again at the last moment – that if she didn't put on the brakes, she'd fly headlong into the chalk pit.

Not something she longed for, death. Not one bit. The sort of thing you realize, in the instance after an accident almost kills you. And after all, she knew a good bit about poison, between her stint in the dispensary during the war and research for her novels. If she'd wanted to be dead, she already would be.

There was a knock on the driver's side window. The man she'd swerved to avoid killing leaned down, staring at her with unnerving calm, as if all this were perfectly normal. Perhaps now he'd kill *her*, but she rolled down the window anyway. Black hair fell into his eyes, and his breath gusted in the cold air. From his coat and jumper she recognized him as the same fellow who'd given Teddy the whittled dog.

'Are you quite all right?' He had a raspy Irish brogue and soulful blue eyes.

'I believe I am.'

'I'm sorry if I startled you.'

'Startled me? My dear, you ran me quite off the road.'

He opened the door to her car, so she could get out. She felt it again, the awareness that perhaps she ought to be afraid of him. The car wobbled precariously, and she saw its front wheels were hanging over the pit. It struck her again with the force of averted tragedy, how very much she wanted to be alive.

'I've come to talk to you about Nan O'Dea,' the young man said.

Oh, the impudence. The way the world was unfolding before her. An awful dream. Wake up, she commanded herself. Wake up, wake up. She closed her eyes, determined to open them and find herself home in bed with her own husband. Even as the cold air insisted she was out on the road in the dead of night, confronted by a stranger wanting to discuss the most intimate horror of her life.

'Mrs Christie,' the Irishman said. 'I think we might be able to help each other. You and I.' He had a nice face. *Très sympathique*, her mother would have said. A handsome young man with an aura of kindness about him, if sadly lacking any humour. She raised her hands and placed them over her face.

'There now,' the Irishman said. She removed her hands and, gently, he touched her cheek just below her eye, where a tear would have fallen. 'We'll have time for tears later, won't we? It's cold and there's some travelling to do.'

'I don't know if my car will start.' As if this were the reason not to go with him. Not even considering that she'd be travelling with this stranger. Not even worrying that she must have gone mad not to at least try to back up and drive away, fast as possible.

'We'll leave it,' the Irishman said. 'That'll give them something to worry about, won't it? As luck would have it, we're both up and about after dark. And I've recently come upon a vehicle nobody seems to be using.'

'Stolen?'

'Abandoned not far from here, on the grass by the road. I've borrowed it.'

'So you'll be returning it, then?' Her voice was sceptical and pointed.

'If I can.'

There was a melancholy to his voice that pinched Agatha's already vulnerable heart. 'How lucky,' she said, suddenly wanting to be forgiving. 'The luck of the Irish, I suppose.'

A rasping sound, the sad echo of a laugh that never was. 'I'm afraid to say I've not found much truth in that expression.'

Ah, she thought, the light dawning. This was Nan's young man. She'd scarcely paid attention to what the girl had said about her past the other day at Simpson's. Now she narrowed her eyes, unsure of what to do. The last thing she needed was another man in love with Nan O'Dea.

Still, she stepped out of the car and placed her hand in his. He nodded, as if proud of her for making the right decision, and she decided to let herself be convinced and give herself over to his care. The scene she'd planned in Godalming would be of no use. But this fellow could be.

'You gather what you need,' he said, 'and I'll bring the other car round.'

Dazed enough to forget her hastily packed suitcase, Agatha transferred the most immediate necessities – her sponge bag, her typewriter – into a roomy Bentley. Before getting into it she stopped a moment, and stared longingly at her own car. You must understand how she adored that vehicle. How proud she was of buying it herself, with money earned from her writing. Perhaps, right now, someone was sitting in front of a fire, unable to sleep, turning the pages of her latest novel, *The Murder of Roger Ackroyd*. The embodiment of that, to her, was the wonderful little car, now teetering on the brink of destruction, just like her life.

Very well, then. She'd leave it behind for another.

The Irishman drove. It always seemed right to Agatha, when a man and woman were in a car together, that the man should drive. The road lay ahead of them, empty and bleak, stars shining down, the moon a waning crescent. The barest wind snuck through the windows, shaking in their frames. This car was not so well kept as her own.

How rarely she ever found herself awake and about in the darkened world. The man sitting next to her, driving, was such an entirely different presence to her husband. And just in that moment, only half awake, only half believing in the ruin her life had become, Agatha realized her skin fit again. She found herself thinking or, more accurately, feeling:

What an adventure.

Here Lies Sister Mary

YEARS AFTER MY stay at the convent – years after my stay at the Bellefort Hotel – I had another baby, a girl whom I named after my Aunt Rosie. I would have liked to have had more children, but, for Archie, one child from each of his wives was enough. He never wanted too much of my attention taken from him. Committed to being the wife he wanted, it was easy enough for me to spend the days lavishing love on my child and the evenings lavishing love on my husband. Unlike Agatha, I never became a writer. For me that possibility fell away.

It's all right. I loved being a mother and I loved my little Rosie. But a hundred babies, a thousand, would never make up for the loss of the first.

Fell away. That's what the nuns told us we'd done. Fallen away.

Mr Mahoney called the convent a charity. *The Sisters will take good care of you.* But to me it felt awfully like the workhouse I was lucky to have avoided. Later, I learned the history. Somewhere between 1900 and 1906, Pelletstown, the first special institution for unwed mothers, had been established in County Dublin. Not long afterwards, the convent at Sunday's Corner

155

followed suit. In exchange for what they called our safe haven, we would labour without pay until our babies were born. Then we would stay on another two or three years, working. Our children would remain in the convent – first in the nursery and then on the other side of that high cement wall – until they were adopted, fostered out, or moved to an orphanage. We were meant to go to the county hospital in Cork City to deliver two weeks before our babies were due, but that spring, a girl's water broke during lawn duty, when she swung a heavy scythe to cut the grass. She gave birth on a mattress by the laundry room with no doctor or nurse, only a few other girls in attendance. Afterwards, the nuns drove her and her baby to hospital in their farm truck. Ten days later, she was back on the front lawn, pulling daisies and weeds, and wielding the scythe where needed.

There were girls who worked the convent farm – tending ducks, milking cows and digging potatoes – under the close watch of the nuns. But I was kept inside the gates. Perhaps the nuns saw escape in my eyes. I tended their graveyard, did the laundry and scrubbed floors on my hands and knees. Each night I fell onto my bed exhausted to the core of my being. From growing a child inside me; from worry; from being so far from home; from waking each day at five for prayers and Mass, then labouring till 6.30 p.m. in the evening. And, perhaps most exhausting of all, from loving Finbarr. From waiting for him to recover, return to consciousness and come fetch me. A rumour persisted among the girls that, a few years ago, someone's beau had shown up and paid the Mother Superior for her release. Father Joseph had married the couple in the parish church. Not all the girls were pregnant by boys they loved. But those who were, myself included, counted on this fantasy as our only hope. I refused to consider Finbarr's death a possibility. We weren't allowed to send or receive letters but surely his parents would tell him where I was, and he'd come for me. I didn't start wishing for him to come for *us* until the first day my baby kicked.

Bess, Fiona, Susanna and I were working in the basement laundry over boiling, soapy cauldrons. The floor was tiled, a pattern of large grey squares and smaller blue and pink squares, a cruel commemoration of the babies most of us wouldn't be allowed to keep. Heat from the fires kept my forehead slick with sweat as I stirred sheets and napkins with a long wooden stick. All of a sudden, my child moved inside my body: unmistakably, distinctly, gracefully. I froze with the magnitude of falling in love. Children have moved in the womb since the dawn of man but never had any child moved in just this way. A somersault, toes grazing my insides, sending up a fountain of bubbles. I stopped, startled, and put my hand on my belly.

Bess stopped stirring and smiled. 'It's like magic, isn't it?'

We weren't supposed to become friends, or talk to each other, or even know each other's names. But of course we did. Girls thrown together find friends sure as night follows day. I'd insisted Bess and Fiona memorize my family's address in London, so we could write to each other if this ever ended.

'Was it real?' I asked Bess, rubbing my hand over the spot where I'd felt the movement.

'Sure it was.' Bess was further along than me, but she was so narrow and slight you could barely see the pregnancy beneath her apron and shapeless dress. 'Did you think you were in all this trouble for the sake of a mirage?'

I laughed. The sound startled me, it had been so long since I'd heard such a sound from myself or anyone around me.

'Can't you be quiet?' Susanna snapped. She hated breaking rules. Susanna was the oldest girl in the convent, somewhere in her thirties. This was her second stay here. Last time her baby had been adopted at six months, and she'd remained another year before being released as a maid to a local family, only to return, pregnant again, five years later.

Sister Mary Clare, the youngest and kindest nun, came in to check on us. She was lenient enough not to chastise us for talking. The room filled with her humming, a haunting Gaelic tune that trailed her like a mist wherever she went. Unlike some of the other nuns, she didn't have a strap attached to her habit. Also unlike the other nuns, she was not Irish but English. The sound of her voice was a comfort to me. On one of my first days at the convent I had asked her how she had come to Ireland.

'My father was Irish,' she'd told me. 'When I was a girl he sent me here to work for relatives.'

My heart jumped with recognition.

The nun said, in a sad and dreamy voice, 'It didn't go as I'd thought.' It was the only time I ever saw her look anything but jolly.

Since that day I'd thought of her less as a nun and more like one of the girls. Sister Mary Clare, I was sure, had arrived at the convent by means of hardship. When she came into the laundry room I didn't hurry back to work but stood exactly as I had been, hands out of the sink, fingers spread wide over my belly.

'Did the baby move?' Sister Mary Clare asked. She stepped close, putting one arm around me, and one soft hand on my stomach.

'Yes.'

'Good work, Mother,' she said, then took out her own handkerchief and wiped my brow. She was only about ten years older than me, with a clear, unlined face, plain but made bright by smiling. None of the other nuns would ever call us 'mother'. They only called us 'girls'.

I set straight back to work. My baby rustled again, and all of a sudden I was not, as I'd thought, alone. There was someone else here with me, a member of my family, the closest person to me there had ever been in the world. Bess turned her eyes back to her washing, but I could see a little smile at the edges of her lips. The two of us, keeping each other company in the love we had for our babies.

Another nun, Sister Mary Declan, poked her head into the room and said, 'Father Joseph's asking for you, Bess.' Unlike her younger colleague, Sister Mary Declan *did* wear a strap tied to her habit and seldom hesitated to use it, no matter how young or pregnant the girl. We cast our eyes downwards. Bess's smile disappeared, but she wiped her hands on her apron and dutifully followed the nun. Sister Mary Clare went along with them.

'Poor dear,' said Fiona, watching Bess leave. 'But I suppose the Father knows what's best for us, doesn't he?'

I couldn't glean from this whether Fiona knew why Father Joseph had summoned Bess. Fiona had grown up in an orphanage, then been released at the age of thirteen to work for distant relatives. A few months later their parish priest brought her here. I never heard Fiona say a word about the boy responsible, The convent burgeoned with girls who'd welcomed young men back from the war. Now the same men were dead from the flu, or fighting the Irish War of Independence, or simply had got on with their lives without a backwards glance.

And, of course, some of us – like Susanna and Fiona, I expected – had not been disappointed by boys we loved, but subjected to something far worse. Fiona's child was a year old now. He had just been moved from the nursery to the other side of the convent. She took comfort in the large raspberry birth-mark on his forehead, which she thought would prevent him being adopted. She never seemed able to think past their time here, and what would come afterwards.

Fiona never questioned the nuns or the priest. *They know best*, she continually muttered to herself. *They know best.*

'Bess will be just fine,' she sang now, stirring her cauldron like a very young, harmless and hopeful witch. 'Her beau will come to get her and they'll be married. I know it, Nan.' Even though I didn't argue, or ask how she knew, she added pointedly, 'I just do.'

The joy of my baby's movement faded. Fiona had red hair and freckles, her fair skin was flush and sweaty from the steam.

'Bess's beau is American,' Fiona told Susanna. 'She met him when she was nursing wounded soldiers at a field hospital.'

'Her mother should never have let her near the soldiers,' Susanna said through clenched teeth. 'And I do wish you two would stop talking.'

'I think her man will come for her,' Fiona said, ignoring the plea for silence. 'I'm praying for it. From what she says he sounds like a good lad.' She let go of her stick. 'Let's take just a moment,' she said, 'and pray for Bess. The Sisters can't get mad if they see that, can they? A little prayer break? For Bess and her child and their happy ever after?'

'The Sisters can get mad at anything they like,' Susanna said, not budging from her station. 'If you don't know that by now, you'll never know anything.'

Susanna was right, but still Fiona and I clasped our hands and pressed our foreheads together. I didn't pray so much as worry. That Father Joseph would turn his attentions from Bess to me. I tried to pretend not to know what happened when he called her to him, but today, thinking of Bess's baby moving inside her the same as mine, I couldn't move my mind away from the horror of it. I worried Finbarr had died, which I knew was all that would ever prevent him from coming to get me.

Magical Finbarr. If anyone could get me out of here, it was him. I closed my eyes, leaning into Fiona, and pictured him, tennis ball high in his hand.

Make a wish.

The two of us – no, the three of us – leaving this place safely and together.

Granted.

Sister Mary Frances blustered in and cracked Fiona across the back with her cane.

'None of that,' the old nun said, as if prayer were something that didn't belong to us anymore, except at the nuns' discretion. 'It's only hard work that will wash your sins away.'

Fiona straightened, smiling instead of wincing. 'You're right, Sister,' she said, her voice sounding sweet and pure. 'I know you're right.'

I returned to my cauldron. Fiona rolled a cart of soaking sheets up to dry on the rooftop. This time of day she might catch a glimpse of her little boy in the yard. She worried because he wasn't walking yet. *Shouldn't he be walking?*, she was sure to ask me, when she returned.

I tried to think of Bess, off with Father Joseph, as if prayers had done any good. As if I had it in me, despite all my sympathies and fondness, to pray for anyone except my baby and myself.

The Disappearance

Day Four
Tuesday, 7 December 1926

Agatha removed her hand from Chilton's the moment he said her name. What a fool she'd been to open the door. Finbarr had told her to keep her head low. He hadn't said not to answer the door because likely it hadn't occurred to him that anyone would come knocking, or that she'd be silly enough to answer if somebody did. But that's what she'd done, instinctively, obedient as ever. Somebody knocks and in the absence of your butler, a polite lady is obliged to answer. What power these customs do have over us, Agatha thought, and steeled her spine ramrod straight, as if that could undo the mess into which good manners had propelled her.

'I'm afraid you're mistaken,' she told him. 'I don't know anyone by that name.'

'I have a photograph of you,' he said. 'It's there in the automobile. Shall I show it to you?'

'A photograph,' she said, waving her hand in front of her face as if moving smoke out of the way. 'One face in a photograph looks very much like another, doesn't it?'

Had they really sent police all the way to Yorkshire to search for her? What a needless fuss. She felt a terrible flurry in her stomach. If they were looking for her here – where no one had any reason to imagine she'd go – where else would they search? Who else would know she'd run off, and why? Oh, she hated to think of her stalwart new benefactors – her new agent and publisher – learning of this whole humiliating mess.

'Mrs Christie,' the man said gently, 'my name's Inspector Frank Chilton. I'm representing the police department in Leeds. I've been charged with looking for you, though I daresay I never thought I'd find you.'

He had a pleasant face and manner. Mild and kind. Agatha saw at once he'd be easy to dismiss. 'I beg your pardon, Inspector Chilton. But I expect you didn't hear me. My name is not Agatha Christie.'

She saw Chilton look past her, to where she'd stationed herself at the long farm table, notebooks piled on it, and her typewriter. She closed the door against herself, blocking his view.

'And your name, then?' He kept his tone kindly, but firm enough to remind her he was a police inspector.

'I don't suppose that's any of your business. My husband will be along shortly. Ah. There he is now.'

She felt herself smile as Finbarr came up the walk, hands in his pockets and colour in his cheeks. An entirely involuntary reaction. They'd been apart very little these last four days. She found herself wanting Chilton to believe she could be married to someone so young and handsome.

'What's this?' Finbarr said, reaching the front stoop. The burlap bag over his shoulder bulged with what she felt sure were apples. Only this morning she'd said how she loved apples, and now here they were. Orange Pippin, she supposed, from the time of year. How she looked forward to biting into the crisp fruit.

'Darling,' she said. It wasn't the first time she'd called him that. He had nightmares. When she was wakened by his cries, she would go to him and calm him. *There, there, darling,* she would say, *you're perfectly safe.*

Finbarr started a little, to hear her use the endearment in daylight, and in front of a stranger. Agatha said, 'This is Inspector Chilton. He seems to have mistaken me for a lady who's gone missing. What did you say her name was? This poor lost lady?'

'Mrs Agatha Christie.'

'Oh dear,' she said. 'Poor thing. I do hope she'll be all right. And I do wish you luck in finding her.' Good manners may have forced her to open the door, but they also made it frightfully easy to manage prying strangers. Follow the script, that was all she had to do.

'So that'll be all, then,' Finbarr said, with a brusque nod at the inspector. He slipped by the man, nodding to Agatha in a polite, deferential manner that no man on earth would use with his wife. He started to close the door but Chilton raised his hand and stopped it.

Finbarr draped an arm around Agatha's shoulder. She smiled again. In the course of a few days they'd discovered a surprising amount in common. Their love of dogs, for instance. *I much prefer them to people, don't you?* And he had agreed before adding, *Most people, anyway.* Last night when she'd woken him from one of his terrible dreams, to comfort him, she'd thought about kissing him. That would serve Nan right, wouldn't it?

Now, looking at Chilton, she was shocked to find herself thinking about kissing him as well. Despite what threat he posed to her continued hideout, he had such a nice, kind way about him. He reminded her of Tommy, the fiancé she'd thrown over for Archie's sake. She refused to blush. Perhaps that was what women did, when they found themselves abandoned by their husbands. Perhaps they thought about kissing new men. She wondered how this impulse jibed with her assurances to Finbarr that they had the same mission, convincing Nan to release Archie from her clutches. Part of her felt nothing would assuage the pain of Archie being with another woman as effectively as being with another man.

'I beg your pardon,' Chilton said. 'But considering the resemblance, I'm afraid I have to insist you tell me your name.'

'Her name's Nan Mahoney,' Finbarr said. How annoying and predictable, for him to supply that name. Agatha's smile disappeared.

'So if I go to the town registry,' Chilton said, 'I'll see this house belongs to the Mahoneys.'

'Of course you will,' Agatha said. At the same time Finbarr said, 'We're renting it.'

They looked at each other. Caught. But what did it matter? She hadn't committed any crime, other than squatting in someone else's house, which didn't seem so very grave.

'Listen,' Chilton said. 'Mrs Christie, I know it's you. But I can give you another day to think things over and prepare yourself. I'll come back in the morning and we can decide together what you'd like to tell your husband. He's very worried, you know.'

Agatha laughed, so harshly she worried she'd erased any doubt he might still have as to her identity.

Finbarr said, 'Good day, inspector.' And he closed the door. Before he took his arm off her shoulders he gave her a little squeeze of comfort. Her protector.

'Not to worry,' he said.

Chilton walked back to the car, his head fairly swimming, trying to sort out what he'd just witnessed. If all of England was a haystack, with hundreds of police officers combing through the stalks, how extraordinary that he should be the one to find the needle. He picked up the photograph and studied it again. It was her, the same lady, he was certain of it. She was alive and would not be discovered at the bottom of any lake. What a happy thing, despite the myriad questions her discovery created, principal among them the identity of the young Irishman, whom so far today Chilton had witnessed with his hands on two unlikely but unprotesting women.

And what should Chilton have done? Marched her at gunpoint back to his car? And should he now go directly to Leeds and inform his friend Sam Lippincott that he'd found her?

No. Better to keep his promise. Give her another day to collect herself. Give himself another day to return to the Bellefort Hotel and soak in the hot pools. Eat Yorkshire pudding and sleep in the bed that was twice as wide and soft as any he'd ever owned. If Mrs Christie were in danger, that would be one thing. But it seemed she was only in a rugged love nest with a handsome Irish bloke.

No. He would not expose Agatha Christie today. He wasn't sure exactly why he'd come to this decision. Perhaps he would change his mind tomorrow. But not today.

The Disappearance

Day Five
Wednesday, 8 December 1926

MARRIAGE HAS A hold not often acknowledged on the popular imagination. I never understood it fully until I was married myself. Whether a marriage begins in duty or convenience, or whether it begins in secret, whispered words and irresistible passion. Even when it begins in resentment, or drizzles into nothing over the years, there's a bond formed that's not easily broken. With his wife missing, Archie buckled under the strain of a yoke he'd believed he'd escaped. Over the last two years, since I'd come along, he'd thought of his wife mostly as Agatha. Now with her missing, possibly in danger, he began thinking of her, rather fervently, as 'my wife'.

Deputy Chief Constable Thompson stood firmly unmoved by Colonel Christie's professions of anguish. 'We know about the girl,' he had announced the day before, arriving at Styles first thing in the morning.

Surely Archie had been tempted to say *What girl?* But he was a smart enough man to know when he was caught. 'I know how this looks,' he'd admitted, mistakenly taking on a tone of authority rather than contrition. 'But I love my wife and would never harm her.' Archie knew he had done no physical harm to Agatha but the deputy chief constable's furious gaze made him feel as though he had. Remembering the emotional pain to which his wife had been subjected, Archie felt simultaneously indignant with innocence and abject with guilt.

'We'll see about that,' Thompson had said, regarding Archie with a scarcely contained rage. If Agatha Christie were found dead, it would be a tragedy, of which the only resulting pleasure could be marching her husband off to jail. He ordered the search to be intensified.

Now Archie sat at his desk, with the copy of the story Agatha had written – typed out but for the title 'The Edge' written across the top in a madwoman's print, as if the pen had nearly punctured the paper. He read it again. The husband came across all right. And the woman, vanquishing her rival, sending her rolling down the cliff to her death. Archie thought of his wife, with a frightened kind of respect: I don't know her, he said to himself. I don't know her at all.

They might be searching for Agatha in every corner of England but, of course, the main hub was Berkshire and Surrey. By Wednesday the counties abounded with hounds and police officers. Even aeroplanes, the first time they'd ever been used to look for a single, missing person. The staff from Coworth House, the largest estate in Sunningdale, took a day off to employ their knowledge of the region, which was naturally far superior to any police force. Professionally tight-lipped, they did not repeat any gossip relayed by the paltry staff at Styles (unaware that Anna had already seen to the matter, just what one could expect from a second-rate housemaid). They were all sure Mrs Christie was now a corpse, and took great umbrage at the idea of anyone other than themselves discovering it.

How disappointing when two first footmen *did* find poor Miss Annabelle Oliver, frozen in a shallow stream, caught up in a snarl of brambles. A great cry went up at the sight of her, followed by disappointment. She was too old and too small to be Agatha Christie. One body would have been valuable. This body, belonging to someone nobody had reported missing, was not.

Archie walked down the road with Peter on a leash. He could hear the aeroplanes overhead, rotors slicing the air. Hounds bayed in the distance, a sound that had become ubiquitous since his wife had disappeared.

If Agatha had done this to drive him mad, hats off to her. Peter pulled disobediently on his leash and Archie yanked him back to his side. The dog had never liked him. But Deputy Chief Constable Thompson had asked Archie to bring her dog to the site where the Morris Cowley had been found. He could have driven but hoped the air – wind, really, cold enough to chap a man's skin – would do something to ease the unrest swirling inside his chest. *What have I done, what have I done?* Blown his life to bits, that's what. Caused this swirling mass, this appalling and unceasing to-do, all about him. The search was like Agatha's anguish come to life. And he had caused it, for the sake of a girl who was good at golf. The newspapers were blaring the news of Agatha's disappearance all the way to the continents. The police knew about his affair, thought they hadn't been able to track down Nan for an interview (he felt grateful to me, for lying low as promised). Still, how much longer before everything else came out, everything he'd done? Once Agatha saw the story of Archie and Nan made public, would she change her mind about wanting him back? When the whole world knew? Or had he ruined his marriage, his whole life, for what he'd begun to think of as nothing, a madness, a dalliance?

Police waited by his wife's car, still at Newlands Corner where they'd pulled it back from the chalk pit. The officers regarded Archie sternly, many of them certain he'd done some foul play. As if that were possible. As if he had it in him. Couldn't they tell how desperate he was to see his wife found?

'Here you go, Peter,' Archie said. The dog pulled on the leash again, in the direction of home. Agatha had spoiled him, allowing him on furniture, feeding him from her plate, walking him with no leash at all. Frustrated, Archie bent over to pick him up. Peter wriggled in his arms, whining. Two of the younger policemen exchanged glances. Amused or disgusted? The dashing colonel could no more control this little dog than he could his wife.

'Come on now, Peter.' Archie placed the dog by the car, but Peter didn't sniff, he didn't do anything but turn round and round in whimpering circles.

'Well,' said the more disapproving of the two officers. 'I suppose that's enough of that.'

'I suppose it is,' Archie said. He unclipped Peter's leash and the dog immediately bolted down the road towards home.

'Hold up there,' a voice called, as Archie started to trudge after the dog. It was Thompson, looking even sterner than usual. There were moments when Archie felt sure the man was just on the brink of throttling him.

Archie opened his mouth to speak but found no voice came out at all. Instead, it was Thompson's voice, obscuring whatever it was he'd meant to say, with the calamitous words: 'There's been a development, I'm afraid. The search has turned up a body.'

A *body*. Agatha? Surely not. To his horror, Archie's knees buckled, his own body, which had always been such a faithful servant to him, committing so humiliating a betrayal. He had to reach out and grab Thompson's collar to keep himself from crumbling to the ground.

Thompson bent at the knees himself, leveraging his weight to keep the colonel upright. He wore an undecided and consternated expression. Was this grief he witnessed, or was it guilt?

My wife, thought Archie. *A body*. It wouldn't do. He couldn't bear it. The world rearranged itself into an inhospitable and unforgiving place. He would have let go the officer, fallen to the road and wept, if only he'd been a different sort of man.

Early that same morning in Yorkshire, Chilton opened the door of his room to see the American woman, Lizzie Clarke, walk down the hall dressed for travelling. He pulled the door closed before she could notice him and saw her rap on a door, a delicate knock, careful to rouse only the occupant and nobody in neighbouring rooms. Once the door had opened then shut, Mrs Clarke disappearing into the room, Chilton removed his shoes and padded down the hall to listen.

'Donny's had a telegram,' the American voice said. 'We have to cut things short. Go back to the States.'

To Chilton's ears, the voice that responded – female, British – sounded as though she knew someone were listening. A little too loud and not quite genuine. 'I do hope everything is all right.'

'Yes,' Mrs Clarke replied. 'Everything is perfect. *Perfect*.'

Chilton imagined the two women, sitting together on the unmade bed, hands clasped. Even with the note of falsehood in the other woman's tone, he sensed a kind of intimacy. He returned to his room and sat on the bench at the foot of his bed to lace his shoes, which he noticed were going about the seams. He would have to tell Lippincott this morning. 'I've found Agatha Christie,' he would say. 'Right as rain. No distress. All she wants is her privacy.'

Perhaps he and Lippincott could be kind about it, and hatch a plan that would suit the authoress. They could tell the husband and no one else, call off the search, let her reappear when she was good and ready.

But even if the law could be convinced to let it rest, the press never would. Newspapers around the world were making a mint off this story. It was Mrs Christie's good luck that someone from the police had found her, instead of someone from the press. Mrs Christie seemed to have chosen the one place in England nobody expected her to be.

And still she'd been found. Such was the world. There was never any hiding for long. He finished dressing and headed down to breakfast. The Clarkes were at the front desk settling up with Mrs Leech.

'How do you do,' he said to the three of them. He pulled out a cigarette and brought it to his lips but did not light it. Mrs Clarke looked uneasy for a scant second, then adjusted herself to a stark inscrutability.

'Good morning,' she said, sharp American 'r'. The husband said nothing, just shuffled bills into Mrs Leech's hand.

'Thank you, Mr Clarke,' said Mrs Leech. 'So good of you to pay in full.' More than one guest had fled since the two deaths, and not all had been so generous. 'Prayers for your safe voyage.'

Mr Clarke turned to Chilton, drawing a match from his pocket and lighting the other man's cigarette. His wife said, 'I'm looking forward to it, actually. Getting back on a ship. I think these hot pools are overrated. No offence,' she said, glancing at

Mrs Leech with apology. 'I just like cold water. Give me the open sea any day over a hot steamy cave.'

The young husband returned the matchbox to his inside pocket and placed a hand between his wife's shoulder blades, manoeuvring her towards the front door as if their exit were a dance.

'Bon voyage,' Chilton said quietly, watching them go. The bellboy pushed a trolley holding their modest collection of luggage. Then he said to Mrs Leech, 'How curious of them to come all this way, only to stay a few days. You'd think they'd at least go and see the continent.'

She asked him if he needed the telephone. In fact, he had not only a need but an obligation. But he found himself saying, 'No thank you. Not just now. But I wonder if you know – are there many abandoned houses in Harrogate?'

'Abandoned, certainly not. Unoccupied, yes, there are a few. Country homes for city folk; they come so rarely I wonder they don't just stay in a hotel. I never did care for the city myself, Mr Chilton.'

'Nor I.' He pulled at the hem of his tweed jacket, which felt loose, as though he'd lost still more weight. It's important to eat, he reminded himself. It's important to work. To go through the motions.

He proceeded to the sparsely populated dining room. Among the few guests, a young woman sat alone, staring intently out the window, a cup of tea cooling untouched on the table in front of her. Chilton walked over directly.

'May I?' he said, pulling out a chair for himself.

What choice did I have but to answer, 'Yes.'

Inspector Chilton had an advantage over me, the kind a police officer enjoys. He didn't know how I was connected to Agatha Christie but he knew I *was* connected. I had no idea he was possessed of such information. I was still fairly reeling from the news Finbarr had given me: that *us* meant him and Agatha, that she was in hiding with him here in Harrogate. How much more would I have reeled if I'd known Chilton shared this knowledge? As it was, he hardly worried me at all.

What did worry me was Finbarr, and the effect his reappearance would have on my future. How could I return to Archie's arms after being in Finbarr's? *One must respect the psychology.* It took a good deal of work on the part of my own psychology, working through warring emotions, to carry out my plan and become Archie's wife. Finbarr's appearance threatened to upend every bit of that.

Three years ago, when I set my sights on Archie, I knew it would never do to approach him. Instead, I placed myself in his line of vision. I found out what he liked and became that, looking away instead of allowing our eyes to meet. The perfect golf swing, the shyest smile. Like following a recipe that results in a beautiful cake, each step worked out just as it was meant.

Chilton didn't seem the sort of man who'd require that sort of game. He was approachable. Humble, but not in a lowly way. In a likeable one. He smiled almost sheepishly as he unfolded his napkin. Everything about him seemed frayed – his clothes, his face and his hair, which needed combing rather badly. He took tea instead of coffee.

'Jitters,' he explained, holding out his one good, slightly trembling hand, 'since the war.'

'I'm sorry.'

Finbarr had no tremors. Each man carried the war differently.

I liked that Chilton announced his weakness rather than attempted to hide it.

He said, 'I see your friend has left.'

'My friend?'

'The American lady, Mrs Clarke.'

'Yes, she did say she was leaving. But we're not particular friends. I only just met her the other day.'

'Did you?'

'Yes. I've never been to America.'

'And her first trip to England?'

'I don't believe we discussed it.'

Chilton looked at me in a way I found unsettling. It was a full, unabashed examination. Not a leer, not at all, but searching, and then assessing what he found. I did not love his questions about Lizzie Clarke but at the same time I found him endearing and, faced with his gaze, I couldn't help but bestow a small smile, as if I needed to comfort him.

The waitress approached our table but he waved her away.

'How do you know I don't want to order something?' I asked. Something I would never say to Archie. Or Finbarr, only because he would never dismiss a waitress without first finding out if I were hungry.

'Do you?'

I shook my head.

'It's an astonishing business,' Chilton said.

'You mean the disappearance? That lady novelist?'

'Why, no. That's not what I meant. Though surely that's astonishing as well.'

'Have they found her?'

'No indeed. Her whereabouts are still very much a mystery.'

'I think it's wonderful,' I said. 'For a lady to become an author.'

He looked surprised by this change in subject. 'Why, yes,' he said. 'I think so too.'

'I used to dream of becoming one myself,' I said. 'But life got in the way.'

Chilton nodded. He wasn't surprised at my confiding. It's the sort of thing that happened, at these hotels, away from the usual world. People told each other things. It's why my fast friendship with Lizzie Clarke was not suspicious.

'But you're still young,' he said. 'Surely you've time to write a hundred books, if you like.'

'Surely.' I clattered my teacup back to its saucer.

'What's astonishing to me,' he said, returning to his purpose, 'is the Marstons.'

'Yes,' I agreed. 'Astonishing. Would you excuse me, Mr Chilton? I've finished here. I do wish you a good day.' I put my napkin on the table and stood. 'If you don't mind, Mr Chilton, I must say, you don't seem at all the type to holiday at a spa.'

'Have I said I'm on holiday?' He tilted his head and for just a moment he did not look unassuming. In fact, he looked rather shrewd.

'No, of course. You're searching for Agatha Christie. I wish you good fortune in that endeavour, Mr Chilton. Good day.'

I left the dining room, unsure of what to do with myself next. The conversation with Mr Chilton left me exhausted. How difficult it is to walk through the world with your insides intact.

Looking back on this stretch of time, not just my days in Harrogate but all the years between the two Great Wars, I often think how fine it should have been. We allowed ourselves to believe evil had been defeated, as if evil never did rise twice. We had so many of the modern conveniences – telephones, automobiles, electric lights – but not *too* many of them, and not too.

readily available. Later there would be an overabundance of noise and glare. We could all be too easily reached. The very stars dimmed from the lights reflected on earth, and you could never do what I'd just done, escape from your ordinary life and fade away, undetectable.

I went up to my room and sat on my bed, picking up *The Great Gatsby* to read its final chapters. My eyes scanned the text but it was my own story that filled my mind. The Clarkes had packed up and gone away. What if I did the same? I could never go back to Ireland. But what if I said to Finbarr, *Forget Bally-cotton. Let's go away somewhere else. Anywhere but Ireland. Anywhere but England.* I could leave Agatha and Archie Christie in the past and take hold, finally, of my own future. Begin anew. As if such a thing were possible.

A distinct sound reached me through the window I didn't remember opening. Perhaps my imagination. Certainly it couldn't have come from the hotel. It might have come from a pram ambling down the road. But I felt certain I heard a baby crying. That sharp, insistent mewl of need and hunger. A pain struck my breasts, stinging, as if they wanted to express milk. I threw my book aside, stood and pulled the window closed. I could never leave England. Not even with Finbarr.

Chilton knew it would not do to let Mrs Christie go undiscovered for long. Resources were being lost. People were worried. He thought it might be less embarrassing to her – that she could rectify everything more quietly – if she allowed him to deliver her home. He decided to go to her straight away and make this offer. The two of them, driving through the countryside. He found himself thinking less about the moment he appeared with her in Sunningdale – a hero – and more about the journey itself. What would they find to talk about, as they drove the country roads?

But when he arrived at the house where he'd discovered Agatha, intent on convincing her of his plan, there was no smoke spiralling from the chimney. Where the car had been hidden there were only the tyre marks it left behind, the branches that had covered it neatly stacked on the grass. Chilton pushed the front door gently, not even touching the knob. It swung open without resistance or complaint. The rooms he walked through were empty of occupants. The ash sat cold in the fireplace. In one bedroom a light scent of lavender lingered. Atop the dresser was a crisp five-pound note.

Chilton sat on the bed and pressed a pillow to his face. Inhaled. By the time the home's rightful occupants returned, there'd be no discernible trace of it, but the next person to sleep on this pillow would dream inexplicably of fields filled with purple flowers.

He might not care for his career anymore, but he still had a modicum of pride, plus Lippincott to consider. Unless he managed to find Agatha a second time, he couldn't possibly reveal, to anyone, the first.

Here Lies Sister Mary

W E SLEPT IN a dormitory on the second floor of the convent, narrow beds in a row, close together. During the day the room was locked so nobody could steal upstairs to rest. At night, once we were in bed, the doors were locked again, the nuns the only ones who had the keys. Sometimes, I still dream about the convent catching fire, all of us locked inside that room with no escape.

It was a restless place to sleep, even in our exhaustion. The nursery was just below us, and we could hear babies wake and cry. When Susanna last stayed here there had been a different Mother Superior. At night the nuns would pin the babies' gowns to their cots and leave them till they could be nursed in the morning. 'It was the worst agony I ever felt,' Susanna said, 'hearing my baby cry with no way to get to her. Of course it's no accident they have us sleeping where we can hear them.'

Punishment, wherever it could be found. The new Mother Superior was kinder, at least when it came to the babies. I'd only ever glimpsed the woman at Mass, so far across the chapel that I had no sense of her colouring, age or features. During her reign, two girls were chosen to work as night attendants. When inconsolable wails reached us, at least we knew the children weren't all alone, but held and rocked. Every morning, the most recently delivered mothers' gowns would be soaked with milk, expressed for their out-of-reach babies.

Of course, the girls cried too, at night. Not just the nursing mothers but girls who'd just arrived, mourning their austere fate. Girls whose babies had been adopted or fostered out, or moved to the adjoining orphanage even though they were not orphans, their mothers mere yards away, longing and toiling and hoping against all expectations. We were a desperate lot, and the desperate seldom sleep well.

Bess's bed was next to mine. I woke one night to hear her sobbing, and sat up to squint through the darkness, making sure it was her. My hands went immediately to my burgeoning belly, the little child kicking and rolling, dancing and thumping. I didn't yet think of my baby as 'her'. But that's how it is in memory. Her, my baby, my little girl. I see her, smiling at me and waving. I wave back. I blow kisses.

'Bess,' I whispered. 'Is that you?' I put my thin blanket aside and went over to her. She startled like a war veteran when I put my hand on her shoulder. 'Hush now, Bess, it's only me. Nan.'

She put her hand over her mouth, shaking, trying to pull herself together.

I sat on the edge of her bed. 'You don't have to stop crying on my account,' I said, and stroked the strands of her cropped hair off her forehead. She had a sweet face, fresh and pretty. It was easy to imagine a young soldier falling in love with her. She should have been out in the world, wearing long hair and fetching clothes. Laughing.

'I can't bear it,' Bess said. 'I thought once I got bigger he'd leave me alone. Move on to someone else. But he won't. He won't.' She pushed herself up on her elbows. Eight months pregnant, at least, but one of those women who carries very small. Her whole figure was slight and spare except for the globe of her belly.

I gathered up Bess's hand and kissed it, searching my mind for something helpful or comforting. 'We could tell Sister Mary Clare.'

Bess didn't have the heart to tell me. Sister Mary Clare already knew. *Come now, it's nothing you haven't done before*, she'd say in a singsong voice. Other times she'd change her tune as if Bess wouldn't remember anything she'd said before. *Of course Father Joseph would never do such a thing. He's a man of God.*

How I wish she had told me but it was kindness that prevented her. She wanted me to hold on to whatever comforts I'd managed to find. Instead, she said, 'And what can Sister Mary Clare do? She's only another woman. None of them can do anything. I should've been brave enough to throw my body off a cliff before they could ever bring me here.'

'Don't say that.' I told her, in a few quiet sentences, about Colleen.

'She was a smart girl, your sister.'

'Please. I mean it. Don't say that.'

'I'm sorry, Nan. I am. I have five brothers and a sister back in Doolin. Every day I think about my little sister Kitty. For all she knows I did throw myself off a cliff. Whatever Da told her, it wasn't that he brought me here.' Bess lay back down on her side. She placed her hands in a 'V' and lay them between her pillow and cheek. 'Kitty wants to be in pictures,' she said. 'She's pretty enough, too. Only twelve years old. I hate not being there with her. I wish I could write to her and say, if you ever get in trouble, don't tell the priest, don't tell Da. Don't tell anyone. Just get yourself away.'

Away to where? I thought, but didn't say. If there was a place in this world that welcomed pregnant, unmarried girls, I hadn't heard of it.

'I hate to think of Father Joseph touching Kitty,' Bess said fiercely. 'I'd have to kill him. I would.'

She started to cry again. I hated myself for feeling terrified that Father Joseph's attentions would turn towards me if he ever lost interest in Bess. A few days earlier I had hid from him, ducking into the kitchens when I saw him walking down the hall with Sister Mary Clare. 'All girls are the same,' I heard him say to her. He sounded as if it made him angry.

'Father, you can't say that,' the young nun replied, with her light and cheerful trill, I would have thought it flirtatious, if I hadn't known that's how she always spoke. 'Why, we nuns are nothing like these girls, are we?'

Father Joseph stopped and touched her arm. 'Surely no,' he said. 'You're the purest angels, tending to the most wretched devils. Snow-white lilies alongside ragwort. A wondrous thing to behold.'

We girls, identical devils. And the nuns, identical angels, each with the same grave awaiting. *Here Lies Sister Mary*. I had seen Sister Mary Frances strap the palms of girls not much older than Bess's little sister Kitty. In the months I'd been here, nobody had touched my palms. I hadn't received a single lash. I kept my head down and did what I was told. Obedience seemed the safest plan. I hadn't learned yet. In this world it's the obedient girls who are most in danger.

Bess moved a hand from under her cheek and I held it. If we were all the same, and if Father Joseph could choose Bess, when indeed she did grow too large, he might choose me. I persisted in that way of thinking, even though it amounted, in my mind, to turning her over to him for the sake of myself. One of the worst aspects of this prison life was the way it could make us ruthless mercenaries, fighting in an army of one.

'I'm sorry,' I told Bess. 'I wish I could help.'

'It's all right.' She moved over and I lay down beside her, facing the opposite direction, both of us squeezed onto the narrow cot, close enough so that, through her belly, pressed into my back, I could feel a great bold kick. We drew in our breaths, hearts lifting at least for a moment.

'Oh, this baby's a strong one,' Bess whispered.

'Could be a boy,' I said. 'Could be, when he's grown, he'll take care of Father Joseph for you.'

'No. I'd never let him. It's my job to protect him. He'll never know a priest and he'll never go to war. I swear it.'

'Have you chosen a name?' Any name we chose wouldn't last. We could see them, the couples who arrived to adopt our babies. In those days women seldom delivered their babies in hospital; they delivered them at home. They stayed in confinement during their last months rather than roam about visibly pregnant. So it was easy not only to steal our children but also to pass them off as their own.

'If it's a girl, I'll name her Genevieve. If it's a boy, Ronan. That means Little Seal. Do you have seals where you come from, Nan?'

'No.' There were seals on the rocks at Ballywilling Beach but I didn't want to come from there anymore. I had abandoned the idea that Ireland belonged to me or me to it. I came from London. My mother's daughter. Not my father's.

'Whenever trouble comes to land, Ronan will swim away. Whenever trouble comes to water, Ronan will return to shore.'

'Why Genevieve?' I asked.

'The patron saint of young girls. So she can look out for herself.'

I hugged my own belly, liking the sound of that.

'No harm can reach this baby ever,' Bess said. 'I'll make sure of it.'

It sounded like what we wanted to be true. Never mind where we were. All the good things would happen. Our young men would return for us. Our babies would stay close to us always and we'd watch them grow. I pictured myself at a kitchen table, my baby playing with Alby at my feet, Finbarr making tea while I filled a notebook with stories. They hadn't taken the wishes out of us, not yet.

All girls are the same. Father Joseph's proclamation dogged us until we could almost believe it was true. There was the occasional rebellion – like the girl who escaped through the open gate when the milk truck arrived. The bells sounded, nuns scurrying everywhere, demanding one door be locked, another opened. We cheered, risking their wrath, and then were disappointed when the escapee returned the same evening, face streaked with dust and tears. A pointless day of walking led to the full realization that there was nowhere for her to go.

'Be glad for a roof over your head,' the nuns told us. 'It's more than most would give you.'

One morning, Bess and I were scrubbing the entry hall. Often the floors they had us clean were already spotless, but summer had begun with plenty of rain, and the girls who'd been working outdoors had tracked a good deal of dirt over the tiles. I left Bess on her hands and knees to fetch more hot water for our buckets, and on my way back, found Sister Mary Clare humming through the corridor.

'Sister,' I said. 'I wonder if I could ask you a favour.'

'My English Rose,' she said, smiling. 'You can ask me anything at all. I hope you know that.'

'Could you send a letter to Ballycotton, to Finbarr Mahoney – just a few lines, to tell him where I am?'

A look of sad hesitation crossed her face.

'You don't have to tell him to come for me,' I assured her. 'You don't have to say anything except, "Nan's at the convent in Sunday's Corner". He'd come for me if he knew, Sister, he'd marry me, I know he would.'

'Sure, and I know it too.' She pressed her hand into my shoulder. Despite the pregnancy there was no flesh for her to grab on to. The diet they gave us was spare at best. Bread in the morning and evening and a thin stew for our midday dinner. 'I'll write to your Finbarr, Nan. I do believe you could be one of the lucky ones after all.'

The nun walked me back to the front entryway. She did not offer to carry one of my buckets, the scalding water sloshing onto my shins and clogs.

'Sister,' Bess said. She struggled to her feet. The stone wall glistened with moisture and so did Bess. Sweat formed in beads on her brow and cheeks. Sister Mary Clare stepped towards her solicitously, the same plump hand rising to touch her cheek.

'I'm feeling poorly,' Bess said. 'Cramped and clammy.'

Sister Mary Clare moved her hand from Bess's cheek to her forehead. 'You don't feel feverish,' she said.

'Please,' Bess said. 'I feel like I'm close to my time. I have pains coursing through my belly like I'm on my monthlies. You need to transfer me to hospital.'

'Oh, is that what I need to do?' Her voice was amused but also warning. Even Sister Mary Clare would not brook impudence from the likes of us.

'I need to go to hospital,' Bess rephrased, the sound of her voice already hopeless.

'Look how tiny you are,' Sister Mary Clare said. 'Why, I can barely tell you're with child. You're nowhere near close, dear, trust me to know what that looks like. We can't have you lying in for weeks like a queen, can we?'

The nun looked from Bess's face to mine and must have been struck by the dismay. 'I'll tell you what,' she said. 'I'll sneak you upstairs for a little rest. Our secret. What do you say to that?'

'Thank you, Sister.' Bess's shoulders sagged.

I took the scrubbing brush from her damp hands. It was unheard of for any girl to be allowed to rest during the day. Not only did I feel glad for Bess but I was also encouraged for myself. Perhaps Sister Mary Clare really would write to Finbarr. I could already see him, striding through the front gates, past the pregnant lawn crew on their knees, straight to the Mother Superior to demand my release.

Bess and Sister Mary Clare walked off together. No other nun would have agreed to it. How lucky we were, that at least one of them was so kind.

Bess knew having a nun beside her wouldn't work as protection. Her heart sank when she saw Father Joseph emerge from the office he used when he visited the convent. Bess didn't believe in prayer anymore but old habits were hard to break. She found herself praying every day for her stomach to bloom into an obstruction. She prayed for a belly a hundred miles wide; the most pregnant woman to ever walk the earth.

'There you are, Bess.' The priest's voice was booming and unashamed.

Despair can be as real as any other trap. Like a fishing net – thrown into the air, widening, then falling to make its catch. In the hallways and in church Father Joseph had a great, smiling face.

Sister Mary Clare said, 'Bess is feeling poorly, Father. I was just taking her upstairs to lie down.'

'She can lie down in here.'

Bess turned to Sister Mary Clare and grabbed her arm. The nun looked down at the grip, then at the priest, who stood with his arms crossed, the picture of fatherly reproach.

'Please,' Bess said, 'he won't listen to me. But he might listen to you.'

Sister Mary Clare laughed, determined to prove she was the jolliest person on earth. 'My goodness,' she said, 'you'd think you were going to your execution, rather than private prayer with the most revered man in County Cork.'

Bess couldn't look at Father Joseph, who, no doubt, beamed at hearing this praise. As if the most revered man in any county would be assigned to ragwort like us. Bess was certain this scene only made him more eager to be alone with her. Instead, she looked at Sister Mary Clare, the enforced cheer on her face, the wilful refusal to see what was right in front of her. Or worse, the refusal to admit what she knew full well.

'Sister,' Bess said, 'can you really believe you'll get to heaven when all this is done?'

The nun wrenched her arm out of Bess's grasp, darkness finally crossing her face. 'Come now, Bess,' she all but hissed.

187

'The Father knows what's best for all of us. You know he does.' She put her hand to the small of Bess's back and propelled her over the threshold.

The office door shut. The priest's face changed. Furious. As if Bess were at fault, forcing him to defile an already defiled girl.

'You said you wanted to lie down. Lie down. There.' He pointed to the floor behind his desk and removed his collar, slapping it down to the floor like something to be conquered and discarded.

'Father,' she said. Her voice cracked. She hated calling him that. 'I really do feel poorly.'

'I've heard that before, haven't I?'

It was no use. The fastest way to get upstairs was to do as she was told. Bess lay down. She closed her eyes.

'None of that, now,' he said. 'Eyes open. Wide open.'

She opened her eyes. When Bess first arrived at the convent, when Father Joseph first began forcing his way into her, she would wait for it to be over. Now, even as she wished for a deliverance that left herself and her baby intact, Bess knew it never would be over. Not after the priest's final grunts and pushes. His righting of his costume and her escape back into the halls. If she ever left this place, if she lived to be a hundred years old. The priest's face would hover over hers, darkening all the moments to come that should have been happiest, even intruding upon her past. When she thought of her brothers she imagined them delivering her to Father Joseph's door. When she thought of her little sister Kitty, only twelve years old, she thought of Father Joseph, ordering her to lie down and keep her eyes open. Until Bess had to push the beloved face out of her mind, to save her from this horror, even if it only existed in her imagination.

'I hate you,' Bess whispered, before she realized the words had left her mouth. She braced, thinking he might hit her, but instead her words seemed to do the trick and bring today's ordeal to one final, thrusting end.

All the while, Sister Mary Clare stood outside in the hall. Waiting. Smiling as if nothing had happened when Bess emerged, shaking, to be led upstairs.

'You see,' Sister Mary Clare sang, musical voice caroming from one stone wall to the next. 'Now your rest will be all the better. Father Joseph always knows just what to do, doesn't he, to restore a girl's soul.'

In our dormitory, Bess lay down on her cot. She heard the door lock with a click and Sister Mary Clare's humming off into the convent. Downstairs in the nursery a baby cried, then another. One of the girls assigned to night duty had been released from the convent only last week, leaving a lone harried attendant tending the babies. But during the day there were plenty of hands, including the nuns, so most wails quieted before too long.

When was the last time Bess had been in a room alone? Truly not very many times in her life, coming from a family as large as hers. Her body ached in pulsing, insistent waves. Next time she'd refuse. Whether or not he was done with her, she was done acquiescing. He might be able to do whatever he wanted to any of us, but he didn't want a scene. He didn't want to hear the things he did spoken out loud. He wanted to move among us as a ruddy, fatherly figure. Pious and jolly. He wasn't so jolly when she flinched away from his meaty hands. He wasn't so jolly when he groaned himself into her. Sometimes she would lie beneath him, her eyes wandering to things she might grab and plunge into his neck. She had her teeth. If she sank them into his jugular – so close and exposed – and pulled hard enough, would a flood of blood open, rushing over her, himself unable to make a noise, falling off her to the side, clutching? Enough time for her to grab something – the thick glass paperweight from his desk, perhaps, or a lamp, or the letter opener – and finish him off.

Downstairs I raked the scrubbing brush back and forth over the tarnished grout, my lower back aching, and thought of Bess. I imagined Sister Mary Clare, accidentally on purpose leaving the door to the dormitory unlocked. And Bess, swift-footed despite her advanced pregnancy, stealing away. An open gate somewhere. Her American soldier waiting outside the convent. She held details about him close, so I didn't know his name, or what he looked like. But he'd arrive still in uniform. Once she was delivered, I'd never see her again, but would not permit myself to miss her. Because her escape would be evidence. Any of us might be rescued at any moment. And one day, I'd be back home in London, and a letter would arrive, across the envelope the address she'd memorized so faithfully. And we could write to each other to say how everything had worked out fine in the end.

Upstairs, Bess had not escaped but had fallen into a sleep she couldn't battle her way out of. She imagined her little sister Kitty standing in the corner of the room. *You must wake, Bess*, Kitty called, and Bess tried like mad to wrest her eyelids open, tried to find the voice in her throat to call back, *You must run, Kitty, you must run away from here*. From far away she heard Sister Mary Declan's footsteps, pounding into the dormitory, furious to hear Bess had been allowed a lie-down. For Bess it was like being at the bottom of a pool, fathoms deep. Far off above her she could see the faint suggestion of light and echoes. But there was no swimming to the top. None at all. She imagined Sister Mary Declan's footsteps belonged to Kitty, not running towards but away from her, fast as she could on coltish twelve-year-old legs, fast and sure and so far away. Now that Kitty was safe, it felt fine for Bess to stay deep under the water. Everything up top was vile and brutal. *Let me stay under*, she thought. *Don't ever make me come back up.*

She didn't know, but finally her American soldier had made his way to her father's door. 'I'll marry her the very hour they let her go,' he promised, when he learned where Bess had landed.

'Bess,' Sister Mary Declan cried. She slapped one cheek, then another, not in anger but genuine fear. Sister Mary Clare looked on, clutching her crucifix. It was important to all the nuns, to believe anyone who called them angels. By evening they would already be offering each other forgiveness, running down the rosary. Naming their sins and flinging them aside, ready to commit more tomorrow.

There was no time for hospital, or even to bring her downstairs to the mattress by the laundry. Susanna and Sister Mary Declan helped Bess deliver as best they could, right there in the dormitory. By the following morning Bess had finally clawed her way to the surface of the water, alive and whole. A miracle.

Another miracle: that same morning her young man appeared on the doorstep of the convent, demanding to see the Mother Superior. In time to walk Bess out of the convent, but too late for their baby boy. Little Ronan was one of the few babies who left the convent in Sunday's Corner in his mother's arms, swaddled in a yellow blanket: perfect and round-faced and stone-cold dead.

The Disappearance

Day Six
Thursday, 9 December 1926

THE BERKSHIRE BLOODHOUNDS weren't doing the job any better than Agatha's dog had done. Deputy Chief Constable Thompson called in a woman from Belgium whose dogs were said to be the best in Europe. These expert hounds followed Agatha's scent in circles, concentrating on the spot where Finbarr had flagged her down, where she'd stepped out of the car, lavender beads of sweat plopping to the earth. The scent ended where it began, as she'd hopped into poor Miss Oliver's car and sped away. The dogs sniffed and bayed uselessly, finally catching a whiff of a rabbit and leading the searchers on another fruitless chase. Even expert dogs are, in the end, dogs.

'Agatha, Agatha,' Archie moaned, taking turns about Styles, the house and its grounds. He found Teddy's hoop, abandoned under a bush at the edge of the property, and gave it a spin. It rolled a few feet, teetered and fell sideways on the grass. He didn't join the searches, not only to avoid his neighbours' suspicious glances, but also because searching seemed to be an admission that there was something to be found – another body, this time Agatha's – and he refused to consider that possibility. She was alive. It would be one of the policemen from an unlikely county to notify them and deliver the happy news: she'd been found, whole and well and ready to come home.

Noel Owen came round to keep him company. They drank late into the evening and took dinner in the sitting room.

'Back when it first began with Nan,' Archie confided, 'it was all so new and exciting. A kind of newness and excitement I believed gone from my life. And I won't lie, the forbidden nature of it, it was all so – so—'

'Irresistible?' Noel was not above prurient interest, though as far as I know he was always true to Ursula, to the extent any man can be.

Oh! The cynicism of that remark. *To the extent any man can be.* It doesn't bear out the way I feel, and what I believe, deep down in my heart. Some men can be true to the greatest extent. Finbarr, for example. He was always true to me, and always would have been, if ever we'd been given our natural chance to be together. If the world had unfolded on its own, without wars and churches. What laughter there would have been. What joy. Dogs and books and children of our own, starting with our eldest, our own darling Genevieve, whom I'd secretly hold in my heart as my favourite, though I'd never let the other children know.

'Irresistible,' Archie agreed with Noel Owen, tasting the word as if it were a kind of poison. 'The things I told myself. About Nan. About my marriage. If I'd been able to look ahead and see this moment, I believe I would have acted differently. I do believe that, Noel.'

Noel had been Archie's friend a long while, and never had he seen him so full of doubts. 'You can't have known Agatha would react this way.' He stood up to pour Archie some more whisky. 'Men leave their wives every day, don't they, without all this wretchedness. Agatha always seemed to have such a good head on her shoulders.'

Archie filled his pipe and stared out the window, everything outside still and quiet, as if the chill had frozen the wind. No branches moved. If Agatha broke through that stillness, if she appeared at the top of the road, a figure coming towards him, calm and resolute, like something of his own invention, he knew he would spring from the house and run to her, but would it be to collect her in an embrace, or to strangle her for what she'd put him through? He reminded himself, uncharacteristically, that he'd put her through plenty.

Now that she was gone, and he had no way to locate her – powerless, impotent, for the first time in his life – she occupied his thoughts as the beautiful face he'd carried through the war. Peach silk. Slim as a reed. Eyes wide with adoration. The stories she scribbled just a pleasing eccentricity, nothing to eclipse anything and everything he'd ever accomplish.

The things they'd come through together, Archie and Agatha – even his relationship with Nan they had gone through together, in their way. Agatha had been a part of it, unwitting, but still a dynamic and important part. Her presence driving the secrecy, the delicious illicitness. Then the way she'd clearly known but held her tongue, waiting for it to end. And then he *had* ended it, but not in the way she'd so patiently awaited, instead in a way that crushed her, and she'd stepped out of his life, out of the world. And all he wanted was for her to come back.

'Oh, A.C.,' Archie said out loud, when Noel left the room. He pressed his hand against the window pane. 'My dear wife. I'll do anything. I'll atone. I won't hold a grudge, for all this worry you've caused, all this uproar and shame. I'll give up the girl. If only you come back whole and well.'

Archie had no talent for magic. The road lay empty, the room sat quiet. The conjuring accomplished nothing.

Meanwhile, in Harrogate, in the course of his autopsy of Mr Marston, the coroner discovered potassium cyanide.

'There was a mark,' the coroner explained in Lippincott's office, the door for once closed. Both Lippincott and Chilton had elected not to see the body again. 'A tiny mark on the man's hip. It was injected, is my thought, right through his trousers. This was not a natural death.'

'What about the wife?' asked Chilton.

'Strychnine,' said the coroner. 'A lethal dose. Ingested, not injected.'

'Both poisons easy enough to obtain,' said Lippincott. 'Any housewife with a wasp or rat problem knows their uses.'

'Indeed.' Chilton pictured the couple, perfectly ordinary in every way. Who on earth would want those two dead? 'It had to have been someone in the dining room, then.'

The coroner nodded in agreement.

'I'd say this points to the wife.' Lippincott was naturally protective of his cousin's livelihood and nothing would empty out the hotel for years to come like a double murder. 'She offed her husband by injecting him with potassium cyanide, then killed herself with the strychnine. Did she seem particularly troubled to you,' he asked Chilton, 'before her husband's death, of course?'

'Quite the contrary. She seemed like someone who'd never known a moment's trouble. Rather jolly. Oblivious. Annoying, really.'

'There, there,' said Lippincott. 'Don't make yourself a suspect.'

The three of them laughed, forgetting themselves and the sombre nature of their discussion.

'But why would she want to kill her husband?' Chilton said.

'Clearly,' said the coroner, whose wife greeted him nightly with a burned dinner and a new list of grievances, 'you've never been married.'

'Do the murderous feelings generally begin on a honeymoon? The woman can't have been more vocal in her adoration.'

'All the more suspicious,' said Lippincott. 'Protesting too much and all that. It's rather clear to me, but as long as you're already there you may as well poke around a bit to confirm my theory. Discreetly. Don't make a fuss about it. See if Mrs Marston confided anything useful to the other ladies. It's a good way for us to get our money's worth out of you.'

Chilton nodded, but instead of driving directly to the hotel to start conducting interviews, he drove down a back road or two, eyes on the winter landscape. The deciduous trees provided a view into the wood. No signs of the young Irishman, or Mrs O'Dea, or Agatha. When his search yielded nothing, he gave up and went to the hotel. He would have a massage, he decided, so long as he was there, and send his mother a postcard telling her he had done so. It would please her to think of him relaxed and happy.

Mrs Leech presided over the front desk, her cheerfulness seeming an effort. Chilton gathered that more guests had precipitously checked out following Mrs Marston's death. Of course, any of those departed guests could be the killer, but now that he thought on it, Chilton tended to agree with Lippincott: the death of the couple was almost certain to have been a family affair.

'I thought I'd book a massage,' he told Mrs Leech.

She smiled warmly, taking up her pen, and said, 'I'm sure you know that won't be included in your gratis accommodation.'

Suddenly the idea of a stranger kneading his naked skin seemed less appealing. Chilton went instead to the baths. He had the place to himself, but despite the solitude and the restorative waters he did not relax a bit. His mind stayed on the roads he'd driven down, frozen and empty, no sign of the black automobile, all the houses with smoke rising from their chimneys inhabited by their rightful owners. It panicked Chilton the way a miscalculation can. He'd had her right before his eyes and had allowed her to slip away. Lippincott had tasked him with finding Agatha Christie as a lark. But what would he say if he knew that Chilton *had* found her, yet managed to daydream the quarry away? Could he do nothing right with the days he had left on earth?

After dinner Chilton took his pipe into the hotel's small library so he could turn to the matter of confirming Lippincott's theory regarding the Marstons. Ladies often complained about cigarettes but seldom pipes – a man with a pipe reminded them of their fathers – and it satisfied his craving while also making him look like he had something to do. The books on the shelves were mostly from the previous century. He perused the spines and landed on *Bleak House*, then settled onto the couch, where anyone who came in would have to sit beside him or across from him in one of the generous and well-worn armchairs. He'd seen Mrs O'Dea carrying a book, and a reader on holiday is soon in need of a new one. If she should venture in, he might also begin to discover her connection to Agatha Christie, killing two birds with one stone.

Before long a young dark-haired woman entered the library, with a cosy pink shawl over her shoulders. Miss Armstrong, Chilton reminded himself, the girl he'd dined with the other evening. She smiled at him perfunctorily and went straight to the bookshelves.

'Not much contemporary fodder,' he said, as she examined the spines. 'You won't find the new Dorothy Sayers, I'm afraid.'

'Oh,' she said. 'I'm not much for detective novels. I like a love story.' She pulled out a dusty copy of *Jane Eyre*, brushed off the cover and sat down, as he'd hoped, in the seat opposite him.

Mrs Leech poked her head into the library. 'Do you two have everything you need?' she asked brightly, anxious to retain the guests she had left. 'Would you like some tea?'

'Tea would be lovely,' Miss Armstrong said. After Mrs Leech's retreat she said to Chilton, 'I love seeing that. Mr and Mrs Leech, I mean. Together, and nobody seeming to mind.'

Chilton nodded, not wanting to tell her there were plenty who minded. Instead, he said, 'People can certainly be beastly about the things that affect them least, can't they?'

'They certainly can. But Mr and Mrs Leech never let that stop them. It's just too romantic, isn't it?'

Mrs Leech returned with the tea tray, all business, not a hint of romance about her. Once she had gone, and their cups were full and steaming, Chilton said, 'Terrible business about the Marstons.'

'Oh,' Miss Armstrong said, closing her book with a snap, as if she'd been dying to talk about it. 'Isn't it awful? And beautiful, in its way? They were star-crossed, Mrs Marston told me. Longing to be together for ever so long. And then just when they finally were . . .' Tears welled up in her dark eyes.

It wasn't that Chilton had lost his powers of observation. He could see things and even assess them. The loveliness of this girl before him, her impeccable manners, the way her eyes were so dark one could barely make out the pupils. He could also note the particular sweetness of a young woman very much wishing for love to enter her life, even as she bravely asserted her own independence. Chilton knew he himself was not the sort of man occupying her daydreams; he also knew he should at least be moved to some sort of emotion. There should be desire lurching forward, to be suppressed, with perhaps a sigh of sadness at what could never be. But regarding Miss Armstrong felt no more personal or emotional than reading a newspaper. He saw everything but felt nothing.

'Did you meet Mrs Marston?' said Miss Armstrong. 'She was chatty and friendly, wasn't she? Oh, I liked her, Mr Chilton. And I feel sure she died of a broken heart.' At this she set down her teacup and brought her hands to cover her face.

Mrs Marston had certainly gone out of her way to make her love story known. Might there have been a method to her garrulousness? Chilton fished the handkerchief out of his pocket and handed it to Miss Armstrong.

This is how I found them when I entered the library. Chilton had appraised me correctly. Having finished *Gatsby*, I longed for something, anything, to distract me from the maelstrom of circumstances at the Bellefort Hotel. If I'd been smart, I would have gone home, as the Clarkes had done. Instead, I'd extended my stay, telling Mrs Leech I'd be keeping the room indefinitely. How could I do anything different, with Finbarr haunting the vicinity?

Miss Armstrong turned to look at me, her eyes widening in

embarrassment, then correcting with that lift of her chin, daring me to judge her. I might almost have thought I'd walked in on a moment of romance if Chilton himself hadn't looked so detached. In fact, he looked more interested in my sudden appearance than the lovely weeping girl before him. This put me immediately on my guard.

'Mrs O'Dea,' he said, and gestured towards his tearful companion.

I sat down next to her and placed my hand on her shoulder. 'Are you all right, Miss Armstrong?'

'You're very kind,' she said, dabbing at her eyes with a shabby handkerchief that couldn't have been her own. 'It's silly. I didn't know them until a few days ago. But talking to Mrs Marston, hearing her story . . . she was already a friend. And they were destined to be together, those two. There's a Chinese legend called Yue Lao, have you heard it? When we're born, the gods tie an invisible thread around our little finger, which connects us to our one true love, no matter what forces try to keep us apart.'

'That's lovely.' To my own ears I sounded insincere. I wasn't immune to that sort of romance. I could believe in a thousand red threads connecting Finbarr and me. I just had a hard time applying this legend to the Marstons.

'It's so sad and awful,' wept Miss Armstrong, 'that they would die like that, right under our noses, right when their threads finally found each other. Just when they were on the brink of happiness.'

'Not on the brink.' I eased the handkerchief out of her grasp and handed it back to Mr Chilton, then gave her my own, which was silk and monogrammed, and far better suited to her delicate skin. A gift from Archie, specially ordered from Harrods. 'They had some days of happiness. Perhaps more than they deserved.'

Miss Armstrong stopped crying abruptly and stared at me, eyes full of rebuke. 'Whatever do you mean by that?'

'You said yourself you hardly knew them,' I pointed out. 'They might have been wretched people.'

Chilton let out a caustic little laugh.

'Why, Mrs Marston seemed the nicest lady in the world,' said Miss Armstrong reproachfully.

'Seeming is different to being,' I said. 'Best not to mourn people whose sins we don't know.'

Miss Armstrong looked at me as if I were the coldest, hardest woman in the world. Which I very well may be. But I should have known better than to reveal it. Nothing is more suspicious than an unfeeling woman.

I stood and went to examine the selection of books. Miss Armstrong held my handkerchief out to me to return it, but I waved it away. 'Keep it,' I said, 'I have loads.'

Chilton and Miss Armstrong busied themselves reading, though the air felt as if they absorbed nothing, just stared at the words on the page, waiting for me to leave so they could discuss my outburst. I should have been more careful but at this point I had no idea Chilton had seen me with Finbarr, let alone that he knew Agatha was hiding in the vicinity. Chilton was keen to keep it that way.

Finally, I settled on a Willy novel that had been all the rage when I was a girl, the first of the *Claudine* books. The edition was in its original French and the effort of translating it would make it all the more diverting. I said a curt goodbye to Chilton and Miss Armstrong.

When I emerged from the library, Mrs Leech looked up from her station behind the front desk. 'Mrs O'Dea,' she said, 'a little boy just came by with a note.'

I snatched it from her fingers, perhaps a little too eagerly. I worried it would be addressed using my first name but the writing on the envelope – bold male handwriting – said *Miss O'Dea*. If Mrs Leech registered the 'Miss' instead of 'Mrs', her face did not betray it. I felt a flush across my neck. It was worth whatever risk I'd taken, to use my real last name, so I could open this envelope and read what it said on the coarse piece of paper, butcher's wrapper.

> *Dearest Nan,*
>
> *Meet me at ten tonight just outside the front door. If I am not precisely on time, trust I'll be there and don't go any further than just past the front door. It's not safe for ladies after dark.*

I floated upstairs and waited obediently for night to fall.

Meanwhile, inside the library, Chilton asked Miss Armstrong if he could see my handkerchief. She handed it over as if eager to be rid of it.

'Rather a nice handkerchief,' he mused aloud, 'for anyone to have loads of.'

'I don't see how she can be so cruel,' Miss Armstrong said fiercely. 'I don't know about you, Mr Chilton, but I was raised not to speak ill of the dead.'

Chilton nodded sadly, as if in agreement, though he had seen enough of the world to know some of the dead earned ill speaking of. He didn't hold it against me. Much later he would tell me he did wonder why my handkerchief was monogrammed with a large cursive N when my name was purported to be Genevieve O'Dea.

The brave or complacent guests remaining at the Bellefort Hotel were exhausted by the hot waters, the spa treatments and the recent tragedy. By the time I came downstairs, nobody was afoot. Even Mrs Leech had left her post. The grandfather clock having finished its ten chimes, everything was quiet the way only a winter night can be, not even birds or bugs rustling. I had bundled into my lace-up boots and woollen coat, mittens and a woollen hat and scarf. I stepped outside, careful to open and close the door soundlessly. It was a well-kept hotel and the door had been recently oiled. It would remain unlocked, I knew. There was so little crime in the English countryside, back then, between the wars. No doubt that was part of the reason so many of us expected a perfectly reasonable explanation for what had happened to the Marstons. Not to mention one thousand men to spare searching for a missing lady novelist.

Not that I knew this, yet, about how large the search had grown. The Leeches didn't keep newspapers at the hotel unless guests requested them. Time at the spa was meant to be time away from the troubles of the world, Mrs Leech said.

My breath gusted out in front of me. The air felt wonderful. It reminded me that Christmas was approaching. When my sisters and I were little we used to wait outside together, staring up at the sky for a glimpse of Father Christmas before our mother bustled us off to bed. 'If you girls are awake, he'll pass our house right by.' We'd eat chestnuts roasted over the fire and go to sleep with sticky fingers, smiles on our faces. It had been the time of year I most looked forward to, more than anything in the world, before summers in Ireland began, and Finbarr.

Just as his name formed in my mind he emerged from the shadows, hands in his pockets. I stepped forward and threw my arms around his neck. He hugged me back, three beats.

'Walk with me,' he said, in his hoarse, whispery voice.

I put my arm through his and we walked away from the hotel, down the road, into the kind of darkness that scarcely exists anymore. Electric lights weren't yet a matter of course out here in the country, and cars didn't often rattle down the road after dark. We had gone a little way when a dog ran out to menace us. Finbarr kneeled and within seconds the giant beast – half collie, half something monstrous – was in his lap, getting his white mane ruffled, shaggy tail wagging joyfully. We continued walking and the dog followed us a while, until Finbarr commanded, 'Go home.' The dog lowered his ears, dejected but obedient, and trotted off in the direction from which he'd come.

'Have you got a dog of your own now?' I asked.

The question couldn't help but burgeon with memories of Alby, so that's how Finbarr answered it. He told me the man who'd bought Alby had joined the IRA. He used the dog to deliver explosives to an RIC barracks and Alby had been blown to bits along with his target. 'Remember how I taught him to crouch so still and not move for anything, no matter what? That was the death of him, Nan. I swear I'll never train another dog so well.'

The pain that erupted in my chest was unbearable, so desperate was I to 'unknow' what Finbarr had just told me. From that moment, for the rest of my life, I'd dream of Alby crouching, watching our tennis games in controlled stillness, only to burst into flames before we could call him back to life.

'It all feels like a long time ago,' Finbarr said. 'But it's not. Eight years since the war ended, twelve years since it started. It's only that the world's changed too much, in ways it shouldn't. And so it's changed how time passes. The trenches were yesterday, or an hour ago. They'll come back again tomorrow. You and me and Alby and Ireland; that was a hundred years ago, and also every day since.'

'And Genevieve?'

'A thousand years ago and just this morning.'

'But not tomorrow?'

'No, Nan. Not tomorrow.'

The tears Miss Armstrong had wanted from me gathered in my eyes. We kept walking, so far that I knew I wouldn't make it back to the Bellefort Hotel this night. Who would even notice? Inspector Chilton, with his sad, watchful eyes and one working arm? What did he think he knew about me? Nothing that could matter enough to change the magic of walking beside Finbarr. When I left the convent, all I'd wanted to do was walk. I would have walked the length of Ireland, and then England; I would have walked from Land's End to Thurso. Not knowing where to look but only that there was nothing in this world for me to do but search and search and search.

Finbarr did not walk with me the length of England, but to a long drive leading to a manor house, the trees on either side so bare that I could see it up ahead in a patch of moonlight. Waiting for us. It was grand but not cavernously so. The country home of some wealthy Londoner, most likely.

'How did you find this place? Do you have permission to stay here?' Even as I spoke I knew he'd found it the same way he'd found our room in the midst of the Armistice celebration. Finbarr magic.

'The house gave me permission to stay,' he told me. 'That's more important than permission from the owners.'

Oak trees bent in a bald canopy overhead, sagging with the memory of their lost leaves, starlight making its way through the branches, creating a kind of mist with our exhaled breath.

'Shall we run to the front door?' Finbarr asked.

I laughed. But all at once, before my voice could object, my body answered. I gave myself a head start by kicking off without warning, my muscles creaky but coming to life against the cold air. Finbarr overtook me quickly but not so quickly that I didn't feel proud, almost at his heels, the good, lost feeling of blood and breath pumping through every ventricle to every cell.

Finbarr finished, slamming against the front door. We walked inside, breathing hard, past the smouldering fire in the front hall.

'Is Mrs Christie here?' I asked.

'Yes. She's here.'

I followed Finbarr up the staircase to what must have been the grandest bedroom, his spare possessions already settled into occupancy, a scarf over a chair, a battered satchel with his father's initials barely visible resting in a corner. Nice of Agatha, I thought, to let him have this room instead of taking it for herself. He kneeled and rebuilt the fire while I stood, watching his face in the glow. My hands cupped their opposite elbows. I knew I should be shivering until the fire crackled in earnest, but instead I felt as warm as I ever had.

Finbarr stood. He took off his coat and tossed it into a corner. He put his arms around me and pulled me close.

'Nan,' he said, 'I know you grieve. I grieve, too. We'll never forget her, but we can have another. We can be together.'

'We can't be together,' I said, even as I let him ease off my coat and felt his lips against my neck. 'Because I have to be with her. I can't go off to live in a different hemisphere to my own child.'

'Nan,' he said, more sharply. He gave my shoulders a little shake, as if trying to wake me. 'I'm right here. But she's gone.

There's no point in looking for something you'll never find, or holding on to something that's already lost.'

Finbarr had never seen or touched our baby. He could love her but he couldn't understand. There was no point in saying so. I didn't want to argue. This night had arrived unexpectedly, a gift out of nowhere, and I just wanted it to continue, separate in time, a little bubble away from the world and everything it had done to us. I would have traded this moment with Finbarr in an instant if it would rearrange the past. But that wasn't possible. So I took it, never mind how it might affect the future. I hadn't packed my contraceptive sponge when I left London. Why would I? But I found myself not caring. Anything that happened this time would be very different from the last.

'Hush, Finbarr,' I said. 'Just hush.'

I silenced him with a kiss that led us to the bed, finally a place and time carved out of all these years, to be together in the way we were always meant to be.

Chilton had learned to walk silently during the war. One of the benefits of not being a tall man, and being slight in build, was that if he led with his heel, moving from the hip, he could walk with hardly any footfall, even with his longest strides.

And the truth was, even if he'd stomped, with no attention to keeping us from knowing he was there, we might not have known he was following us, so absorbed were we in each other.

But follow us he did, undetected, even when Finbarr turned to point the dog towards home. Chilton froze then, arms by his side, as if he could make himself invisible even to an animal. When Finbarr turned, and we resumed our walk, Chilton didn't hesitate before resuming his stride. A sad pair, weren't we?

Chilton could tell, he knew, we'd been separated by the war, only now coming back together. What he couldn't figure out was our connection to Agatha Christie. He just knew we'd lead him directly to her. And so we did.

Once we'd turned up the drive of the house Chilton had secured our destination, so he began to take greater heed lest we discover him. He waited by the gate that Finbarr – country boy, mindful of fences – had closed and latched behind us. When we were far enough in the distance for him to be sure we wouldn't hear it creak, Chilton opened the gate and walked down the road, noting, as I had, the bare branch canopy, and thinking how lovely it must be in spring and summer, when everything was in bloom. He breathed in the night air to calm himself – anxiety taking him unawares as it so often did; the feeling that someone might be watching him, might be lurking, behind any shadow. Yorkshire was fine but Chilton had grown up by the sea. That was the thing, the only thing: to hear the waves upon the shore. To walk upon the rocks at Churston Cove and see the seals sunning there. To thrust your head into the salt water, even in the coldest months, and let its chilling shock clear your mind.

He stood before the house, a lovely old building, a great stone box, shimmering with windows under the low light of stars. From behind one upstairs window a flicker of light grew; that would be the Irish fellow, stoking the fire for an evening with Mrs O'Dea, if that were indeed her name. Whatever had separated us, Chilton hoped it could be sorted out, that we could be together. He had lost his own sweetheart because of the war. Katherine had waited for him patiently, praying for his return, but her prayers hadn't been complete enough, because a different man had returned in his place from the one she loved. *I scarcely recognize you, Frank*, she'd wept. Not long after she broke things off, she married the florist's son, who was set to inherit the business and hadn't been to war on account of blindness in one eye. It was one of the reasons Chilton had left Brixham for Leeds, years ago. One day he'd walked by the flower shop and had seen Katherine arranging a vase full of peonies, round with expecting a child. He'd decided to take himself away as if not seeing something spared you from its sorrow.

Torquay was close enough to Brixham for Agatha Christie to have bought flowers from that shop, even from Katherine herself. Or likely not. Likely it was a servant's job – to buy flowers.

Once over the threshold of the manor, the door shut quietly behind him. Inside it was draughty and cold. There were so few furnishings – there was so little sign of life – Chilton thought it might be waiting for sale, or to be leased. It didn't have any air of waiting for its own family to return. He adjusted his scarf, then set about searching. It was a large house but not prohibitively so. He could make a quick turn downstairs to the kitchen, wine cellar (amply stocked for a house that seemed so deserted) and housekeeper's office. Then through the main floor into the parlour and library. He peered into every room except for the one the couple occupied, marked by the flicker from underneath the doorway. Light voices carried into the hall, including a soft laugh that gladdened him. It was difficult to imagine either of those two laughing, both so haunted and earnest.

In the attic there was a modest servants' quarters, with a row of closed doors. Beneath one of them, some movement, faint light, as though from a single candle. He knocked quietly, using only two of his knuckles.

'Yes, darling,' came the voice, weary and slightly worried, like a mother addressing a child out of bed in the middle of the night. In his own family it had not been he but his youngest brother who woke their mother after dark. She was always sweet about it. How she loved all three of her boys.

Chilton knew Agatha's endearment, and its implied invitation to enter wasn't for him. Still, he pushed the door open. And there she sat, in a hard wooden chair – wearing a man's pyjamas, hair loose and curling, lovely in the poorly lit room. There were two single beds, only one of them made up. On the dressing table, which she was using as a desk, sat a typewriter and two lit, dripping candlesticks in tarnished silver holders. Stacks of paper were piled on a chest of drawers. More stacks of paper sat on the bare bed. Agatha stared at Chilton, fountain pen in hand, poised as if in mid-sentence.

'Oh drat,' she said. She did not put down her pen.

He walked into the room and sat down at the foot of the bare bed, careful not to disturb her papers. He did not remove his coat. There was a small stove in the corner, alight with coal, but he suspected it would be out by morning. He imagined her waking with a shiver, breath visible. Would she rekindle the fire herself or call for the Irishman, the geography of the house revised but not their roles?

'Mrs Mahoney,' Chilton said, with no faint measure of sarcasm. She had to strain backwards in her chair to face him.

'Is this how the Yorkshire police conduct themselves?' There was a practised tone of upper-crust umbrage in her voice but he could tell her heart wasn't in it. 'Marching into a lady's bedroom in the middle of the night?'

'I did knock,' he said. 'You were expecting your husband?'

A sad look crossed her face. Chilton did not mean to make her cry. At least, as a man, he did not. As an inspector, he recognized emotional frailty might lead to an outpouring of information.

'I'm afraid,' he pressed on, 'your husband is downstairs in one of the bedrooms with another lady. I do hate to be the bearer of such unfortunate news.'

Finally, she released her pen, placing it on the bedside table with the exhalation of someone whose concentration has been truly and unwelcomely wrecked.

'Let's not play games,' she said. 'You know very well he's not my husband.'

'But wasn't it he you meant when you said *darling*? He's not—'

'Don't you dare say it. I'm not nearly old enough to be Finbarr's mother.'

'I was going to say, your brother.'

'He has become very like a brother to me, and is indeed very darling. Though I don't see what business it is of yours.'

'What business it is of mine, Mrs Christie,' Chilton switched to her true name, though she had not yet confirmed her identity, 'is that I am employed by the Yorkshire police. There are a good many officers searching for you.'

'A good many? Searching for me? In Yorkshire?'

'Yorkshire and everywhere else in England.'

Agatha frowned. She couldn't even curse her bad luck at landing in Yorkshire. If she'd run off to Derbyshire or Cumberland or Norfolk, there would be police to come knocking on the door of her hideout.

'Gracious,' Agatha said, exhausted by the news. 'What a fuss.'

'So you admit, you're Mrs Agatha Christie?'

'I admit no such thing.' But she looked doubtful.

If Miss O'Dea (he had begun thinking of me as *Miss* almost without considering it) or any other woman had done what Agatha did next, Chilton would have been on guard, considering it an attempt at manipulation. But when she reached out her hand, touching his arm, closing her fingers around the thick woollen cloth, he recognized the gesture as not woman to man, but human to human. A genuine and urgent entreaty.

'Mr Chilton,' she said, 'have you ever been in trouble? Real trouble, the kind that comes not only from without but also from some place within? Some place you never even recognized?'

Her face looked open and painfully tender. Thirty-six is an age one looks back on as young. But at the time, living in thirty-six-year-old skin, it doesn't feel young. Women start believing themselves old so soon, don't they? Agatha didn't realize it was her youth that allowed her to sit for hours in that comfortless rock of a chair, staring at her pages without need of spectacles, nary a twinge from the small of her back. One day far into the future she would look back on this time in her life and understand she had not been old, or even middle aged, but *young*, with the bulk of her life ahead of her, not to mention the best of it.

She trained her sharp eyes upon Mr Chilton, assessing him frankly as she let go of his sleeve.

What a different life it had been for Agatha since she'd gone on the run with Finbarr. What a different person it had made her already. Staying in an empty house without permission or even knowing the owner's identity. Like an outlaw. This time she wouldn't bother leaving money, no matter how much of the household she helped herself to. She had chosen a servant's room for the sheer austerity of it, as well as the privacy. Sitting here now, with a stranger, a man, she felt no fear whatsoever, nor worry about impropriety. She had sidestepped right out of the world as she'd always known it and had landed someplace where, seemingly, nothing mattered, not even great search parties, elsewhere, all for her benefit.

'Mr Chilton,' she said.

He heard her, and was struck again at the lack of ploy. A beautiful rawness exhibited either her character or what her character had been reduced – or elevated – to, thanks to whatever trauma it was that drove her.

One of the difficulties of having been to war: the impossibility of appreciating someone else's trauma at first glance. It all seems so insignificant. Now, though, faced with her lovely furrowed brow, sympathy began to stir.

'Is there anyone else here,' she said, 'in Harrogate, looking for me?'

'No,' he said. 'This area is my purview. And you might imagine the bulk of the search is closer to home. Your home. Dragging ponds and so forth.'

'They haven't told Teddy, have they? My daughter. They haven't passed that worry on to her?' She stood up, the space where she sat no longer enough to contain the flood of concern.

'I wouldn't know about that,' he said, and then, because placation was useful under these circumstances (even if he hadn't precisely identified how to characterize these circumstances), he added, 'I imagine not.' He had never seen the child but could picture her, cossetted, protected from every bit of news or information that might cause distress, for the sake of the parents perhaps more than the child. What's more inconvenient than another person's distress?

He wondered if Agatha Christie had ever in her life been as willing to wear her emotions so plainly on her face.

She made an effort to collect these emotions back to invisibility. 'Let's not play games, Mr Chilton.' Her voice sounded like she wanted to infuse it with accustomed authority, and yet it shook. The candle on her desk fluttered. The stove needed more coal.

'That's the second time you've said that. You needn't say it again. I've no fondness for games. I only want to deliver you safely home.' When she didn't reply he added, 'Mrs Christie. Isn't that enough of all this? You've given your husband a fright. He's longing to see you. Surely it's time to put an end to it all and go home.'

'Did you see that girl?' Agatha said. 'The one you said came in with Mr Mahoney?'

Now, they were getting somewhere. A mystery about to be solved.

'She happens to be my husband's mistress. My actual husband, Colonel Christie. She imagines she's shortly to be his wife.'

The situation began to take a shape, albeit an unreasonable one. Chilton said, 'She seems to have hit upon a hiccup, in that regard.'

The house was still but also electric, with an awareness of the floor beneath them and all it held. Those two young lovers, at last reunited (this much was clear). Not only what took place physically but the emotion swirling around them, oozing out from under the door, floating through the house like a new and intoxicating form of oxygen. He'd scarcely noticed that he had shifted to thinking of her as Agatha rather than Mrs Christie. In that moment the mist surrounded them, intimate in its proximity.

(The Timeless Manor, Agatha and I named it later. I've never been back to Harrogate, or to this manor house. But sometimes I think if I did, if I tracked the coordinates precisely, I would find an empty stretch of moor and heather and bramble, the house itself having secreted itself into the mist for another hundred years.)

'Do you think she's beautiful?' Agatha asked. 'That – girl.'

She'd been on the brink of using a different word, Chilton

could tell. He answered with a lack of propriety and a wealth of honesty, because both seemed to be what she needed.

'Not as beautiful as you.'

For a moment, based on the fervency that held every one of Agatha's features absolutely quiet, he thought she might lean over and kiss him.

But she didn't. She only said, 'Please don't tell anybody you've found me. Not yet. Give me a day or two more.'

He knew he should be objecting, cajoling, insisting. Rejecting the notion – to let her remain concealed – entirely. Instead, Chilton got to his feet with an air of acquiescing. It wasn't as though a murder had been committed, after all. Why rouse people out of their beds with the shrill invasion of ringing telephones? She was a grown woman of means and station, free to make her own decisions. And he seemed to be rather enjoying himself. He seemed to be not wanting any of this to end. If he did his duty, and reported her found, the odds of him ever seeing her again stood slim.

'I promise I won't tell anyone,' he said, 'for now. If you promise not to move again. Stay here, please, where I can find you if needs be.'

'Done,' she said. 'I promise.'

She held out her hand for him to shake. Soft, cool skin.

'Poor Finbarr,' she said. 'I do hope Nan's not toying with him.'

'You're tender-hearted.'

Agatha laughed. In agreement, he realized. 'I expect that makes two of us,' she said.

Chilton had considered his heart so utterly undetectable for so long, it surprised him to believe her. 'Do you know,' he said, 'I thought earlier, for a moment, when you were looking at me so intently – I almost believed you were about to kiss me.'

215

'I haven't kissed a man other than my husband in years. Not since the day we met.'

'You've been a good wife.'

Agatha nodded vigorously. It made her furious to think what a good wife she'd been. To Chilton she looked breathlessly young and full of thoughts he couldn't read. It reminded him of his girl, Katherine, before the war. He felt his mind start to reach, by habit, for the next dark idea to follow, the bitter side of the world. And stopped himself.

'Mrs Christie,' he said.

'Call me Agatha.' She closed the distance between them and kissed him, a tentative but time-consuming kiss. Chilton didn't dare lift an arm to her waist. He was afraid if he moved at all, she'd realize what she was doing and it would end – her soft lips on his, her hands resting ever so lightly on his chest. Both their mouths open just enough to inhale each other's breath. She tasted like roses and spring grass.

'Agatha,' Mr Chilton said, when finally she stepped away.

'You'd better go now.' It almost wounded him, how even and unphased her voice sounded.

'Yes.' He boasted no such calm. His voice cracked like a twelve-year-old boy's.

'But you'll keep your promise? And tell no one?'

'Yes,' he said again.

Chilton closed the door behind him. He walked down the stairs and through the front door, feeling like a ghost, as if, instead of stepping, he were gliding, feet still and floating an inch or more above the ground.

The Disappearance

Day Seven
Friday, 10 December 1926

S IR ARTHUR CONAN Doyle loved a mystery too much to
admit he'd never heard of Agatha Christie prior to her
disappearance. There were whispers of a publicity stunt and so
what? If this was a publicity stunt, it was a damn good one.

People do like to be the ones to solve problems. The more
people trying to crack a case, the more one wants to be the man
to do it.

Donald Fraser, Agatha's new agent, cleared his schedule to
take a meeting with Conan Doyle. The celebrated creator of
Sherlock Holmes! Even if he didn't see how Sir Arthur could
help in discovering Agatha, perhaps the author could be per-
suaded to abandon his current agent and join Fraser's list?

Not that Fraser's feelings were mercenary where Agatha was
concerned. He was worried. And he felt horrible for Mr Christie.
Fraser's own wife had run off with one of his writers last spring.
Fraser fully expected Agatha to have done something similar.
She always conducted herself as an unassailable lady but then so
had his wife.

Fraser did not have confidence Conan Doyle could discover
what every police officer in England had not. The man was an
author, not a detective. What's easier than solving a puzzle of

your own invention? Authors created problems, they didn't solve them. Another mystery writer of the day, Dorothy Sayers, had already invited herself to Sunningdale to search for clues and *test the energy*. Agatha Christie was not the sort to meddle in such nonsense. She wouldn't want charlatans involved, Fraser felt sure.

Conan Doyle at sixty-seven (a mere four years from joining the spiritual realm himself) cut a handsome and confident figure. It was almost endearing, that someone so stalwart could believe in messages from the beyond. Once it became clear there would be no wooing him away from his current representation, Fraser resolved to get the meeting done with. The whole business made him sad. He wanted Agatha Christie found as much as anyone and couldn't bear wasting time about it.

'Have you got anything of hers?' Conan Doyle's moustache sat wonderfully still on his face, no matter how animated he became. 'Personal possessions she might have left behind? Clothing is best. A handwritten note might do.'

Fraser opened his desk drawer, where a lovely pair of leather gloves had lain going on nine months, waiting for their owner's return. He hesitated before handing them over.

'And may I enquire after your plans?' said Fraser. 'The hounds have already got her scent, you know. There's a veritable army in Berkshire, searching for her.' He mentioned Dorothy Sayers' involvement and Conan Doyle waved it away as ridiculous.

'She has no idea what to look for.' He snatched at the gloves as Fraser tentatively withdrew them. 'A spiritual fingerprint is what's needed. I've been in touch with Horace Leaf.'

Fraser blinked, indicating the name meant nothing to him.

'My good man, he's only the most powerful clairvoyant in Europe.' How interesting that Conan Doyle of all people employed spiritualism – mediums and divinations – rather than deductive reasoning. 'And to our great good fortune he happens to reside in London. Have these gloves been worn recently?'

'Oh, very recently,' Fraser said. 'Mrs Christie was here just a day before she went missing. Sitting in that very chair.'

Conan Doyle nodded, stroking the armrests as though collecting molecules Agatha had left behind. He held the gloves up as if he'd found them himself, a most important clue. 'These will do nicely,' he said. 'Horace Leaf will solve this. We'll find Agatha Christie, alive or dead. By morning, we'll know her whereabouts. You can be certain of that.'

Fraser felt no guilt whatsoever. If Mr Leaf had any powers at all, the first thing he ought to divine was that the gloves belonged to Mrs Fraser, who'd belonged to Mr Fraser, until she'd absconded to Devonshire and broken her devoted husband's heart.

The heavy door shut. Fraser stared at it, full of melancholy. Perhaps he'd go by Harrods and buy Mrs Fraser a new pair, send them to her in Devonshire. As a present. Her hands might be cold.

It surprised Fraser that he hadn't felt star struck meeting Sherlock Holmes's creator, only moved by the impermanence of life here on earth. Agatha Christie had a new novel, *The Big Four*, coming out this January. Perhaps she'd be courteous enough to return to her husband by then. Or perhaps the more macabre imaginings would prove correct, and a corpse, rather than the woman, would turn up. Either way – whether or not anyone saw her again – by January she would be a household name in England, indeed if not the whole world. Which couldn't hurt book sales.

Fraser sighed, made melancholy by his avarice. Nothing in life unfolds the way you think it will, does it?

In bed at the Timeless Manor, I propped myself up on my elbow, eyes trained on Finbarr's sleeping form, so I would see his face in the first light. The brick we'd heated in the fire to keep us warm had gone cold at our feet. The heavy curtains were drawn and the room stood black with the late morning darkness of winter. By the time sunlight speckled into the room, his eyes were open, staring back at me. I thought of the night in Ireland I lay beside him, the only other time we'd slept all night in the same bed.

'Last time we slept together,' I said, 'you never opened your eyes in the morning.'

He collected my hands and held them on top of his heart. 'If I had, I would've married you that day.'

Tears filled my eyes. 'We'd be together now.'

'We *are* together now.'

'Not for long,' I said. 'And not all of us.'

He sat up. I noticed for the first time something I'd missed the night before. His thick black hair was tamed and cropped. The back of his neck shaved. It gave him the unaccustomed and misleading look of order. It gave me proof of what seemed an impossibility: Agatha Christie was here, truly here. In this very house. With us. Living – as I'd never had the chance to do – with Finbarr Mahoney.

'Did she cut your hair?' I pictured Agatha's hands blowing the stubborn wisps off the back of his neck. Running her fingers through the thick silk strands to hold, snip and release. Her hands, brushing the last of it off his shoulders.

'She did,' he said, running his hand over his scalp as if just remembering. 'Do you like it?'

'I like it long.' My head dropped back to the stale, bare pillow. The house was outfitted so meanly it was as if we were camping. Outlaws and borrowers. Finbarr got up to put another log on the fire. I stared at the ceiling, which had medallions carved into it, unnecessarily ornate. I had never once thought of Archie's hands on his wife with any kind of jealousy. But how I hated the thought of Agatha's hands on Finbarr. It gave me a clearer glimpse of how it must feel for her, Archie's hands on me, doing far more than cutting my hair.

'And she's here in this house, right now?'

'Of course. I've already said so. Where else would she be?'

'Her own fine house in Torquay. Or a fine hotel. She's got plenty of money, you know, she can well afford it.'

'Like you're affording it?'

I didn't answer. Finbarr got back into bed. 'She loves her husband, Nan. She wants him back. Give him back to her and come away with me. We can do what we should have done directly after the war.'

'Oh, Finbarr.'

'We can go back to Ballycotton.'

'You're daft if you think I'm ever setting foot in Ireland.'

'You can hate Ireland for what it did to you,' Finbarr said. 'But I'm Ireland too. Do you hate me, Nan?'

'Never. You know that.'

'And Ireland's not the only country where these things happen.'

'But it's where it happened to me.'

He closed his eyes. I stroked the cropped hair off his forehead, fingernails grazing his scalp, willing it to grow into its usual floppy disarray. And I felt what I always did. That he was my favourite person on earth, the one in whose presence I most belonged. At the same time, I loved Genevieve more.

'Finbarr,' I whispered, to erase the hardness of what I'd just said. 'You're my favourite. You're still my favourite.'

He opened his eyes. Although his interior weather had gone cloudy, I could see it like a memory, the old insistence on sunlight. Perhaps I could bring it back to him. And so we returned to lips and hands and furtive sentiments.

We couldn't hear Agatha, upstairs, clacking away on her typewriter. She knew it was mad to stay here, to not reveal her whereabouts. She ought to get in Miss Oliver's car and drive straight to the police station and turn herself in.

Turn herself in! She baulked with indignation at her own interior words. What crime had she committed? None at all. She had every right to storm out of the world.

And still. With so many people searching and worrying, she knew she should return home immediately. For the same reason, she knew she could never return at all. Face all those people? Provide an explanation? Look again into Archie's face and see it entirely devoid of love? Impossible.

She hoped she could trust Chilton to keep his word. Last night his body had thrummed with respectful restraint. His lips were softer than Archie's. He didn't smell like any kind of soap or fancy emollients, just himself, a good grassy smell, a touch of salt water. She herself had traded her scent in these last few days, the last of the lavender fading in favour of woodsmoke and good old-fashioned sweat.

No matter that Mr Chilton was a police inspector. She could trust him to keep her secret. She knew she could.

Chilton was also awake at first light, not having changed his clothes or slept a wink. He could hardly remember the last time he'd kissed a woman. Ridiculous to feel happy. This was a conundrum. The whole world looking for a woman he'd found, and what had he done but kiss her and promise to keep her whereabouts a secret? However the years may have changed him, they certainly hadn't made him any smarter.

From overhead he heard an unexpected thump that put him on immediate alert. One doesn't wake to screaming one day without expecting more of the same. But after a few moments passed with only quiet, he allowed himself to breathe again. Today he would focus on the Marstons, so he could confirm Lippincott's theory and make sure there wasn't a murderer on the loose. Harm could be wrought by inaction as much as action. And since the war, Chilton had made an oath to himself to do no more harm in the world.

It's not something you imagine, as a boy, even as you pretend at swords or gunfire. The lives that will end at your hands. It was a German boy from a trench raid who stuck most consistently in Chilton's memory. The boy had been crawling out of the trenches on his hands and knees, and Chilton stooped to bayonet him through the heart. How surprised the boy looked, as if no one had told him going off to war might result in this outcome. Chilton felt so terrible, he'd kneeled to give him a drink of water from his canteen, though for this boy there was no more wanting water, or wanting anything. *What are you doing, mate?* a corporal had said, tossing a bomb into the trenches. Chilton screwed the top back onto his canteen. The boy was so young he still had roses in his cheeks – translucent and girlish skin, as if he'd never shaved. Later, when Chilton heard his youngest brother had also been bayoneted, the two men swapped faces, and it was Malcolm, his baby brother, everybody's favourite, eyes glossing over with the shock of it. Young enough to be immortal amid the blaring canons. Stupid bloody idiots we all were, Chilton thought. We walked over corpses and still believed death might not touch us.

From upstairs the silence was again interrupted. Chilton heard a shout, instantly muffled, followed by a door opening and closing. He hastened upstairs, quickly but not running, to avoid the pounding of footsteps that could wake the entire hotel. In the upstairs hall he found Mr and Mrs Race, such a beautiful pair, both faces flushed – the husband's with rage, the wife's with anguish. Mr Race had his hand around Mrs Race's wrist, a painful grasp that Chilton knew would leave a mark.

'There now, let her go.' Chilton's voice was low and calm, as he might speak to a menacing dog while backing away. Except in this case he didn't back away, but took a step closer.

'This has nothing to with you, sir,' Race said. 'I suggest you return to your room.'

'Good God, man. She's your wife. That's no way to behave towards her.'

Mrs Race wrenched her hand from her husband and held it to her chest. Her husband made a motion as if to grab her again and Chilton took another step towards him.

'Before you wake the entire hotel,' Chilton said, his voice still steady, 'why don't I escort Mrs Race to the kitchen for a cup of tea, while you go back to your room and cool off?'

The couple focused on Chilton for the first time. He saw

them registering that he was fully clothed, including his over-coat, while the two of them wore night clothes, their attire, if not their behaviour, far more appropriate for the time of day.

'Very well,' Mrs Race said. She smoothed her hair back in one graceful motion. 'I could do with a cup of tea. Thank you, Mr Chilton.'

Chilton had promised her tea but the hotel staff had not yet convened. Instead of the kitchen he brought her to the drawing room just off the front hall. Chilton's nerves felt awfully frayed – too frayed, he thought, to calm someone else down. The young woman paced the small room, arms tight around her waist. He reached into his interior jacket pocket for a cigarette. When he lit it she jerked her head towards him, as if she'd forgotten he were there. Chilton stood, holding the open cigarette case towards her. She took one. He returned the case to his pocket and lit it for her. Always an intimate moment. He noted her wrist was not marked, as he feared it would be, but smooth and unharmed. Her bright blonde hair was shoulder length and silken. Uncurled and mussed from sleep. One of those women who probably don't know they're more beautiful without make-up, or done-up hair. Like Agatha Christie. A surprising, involuntary smile twitched his lip at the thought of her.

Mrs Race inhaled her cigarette deeply, hungrily, then blew an expert stream of smoke to the side.

'It might be more useful to pour you a brandy,' Chilton said. 'I've seen where Mrs Leech keeps a bottle behind the reception desk, though I can't account to its quality.'

'That sounds grand,' she said, marching over to a couch and collapsing onto it. 'Might as well become the sort of person who pours a scoop and lights a cigarette before the sun's properly risen. You see what I've let this marriage make me, Mr Chilton?'

'I'm afraid you've married a brute.'

'I'm afraid I have.' She spoke through clenched teeth, staring at some point past him. 'And now I'm stuck with him. My family would never abide a divorce. They're not much for scandal.'

'Did you know what he was like?' Chilton asked. 'Before you married him?'

Mrs Race inhaled deeply from her cigarette. 'I had my suspicions.'

'Then may I ask why you went through with it?'

'No,' she said. 'No you may not, Mr Chilton.'

'Perhaps you can fill me in on another matter, then. I'm curious about the other day. In the dining room. Poor Mr Marston. You were quite heroic.'

'Not at all,' she said.

'I wonder if you had the chance to talk to either of that couple. Before all the . . . unfortunateness.'

'I did not. I've been rather preoccupied with my own unfortunateness.' She stubbed out her cigarette, harder than was necessary, in the porcelain ashtray on the coffee table. Then she stood. 'Thank you for your care, Mr Chilton, but I'm off to face the music. Life's not a fairy tale. I thought that was something you old people learned during the war.'

She glided out of the room, head held high, as if she had been a dancer rather than a nurse. Chilton inhaled his cigarette to find it already worn down to his fingertips. The small burn shook him awake, nearly taking the place of a goodnight's sleep, or any night's sleep.

Back at the Timeless Manor, as she had already begun think-ing of it, Agatha sat downstairs at the long servants' dining table in the kitchen. She did not consider returning to Sun-ningdale. Unlike Styles, this house had a good energy. Or perhaps she had brought the good energy with her. Not just she, but Finbarr, brimming with the most unexpected good energy since they'd left Newlands Corner on the wind of excitement, leaving responsibilities behind. She could worry about Teddy but chose not to. The girl would be diligently cared for by Honoria. She would *not* worry about Archie and indeed had to admit it gave her pleasure, having him worrying about her for a change.

Certain elements of the world had fallen away. She was writ-ing as she always did, without thought of readers or agents or editors. Agatha wrote to entertain herself, the same way she'd made up stories in her head as a child, spinning her hoop round the monkey puzzle tree at Ashfield and inventing characters. Writing a book was a different world to live in. And she dearly needed a different world.

These past days, she dressed herself from the same collection of men's clothes she'd taken from the previous house, plus Miss Oliver's warm and well-worn coat. Vanity, gone. She still wore her pearl necklace, it had belonged to her mother, but her pearl ring she had pushed to the back of an empty drawer in the ser-vants' room where she was bunking. This morning she had glanced at herself in the mirror, hair unwashed, man's clothing, and thought she could walk right by nearly any of her acquaint-ances and only those who knew her best would recognize her. And who were those people who knew her best? She couldn't come up with a single person, not even Honoria – a paid com-panion, if she was honest – who understood her as well, or with whom she had such ease, as the Irishman who'd spirited her away.

Even in this house, large as it was, Agatha could hear Finbarr's nightmares. Every night since they'd run off together, until Nan showed up, she had left her own bed to place her hands on his shoulders. *Finbarr, darling, wake up.* All at once his eyes would open, taking her in, and breathing in gratitude. Twice he'd put his arms around her and held her close. It was a shock to find herself clasped against him and at the same time it wasn't. She didn't believe in reincarnation but if she did, she would have thought they'd known each other, Finbarr and she, in a previous life. An unlikely pair in theory but in practice perfectly likely. It made her realize how large her husband had loomed. He had somehow become to her the face of all men, and the way he looked upon her reflected how she appeared to all men. Finbarr represented an entirely different species, and here she had fallen into this strange but perfectly natural step with him.

Which meant that she could fall in step with another. Her mother wouldn't have liked the thought of her married to a police inspector. But her mother wasn't here to object, was she? Agatha found herself laughing – horrifying and such a relief, to laugh so quickly on the heels of remembering her mother's death.

'Something funny?'

It was me, standing there in the doorway. Flushed from lovemaking, my hair amiss, my chin raised in near defiance. The sight of me hardly moved her at all. She didn't envy me, or want to hurt me. She didn't even find my presence a particular intrusion. Another fugitive. So long as I agreed to keep my silence, I might as well come aboard. She seemed to have forgotten already – the mission for which Finbarr had enjoined her.

'Hello, Nan,' she said.

'Hello, Mrs Christie.'

I didn't feel as sanguine about her, in this moment, as she did about me. It made me furious somehow. To see her at the servants' table. She who'd grown up in cavernous houses that had names. Whose idea of financial hardship was a hundred pounds a year for doing nothing. A five-room flat with a butler and a maid. A life of wanting things – a writing career, a husband, a child – and having them delivered to her, as if the wanting naturally equalled the having. For the sake of a woman like her a hundred more always suffered.

'Come now,' she said. I couldn't account for her cheery disposition. 'Call me Agatha, would you. Surely at this point we can dispense with formality. Both of us on the lam.'

'I'm not on the lam. I'm on holiday.'

'It's rather an unusual holiday. I wonder what Archie would say about it?' When I didn't answer she said, 'There. I knew you didn't love him.'

I sat down at the table as Agatha stood to get another teacup. 'I'm afraid there's no milk,' she said, pouring for me.

'I don't suppose Archie would have any right to say anything about it, would he? Not yet.'

'True enough.' She could have told me about her last night with Archie but she didn't. It was the first time she and I had been together since the artifice had finally lifted for good. I suppose she liked having a bit of her own artifice. I expected her to start straight in on demands that I relinquish Archie but she just sat there, sipping tea, watching me do the same. It softened me towards her somehow. Perhaps if I didn't begrudge her good fortune, I'd finally be due some of my own.

'What are the provisions like here?' I asked. 'Would they last a while?'

'There's tinned fruit. Tinned tongue and kippers. Sardines. Loads of wine, if that's what you're about. Finbarr's been on some scavenges in town for fresh food. Apples and cheese. We have enough to last a while. But not forever, of course. And we don't know when the proper owners will return.'

'It doesn't look like they intend to any time soon, does it?'

'No. But there's no predicting what people will do.'

'There's a part of me,' I confided, 'that could just go upstairs. Never eat or drink again. Wither away to a skeleton in his arms.'

'Like Elvira Madigan and Sixten Sparre? Terrible story. If we could talk to their ghosts, I'm sure they'd tell us it hadn't been at all worth it. I never did go in much for romances. Especially not the tragic ones.'

'Neither did I,' I lied. If the idea of me dead in Finbarr's arms – dead anywhere – pleased her, paving the road back to her husband, her face did not betray it.

'Finbarr tells me you want to be a writer.'

'Does he?' How humiliating. I wondered what else he'd told her. 'That used to be true, I suppose.'

Finbarr bustled in just then. Full of business and energy. 'Good morning, Agatha,' he said, as if they were absolute equals, the best of friends.

'Good morning, dear Finbarr,' she said with authentic warmth, and I remembered how everyone always loved him. I used to think it was because of his insistent happiness. But now that was gone and still the love he inspired remained.

Several minutes of domestic exchanges transpired. Finbarr produced a loaf of bread from the pantry, and Agatha found some marmalade and poured him some tea. It was a remarkable thing to witness. I sat, not helping, and eventually food was placed before me.

'Have you heard from our man, then?' Agatha asked me, when all was settled again.

I glanced at Finbarr, whose face refused to darken, or to acknowledge anyone else as my man.

'I haven't,' I said. 'Not for days. He doesn't know where I am.'

'That makes two of us.'

'He's terribly worried about you,' I said.

'How do you know, if you haven't heard from him?'

'Well, he was, last time we spoke.'

'I might have considered that good news a few days ago. Now I find myself not much caring, if I'm to be honest.'

I had no way of knowing the smile on her face owed itself at least in part to last night's kiss with Chilton. I only thought, Poor Archie. Last week with two women intent on his attentions, this week with none.

'Finbarr has some things he'd like me to say to you,' said Agatha.

'Does he?'

'Before I begin, I'd like to remind you. In my whole life no one's hurt me as much as you have.'

Partly because I couldn't bear Finbarr watching this interaction, I brought my hands up to cover my face. Agatha reached across the table and pulled them away. 'We're not going to do that,' she said. 'We're not going to have me comforting you for all the wrongs you've done me.'

I looked at Finbarr. He had his eyes focused on Agatha, counting on her to say what he wanted and set everything to right.

'There've been some wrongs done to me as well.' I knew my voice sounded ominous but I didn't care. 'I lost something much more valuable than a husband.'

'Finbarr's filled me in on some of your history. Things I didn't know. I daresay Archie doesn't even know. Does he?'

Was this a threat? I moved to shoot an accusing glare at Finbarr, for telling Agatha what so few people knew. Then she said something that surprised me: 'I'm sorry about what happened to you in Ireland.' She still had her hands over mine. 'Dreadfully sorry. A travesty. Abhorrent. An outrage.'

It occurred to me this was the first apology I had ever received, from anyone, regarding my stay at Sunday's Corner. And I knew, and know still, it wasn't connected to what she said next.

'You won't tell anyone where I am?'

'No,' I promised. 'I won't.'

In all the years since Agatha Christie disappeared, amidst all the conjecture about her state of mind, and her activities, and her motives, not one single person has ever come to me for answers. People like to follow a very particular script. It never occurred to anyone that she and I might, after all, be friends. That the reason she stayed quiet, forever and always, was not to protect herself, but me.

Eventually, she would move beyond all this. She would marry again (a significantly younger man) and become successful beyond anyone's wildest imaginings. Things would work out for her in ways they never would work out for me. In ways they seldom work out for anyone.

For now we sat, staring at each other across the narrow table, the fire in the stove crackling cosiness. Refusing to say what the other most wanted to hear. While Finbarr sat with us, thinking his mission well on its way to accomplished, not knowing that one day soon, no matter what was said and done, my name would be Mrs Christie, too.

Here Lies Sister Mary

FATHER JOSEPH LOVED England. In 1919 this made him an unusual Irishman. That June a small British patrol was attacked in Rathclaren and during his sermon he interrupted his usual screed against lust to bellow his opposition. 'Crown and country,' he said, pounding the podium. 'It's what we went to war to defend, and now these ninnies are trying to upend it all.'

'It's a relief, isn't it,' Sister Mary Clare said to me one afternoon, 'that they don't hold being English against us. I've sometimes thought about going home, to an English order. But with Father Joseph in charge it hardly seems necessary.' She smiled more to herself than at me. 'In truth I believe it makes me his favourite. My being English.'

She was walking beside me as all the girls filed through the corridor for Holy Hour, a ritual that took place on the first Friday of every month. Sister Mary Declan looked back at me and frowned, but it was a nun talking to me, not another girl, so I went ahead and answered.

'Does it?' I tried to make my tone sound idle, but felt the blood leave my face, worried that being English might draw his attention to me.

'It's just a flash in the pan, all this IRA business,' Sister Mary

234

Clare went on, not noticing my discomfort. 'I'll be shocked if it lasts another month. You'd think these boys might have had enough fighting, mightn't you, seen enough horror, to be causing more of it in their own country.'

'Does Father Joseph know about me? Being English?'

'I've never heard him say a word about you one way or the other.'

Her words should have given me relief. And I did seem to be invisible to Father Joseph – as if a magic cloak protected me from his notice – but I remained terrified this would change.

Sister Mary Clare squeezed my hand and walked away before we entered the chapel, humming her usual, eerie tune. She had a pretty voice, even though she never attached words to her songs. I could hear her as I stood with my fellow penitents, still as could be, for fifteen minutes, our arms outstretched at our sides as if we were hanging on the cross. If anyone twitched, Sister Mary Declan made us start again. On this day we were in the chapel for a full hour. It was hard work not to tremble, thinking of the priest's love of England. I could feel my baby's little hands, pressing against the walls of my womb, and I was grateful she hadn't ever glimpsed the world outside.

A new girl arrived on a Tuesday and on the Friday she escaped, exactly how nobody could say. She simply vanished from our midst without a confiding word to anyone. The bells clanged and the nuns flurried. I took heart when she never returned. The next day, working in the nuns' graveyard, I looked through the bars to ascertain the route she'd taken. Through the fence that surrounded the graves I could see the entrance to the convent, the wrought-iron gate that opened to let in visitors. And I noticed at the corner, where the gate met the cement wall, one bar had rotted away and fallen into the high grass. The space it left was still too small for my pregnant self to slip through. But I wouldn't be pregnant forever.

The two other girls worked in obedient silence, pulling weeds and cleaning lichen from the headstones. I kneeled and pulled the bar into place, lodging it in so the cracks wouldn't be visible unless examined closely.

That afternoon Sister Mary Clare sat down beside me in the sewing room, where I worked alongside a group of girls, mending old uniforms. Other girls – who unlike me were handy with knitting needles – worked on the tiny matinee coats the babies would wear to keep warm. I prayed my baby would never have one of these. I'd get out of here too soon for the nuns to dress her. Whatever clothes my child wore, they would not be manufactured at this convent.

'Dear Nan,' Sister Mary Clare said, perched on the same backless stool the rest of us used. 'You don't seem yourself.' She patted my arm. Two nuns came in carrying babies, and the girls they belonged to put their knitting aside to nurse them.

'What would you have been,' I asked Sister Mary Clare, as I executed a clumsy stitch, 'if you hadn't been a nun?'

'Why, a mother, of course.' She smiled over at the nursing babies then quoted Coleridge, though at the time I believed they were her own words. 'A mother is a mother still, the holiest thing alive.'

I let my work drop into my lap and covered my face with my hands, thinking of Bess. Was she still the holiest thing alive, now that her baby was dead? 'Bess,' I said. 'Poor Bess.'

'There, there. Don't you worry about Bess. Why, she's a wife now. She can have another baby, one that can be baptized properly. She can have ten babies, all fat and happy, gathered round her feet.'

I broke down sobbing, and Sister Mary Clare rubbed my back in gentle circles. She would have been a good mother. 'Take heart. Bess's young man turned up for her. Could be yours will too. He'll have read the letter I sent him by now.' She handed me a handkerchief and I blew my nose.

'Here,' she said, reaching into her sleeve. 'I've brought you a treat.' She pressed a piece of soda bread into my hand, still warm, and slathered with fresh butter, a luxury I hadn't seen since I left home. I looked at the other girls apologetically.

'Go ahead and eat,' she said. 'Your friends don't begrudge you a treat, do you, girls?'

None of them looked up to meet her challenging gaze. *I should have seen it.* But I couldn't afford to. I bit into the soda bread, butter melting on my tongue. It tasted so good I had to stop myself telling the nun I loved her.

That night I dreamed of Father Joseph's jowly face hovering over mine. His veiny hands pawing at me. His groans and snorts.

'No, no, no!'

I woke already siting up. My hands, covering my face, smelled like they belonged to someone else. This place was wholly foreign. Fiona sat next to me, patting my back, not asking. We all had identical dreams, good and bad. In this way and perhaps only this way, Father Joseph's theory of our sameness was correct.

'Tell me,' I whispered. She recited my parents' address in London, her voice light and cheerful as a fairy's.

There were so many more of us than there were of them.

What if we'd banded together? An uprising? A hundred girls rising up against the handful of nuns and one lecherous priest? We had more to fight for than any soldier in the IRA. We could have taken our captors down and marched back into the world, our youth and our children reclaimed.

Bess and her American were married before travelling across the Atlantic, by an Anglican priest in London. They settled in Philadelphia. Did her parents back in Doolin weep when she never returned? Or did they rejoice at being done with her sin and shame?

She didn't care about that anymore. She missed her brothers and would always love her little sister, but the only sins she still believed in were the ones that had been committed against her. She'd never set foot in any church again as long as she lived.

At night she clung to her new husband. She never blamed him for arriving too late. They were a single unit in this, their loss, and the crimes that had been done to them both. But one crime done to Bess she bore entirely alone. She bore it daily, and nightly, unable to expel the memory of the priest's invasion.

And then there were her arms that ached the way only a mother's can, when they're empty of her child and always will be.

'Ronan,' she said, throughout the day, mostly when no one could hear her. In different tones. Fondly. Scolding. Laughing. Proud. As if his ghost accompanied her, the way he himself would have, had he been there, beside her, the reflection of all the emotions she should have experienced, rather than the ones she did.

The Disappearance

Day Seven
Friday, 10 December 1926

I T RAINED IN Sunningdale on Friday morning. The temperature had warmed. Teddy stood in the window of the nursery, holding a stuffed rabbit Agatha had named Touchstone. She'd given it to Teddy before she and Archie left to travel around the world. 'Some of my love is stored inside him,' she'd told Teddy, tying a blue ribbon around its neck. 'As long as you hold him, my love is always with you. Whenever you hug him, I'm hugging you back.'

'Touchstone is a girl, not a boy,' Teddy insisted. She didn't much care for men. It was women who took care of her. Every toy with a face was a she. Sonny, the little whittled dog, was a she.

Despite the rain, Sunningdale crawled with people. Teddy watched the pelting rain clutter her window. She saw scattered people in raincoats but didn't find them alarming; she was used to fusses on the property that had nothing to do with her. She put Touchstone down. Her mother's dog stood at her ankle and she lifted him up so he could look out the window, too. Peter yapped twice at the sight of strangers then settled into a resigned cuddle. Usually, when Agatha travelled, she took the dog with her. Teddy was glad she'd left him behind this time, it was fun to have him all to herself, always right beside her. He barked, his funny little *arf*, as someone new trudged up the drive.

'There, there,' Teddy said to Peter. 'There's no need to bother about all that.' She turned from the window and set to dressing for school. Likely, she and Honoria would drive instead of walk, considering the weather.

The press had dubbed the search for Agatha *The Great Hunt*. As if it were a novel or a film. A sporting event, a national pastime. Or a war. Police officers and civic-minded citizens spread out all over England, doing their part.

'Rather grand of you to dub this hunt *great*,' Archie raged at Thompson, holding up a newspaper with the phrase emblazoned in a giant headline. 'You haven't turned up so much as a thumbprint.'

Thompson crossed his arms and regarded Archie, who had marched into his office at Berkshire Police Headquarters as if to scold an underling. Thompson certainly hoped Agatha Christie was found alive but that seemed more unlikely with every passing day. Living people turned up quickly. Dead people took their time, especially if a murderer had taken pains to hide them.

'You're finding every dead woman in England,' Archie went on, unfairly. Only one dead woman had been found, poor Miss Annabelle Oliver. 'Except the one you're actually searching for.'

Thompson attempted to raise an eyebrow and failed. A gesture Archie had in his repertoire and it galled the officer to realize he'd tried to imitate it.

'Searching for a dead woman, are we?' Thompson's tone meant to remind Archie of who was in charge of whom, and who knew what.

'No,' Archie insisted. 'She's alive. I know she is.'

'You're right to know we're not awfully good at finding women. You know who else we haven't managed to locate? A Miss Nan O'Dea. She seems to have gone missing from her place of employment as well as her flat.' He didn't tell Archie that he wasn't worried about my wellbeing. An officer had stopped in to the Imperial British Rubber Company and learned that I'd phoned to say my holiday would last a few days longer than expected. It would do just as well, Thompson thought, to wait on interviewing me until after a murder was confirmed.

'There's no need to trouble Nan,' Archie said. 'No need at all. She's the last person to know where Agatha's disappeared to.'

'And who would you say is the first?'

A dark, sorrowful look crossed Archie's face and he disappointed Thompson by breaking down in tears. Even if Archie Christie turned out not to be behind his wife's disappearance, the constable wished to waste no sympathy on him. Yesterday Archie had given a rather unfortunate interview to the *Daily Mail*, insisting his wife would never do harm to herself but adding that if she did, it would most certainly be with poison. Like so many men who believed themselves above reproach in deed and word, the manifest destiny of mattering in the world, Archie had no inkling of how to edit himself. Thompson, like so many men in positions of power who nonetheless found themselves tacitly subordinate to the Archies of the world, enjoyed imagining his downfall. He did not wish to feel a drop of kindness towards him, so it was most inconvenient that Archie Christie's tears appeared to spring from genuine, uncontrollable agony.

Archie drove to his mother's through the rain, shivering. He'd left Styles without his coat, most unlike him. He'd broken down in tears in front of another man and he didn't feel shame, or embarrassment, or anything except the nagging, overriding, maddening question. *Where is she?*

He regretted the interview he'd given to the *Mail*. As if the police weren't looking at him sideways already. No more press, Archie vowed, thinking not of himself but his wife. She was shy. *Shy.* The idea some of the officers floated, that this might be a publicity stunt, was utterly preposterous. His wife would never do such a thing. If she were alive, how could she possibly avoid seeing the newspaper articles, splashed across England – the world! – screaming her name? She would be horrified. At first glance of a headline – blaring her age! – she would ring Archie, or turn herself into the police, or simply board a train and come home. This was what worried him most. Where could she be that the publicity had not reached her? The only place he could think of was dead.

Dorothy Sayers, who fancied herself a medium as well as a novelist, had come to the Silent Pool and claimed to sense Agatha's absence from the region. Now *that* was a publicity stunt, atrocious woman, hopping on the coat tails of the sort of infamy tailor made to sell detective novels by the bushel. Sir Arthur Conan Doyle had phoned to deliver the sad news that he'd consulted a psychic who'd assured him Agatha no longer inhabited our mortal realm. 'We're working on direct word from her,' Conan Doyle had said, and Archie rang off without a word, Order of the British Empire be damned. Oh, it was all nonsense, this idea that spirits could communicate what hundreds of living men could not find with their own hands and eyes.

Still, when Archie reached his mother's house, he switched

off the ignition and leaned his cheek against the glass of the driver's side window. He closed his eyes and tried to sense whether or not Agatha was gone from this world. Can a man live with a woman for so many years, sleep beside her so many nights, without the molecules in his body palpably rearranging themselves in the event of her death? He forgot they had ever separated, in body or affection. He forgot *divorce* was a word that existed in the English language.

She's alive, he thought. I know she is.

Agatha was shy and lovely and thoughtful and proper. Agatha was considerate. Agatha would be horrified, knowing what a fuss had risen, all in her name. She couldn't possibly be alive and avoid seeing a newspaper. And she couldn't possibly see a newspaper and not come rushing home.

Yet she *was* alive. She had to be.

'I *never* wanted you to marry that woman, did I?'

Peg Helmsley, as she made this grand understatement, held out her silver-handled cane and thrust it in the air towards him, like a sword. Years ago, when Archie had first given his mother the news of his engagement, Peg had forbid it absolutely. He was nothing but a young subaltern and couldn't expect a penny from her. What's more, she'd disapproved of Agatha's Peter Pan collars. Showing off her neck! Peg was from a strict Irish Catholic family, one of twelve children. The bare-necked Agatha, who'd already been engaged once before, might as well have been a chorus girl. When they'd gone ahead and married, despite her objections, Peg had burst into tears and had taken to her bed for days.

'You can hardly blame this on Agatha,' Archie said. Part of

243

him did blame Agatha. If only she'd handled his affair with a stiff upper lip, like she was raised to do. Then all he'd be contending with, as far as his mother was concerned, was the unavoidably violent reaction she'd have upon discovering Nan.

Peg lowered her cane. Her second husband, William, was off on a walk. It was just the two of them, Archie and her, the perfect time for a confession. She stepped close to her son and closed her hand in his lapel.

'You haven't done something dreadful, have you, Archie?'

'Good God, Mother. Of course I haven't.' He stepped back so sharply the old woman lurched forward unsteadily. Archie took his mother by the elbows and helped her into a chair.

'I've had to stop William bringing in the papers,' Peg said, with an indignant thump of her cane. 'A person could have a stroke, couldn't she, reading about her own family in the papers. It's a humiliation, is what it is. Oh, if Agatha isn't dead, I will be so cross with her.'

Archie sank onto the settee across from her. He would have nodded in agreement if it hadn't hit him so hard, his own mother believing he could kill his wife. But then his answer, *Of course I haven't*, wasn't precisely true. He *had* done something dreadful to Agatha, and that had spurred her going missing. He remembered the marks on her wrists and his callousness towards them. The one and only thing he hadn't done to his wife, at this point, was murder.

At home in the evening, Archie smoked his pipe and poured whisky after whisky until sentimentality overtook him. He climbed the stairs to Teddy's room, where she lay sleeping with deep, untroubled breath. It was the first he'd seen of her all day

– perhaps several days – the two of them rattling in different corners of the house, her caretaking not Archie's duty. He sat down on the bed. Peter lay beside her. Archie would have stroked Teddy's brow but he didn't want to wake her, so instead he picked up the stuffed rabbit Agatha had given her and sobbed into the velvety fur.

Teddy lay there, eyes closed shut so he wouldn't know she was awake. It made her uncomfortable, having Archie there. Hearing him cry, for goodness' sake; fathers weren't meant to cry.

Not that she felt afraid of him. She didn't feel afraid of anyone. Thanks to the life Agatha and Archie gave her, Teddy never did find out what men can be.

Back to morning:

It rained in Harrogate, too, pelting the windows of the Timeless Manor. After breakfast, Finbarr, Agatha and I walked upstairs, Agatha continuing on to the top floor to write. I wanted to return to the bedroom but Finbarr shook his head. 'They'll worry about you at the hotel. Best not to draw too much attention. Unless you'd rather leave England with me today?'

'Of course that's what I'd rather do,' I said in a tone that indicated clearly it's not what I *would* do.

He drove me back to the hotel in Miss Oliver's Bentley. When I walked into the lobby, Mrs Leech proved him right by saying, 'There you are, Mrs O'Dea. We were almost ready to set the hounds out after you.'

'So sorry,' I said. 'I do love walking in your beautiful countryside.'

'In this weather? That'll be the death of you. Why don't you book a treatment, Mrs O'Dea?'

I promised I might later and she sent me into the dining room. Breakfast had passed but there were tea and scones on the sideboard. I wasn't particularly hungry but I sat myself down, staring out of the long windows. My whole body thrummed with Finbarr. I sipped my tea, gone a little cold.

'Mrs O'Dea. May I join you?'

It was Chilton, rumpled and handsome and blurred about the edges. I hadn't heard him come in – more like a ghost than a man.

'You're something of a prowler, aren't you?' I said.

'Not at all.' He sat down, though I hadn't said yes. 'Mrs Leech tells me you extended your stay.'

'Did she? How indiscreet of her.'

'She was worried about you. And apparently I'm the expert on missing women.'

Chilton had this way about him that made everything he said sound like a musing rather than a pronouncement. An interior loveliness, a willingness to question himself, apparent on his exterior. I expected I would feel fond of him right up to the moment he clapped my wrists in handcuffs. Perhaps even afterwards. Mr Chilton was not the sort of man one blamed. He was swept up by the world like the rest of us, doing his best to muddle through it. He was so entirely unthreatening to me that I couldn't have been taken more off guard when he said, 'I've been to the coroner.'

'Have you?'

'Yes. Poor Mr and Mrs Marston. I never got the chance to meet them properly. Did you?'

'No,' I said. 'Frightful business. You hear of it often, don't you? One half of a married couple dies, and the other follows for grief. Would you excuse me, Mr Chilton? I think I'd like to lie down a while.'

I stood and pushed back my chair, too abruptly. It scraped horribly. Behind my throbbing temple, the beginnings of a headache. One couldn't function on so little sleep.

'Goodnight, Mr Chilton,' I said, and then amended it to, 'Good morning.'

Chilton watched me leave, thoughtful. He lit a cigarette. He picked up the uneaten scone I'd abandoned and took a bite. Disappointed, somehow, that I didn't seem to know he'd been at the manor last night. Did he imagine Agatha and me, gossiping about their kiss like schoolgirls?

The rain let up. He touched his lips and stood to leave the dining room. He thought to get some sleep but changed his mind and walked to the Harrogate library. It was a small and cosy building, overseen by a white-haired librarian who greeted Chilton as he entered. He asked her if she knew offhand whether they had any books by Agatha Christie.

'All checked out,' the librarian said. Her name was Miss Barnard. She held up the daily paper and showed him a picture of Agatha, with a wide-eyed little girl sitting in her lap. 'Quite an interest in that lady these days. What with her tragic disappearance.'

Miss Barnard pointed him towards a table stacked with an array of new novels. Chilton looked through them, thinking he'd try to find something more to my liking than the Willy novel he'd seen me take from the shelves at the Bellefort. He could tell I'd chosen the book without enthusiasm, and believed it would behove him to make friends with me despite my resistance. After some perusal he landed upon *The Silver Spoon*, John Galsworthy's latest instalment of *The Forsyte Saga*. As he tucked the novel under his good arm, his eyes landed upon a woman, sitting at a table in the next room, a stack of books in front of her, studying the open one intently: Mrs Agatha Christie. For the outing she had changed into her own clothes, skirt and stockings. They were much the worse for wear, wrinkled and muddied about the hem, making her appearance almost as conspicuous as if she'd been wearing her man's clothes.

Chilton crossed into the alcove on swift feet. She was so engrossed that it took her a moment to look up at him.

'Why, Mr Chilton,' she said, and turned wonderfully, beautifully red. As if surprised by the way her face warmed, she touched her cheek, then removed her hand quickly, further embarrassed at being so transparent.

'Please,' he said. 'Call me Frank.'

With no spoken agreement, the two stood. Agatha put on a long woollen coat, rather the wrong size for her, too wide and too short. Chilton helped her to gather up her stack of books and they went together to the desk. Chilton started with surprise to hear Agatha give her name as Mrs O'Dea.

Miss Barnard looked up with a smile. Then something in her face changed. 'My goodness,' she said. 'You look just like the missing authoress. The one he was asking after.' She pointed to Chilton, then turned the newspaper towards them, again showing the picture.

This was Chilton's fault. He should have warned her, kept her from showing herself to the librarian. He watched as Agatha brought her hands to her pearl necklace, paling almost as dramatically as she had coloured earlier. By way of coming to her rescue, he put his arm around her shoulders. 'Darling, there is a bit of a resemblance, isn't there?' To the librarian he said, 'My wife hates being told she looks like anyone else. Wants to be an original.'

Dubious, Miss Barnard returned her eyes to the picture, then back to Agatha. 'Well,' she said, half convinced, 'I do hope they find the poor lady alive. Seems unlikely at this point, doesn't it?'

'Yes indeed,' Chilton said.

Agatha, absent her stack of books, had already turned and headed for the door. Chilton gathered everything – including my Galsworthy – and bade goodbye to the librarian.

'You're certainly not cut out for this,' he scolded, when he caught up with Agatha outside. 'Not much of a poker player either, I would suppose.'

'Did you see that headline? My photograph? *The Great Hunt?* How can I ever go back? How can I ever face the world again?' She covered her face with gloved hands, then stepped forwards and pressed the crown of her head against Chilton's chest. He wasn't much taller than she so she had to stoop to do so. Chilton lifted his arm to hold her and the books clattered to the ground. From where they stood, he could see the librarian, standing in the window, watching them.

'Agatha,' he said.

She stepped back and they kneeled together to pick up the books.

'Will you drive me back to the manor?' she said. 'I don't feel fit to do it myself.'

Chilton cranked up the Bentley while Agatha settled in the passenger seat. Miss Oliver's coat smelled like rosewater. The Bentley was too large for Agatha's taste. How she missed her own little car. She thought of it left in so precarious a spot and hoped it was all right. She hoped that some good soul – Archie, even – had pushed it back onto the road and driven it home where it belonged. When she was a girl, in the tidal wave of financial wreckage following her father's death – and the other times in her life, early in her marriage, for example, when the spectre of money troubles loomed, her mother-in-law's warnings bearing out, numbers not properly arranging themselves in the ledger – what if someone had told her then that one day, she herself would make enough money, by her own hands, to purchase such a thing: her dear Morris Cowley? Would she ever see it again? Was it worth leaving it behind, along with everything else – Teddy – to never have to face the questions the whole world would ask if she reappeared?

When Chilton got behind the wheel she said, 'I can't bear going home and facing the world. But how can I do anything else? The more time they spend looking for me, the worse it will be. You should drive me to police headquarters straight away. Just end this whole thing here and now.'

'I don't find myself able to do that. Not yet.'

So many police, so many people, discharged in the search for her. What luck, that such a lovely one had been successful. She reached over and grabbed Chilton's hand. 'I don't like romances,' she said. 'They ring false to me. Especially when people meet and fall in love at a glance.'

'What about several glances?'

She laughed and let go of his hand. They both sat and stared out the windscreen for several minutes. Then she said, 'She's still watching. The librarian. You'd better drive.'

Back at the Bellefort I had not gone upstairs to lie down, as I'd told Chilton, but only to change my clothes. Having made an appearance at the hotel, assuring the general public of my remaining presence in the world, I escaped from it again almost at once. The day had warmed. The rain had lifted. *Solvitur*

ambulando. When I reached the Timeless Manor's drive I ran the length of it.

'Look what I found,' Finbarr said, meeting me on the lawn outside, as if he'd known I would come straight back. It was a tennis net, rackets and balls. He set it up and we played two sets, me winning them both handily.

A big black car came sputtering up the drive. I lifted my hand to shade my eyes. There in the driver's seat sat Mr Chilton. All the workings of my body halted. No breath to my lungs or blood from my heart. Agatha had been found. Was Chilton here to arrest Finbarr? All of us, for trespassing? Worst of all, regardless of what happened next, would this time come to an abrupt end, all of us returning to life as it had been unspooling?

Instead, Finbarr called out, as the two of them emerged from the automobile. Cheerful as you please, as if he'd known the man for ages, he said, 'Do you play, Mr Chilton?'

And Chilton said, absolutely casual, 'I did once or twice before the war. Afraid I'm a bit of a liability now.' He indicated his bad arm.

'It's just for fun,' Finbarr said.

Chilton nodded. He looked at me as though he'd fully expected to find me here. 'Hello, Miss O'Dea.' He pronounced the *Miss* pointedly.

'I haven't got an eye for balls,' Agatha said. 'I never had.' Still, she went upstairs to change back into her men's clothes. Finbarr, Chilton and I stood on the grass. I wanted to ask Chilton when he'd discovered Agatha, but something silenced me. I didn't want to say anything, lest I break whatever spell allowed this to happen – all of us discovered, and yet not ruined. I felt a burst of love for Chilton, that he had found her and yet apparently had no intention of alerting the world.

'It's rather magical here,' I said, instead of posing any questions.

'Indeed it is,' Chilton agreed.

Agatha returned. Since I was the best player, I took Chilton as my partner. For once I held back on my need to win, letting Chilton swing at balls I could easily have reached. Despite her disclaimer, Agatha played quite nicely. All the upper-crust girls were passable at tennis. The four of us played while our hands reddened and chapped along with our cheeks. But the same magic that brought us all here together without spelling disaster seemed to keep us warm enough, half-dead tennis balls tossed in the air, scores called out, the pop and whack of slicing rackets.

How long did we play? How does one measure time in a place where time has vanished? At some point the shaggy dog from down the road leaped out from the bushes. He stole our ball in mid play, running off with it, and though we could easily have given it up for lost Finbarr and I re-enacted our youth by chasing after him, calling to him, running in mad circles until the dog tired and dropped the ball at Finbarr's feet. The two of us collapsed in a laughing heap, ruffling the dog's fur and letting him lick our chins. Finbarr scooped up the ball and stood.

'Make a wish.'

He could see from my face. I knew how this game worked. You can declare a wish granted but that doesn't make it so. He dropped the ball, the laughter gone. Finbarr's magic powers had their limits, and they were fatal ones. I looked off, into the trees, not ready to face the broken spell.

252

By the time we thought to look around us, Agatha and Chilton were gone.

In silent agreement they had walked up to the top floor, where Agatha lay down on the bed she hadn't bothered to make that morning, used as she was to someone else performing that task. Chilton rekindled the fire, then lay down beside her. She did not object. Nothing real existed. It was a span out of time. No consequences. She acknowledged what she ought to be feeling – the rekindled romance between Finbarr and me could represent her road back to Archie. Instead, she felt something different and altogether more liberating.

She could allow herself to kiss Chilton. She could allow him to remove her clothes, and she could even assist him with the garments that required more than one hand. She could take him inside her and enjoy it immensely. If she became pregnant and went back to Archie, she could pass the child off as his and that would serve him right. If she became pregnant and Chilton disappeared from her life, and she and Archie divorced, her marriage would still protect her, as would her money, the living she was quite capable of making on her own. Among Agatha's enviable qualities, perhaps the most significant was her ability to thrive in this man's world. Following the rules but managing also to rise above them.

Her new novel was coming out in one month. As aghast as the headlines made her, in the new flat calm of throwing aside all social mores she allowed herself to think, how many more people will recognize my name, now, when they see *The Big Four* in a bookshop's window? Curiosity so often amounted to money spent.

But that was a secondary point of thought. The main point was this bubble, away from every ordinary concern.

A while later, when Chilton lay staring at the ceiling and Agatha lay naked in his arms, several thick blankets piled on top of them, he said, 'I have to ask. You've told me Miss O'Dea is your husband's mistress.'

'Yes.' A small sigh. Nobody wanted the past or world at large to intrude on such a moment.

'But that's not the only point of connection. Is it?'

'No,' she said frankly. 'Miss O'Dea is my husband's mistress because she believes my daughter belongs to her.'

And so she told Chilton everything Finbarr had told her, about my time in Ireland, and how it all ended.

Here Lies Sister Mary

M Y LITTLE GIRL was born on 5 August 1919 at the county hospital in Cork City. They say first children come slow and hard, but not mine. A few hours, that's all. Susanna had warned me I wouldn't get stitched afterwards – punishment wherever it could be found was encouraged for the girls from Sunday's Corner, even at hospital – but the midwife who attended me was kind. She had green eyes and freckles that reminded me of my mother and Colleen. Nothing in the way she treated me indicated she knew where I'd come from, though certainly she did know, from my short hair and grey uniform, not to mention the desperation with which I reached for my child, as if I'd never be allowed to hold her again.

'What will you name her, then?' the midwife asked, so gently I could believe whatever name I chose would stand forever.

'Genevieve,' I whispered, running my fingers down her tiny nose, flattened from her battle into the world. We memorized each other's faces as she nursed for the first time. *A mother is a mother still, the holiest thing alive.*

'Will you send a letter for me?' I whispered to the midwife. At the same time sifting through my options since Sister Mary

Clare's letter to Finbarr hadn't worked. My mother. Megs or Louisa. Aunt Rosie.

The midwife's face darkened with sadness. 'Hold your baby, sweetness,' she said, by way of saying no. 'Give her all the love you can.'

And so I did, all the ten glorious days I lay in at the hospital. There was a cot beside my bed, but Genevieve didn't occupy it a single time. Instead, we slept cradled together, the scent of colostrum and then milk wafting from her lips as she exhaled her tiny, contented breath across my chin.

You might be thinking: those ten days were my chance. There was no iron gate. At night I wasn't locked in. Of course I did think about an escape. But these thoughts led to images of myself, out on the road in the dark, clutching a helpless new-born. Not a penny to my name. My hair and clothes announcing my identity to the world, begging me to be returned to the convent, or some place even worse.

So I bided my time obediently. I returned to the convent, lying on my bed in the dormitory that first night while Genevieve lay unreachable in the room below. I thought I'd known what the other girls experienced, hearing their babies cry while unable to go to them. I thought I'd been sharing in their grief. But I hadn't known the half of it. If I could have made my way out a window and scaled down the wall to the nursery, I would have. Instead, I held my rock-hard breasts, determined that not a drop be released until I could get to her. But then a cry would come through the floorboards and I'd know it was Genevieve, and the milk would let down without my baby to catch it.

'Such a good nurser,' Sister Mary Clare cooed, in the morning, as Genevieve gulped with desperate relief, her little cheeks hollowing out with the effort, her face flushed red and sorrowful from her first night away from her mother.

'Please,' I begged the nun, 'you've only one night attendant. Don't you need another? Couldn't that be me?'

'It's not usually new mothers who get that job,' Sister Mary Clare said, dubious.

'Please. I'll work so hard. I'll be so good. I promise you.'

'I'll see what I can do.' She chucked my chin, eyes alight with fondness.

That night I lay in bed, desperately needing to sleep but only able to listen to my baby cry. I got out of bed and went to the door, rattling the knob despite having heard the key turn hours earlier. It stood firmly locked against me.

'It's no use,' Susanna whispered from her cot. She was due any day now. Years later when I was pregnant the second time, married to Archie, I would sleep with no fewer than five pillows, propped all around me. Susanna lay on her side, the thin pillow meant for her head clutched against her belly.

I perched on her bed and gently rubbed the small of her back, thinking she'd shoo me away but instead she sighed with relief. Closing my eyes, I saw the difficult but preferable future I'd scuttled by coming to Ireland in search of Finbarr. The one where I'd taken my grandmother's wedding ring and run away with its shining virtue on my finger. Boarded a ship to America, given birth in New York City, or San Francisco, as a war widow. I could have been anybody except the girl who'd put her own and her child's fate into the hands of foreign strangers.

In the morning, Sister Mary Declan escorted me and the other nursing mothers to our babies to feed them before prayers.

As I settled on a stool with Genevieve, Sister Mary Clare marched in, a triumphant smile on her face.

'I've done it, Nan,' she said. 'The Mother Superior has given her permission. You can be a night attendant, starting this very evening.'

I clutched Genevieve tightly enough to unlatch her. Her eyes blinked open in frustration, and I saw they had changed from the steel grey of a newborn to the shocking, layered blue of her father's.

'There, there,' I said, wiping the dribble from her chin and bringing her back to drink her fill. 'Did you hear that? We're going to be all right. We're going to be together.'

I refused to sign the papers Sister Mary Declan thrust before me, agreeing to let the Church put Genevieve up for adoption.

'Is that what you want, then,' Sister Mary Declan scolded, 'that she should grow up in an orphanage? If you truly loved her, you'd let her have proper parents.'

'She *has* proper parents.'

Sister Mary Declan gave me a lash with her strap for that but it was half-hearted. She still had enough humanity to feel sorry for me. Looking back on any kindness the nuns showed me, I feel a fury. It was those small kindnesses – as if refraining from beating me were a kindness – that kept me there too long.

I was so grateful for small favours. Like Father Joseph walking by me without a second glance. Like being allowed to stay up all night long, tending Genevieve and the other babies in the nursery. Any time a baby cried I would think of its mother, listening upstairs, and cuddle and rock the poor thing until there was quiet. After my night duty I would nurse and bathe Genevieve, go to prayers and Mass, then up to the dormitories to sleep until our midday meal, then return to work scrubbing floors or washing clothes until evening.

Sister Mary Clare continued to sneak extra food to me. 'Don't worry,' she would say, placing a biscuit or a boiled egg into my hand. 'I'll keep Genevieve hidden for you. Nobody will adopt her, I promise you that. Your young man will arrive any day. Pretty as ever, I told him you were. You'll be one of the lucky ones. I know you will.'

Susanna went off to the county hospital to give birth, returned to us for three weeks, and then was sent to a Magdalene Laundry in Limerick. Her baby boy stayed on at the convent.

'We can't have a second offender staying on too long, contaminating the rest of you girls,' said Sister Mary Declan, when they sent Susanna away. Sunday's Corner and Pelletstown were twentieth-century inventions, specifically for mothers and babies. The Magdalene Laundries had originally been established to incarcerate prostitutes, but as the Irish State closed in on its independence, they increasingly became a repository for any girl suspected of sexual impropriety. This could include girls who were considered flirtatious, or too pretty. Girls who made the mistake of telling a priest or family member they'd been molested. Girls with nowhere to go after their debt was worked off. Girls like Susanna, who'd proven themselves beyond redemption by landing at Sunday's Corner twice. *Fallen away*.

For all I know, Susanna spent her whole life at the Magdalene Laundry. She wouldn't have been the first woman to do so, nor the last.

Meanwhile, Fiona's little son was adopted, and the nuns

refused to tell her where he'd gone. Her cheerful words persisted. When she said, 'The nuns know best. He'll have a better life than I could ever give him,' her hands shook, and her fair skin looked whiter still. Sometimes she'd step forwards to bring the laundry to the rooftop, then freeze, remembering her little boy was no longer there for her to see and worry over.

'Tell me,' I'd say, in the moments she looked about to crumble. And she'd recite my parents' London address, a soothing mantra, representing a time that might come after the convent.

Once a week in the nuns' graveyard, autumn chill creeping into the air – I would check to make sure the rotted bar hadn't been repaired. The winter before, I'd arrived with a young woman's hands. Soon I'd leave with an old one's, dried and cracked. But I was strong, and it was better to go in the cooling weeks of autumn before bitter cold set in. My hands were old but I was not. Beneath my shapeless dress the bulk of my pregnancy had diminished with hard work, nursing and scant meals.

Tomorrow, I said to myself, day after day. Tomorrow I'll steal from the nursery, out into the graveyard. I'll pass Genevieve through the bars of the gate, lay her on the grass, then squeeze myself through. Scoop her up and find my way to the boat that will carry us home to England. If I have to steal, or sell my body, I'll do it. Anything to get us away free and clear.

Susanna's son and Genevieve were the only babies under four months old. At night the older babies could be soothed if we rocked them, or let them suck our fingers. During the day the nuns fed Susanna's baby milk-soaked bread, though he was barely six weeks old. At night when he cried, I would scoop him from his cot and nurse him myself.

One morning after Mass, Sister Mary Clare looked over my shoulder as I bathed Genevieve. 'How fat and rosy she is,' the nun exclaimed.

So many of the other babies were thin and pale from feedings spaced too far apart. But Genevieve looked as healthy as any babe under her own mother's care. Her bright blue eyes blinked away water as I dabbed gently at her face. I lifted her from the soapy basin up into the air, then back down so I could nibble her cheek, and she giggled for the first time.

'Oh,' said the nun. 'Is there a more glorious sound in the world than a baby's first laugh?'

I did it again, lifted Genevieve, then rushed her down to nibble her cheek, and she laughed, a belly-shaking, chortling sound. My own laughter scratched my throat, the muscles shaky. I had a flash of remembrance, how much I had loved my mother when I was a small child. The overwhelming joy and safety of her presence. I longed for Mum's green eyes and freckly face, and for her to see me now, with my own baby, loving me in just the same way.

Over and over, I lifted Genevieve up then down, the baby laughing, the nun laughing, me laughing, breathing in my baby's spicy scent with each nibble, until the front of my apron was splashed through with water. I cast a look of smiling comradery at Sister Mary Clare. She was no substitute for my mother but it was nice to have someone laughing along with us, a witness.

Finally, Sister Mary Clare took Genevieve from me, wrapping her in a towel. 'You go off to rest,' she said. 'I'll find a special treat to bring you later.'

Sister Mary Declan arrived to escort the other night attendant and me upstairs to be locked in the dormitory for our few hours of sleep. I cast one last glance over my shoulder to see Sister Mary Clare cooing sweetly at my Genevieve as she carried her away.

That afternoon, I pushed a cart of wet linens to the flat roof above the conservatory, hanging out the sheets to dry in the sun. From up there I saw a man step out of an automobile, with a regal bearing and slicked-back hair. From three storeys above, the details I noted were ones of outline, the sheen of wealth that radiated even to where I watched from a distance. A certain kind of girl would have thought him dashing. But dashing didn't interest me. It never would.

Still, there was something about the man, and he stayed in my mind, though I barely caught a glimpse of his upturned face. When I brought the next load of wet sheets up to the roof to dry, I saw his car had gone. On my way back to the laundry room, I slipped into the nursery. Ordinarily, I never went where I wasn't meant to during the day, for fear of running into Father Joseph, or losing my nights with Genevieve. But something urgent drove me and I hurried under the high archways and over the multi-coloured tiles, stepping carefully so the wood-soled shoes wouldn't clomp. It would be trouble if another nun were in the nursery, but if it were Sister Mary Clare, she wouldn't mind my breaking rules. She was in on the joy of it, Genevieve's laughter.

When I got there, my baby's cot lay bare and empty. No sheets, just a tiny stained mattress where countless other babies had lain. Sister Mary Clare walked towards me with her arms outstretched, a look of consternated sympathy puckering her jolly young face. And something else: a twinkle in her eye. I saw it. Whatever she was about to tell me would account for the day's excitement. A bolt of understanding landed in my heart with the first murderous twinge.

'Where is my baby?' I demanded.

In another cot a little boy old enough to stand pulled himself to his feet, bright copper hair in disarray. He held out his arms to be picked up and Sister Mary Clare swerved away from me as if to accommodate him. I grabbed her billowy sleeve.

'Where's Genevieve? Bring me to her right now, please.'

The nun was the barest bit shorter than me but considerably broader. 'Oh, Nan,' she said. 'Poor, dear Nan. Don't you worry about that baby.'

The other nuns always did that. Called our children 'the baby' or 'that baby', as if they were still in utero and would only be born when delivered to their counterfeit parents or transferred next door to the orphanage. But at least in my presence, until this moment, Sister Mary Clare had always called my baby Genevieve.

'Your baby is gone,' she said. 'To the nicest family, Nan. They'll give her a wonderful life.'

'You can't adopt her to anyone else. She's mine.'

'There, dear. Of course she'll always carry you in her heart.'

'Where is she right at this moment?'

'Now, Nan,' she said. 'I'm not supposed to tell you. I could get into great trouble for doing so, but I believe this will please you. It's an English family who's adopted her. A lovely English family, she'll be raised right and proper.'

'Where in England?' It came out as a bellow. A scarcely contained roar. To my own ears I sounded like an animal. How must I have sounded to Sister Mary Clare? Fierce enough for her to take a step backwards, looking less confident in her ability to soothe me.

How could I ever have believed her? I felt seduced. My hand still clutched the fabric of her sleeve. I closed the distance between us, my nose almost touching hers.

'You bring me to my baby right now.' Not a bellow this time but a growl. I finished the sentence in my thoughts: or I swear to God I will kill you where you stand.

Now she saw it. Now she was afraid. As if the threat hadn't just been in my head, but I'd said it aloud. The jolliness disappeared from her face along with the sympathy. I stepped closer. She stepped away. Now she was near enough to the wall to feel its cold stone through her habit. Genevieve's molecules still inhabited this room. Her laughter still echoed from its stones.

It was the man I'd seen earlier. I knew it. Had they brought her directly to him? Or had they let him shop, as if for a puppy? Perhaps he had walked up and down the rows of cots, peering into every one, until my Genevieve's bright blue eyes stared back at him. So alert. So beautiful. So plump and rosy on mother's milk. Worth any price the nuns asked. Perhaps she'd performed her new trick for him and laughed. Enchanting. *I'll take this one*.

And Sister Mary Clare handed my baby right over to him. Genevieve, bundled into a stranger's arms and carried away. And all the while I was working in the very same building.

The nun stared straight at me. You'd think the shape of my face would be something she'd remember her whole life, but her eyes never took me in. Not really. All she saw was her counterfeit kindness, reflected back at her as something real. Her gaze was no more authentic than the studied furrow in her brow, now, as if she cared about me. As if she hadn't presided, jolly and smiling, over the kidnapping of my child.

A criminal. In the course of this story thus far I have described to you a variety of crimes. But none – *none* – is more heinous, more violent, more unconscionable, than this one. The theft of my baby. Nothing I could unleash upon Sister Mary Clare could ever equal what she'd just done to me.

My fingers twitched. They rose, almost without me. I placed both hands around her neck. How satisfying her gasps – first of shock and then of pain. She tried to gasp but couldn't. No oxygen for her, my hands saw to that. Her eyes bulged. Her hands came up to claw at my arms but I worked with the strength of a mother protecting her child – too late but none the weaker. She tried to bat me away but her blows were like air, as if she knew she had no right to defend herself.

It felt good. It felt like the beginning. I would kill her and then I would leave the convent and find the rich, slick-haired man and retrieve my baby. But first this sweet task, choking Sister Mary Clare until her face turned blue. Once she was dead, I would smash her head against the stone wall, one sharp blow. When she fell to the floor, I'd smash her head a final time, breaking it open on the hard-tile floor, that cruel pink and blue. Sister Mary Clare made a gurgled sound of fear, which only fuelled the pleasure I took in harming her. *Soon you will be dead.*

I could feel her pulse beneath my hands, steady and stoppable. Slowing down. Against my palms, her throat tried to gurgle but couldn't. I pressed harder. Her eyes bulged. Good. Excellent. Good. I'd scarcely known my own strength. It was the first religious moment I'd encountered between these hallowed walls.

Then a baby cried. Perhaps it was Susanna's baby. That distinct hungry mewl, sharp and desperate. My milk let down with a searing sting, soaking through my shirt and apron. I let go of the nun. Sister Mary Clare raised her hands to her throat, stroking away what damage I'd done, reclaiming the room's oxygen with great honking inhalations. I could see welts, red now; by evening they would be black and blue. She stared at my chest, milk spilling through my dress and apron, its sweet smell filling the room.

How far away was Genevieve at that moment? Every second brought her further and further from my arms. If I raised my hands again, if I killed Sister Mary Clare, I'd be incarcerated for good. There would be a trial. My parents would discover my whereabouts through newspapers. The harlot who strangled a bride of Christ. I would spend the rest of my life in prison, if I was lucky enough not to be executed.

So I kicked off the clogs and ran from the nursery with my soiled apron, in my stockinged feet. Out of the convent. Into the nuns' graveyard. The children from the orphanage played in the yard, I could hear their voices rising up into the air. When I got to the iron gate, I only had to kick the bar, turn sideways and squeeze myself through, just as I'd practised. I ran away from the road, across the fields. After a while, in the distance, I heard the convent's bells and then a constable's siren.

The bells were for me. I knew the nuns would be scurrying and exclaiming and running in useless circles. But the sirens sounded for a different reason. Luckily for me, the police were engaged elsewhere. An RIC patrol had been ambushed in Cobh and every available officer was rushing in that direction. Every girl in the convent could have escaped without capture, if only I'd known to tell them.

First I ran, faster than ever, joyless. I flung off my cap and my apron, in motion, never missing a stride. I ran off the road, through fields. Not the barest slip or side sprain of an ankle. Clean, fast strides, like I'd been in training. I passed a farmhouse where laundry dried on the line, swaying in the cool crisp afternoon. I should have stopped and stolen clothes, disguised myself. The front of my dress was soaked through with milk, drying from my flight and the sun. But I didn't stop. I ran and I ran.

'Whoa, there darling,' a woman said.

I hadn't seen her, leaning against a barn. Wearing trousers and a thick jacket, a cigarette in one hand, the other raised up in the air as she stepped out in front of me, stopping me short. She had wild grey curls and a wind-burned face, standing close enough for me to smell last night's whiskey on her breath.

'Please,' I said. 'Please let me go.'

Her eyes landed on my chest, the milk stains dried by now, then travelled to my shredded stockings and feet. She blew out a stream of smoke then dropped her cigarette dangerously into the hay. Took a moment to stamp it out.

'And where is it you're going, then?'

'I don't suppose I need to tell you.' I sounded more weepy than defiant. Nothing had ever felt more incorrect than standing still. I had to run, away and also towards.

The woman took off her coat and placed it over my shoulders. 'I know where you'll be going,' she said, raspy voice wanting to be kind, forcing itself to be stern. 'Straight to the boy who got you here in the first place. But you mustn't go to him, dear. Listen to you. Sounding like England. That's where you belong, then, isn't it?'

Her name was Vera and she brought me inside, gave me a change of clothes and fed me. I think she told me about her life, the friend she lived with and her feelings about the nuns and what they called charity. I didn't hear any of it. For the longest time I didn't hear a word anyone said to me. I was a shoeless girl on foot, desperate to win a race against cars and boats. From the moment I discovered I was pregnant I had only ever been a girl on foot.

At some point another woman arrived, also wearing a man's work clothes and smelling of smoke and whiskey. 'Good gracious,' she said, at the sight of me.

'That's Martha,' Vera told me.

Martha looked directly at my breasts, swollen to lopsided rocks with breast milk. 'Come with me, love,' she said. 'I can help you with that.'

She brought me into the small bedroom and unwound a cloth bandage for me to wrap around my breasts. 'You want to let the milk out a little bit, every now and then,' she said. 'Enough to relieve the pressure, but not so much to keep you producing.'

Thinking about it now I wonder what babies were in her past, whose milk she'd had to stop. But I didn't wonder at the time. Vera and Martha emptied a biscuit jar of pound notes and shillings. They bundled me up in what may have been one of their best coats. Vera's shoes fit me better; she gave me a pair of soft-leather boots. Then they loaded me into the back of their wagon.

'Lie low and still,' Vera instructed.

And so I left Sunday's Corner the same way I'd arrived, in a horse-drawn carriage. Martha sang as she drove the horses, the same tune Sister Mary Clare used to hum, echoing like bagpipes through the stairwells and hallways of the convent. Finally I learned the words:

> 'Come, all you fair and tender girls
> That flourish in your prime
> Beware, beware, keep your garden fair
> Let no man steal your thyme.'

The song and the women carried me to the train station where they bought my ticket to Dublin and gave me the rest of the money for the boat back to England.

'How will I ever repay you?' I asked.

'Be well,' Vera said, 'and be happy.'

Martha's dress was far too big. I kept the good coat buttoned to my chin. When the boat docked in Liverpool, a group of English soldiers waited to be dispatched to Ireland. And I wondered, in the history of the world, had one soldier ever been sent to win back a mother's stolen child? In the coming months I'd search for Genevieve in the most illogical ways. I walked from London all the way to Croxley Green, straight through the night, the soles of my shoes worn down, speckled with holes. I peered into every pram, wary mothers or nannies rolling them back, pulling up the hood.

Once you've lost a baby their cries will reach you anywhere. Across miles of parkland. From an open window two streets away. You wake in the middle of the night and find yourself in the wrong place, you're supposed to be elsewhere, *with* someone. Wherever she is, you know she's waking too, blue eyes opening in the dark, searching for the one person in the world who answers to the name. Mother. Not a pretender. Her own real, true mother. The body knows, even when the mind does not.

When, finally, I made it home, grey-faced and ruined, I found a stack of letters from Finbarr waiting for me, some of them with money enclosed – for the journey to Ireland he didn't know I'd already taken.

'Why won't you answer, Nan?' he wrote, again and again.

His parents never told him how I'd landed on their doorstep. He knew nothing about the night I'd lain beside him, holding myself against his feverish body. Sister Mary Clare had never written to him, I was sure, and even if she had, the Mahoneys would have thrown the letter away.

'If you don't love me anymore,' he finally wrote, in a letter that landed in England before I did, 'I want to hear you say it to my face. I'll come to London to hear you say it.'

I picked up pencil and paper to write back to him. But there was too much to say. Too much sorrow to deliver.

When my mother wrote to Aunt Rosie to tell her what had happened, Rosie travelled from Dublin to Sunday's Corner and insisted on speaking to the Mother Superior, who sat her down and showed her a death certificate.

Mother: Nan O'Dea.

Baby girl: deceased. And there, written beside the word, was the same day in November they'd sent her off with the man I'd seen from the rooftop

It was Sister Mary Clare's handiwork. I knew it.

'I'm so sorry, Nan,' my mother sobbed, when she told me. Never having seen Genevieve that day, the laughing picture of health.

'She's not dead,' I promised.

My mother looked at me, sorrowful for my loss, and possibly my delusion.

What could I do then but walk, all over London and beyond, refusing to rejoice in my freedom, wanting to search for Genevieve but not knowing where to begin? I clutched my body, cruelly bounced back to what it had been before, my stomach flat and smooth, my milk dried up.

If I'd been right enough in the head to track time, I could tell you the date I returned home to find Finbarr, sitting on the curb in front of our building, a satchel at his feet. It was the only time in my life where my heart didn't leap at the sight of him. There was nothing I could do but break *his* heart once by telling him about Genevieve, and twice by sending him away.

If only he'd come for me just a little later, when I was at least able to pretend to be my old self. By the following spring, I was working a few afternoons at Buttons and Bits. Megs was already training as a nurse. Louisa, still home but already engaged, was taking a secretarial course. At our kitchen table she taught me the shorthand and typing that would one day lead to my job at the British Rubber Company. By that summer, I could walk through the world and present a face that didn't look entirely broken, or constantly searching.

I was, though. Constantly searching. Did I ever stop? No. Did I ever plan to stop – did I ever think there would come a time, or a moment, when I'd admit defeat and the impossibility of my quest? Of course not.

Four years after my return to England, quite by chance, I found her. Unmistakable. I was visiting my sister Megs at her new home in Torquay, where she worked as a nurse.

Megs took a day off and we went for a walk on the beach. A little girl ran towards us with the peripatetic zigzag of small children. At first I thought the child was on her own but as my eyes searched through the sunlight I saw two women a long way behind her, so distant I could barely make out their forms. When the little girl found Megs and me in her way, instead of running around us, she threw her arms around my legs.

'Oh,' I said, looking down into a pair of bright blue eyes. She had a high forehead and shiny dark hair cascading backwards as she looked up at me. Sweet, pointed little chin. I knew her in an instant. And she knew me, too. I know she did.

'Nan,' Megs said sharply, as I stooped to gather the little girl in my arms. 'You can't just pick up other people's children.'

The little girl didn't agree. She returned my embrace as if she remembered the last time her mother had held her. Her real mother.

'Teddy,' one of the women called out. 'Look here, Teddy, we must head back to Ashfield.'

The child's consciousness returned to her present-day life. She squirmed out of my arms and ran back to the women, who turned and walked off in the other direction. I grabbed Megs's arm to steady myself.

'There, there,' Megs said. 'You'll have one of your own one day, Nan, you will.'

'I already have one of my own,' is what I said out loud. Inwardly I said *Ashfield*, again and again in my mind, memorising it without a doubt, and vowing to discover all there was to know about the people who lived there.

Was she beautiful?

Yes. More beautiful than you can imagine.

The day Finbarr finally came to fetch me, I sent him away, returning the money he'd sent me against his protestations. We had barely talked an hour before he trudged off, out of sight, heavy with the added sorrow I'd given him.

'You'll always know where I am,' Finbarr said before he left, tears streaming down his face. 'I'll never live anywhere without sending you word. You'll change your mind one day. I know you will.'

A mother bat can find her pup in a cave full of thousands, even without eyes that see. When your child has been stolen you measure her age by the days that pass. You look into the faces of other children, to make sure. You do this so many times you know with your whole being, you haven't made a mistake when at last you find her.

Sometimes I wonder if Agatha learned it from me. About the worst violence you can do to a person. What you might be driven to in its aftermath. The wars that can be started, the justice that must be served. All for the sake of avenging a child.

Part Three

Part Three

16 September 1926

Dearest Finbarr,

I hope this letter finds you well after all these years. My goodness, I hope it finds you at all, and that you will be happy to hear from me. I must admit that even after all that's happened, even though I haven't answered your letters, whenever I see your name on an envelope (whenever I see the words, 'Love, Finbarr' written across the bottom of a page), my heart somersaults backwards up to the sky.

And so I must tell you what I'd promised myself I wouldn't, which I take a risk in doing. I have found our baby, our girl, our darling Genevieve. I have seen her and even held her in my arms. She is happy and healthy and living with 'parents' at a house called 'Styles' in Sunningdale, Berkshire. If you could only see her! She has your eyes, Finbarr. She's smart and brave and beautiful. She loves dogs and books. In that way at least one of our wishes has come true.

The people who have her are named Archibald and Agatha Christie. And here is the difficult part. Archie Christie plans to leave his wife and marry me. Did I engineer this? Did I plan it? Yes. To you alone I confess that I did. For the only

277

reason that could excuse me. To be a part of my own child's life.

If I received such a letter from you, if you told me you were about to marry, it would cause me great sorrow but I would thank you for telling me yourself. I hope you understand this is all I can do. It's too late to take her away from the only family she's known. At least this way I can be her stepmother. At least I can land my eyes upon her, and embrace her, and call her by her real name when she's asleep.

I don't love Archie. But I can't afford to hate him despite his role in all that happened. He's my only road back to Genevieve. So I do what must be done. And Finbarr: nothing could be like us, could it? My heart belongs, as ever, to you.

Love,
Nan

The Disappearance

Day Eight
Saturday, 11 December 1926

Finbarr caught Agatha at the top of the stairs on the first floor, his hand on her elbow, urgent but gentle. The house was dark, just after midnight. She and Chilton had missed their dinner. She'd only wanted to gather some tins of food to sustain them.

'Agatha,' Finbarr said, his hoarse voice full of urgency. 'Please don't say you've decided not to help me after all?'

She looked at him, his face barely visible in the flicker of the candle she held, but strikingly earnest. She thought, What a fool Nan is. Any woman with her wits about her would run away with him the moment he asked. The conviction with which she thought this, while Chilton sat waiting for her upstairs, could almost make her sympathize with Archie, the twin desires, the divided loyalty.

'All it would take is one word from you,' Finbarr said. 'Tell her. That your daughter is your daughter. That she's not Genevieve.'

'One word! I could offer ten thousand words and she'd never believe me. I could show her a birth certificate and she'd say it was forged. Don't you see she's been convinced of this for years now? To accept any evidence to the contrary would be to lose her child all over again.'

Did Finbarr stop in that moment, or any moment, and consider whether *he* believed Agatha's denials that Teddy and Genevieve were the same person? That when Agatha said *her* child, she also meant *his* child? I doubt he did. It would have been too contrary to his primary goal. I had already told him Teddy's birthday was the same as Genevieve's. That Archie's mother came from County Cork, so he'd have known the perfect place to collect a baby to pass off as his own.

The nuns wouldn't give a baby to Protestants, Finbarr had said.

Archie's mother is a Catholic. And please don't ever think to tell me what nuns wouldn't do.

That face. Finbarr had kneeled in front of Teddy when he'd given her the whittled dog. His own eyes, looking back at him. How could he not have seen it?

A person does adhere to the mission at hand. We believe what furthers our own cause. I don't blame Finbarr for this. What was stolen from me was stolen from him, too, even more completely, so that he never understood what he had to fight for. He thought he only had to fight for me.

'That's why you've got to convince her,' he said to Agatha. 'You haven't even tried.'

Agatha looked away, off into the dark distance. Frustratingly silent.

'Tell her, then, how it's hurting you,' he said. 'To lose your husband.' I never heard Finbarr say Archie's name, not once. 'Nan's not cruel. Tell her you can't live without him.'

'But I think perhaps I can live without him. You can live without her, too.'

'I know I can. I've done it all this while, haven't I? But I don't want to, Agatha. Don't you want your husband anymore?'

'I can't say that I do. Not entirely.' And then, she wasn't sure if it was to assuage him or if it were true: 'I don't know, Finbarr. I'm sorry, I just don't know.'

He let go of her elbow and touched her cheek with the coarse, lovely flat of his palm. And then he turned and walked away. She hated the sag of his shoulders. She wanted to give him hope, she did. But not enough to relinquish her own.

When daylight arrived, the first thing Agatha felt was a rush of happiness. How wonderfully foreign it all was, and what a release. Casting all propriety aside could almost eliminate the question: What would she do now? Having left the world so publicly, how could she return privately?

'Can one woman cause such a fuss,' she said to Chilton that morning, lying in his arms under a mountain of scratchy wool blankets, 'and then just return without any explanation?'

'Absolutely not.' Chilton had a complicated way of wrapping both arms around her, using the good to hoist the bad. In this way he managed to clasp too tightly for her to sit up and look at his face. 'It's quite clear you can never go back. You'll have to stay with me.'

She touched her fingers to his lips, eyes fixed on the ceiling.

'I've had a murder to solve, you know,' Chilton told her.

She broke free from his grasp and sat up so she could face him. This was the first she'd heard of it. Chilton told her about the Marstons.

'How sad,' Agatha said, and tears did come to her eyes. She'd forgotten the wider world and its inhabitants in the midst of her various conundrums.

'What do you think?' Chilton asked. 'You write detective novels. Should I agree with Lippincott's theory and call it a day?'

'Oh, I couldn't possibly solve a crime I hadn't invented. The point of a good detective story is to make it all obvious. You throw in enough variables so the reader doubts his own solution, and then at the end he can be pleased with himself for figuring it out. In life I imagine Occam's razor applies. The simplest solution is usually correct.'

Chilton smiled. It pleased him enormously, to listen to her.

'What do you think?' she asked. 'Do you suppose your man Lippincott is right about the wife? There's no reason to suspect anyone else, is there?'

'To be perfectly honest I find myself not caring as I should.'

She kissed him.

'I'd like to read your books,' he went on. 'I'd like to read every word you've ever written.'

Agatha smiled and pressed her forehead to his. 'I'm not at all ready to go home,' she said, and their kissing recommenced in earnest.

Who would have known it was possible to make love so rapturously and still entertain so many thoughts? Agatha kept her eyes open. Taking in the Spartan room and the man who'd been a stranger mere days before. She thought she would always be grateful for this span of time, and then she thought she might make it last forever. She could start calling herself Mrs Chilton today, and the two of them could go off somewhere together where nobody knew either of them. She would never have to associate herself with that terrible word, divorce, or face the music from running away and causing such a brouhaha. Back in Berkshire, Teddy would bear a scar, but we all acquire those along the way, don't we, despite anyone's best efforts. Nan would take up the mother mantle with a fervour few daughters had ever seen.

Eventually, if Agatha remained hidden, the world would

forget she'd ever gone missing, or existed in the first place. She imagined herself shedding everything. Her old life scattered to the wind, melting into the air as mist off the sea. Nan could claim it all – the house, the husband, the child. Of course, this would prove terrible for Finbarr. But sometimes a person had to think of herself.

She could sidestep into a new existence, taking nothing but the writing with her. She could start fresh under a new name. She could change her hair, starve or stuff herself till she was unrecognizable, the woman she'd been before nothing but an unsolved mystery. While Mrs Chilton clattered away on the typewriter, and took long walks on the beach, and rolled under the covers with her gentle husband who adored – who *worshipped* her.

'Darling Agatha,' Chilton said, lips against her ear.

It felt so good to be darling, being lost didn't matter.

A little while later, Chilton drove back to the Bellefort through the damp, late morning, his frayed woollen coat on the seat beside him, one chapped hand on the steering wheel. The rain from Sunningdale had made its way north, falling gently. A smile contoured his face, twitching at his lips. He didn't know the turn Agatha's fantasies had taken – running away with him and becoming Mrs Chilton. But he would have agreed to it in a heartbeat.

For the first time since the war he felt as though he might have recovered something of himself. Not his innocence, never his brothers, but something wonderfully important. A will to live beyond the need to spare his mother further pain. Only a few days prior, if he'd heard word of his mother's death, he might have boarded a train home, kissed her corpse's forehead, then turned his father's old Purdey shotgun on himself and drawn the trigger with relief. At last.

Now, though. Now he felt like he might stick around another few days, just to see what happened. When he held Agatha in both his arms, good and bad, Chilton believed, the way a person does in that first miracle of reciprocated ardour, that one night of passion could translate to forever. And why not run off with her now? As far as the whole world was concerned, she was already gone.

When Chilton parked his car at the hotel, he saw Mr Race, smoking and pacing out front, thin curls of smoke followed by thicker exhalations of breath. The sight made Chilton realize he'd forgotten to smoke himself, for hours, even for an entire day. He reached into his inner coat pocket for his cigarette case and then stopped himself. He wanted nothing in common with Mr Race, whom he imagined to be the same breed as Archie Christie. The kind of man for whom Chilton felt nothing but disdain. Not that they'd care or notice. They considered disdain their own particular province. Belligerent and concerned only with themselves, even at their most generous. *Men who served in the trenches and men who served in the air.* Race may have been too young to belong to either group but Chilton placed him firmly in the latter.

I must say, Chilton's opinion of Archie was unfair, having never so much as laid eyes on him, let alone having spent the better part of the night and morning making love to his wife. He knew that. But clinging to his bad idea of the man was part and parcel of clinging to the woman.

As Chilton stepped out of the car, he saw Race do something that surprised him. He dropped his cigarette to the dirt, ground it up with his foot, then scooped up the remains, tucking it into his palm as if he meant to throw it away later. Chilton hadn't pegged him as the sort to clear away his own mess. Mrs Race emerged from the hotel a moment later, bundled up in a hat and coat. Upon seeing her husband, she broke into the happiest smile and stepped immediately into his arms, looking up at him with profound delight.

Chilton knew enough of the world not to be surprised by a woman returning to a beastly husband. But something about this did not look right. They might have been two entirely different people. Mr Race, who had seen Chilton, seemed aware of the discrepancy. He placed his hands on his wife's shoulders, and she looked over to see Chilton. Whereupon she stepped back rather abruptly.

'Good day, Mrs Race,' Chilton called out, trying his best to be jaunty. 'Mr Race.'

They murmured hello, newly subdued.

Inside the hotel, Chilton waited a moment. Then he stepped back outside. The Races were gone. He walked quietly round the back, where they stood together, quite close, holding on to each other's elbows. They appeared not only loving, but trusting and intimate.

He didn't dare creep close enough to hear what they were saying, or they surely would have seen him. But from where he stood, observing in secret, he tried to listen. And although no words became distinct, he could have sworn they both spoke with Irish brogues.

Earlier, Finbarr and I had driven back to the hotel in the grey winter dawn.

'I've been thinking,' I said. 'Can't a person train dogs in England as well as Ireland?'

He pulled the car over to the side of the road and turned towards me. 'What are you saying, Nan?'

I saw I'd given him false hope. I couldn't offer him precisely what he wanted. But I could offer him a version of it. 'I'm saying—' I stopped trying to think how to word it. 'My plan could stay in place. And you could be a part of it. Think, Finbarr. Archie travels. He works all day. Why, just two years ago, he left England for an entire year. We could be together often as not. I could even bring Genevieve to you sometimes.'

'Good Lord, Nan, what have you become?'

The pilot light of shame, always ready to be struck into full flame, flickered inside me. I doused it with anger. 'I've become what I've been since August 1919. A mother who loves her child. And a woman who's ready to do what's necessary. That's what I've become.'

He didn't move for a long moment. 'We could take her, then,' he finally said. 'The two of us. Out of England, to anywhere you like, and raise her as our own.'

'How can I do that to her, Finbarr? Kidnap her? If she were still a baby, fine, but now? What would that do to her? And if there's an army searching for Agatha Christie, what will there be to search for her child? I've no way to prove she's mine. It's too late for that kind of justice. I wish it weren't, but it is.'

'And what if you discover a month from now you're carrying my child again? What will you do, then?'

(Oh, Finbarr. Oh, Reader. Must I know and provide an answer for everything?)

I closed my eyes against tears and he gathered me up in his arms. Holding me tight, he spoke into my ear. 'How can you stand that man touching you, if you truly believe he stole our child?'

I was silent a while, as if reasoning it out in that moment, though in truth I'd thought it through a long time ago. I didn't blame Archie, not fully. He'd availed himself of something readily on offer, without considering how it came to be so. The way all men like him do. He might inhabit the world unthinkingly, in the manner men of his station were allowed. But Archie hadn't invented the world; he'd only been born into it like the rest of us.

'It's the same way a diplomat makes peace after war,' I said. 'And having me as his wife will be punishment enough. Especially if you live nearby.'

'I'm not meant for that. To be on the sly. I'm meant to be your husband. You know that, Nan. What's more, I'm not sure I could lay eyes on that man without killing him.'

This might have been hyperbole but I knew that urge well enough to take him at his word. And, of course, I couldn't risk it, Finbarr losing his freedom over killing Archie. Or Archie being killed, for that matter. Whatever he was guilty of, nothing he'd done was terrible enough to merit death as punishment.

'The only answer,' Finbarr said, still holding on, 'is for us to leave this place together.'

I didn't agree out loud. Neither did I disagree. Somewhere in our embrace, in the tightening of his grip on me, I could feel Finbarr take heart in my silence.

By the time Chilton arrived at the Bellefort, I was already back in my room. He knocked on my door, and when I opened it, he pressed the Galsworthy novel into my hands.

'Thank you,' I said. 'How very kind. Though I don't imagine I'll have time to read it before it needs to be returned. I do need to get back to London before long.'

'Do you?' he said. 'I thought perhaps you'd be returning to Ireland with Mr Mahoney.'

'I will never return to Ireland.'

Chilton must have noticed, I didn't say I'd never go away with Finbarr. 'Speaking of Ireland,' he said, 'I must tell you the strangest thing. I heard Mr and Mrs Race talking just now and it was as if they were two entirely different people. Not only kind to each other, but also sounding as though they'd just got off the boat from Dublin.'

My face went hot and my eyes flooded. I didn't want him in my room. 'You know, Mr Chilton, if you've opted not to reveal Mrs Christie's whereabouts, shouldn't *you* be going back home?'

'I imagine my reasons for staying are similar to yours.' He said it kindly. He said everything kindly. But that didn't necessarily bode kindness, did it?

'Won't you be in terrible trouble,' I said pointedly, 'when they find out she was here all along?'

'It's not trouble if you're never caught, is it?'

I remembered my hands around Sister Mary Clare's throat. I imagined a gravestone behind the convent, marked like all the rest. *Here Lies Sister Mary*. But this one was just for her.

Down the hall a door opened. Young Miss Armstrong emerged, her black hair loose, her face bright and clean of any troubling past. If only I could have willed my soul out of my own body and into hers, and lived my whole life differently.

'Oh, Mr Chilton,' I said, and the floorboards rushed to meet my face.

Chilton hadn't meant to upset me, at least not to this degree. It was part of his job to disarm people, make them vulnerable and get them talking. He did it almost by force of habit. What was less practised was disarming himself. Before I hit the floor he reached out his good arm – sufficient only in protecting my head from a more severe blow.

'My goodness,' said Miss Armstrong, bustling to my side. 'Shall we get her into bed?'

'No.' I sat up and pulled at the collar of my dress. 'I'm fine.' I shrugged away from both pairs of hands. 'I just need some air. Some room and some air.'

'Let me at least walk you downstairs for luncheon,' Miss Armstrong said. 'The combination of cold air and hot water is said to be so healthful. But I've been feeling rather light-headed since we arrived. Perhaps that's what killed the Marstons. Some kind of shock to their system. It must be all the worse, for old people.' She glanced at Chilton as if in concerned warning.

Chilton remained focused on me. 'You're sure you're all right?'

'Perfectly fine. Just feeling a bit ridiculous.'

'Is that nurse afoot?' asked Miss Armstrong. 'Mrs Race?'

'I don't believe she is,' Chilton said. 'Perhaps you can consult with her later.'

'That won't be necessary,' I said.

Accepting Miss Armstrong's hand, I got to my feet. I would eat to oblige them. And then steal away to see Finbarr. I should have returned to London already. One more day, I kept telling myself. Just give me one more day.

Chilton watched as Miss Armstrong and I walked off, her arm wrapped around me with genuine concern. People can be so kind, he thought. Women especially. The way one woman naturally allows another to lean on her in times of trouble.

The Disappearance

Last Day Seen
Friday, 3 December 1926

WOULD IT SURPRISE you to know that most women, if they saw Finbarr and Archie side by side, would choose Archie as the handsomer? Especially after the war, once Finbarr had lost his joyful gleam.

Whereas the years had made me more attractive than I'd been as a girl. Something about the way I learned to conceal my shattered self. It made me fascinating to men.

'Oh, Nan,' Archie said, taking me into his arms that night at the Owens', before we knew what tomorrow held. If you can see your way to never minding, that he'd taken his own wife in much the same way not twenty-four hours earlier, then try to understand: he loved me, he did.

Do you think, as Finbarr did, I should have hated Archie? Perhaps I did. When it all started I did, I'm sure of it. Looking back now, it's hard to say. I married the man, after all. I bore him a child whom I love as dearly and deeply as the one I lost. Thousands of days and hundreds of thousands of hours have been spent alongside him, both waking and sleeping. From this particular hour the only answer I can give, as to whether I hated him, is sometimes. And in some ways. If that's what you'd like to call hate.

The way a certain man can walk through the world. If in that day and country Archie had been allowed more than one wife, he might have had ten and loved us all, with waxing and waning preferences. Which is not to say he loved Agatha or me as possessions. He did *see* us in his way. On the golf course he would stand back, arms crossed, assessing my swing, my form, the arc of the ball I propelled. 'Ripping,' he would say, for all to hear. And when we were alone: 'Ripping, gorgeous girl.'

I could have won at golf with Archie but I never let myself. He wanted me to be good but not better than him. He liked to watch me play tennis at the club, against other women. And it pleased me that this aspect of myself pleased him. My plan to land Archie was born of urgency but that didn't mean I never found pleasure in it. Running again, swinging a racket, winning.

Funktionslust. It's a German word for the joy of doing what one does best. Seducing Archie, stealing him away from his wife, had a very specific purpose. But as it turned out, I was good at it. Better than good. It might have been a tennis match. No other woman at the club, no other woman anywhere, could touch me.

'Oh, Nan,' Archie said. Smooth hands down my smoother side. He had good lips, Archie did, tasting like Scotch in the evening. By now I'd learned how to arch and whisper, how to climb and conquer. The night before Archie's wife disappeared I could sense the night before, enough to understand the imperative of reclaiming him. Now that he'd decided to move forward there could be no more lapses or wavering. My claim on him as a shark, swim or die.

I clamped my hand over Archie's mouth, hard enough for it to hurt him. 'Hush,' I commanded.

'Nan,' he answered, a tight gurgle. And then, when all had come to rest, 'I love you.'

The covers had been thrown to the floor and my head rested on his slick chest, his breath still coming out hard and forced.

'Dear Nan,' Archie said. 'How I love you.'

In nine days' time it would finally occur to Archie to wonder in earnest. Where had I gone?

He would have an afternoon to escape the confines of Styles and the chaos of the fruitless search. He would travel to London.

Turning his collar up against the cold, he would march down city streets to my flat. Walk up the steps and rap on my door. Hold his ear against it when there was no answer. The silence inside sounding like it had taken time to build. An uninhabited place.

Nothing in the world removes the ills a wife causes like the balm of a mistress. Even as Archie listened for me, he thought if I were to swing the door open and welcome him inside with a seductive smile, I'd be nothing but a poor substitute, the satisfaction I offered him temporary, fleeting. Only enough to carry him through this terrible grief until his wife was found.

My door sat sealed, the room on the other side of it soundless. My neighbour, old Mrs Kettering, opened the door. It wasn't the first time she'd seen Archie and she frowned at him as she always did. He responded with a placating smile. People like her, who'd witnessed us together, might be trouble down the road.

Still the question bubbled up inside of him, impossible not to ask. 'Good afternoon, Mrs Kettering. I wonder, have you seen Miss O'Dea?'

'Not for days,' she said. 'More than a week, I'd say. Not a

glimpse of her nor a peep from her. Here's hoping she's run off with some bloke her own age.' She bestowed one last, hawk-like glare before slamming the door behind her and stamping down the stairs. There are too many women in the world helping men with their dirty work. But so many more taking each other's side in unexpected moments.

Equally unexpected, Archie would find the moment of reprieve he'd wanted. For the first time in days, his mind went blank with sheer perplexity. The question eclipsed emotion, for just one moment. *Where had Nan gone?*

He hurried down the stairs to the street. Walked quickly, his breath coming out in gusts. Willing his hands not to rise and cover his face. Any tears in his eyes could be explained away by the cold. Miles away in Harrogate, I wasn't thinking of Archie. Hardly a bit. Hardly at all.

While he was thinking: How peculiar, and what has precipitated this? The Age of Disappearing Women.

The age of disappearing women did not begin with Agatha Christie. It had begun long before Agatha hopped into a car and motored away from Newlands Corner with Finbarr. And it would continue for quite a bit longer. We disappeared from schools. From our hometowns. From our families and our jobs. One day we would be going about our business, sitting in class, or laughing with friends, or walking hand in hand with a beau. Then, poof.

What ever happened to that girl? Don't you remember her? Where did she go?

In America we went to Florence Crittenton homes. In England to Clark's House, or any of the various homes run mostly by the Anglican Church. In Australian hospitals, babies were taken from mothers who were drugged, incapacitated, unwilling. And, of course, some of us didn't go anywhere at all. We bled to death on butchers' tables. We jumped off bridges.

The age of disappearing women. It had been going on forever. Thousands of us vanished, with not a single police officer searching. Not a word from the newspapers. Only our long absences and quiet returns. If we ever returned at all.

Before Agatha disappeared, before I knew Finbarr had returned to Britain, the plan I'd authored was well underway. In the Owens' house, in the borrowed bed, my arms wrapped tight around Archie. The overriding element was mercenary, true. But there were other elements.

'I love you, Nan,' Archie said, as if he couldn't say it enough, as if the words needed to be repeated ad infinitum until the world conspired to let this moment last, the delicious, breathless secret of it.

I loved him too. If that's what you'd like to call love.

The Disappearance

Day Eight
Saturday, 11 December 1926

IN THE MIDST of all the maelstrom, Agatha's work was another place for her to go. A world to visit apart from her own. She could lose herself there no matter what occurred. In the Timeless Manor the typewriter keys clicked and clacked. Let them search. Let Archie worry. When her fingers flew over the typewriter keys it was the whole world that vanished. Not her.

I was not so lucky. In Harrogate, in the moments without Finbarr, my mind assaulted me with fear, worry and misgivings. I tried to concentrate on reading the novel Chilton had given me. I'd barely fought my way to the second chapter when a rap came on my door. I opened it to find Mrs Leech.

'There's a man downstairs to see you.' I knew from the way her brow cocked, not sure of the propriety, that it was Finbarr, and my face changed so suddenly – lighting up – that Mrs Leech smiled.

'You're not really married, are you, Miss O'Dea?'

'No,' I admitted. 'I'm not.'

'There, there.' She patted my shoulder to comfort me. Anyone who's been in love knows it's a state that requires comforting. 'You go on downstairs. Tell him to cheer up, that's all. And you mustn't bring him to your room. We're not that kind of hotel.'

'Of course. Thank you, Mrs Leech.'

In the lobby Finbarr sat on the settee, his pea coat open, rubbing his hands across his knees. He stood, and we walked outside together into the cold, where I stepped into him, sliding my hands into his coat pocket. I felt a square of paper, glossy against my fingertips, and pulled out the photograph I'd sent him, years ago. It was bent and battered, tearing around the edges. Tiny holes at its corners gathered upon themselves, indicating it had been pinned to more than one wall.

Have you ever looked at a picture of someone – from when they were very young – and thought: how sad? All that promise, all that hope. The girl looking back at me from that photograph may have known sadness (her broken mother, stiff upper lip, bringing her to have the picture made) but she didn't know where her own road would lead. She grieved for her sister but felt sure no such fate would ever befall her. She knew the war was on but didn't quite believe it. How could any war reach English shores? Impossible. If I had presented that girl with any of the obstacles approaching her as predictions – she would have offered intractable solutions to each one. The face staring back at me believed better things lay ahead. Making a picture for a soldier, who'd return from the war exactly as he had been, to marry her, escorting her off to Ireland and perpetual happiness.

'I wish I had a picture of you from that time,' I said. 'Why is it girls send pictures to soldiers but not the other way round?'

'Listen to me, Nan.' Finbarr took the picture back from me carefully, a precious relic, and returned it to his pocket. 'Come away with me now and I won't carry this with me anymore. We'll have a new one taken. We'll put this one in a book to show our children.'

'But then I'll never be able to show myself again. To our child.'

'We've both become things we never saw for ourselves,' he persisted. 'I never wanted to go to war. I never wanted to fall sick. I never wanted to leave my own country, or even Ballycotton. What I never wanted most of all were the things that happened to you.'

I grabbed his hands and kissed them.

'I'll tell you something terrible,' he went on. 'If I had a choice, to make every man that died in war, from 1914 till now – Irishmen, Englishmen, Australians, Germans, Turks, all of them – if I had the choice to go back in time and let them live, or put our baby back in your arms, they'd all remain dead, every last one of them.'

'If you can see that, Finbarr, can't you see I need to continue?'

'There's only one road back to you, the real you. The road back to yourself, Nan. And that's with me.'

'But I don't want the road back to me. I want the road to Genevieve.'

For the first time in a long while I pictured my daughter's face not as the little girl purported to belong to the Christies, but the baby I'd last seen, seven years ago, carried away by Sister Mary Clare. I breathed in, unexpectedly harsh, like my own lungs had received a dose of mustard gas. Perhaps the kindest thing Agatha Christie could do – not only for Finbarr, but for me – was to convince me the child was indeed hers.

By the time Chilton reached the Timeless Manor's second floor, the sound of Agatha's typewriter was audible. A cheerful and industrious *click clack click clack*. He could imagine the way it would fill a house of his own. Every evening he would come home and put on a kettle, the sound of the typewriter from the other room, she so absorbed that she wouldn't know he'd arrived, until he came into the room with a steaming mug of tea. *Oh, darling,* she would say, *the day was lost to me.* That would be fine with Chilton. He was used to doing for himself and would be glad to do for her, too. *You keep writing,* he'd say. *I'll take care of dinner.*

Now she answered his knock, industry ceasing, her face alight with the joy of seeing him. Once he was no longer a novelty, disturbing her work would be something they'd quarrel about. It pleased Chilton to think of it, how he'd have to learn to tiptoe. He'd become adept at removing the kettle just before it whistled, slipping a mug quietly on the table beside her, and still she'd scold him for breaking her concentration. *Must you always interrupt me?* He'd kiss the crown of her head and steal away, leaving her to her work.

But for now she stepped aside and let him in. He flopped onto the narrow bed – their bed, he thought of it now – and reached for a piece of typewritten paper on top of a neat stack on the second bare bed. Agatha snapped it out of his hand, put it back where it belonged and returned to her seat.

'But when can I read it?'

'When it's printed, bound and sewn, and not a moment sooner.'

She went back to typing, a twitching smile betraying how his interest pleased her.

While she clicked and clacked she told her about what he'd witnessed between Mr and Mrs Race.

'Are you listening?' he asked, after a while. 'Or are you writing?'

'I'm doing both.' But she stood, and collected the missing pieces of him by falling onto the bed. It had been years since he'd felt he had two arms but Agatha wrapped them both around herself. 'I never knew kissing could be such fun,' she said, after much agreeable time had passed.

But she had known, hadn't she? Agatha had learned how much fun kissing could be years ago, in her early days with Archie, when he was a different man, when his invincibility had the power to protect her rather than harm. What she hadn't known, really, is how bereavement can shift. How it can open up the world to a place where there's nothing to lose and you can make a grab for joy in the form of a rumpled, but really rather lovely police inspector.

Chilton went down to the larder and returned with two tins of tongue. She had already made a vow never to eat tinned tongue again but she found herself starving, so much so that even this poor, repetitive food tasted wonderful.

'Do you know what I'd like to do?' Agatha said. 'Go to the baths.'

'A long walk in the cold followed by grotesquely hot water?'

'What could be better?'

They walked briskly, arm in arm. There were few cars on the road. A young farrier driving a horse-drawn carriage stopped and offered a ride. They said no at first but changed their minds, running after him, calling to him and climbing in the back when he drew his team of two bay mares to a halt. Agatha sat on a bale of hay amidst clanking tools, petting a panting Labrador who cuddled up beside her. She laughed when the dog licked her chin, and kissed him back for good measure. The cold made colour rise in her cheeks. Her laughter sounded like wind chimes.

'Tell me, Mr Chilton,' she said, raising her voice above the clatter of hooves and jingled metal. 'How do you feel about dogs?'

'I think they're just fine,' he said. As Agatha put her arms around the beast and pressed her face into its dirty fur, he decided to be more emphatic. 'I love them.' And then he added, 'You look wonderful. You look like a young girl.'

It was the wrong thing to say. Her smile vanished and her colour waned. 'But I'm not a young girl.' As soon as she spoke the words it became so. Lines on her brow, a shadow across her jaw.

The farrier let them off at the Karnak Baths and Spa, and they parted quietly, Chilton to the dressing room and Agatha to the gift shop to buy a bathing dress. This would mean showing herself to more people, but who was observant enough to connect the proper woman in the photographs to the one before them, with her wind-mussed hair and men's clothing? She buttoned Miss Oliver's plain woollen coat to her chin in the hopes of not looking quite so odd. In the shop she bought the most modest bathing dress she could find, a green and blue V-neck that just skimmed her knees. She bought a matching cap, too.

Unlike the segregated caves at the Bellefort, the Karnak's baths were open to men and women in an airy atrium, humid and dripping with ferns, the fog from hot water and human breath obscuring what should have been visible through the glass ceiling. Chilton was already soaking when Agatha returned from the dressing room, wearing a thick dressing gown issued by the establishment. Steam rose around them as she removed the dressing gown and stepped gingerly into the hot water, flinching in pain and pleasure as she lowered herself in, smiling at him once again.

Chilton felt a restriction in his throat. A catch. He regretted leaving the manor. Outside in the world time revealed itself as fleeting in a way no amount of wishing could reverse.

'Agatha,' he said.

She glanced with concern at the other bathers, worried they'd hear her name and connect it to the morning's headlines. But the only person who seemed to have noticed was a young woman with kindly eyes, not bothering with a cap but with her black hair piled high on her head: Miss Cornelia Armstrong.

'Oh, hello,' Miss Armstrong said, ever sweet-natured. 'You must be Mrs Chilton. Come to join your husband?'

Agatha smiled. It pleased Chilton no end that she might like the sound of that: Mrs Chilton.

'Yes,' Agatha said. 'He claimed this was a trip for work but to me it sounded like a holiday. So I thought I'd join in.'

Chilton said to Miss Armstrong, 'I thought you'd gone off these hot waters.'

'Oh, not at all, Mr Chilton. One must keep trying new things, and soldier through. And when I thought how my mother would object to this particular bath I couldn't resist. Men and women bathing together. Quite scandalous.' Miss Armstrong spoke the last as if it were the most delightful word in the English language. 'I'm determined to enjoy myself despite the bad business with the Marstons.' She turned back to Agatha. 'Has your husband told you? About all that's been going on at our little hotel?'

'Yes,' said Agatha. 'How awfully sad.'

'You've no idea. That is, I'm sure a man wouldn't tell it right. Their love story was something special. All those years of longing to be together. And then when they finally were, when the moment they'd longed for arrived, all the years ahead of them were taken away. Just like that. There's a lesson in that, don't you think, Mrs Chilton? A person can't waste time being unhappy.'

301

'Quite right,' Agatha said. 'I far prefer to waste my time being happy.'

Chilton thought, if I can talk her into boarding a train, first thing in the morning, we could waste the rest of our lives being happy.

For the moment what seemed to make Cornelia Armstrong happy was waxing sorrowful about the Marstons' untimely end. She moved over to sit directly beside Agatha. Chilton felt thankful none of the hotel guests were privy to the information about the poison that had been discovered in both Marstons.

'Do you know,' Miss Armstrong said to Agatha, 'that before marrying Mr Marston, Mrs Marston had been a nun?'

'You don't say?' Agatha looked to Mr Chilton, interest changing from polite to sincere.

'She told me so herself. She asked me not to tell anyone. But I suppose that doesn't matter now.'

'I suppose not.' Chilton poised himself, the way he did when someone was about to reveal something important, hoping the acceleration of his heartbeat wasn't detectible.

'She had been a nun,' Miss Armstrong said, her voice giddy with the romance of it. 'And Mr Marston, he had been a priest. Oh, it sounds like a novel, doesn't it? The two of them torn and in love, all those years working side by side until they couldn't bear it a moment longer. They'd only just renounced their vows and run off, so they could be together.' She lowered her voice to a whisper. 'You know, I'm not sure they'd even married yet, really. But that could just be me wanting more scandal.' She laughed, a gentle twitter that might have been delightful, this show of happiness from the lovely young woman, if only it didn't spell possible doom for another.

302

'Do you happen to know,' Chilton said carefully, 'what sort of order they'd come from?'

'An orphanage.' Miss Armstrong spoke warmly, as if this were the most philanthropic venture she could imagine. 'She was such a loving person, Mrs Marston, you could see it plain as day. I'm sure she took wonderful care of all those children.'

'I'm sure she did,' said Mr Chilton. 'Did she say where this orphanage was located?'

'County Cork, in Ireland. And I remember the name of the town. So poetic.'

Before Miss Armstrong could speak the words, Sunday's Corner, Chilton looked over at Agatha. He could see from her face that in her mind as well as in his, everything had just come clear.

Perhaps you surmised in that moment, along with Chilton and Agatha: Mrs Marston and Sister Mary Clare were one and the same. Or perhaps you figured it out pages and pages ago. I wasn't finished, that day in Sunday's Corner, when my fingers circled around Sister Mary Clare's throat.

In the baths, the world dripped with warm moisture. The ceiling was good and high, no need for claustrophobia as Chilton made the connection he'd felt certain was there, between his two cases and the element that connected them both. Me.

'Funny,' Agatha murmured. 'My mother-in-law comes not far from Sunday's Corner.'

'Oh,' Miss Armstrong said, turning to Chilton. 'Is your mother Irish?' At his vague nod she said to Agatha, 'Mrs Marston was such a jolly person. Wasn't she, Mr Chilton?'

He nodded again, just as dishonestly. Mrs Marston had the

precise sort of jolliness he'd never believed in. The sort that masked something, or else the lack of something. He wished there were a way to convey this to young Miss Armstrong. It seemed an important lesson for a young person. It wasn't only the angry people that should make one wary. The jolly ones could be even more dangerous.

'And where do you return to, Miss Armstrong,' Agatha asked, 'when you go home?'

'Mundesley.'

'Lovely,' said Agatha. 'How I prefer the sea, Miss Armstrong, to this countryside. Even in the winter. I don't care what sort of natural springs a place has to offer, or how they try to lure me. This is all well and good but there's no place so refreshing as the sea. Do you know, my mother believed salt water cured everything, from spots to heart disease?'

'My father says the same,' said Miss Armstrong.

'Give me a plunge in the cold brine.' Agatha actually looked cosy, even refreshed, by the hot water. She sank low so that it covered her ears for a moment, as if someone might contradict her and she didn't want to hear it.

From outside a cold wind blew, strong enough for a little chill to creep in, the glass ceiling rattling as if flimsier than promised. Agatha's love song to the seaside was a welcome sound to Chilton. Very welcome indeed.

Chilton and Agatha bundled back into their clothes and headed outside with their hair still damp. Strands froze; Agatha scrunched a handful to hear them crackle.

'You know what I like to imagine?' she said, as they walked towards the road.

Neither had discussed what they'd learned, not yet, only come to a silent agreement. That's love, thought Chilton, when your mind works in concert.

Agatha seemed to know better than him, at the moment there were more important things to think of than their romance. She said, 'I like to imagine it wasn't just Nan. That every single woman staying at the Bellefort had a hand in it. When you think of all the girls who passed through that place, and others like it. Seems a pity for just one to have revenge when so many deserve it.'

This was the last thing Chilton expected. He said, 'I suppose I'll have to get a confession out of Nan.'

'You'll do no such thing.'

'But Agatha. This is murder we're talking about, not a game.'

'What some call murder others might call justice.'

Chilton stopped walking but Agatha continued, firm and determined footsteps. He put his hands in his pockets – first hoisting the useless one – and thought of the killing he'd done in the war. The bodies beneath his feet as he ran through no man's land. All of it sanctioned, in fact demanded, by the world. Perhaps a woman has a different kind of measuring stick. For when it might be acceptable, or even necessary, to commit a murder.

Here Lies Sister Mary

NOT LONG AFTER my escape, Fiona was released from the convent to work as a housemaid for a family in Sunday's Corner. She dutifully attended Father Joseph's services at the parish church. Her misspelled letters to me swelled with her old false cheer, claiming she couldn't be happier or safer, and that she prayed every day for her little boy. 'I hope he's never told where he came from,' she wrote. 'The nuns always knew what was best for us, didn't they?'

Upon reading that line, I ripped Fiona's letter into a hundred pieces, the fiercely torn shreds turning up for weeks when I swept my room.

'Don't be angry at Fiona,' Bess wrote. 'She was raised by the nuns. If believing in them keeps her from going mad, who are we to take that away from her?'

I couldn't stop myself sitting down and writing to tell Fiona how her little boy would always have a memory of her, deep in his bones and blood. That's how it works with humans. 'A baby never entirely leaves a mother's womb,' I wrote. 'Traces of your boy – the very cells that comprise his living form – are still contained inside of you.'

She wrote back to tell me the roses that year were the most

beautiful she'd ever seen. And she'd gone to the convent to buy milk and radishes for her household, and all the nuns seemed wonderfully well.

In Philadelphia, Bess tried to be happy. It shouldn't have been so difficult. Her husband was a kind man who adored her, and he found good work as the manager of a shipyard. They lived in a white clapboard house in a pleasant neighbourhood. There were two bedrooms waiting to be filled with children: her husband wanted two boys, two girls. But when Bess walked into these rooms, she didn't see them as empty of future children, the family she couldn't convince herself to start. She saw them empty of Ronan, who'd kicked and swum inside her, promising his arrival, and then emerged as a cold, unbreathing bundle.

'Do you remember how beautiful he was?' she would ask her husband late at night. He held her close in his arms and kissed her hair, and hoped one day she could find a way to move past it all.

'But I can't move past it,' she confessed to her doctor. He was bald, with shockingly dark eyebrows and a compassionate bearing. 'It's left me so afraid.'

'You're perfectly healthy,' Dr Levine promised her. 'There's no need to be afraid. You're young.'

'Do you think,' she said, 'that it was the priest who caused it? The stillbirth?' She had told Dr Levine what she'd endured, on previous visits, to explain scarring he'd found when he first examined her and worried her husband was the perpetrator.

He raised his eyes to the ceiling before answering. Thinking. Wanting to give her an honest answer.

'I can't say for certain one way or the other,' he finally said. 'But I do know it can't have helped.'

She wept, and he patted her shoulder. Bess hadn't left Ireland unable to accept human touch from a man. She could take comfort from Dr Levine's kind thumping. She could enjoy making love with her husband. Father Joseph hadn't taken that away from her.

But she couldn't recover what she believed with all her heart he *had* taken from her. She would walk outside her cosy house, a mug of coffee in her hand (a full-fledged American now, no more tea), to wave goodbye to her husband as he walked off to catch the train to work. Once he was out of sight, the mothers began emerging, to play in the pretty yards with their children. Bess would see, so clearly, her Ronan. Whatever age he would have been. Riding in a pram. Toddling after a cat in the garden. Rolling a toy truck along the drive. Chalking the sidewalk.

He should be here. He should be here, he should be here, he should be here.

'I want to leave my old life behind,' she wrote to me. 'I send letters to you and Fiona and my sister Kitty. Apart from that I'm only interested in what's here for me, here and now.'

Even as she wrote the words she knew they weren't entirely true. Bess wanted children. She would have happily, joyfully filled those rooms upstairs. But not while Father Joseph drew breath and Ronan didn't. The hatred in her heart had nothing to do with being a mother. And only one thing in the world would vanquish it.

Such a thing never seemed possible. Until a letter from Fiona arrived with the gossip from Sunday's Corner. Sister Mary Clare and Father Joseph had fallen in love and renounced their vows.

'She was in the village, chatty as ever,' Fiona wrote. 'She told me they'd be married next month and then leave for Yorkshire to honeymoon at a place called the Bellefort Hotel. She told me I might as well start calling her Mrs Marston as that would be her name soon enough.'

Bess could easily imagine the cheery laugh that followed. A plan had to be hatched quickly. But she knew it would be easier to complete, now that Sister Mary Clare and Father Joseph would be together, in England. And she'd have such a willing accomplice in me.

The Disappearance

Day Five
Wednesday, 8 December 1926

Bess and I knew perfectly well Chilton was listening at the door. Not because we'd heard him – he was quieter than a mouse – but because we expected him to be watching us. We'd known we'd be facing perils enough, with our plans to murder two seemingly innocent people. Little did we know we'd also have to contend with my lover's wife and the inspector who was searching for her. Not to mention Finbarr, come to reclaim me.

'Donny's had a telegram,' Bess said, so loudly I nearly laughed at the contrivance of it. 'We have to cut things short. Go back to the States.'

She sat down on the bed beside me and clasped my hand. We stared at each other, eyes full. No matter what happened next, it had been worth it.

The poisons had been easy enough to obtain, though potassium cyanide was an odd purchase for winter, with no wasps afoot. I went to two different shops in London, one for the potassium cyanide and another for the strychnine, the beauty of a populous city, where nobody would remember me, or think to connect the substances with any death in Yorkshire. Archie may not have read Agatha's books but I had. I knew poison was the best way to accomplish a quick and easy murder – easy to perpetrate but not to solve.

Sister Mary Clare, now Mrs Marston, was so untrue and unthinking in her every word and deed. At the Bellefort Hotel she stared directly at me. Never into my face. Only glancing at the surface. Bess, too, she trained her eyes on both of us and spoke about herself. Just like at the convent, she smiled, she chatted, she landed her plump hands on our shoulders as if she believed herself fond of us. But when we appeared in her life again, there was nothing about either of us she recognized. To her all girls were the same.

It was Hamlet, wasn't it, who said: 'One may smile and smile and be a villain.'

To the man who'd never bothered to smile, at least at us – the ragwort – some girls stood out. Father Joseph knew Bess the moment he laid eyes on her. In the hotel dining room, doing what needed to be done, Bess had felt no fear. None at all. Only a gladness at witnessing his discomfort. Knowing he'd be dead before he could alert his wife to our identity.

Bess's sister Kitty and her husband Carmichael, posing as an unhappy English couple, had caused the necessary diversion – a great row that commanded the attention of everyone present. Bess had been able to step forward and plunge the syringe into Father Joseph's flank, then secret it back into the pocket of her dress almost before he felt the prick. Kitty – pretending to be a nurse – had flown to his side, not to help him, but to make sure he was dead. She had a secondary needle waiting in her own pocket just in case, but that proved unnecessary.

Bess couldn't call it gladness, exactly, watching the man die. She wasn't a cruel person. It was a distasteful but necessary task. The world had offered no justice so we made our own.

Kitty, the little girl Bess had told me about in Ireland – the pretty twelve-year-old who'd wanted to be in pictures – had grown up to marry a young man blessed not only with a family fortune, but also with theatrical aspirations of his own. With his help Kitty pulled off the greatest performance of her career before it even began. She and Carmichael stayed on at the hotel afterwards, continuing the ruse, so no one would suspect their row was connected to Mr Marston's collapse.

In my room at the Bellefort, with Chilton's ear pressed against the door, I said, also loudly, 'I do hope everything is all right.'

'Yes,' Bess said. 'Everything is perfect. *Perfect*.' Then, in a whisper that wouldn't be heard no matter how closely Chilton hovered: 'Kitty and Carmichael will stay on, and they've paid for your room through to the end of next week. But we're leaving. Back to America. You should come with us.'

I shook my head, vehement.

She said, 'Stay in England, if you must. But go back to London. Get out of here, fast as you can.'

'That would only make me look guilty, wouldn't it?' But I wasn't thinking about looking guilty. I was thinking about Finbarr's arms, a brisk walk away. Soon enough I'd have to face my whole life without him. But I couldn't do it just yet. I needed just a little while longer. Even if it did increase my risk of being caught.

Bess and I embraced, hands clutching at the other's clothes, faces buried in each other's necks. We had done what we'd come to do. Now the world would unfold however it needed to. Having removed Father Joseph from the world, Bess could go on with her life. In fact, we didn't know she was leaving England already pregnant with a little girl who'd be born – the squalling picture of health – that September.

❧

And I had taken care of Sister Mary Clare. By bringing a steaming cup of tea to her door and gently rapping.

'Oh my dear,' the former nun said, when I peeked into the room. 'How good of you to come to me. I'm afraid I shan't sleep a wink tonight. Not one wink.' Her face was swollen and blotchy. She covered it with her hands and wept some more.

I walked to her bed and sat down, pressing the cup into her hands. 'Drink this,' I said in my most soothing voice. 'There's a bit of brandy in it.' I wore a dressing gown, my hair loose. Hers was gathered up under a nightcap. I could see the gleam of cream upon her face, still tending to the usual ministrations, imagining a tomorrow despite her bereavement.

'Oh, you're a darling,' she said to me. 'That doctor gave me a sleeping draught but my nerves are overcoming it.' She took the cup and sipped. The English love of tea as solution to life's ills does make us easy to poison.

'I can't say where I'll go tomorrow,' she said. 'We had a plan, Mr Marston and I, for where we'd go next. Manchester, where I lived as a girl, before I was sent off to Ireland.' She was speaking to herself, not realizing I'd heard this story before. 'But my family's not there anymore. How can I do it without Mr Marston? I've never lived alone, you see. I used to be a nun, if you can believe that.'

'Oh, I believe it, Mrs Marston. I do.'

She cried and sipped, cried and sipped. I sat beside her and patted her knee. It had only been seven years, and not years that particularly age a person. At twenty-seven I looked passably as I had at twenty. She'd seen me every day for months. She'd been with me when Genevieve first laughed. She was the last person I ever saw holding my baby. I stared and stared, willing her to stare back. The ghosts that ought to have haunted her fluttered away, unthinking.

'You're a dear,' she said, handing me the empty cup.

I put it on the bedside table. Later, I would be sure to wipe it clean of fingerprints and residue. Sister Mary Clare lay back. She reached out and clasped my hand. 'You'll stay with me, won't you? Until I fall asleep.'

'Of course I will.'

Her eyes fluttered closed. If I waited, the poison would kill her. But unlike Bess, I wanted hands on my quarry. The coroner would find the strychnine. But I'd have her dead before it did its work. I hummed a few bars of the same haunting tune she was always so fond of, but even that didn't make her realize. She smiled a bit and said – very quiet, eyes still closed – 'Oh, I do love that song.'

A few more moments passed. The clock downstairs chimed but I didn't count the hour. I picked up a pillow, no doubt it had lain beneath Father Joseph's head the night before. Then I tapped her to make sure she hadn't fallen asleep. Her eyes fluttered open. I smiled, dearly wanting her to see love and kindness in my face. She managed a wan, thankful smile in return. Then down came the pillow.

I took one risk, in the middle, taking the pillow away for the barest second. Sister Mary Clare rewarded me with the second honest expression of her life: fear and shock and anguish. I could have told her who I was, in that moment. But I liked adding confusion to the terrible emotions overcoming her. So I pressed the pillow back down. I held the woman down. Until she stopped struggling. Until she stopped causing harm. Until her body came to rest, and her breath ceased to flow. When I pulled the pillow away her face held no false cheer, no false kindness. Her lips spoke no empty promises. All she had were eyes newly made of glass, open but not seeing. Her mouth open, frozen in its useless attempt to find oxygen.

For years I'd been swept in directions I never meant to go. I'd made mistakes, acting by accident or imperative. Finally, in this moment, I was the author of my story. The universe must not have held it against me, because I was rewarded almost at once with my days in the Timeless Manor.

When Sister Mary Clare lay dead before me, how the air metamorphosed. Particles that had been charged became inert. The rage inside me quieted. A violent storm had ended.

The urge to murder. It never left me until the job was done.

The Disappearance

Day Eight
Saturday, 11 December 1926

FINBARR WAS DOWNSTAIRS stoking the kitchen fire when Chilton and Agatha returned to the Timeless Manor. On the table were bottles of wine – he had helped himself to the collection in the cellar – along with a tray that held three loaves of fresh bread, various kinds of sausage, a wheel of Swaledale cheese and tins of peaches.

'You said you were tired of tongue,' he told Agatha. 'So I went on a little scouting mission.'

'Aren't you a darling,' she said.

Chilton frowned the slightest bit, looking from one to the other. Agatha sat, weary, the force of these days away, this time away, still not seeing the future take any shape she could recognize. Chilton pulled out a chair and sat beside her. In a calm voice he told Finbarr what they'd pieced together. The Marstons' true identity and my hand in their murder.

Finbarr listened, his face unmoving and inscrutable. When Chilton had finished he said, 'Good.'

'Good?' said Chilton. 'Come now, man. You can't mean that.'

'But I do mean it.'

Agatha poured wine into a teacup. This seemed the right night to make an exception to her abstinence. It occurred to her she ought to be glad of the thought, me headed to jail, which would not only get me out of the way but also punish me for the pain I'd caused her. But even before our escape, accidentally mutual, such a thing wouldn't have made her glad. She wasn't that sort of person and never would be. She might be capable of imagining other people's plots of revenge and the bitterness that drove them. She could even sympathize with mine. But she never could carry them out herself. She was better than me in that way. Or else just luckier.

'What happens next, then?' Finbarr asked.

'I'm afraid I'll have to tell the Yorkshire police what I know,' Chilton said. 'About who the Marstons are. And what Nan and her friend are guilty of. I'm afraid the inquest will take it from there.'

'Not today,' Finbarr said. Agatha heard the rasp of mustard gas strangling his voice, worse than usual.

'Yes,' she agreed. 'Not today.'

'But Agatha.' Chilton turned to her as if Finbarr couldn't hear. 'That will give him the time he needs to escape with her.'

'Would that be so bad?' Agatha said. 'Sometimes an escape is precisely what's needed.'

Chilton looked dubious. How many of his duties would he let float away before all this was over? What if Agatha wanted Nan to escape to form a road back to her husband? Though surely my arrest would net the same result. Archie would not have stood by me through a murder trial. He might not have stood by me if he heard me speak with the working-class accent I'd so carefully expunged.

'One more day,' Agatha said, softy, delightfully aware of the romantic power she had over Chilton. 'Perhaps two.'

One more day undiscovered. Perhaps two. One more day

exempt from time and repercussion. One more day dispensing with propriety and responsibilities. One more day as if her mother had never died, and her husband had never left her – indeed, as if both of them had never existed at all, to cause her joy or pain. Why not two more days? Why not a thousand?

'One more day,' she said again. 'Just one. We'll decide tomorrow. We'll make a plan?' The question mark was a brilliant stroke. Implying he was in a position to argue.

'Come with me,' Finbarr said, as if they'd all reached an agreement. He picked up the tray and left the kitchen, moving his head ever so slightly, indicating that Chilton should collect the wine.

Upstairs the great room was nearly empty of furniture except for a settee covered by a dust sheet and a cluster of large pillows thrown to the floor (as if we had not been the first squatters the Timeless Manor had seen and someone else had sojourned here, and made free with what could be found). On the floor beside the settee sat a Victrola – of the gramophone variety, old fashioned even for the time, with a great mahogany horn.

'I found it in the butler's pantry,' Finbarr said. He wound it up and placed the needle on its record, and scratchy big band music filled the cavernous room.

To join the party, I had but to follow the music. Finbarr lounged on the floor against one of the big pillows, a goblet filled with wine in one hand. Chilton and Agatha were dancing, her face aglow from the firelight and the day in the baths, looking as lovely in her trousers and jumper as she ever had wearing any gown in any ballroom.

Three faces turned towards me, fondly, withholding the

devastating information. Tomorrow. It could all be saved until tomorrow. For now we would let our disappearance extend a little longer. It would continue into the night and small hours of the morning. One thing we'd learned since discovering this place: there was nothing in the world that couldn't wait.

'Oh, Nan,' Agatha said, as Chilton dipped her, her head thrown back, her tone joyful, as if I were her best friend in all the world. 'Come and have some wine and cheese, come and have a dance. For who knows what tomorrow will bring?'

Remarkably, my ears did not hear this as ominous. It sounded like an invitation. If I had been a different sort of person, raised in a different time and country, I might have told her I loved her. And she might have said it back. Instead, the two of us smiled at each other. Not rivals but landsmen. A shared sorrow can create unexpected warmth, even as it illuminates all the ways our world is ruined.

The Disappearance

Days Nine and Ten
Sunday, 12 December and Monday, 13 December 1926

THE MACHINERY OF the world had already started grinding against our remaining undiscovered. The Harrogate librarian, Miss Barnard, picked up newspapers with increasing fervour, looking at every new photograph and thinking that she knew – she absolutely knew – the woman she'd seen was the missing mystery writer. Finally, she telephoned the police department in Leeds. The officer who answered, hearing the emotional certainty in her voice, utterly dismissed her concerns. But still. A seed had been planted.

Inside the Timeless Manor, though, everything was beautiful.

That night we stayed up past dawn, the records singing, the wine flowing, the four of us twirling and laughing and dancing. Agatha felt young again. Truly young – once again the girl who had slid off her horse when her hair flew off into the wind, to collect it with gales of laughter. All the house parties she'd attended as a girl, jumping from one to the next – sometimes out of necessity, because the money had run out and Ashfield was let. Without society Agatha would have had nowhere to go. But when she was a guest, everything was taken care of, everything was bright and gay and fun. But never so much fun as this. Nobody, ever, like Finbarr. Nobody like Chilton, certainly, with his hand at her waist, travelling at will. A strange, gorgeous echo of her old life but with the oddest most unlikely people, and no rules at all.

What would her mother say? Liberating to have that question melt into the air, unanswered, unimportant. How it used to hover over her every move. How she had watched herself, even in her youth. Never too much to drink, if anything at all. Don't say this. Don't say that. Don't wander upstairs into a bedroom with a man not your husband to do whatever the two of you please. Now her mother was gone but life did go on in new ways. Humane ways. That was the thing. To be sensible and to be humane. Even if it appeared at the moment she wasn't particularly sensible anymore. For what seemed the first time in her life – and only for this short window – Agatha owned her own virtue, and thereby her own fate.

When she and Chilton had disappeared upstairs, Finbarr and I stayed behind, dancing a while longer. So I forgot to return to the Bellefort Hotel, my room there empty yet again. Kitty and Carmichael would have left by now. The ruse of their misery had gone on long enough to fool everyone; nobody would ever think back and recognize it as a diversion. They didn't return to Ireland, but headed to America, to stop in Philadelphia with Lizzie and Donny, then on to New York, both of them destined for the stage. Before they left they made sure my room was paid for a few more days. Mrs Leech would never give them up as my benefactors. And she wouldn't send anyone hunting for me, at least not yet. She knew about Finbarr, young lovers. She'd shake her head with a secret smile, remembering a time when her romance had seemed impossible, too.

Morning light had long since arrived by the time we went to sleep. All our heads fuzzy with wine and giddy with love. Nobody got around, that day, to accusing me of murder.

On Monday morning in Sunningdale, Teddy woke, horrified to find her father sleeping beside her, on top of the covers, still wearing his suit and even his shoes, his mouth open, spittle winding its way from his mouth to the pillow. She jumped out of bed, quick as she could, collected Touchstone and held her close to her chest.

'Colonel Christie!' she exclaimed, deciding only the most formal address would do.

Archie started awake and swung his feet to the floor. 'Dear me,' he said. 'I must have fallen asleep.'

'Indeed.' The little girl's face looked dark with rebuke.

Archie lifted a hand to his brow. Unruly curls loose on his forehead. Reflected in Teddy's glare, he had no way of knowing he'd never been handsomer, in all his undone vulnerability. He had no interest in being vulnerable. Over the past ten days he'd become everything he most detested – melancholic, sickly, ineffectual.

'I only want to be happy,' he told Teddy, hanging his head, hating the pathetic sound of his voice.

Because she was a kind child, Teddy patted the top of his head.

'And so you shall be,' she promised.

Like Miss Barnard, the woman who worked at the Karnak gift shop had been thinking about Agatha Christie. But she waited until Monday to say anything, Sunday not being a proper time to cause any kind of upheaval.

'I've seen that missing lady novelist with my own eyes,' Miss Harley announced, when she walked into the Leeds Police Headquarters. She was a middle-aged lady, unlucky in love, always rheumy with remembering the man who should have proposed before he left for the Boer War, never to be heard from again.

The young fellow at the front desk called Lippincott over.

'Are you quite sure?' Lippincott demanded, assessing Miss Harley to no particular advantage. 'I've got a man reporting daily on that case.' In fact, he realized, he had not heard from Chilton in several days. 'He says he's not seen head or tail of her.'

'Well, I've seen the head and the tail.' The wattle on Miss Harley's neck became tremulous with indignation. 'She was in the hotel gift shop, staring right at me, looking just like her picture. She bought a bathing dress and picture postcard. I thought I might be imagining things but I saw another photograph of her in the papers today and it was her. I just know it was.'

That's what you get when you don't take matters in your own hands, thought Lippincott. He headed over to the library to question Miss Barnard.

'Oh, I'm quite sure it was her,' Miss Barnard said, thankful to be heard finally. 'She went awfully pale when I pointed out the resemblance. Can you say someone has a resemblance to herself?' Miss Barnard laughed, then stopped abruptly when she saw Lippincott was unamused. 'Took some books out, too. Detective novels, mostly.'

'What name did she give?'

'Mrs O'Dea. Said she was staying at the Bellefort Hotel and Spa.'

'The Bellefort!'

The thought of Agatha Christie right under Chilton's nose this whole time – not to mention Lippincott's own family – was more than any man could bear. Fond of Chilton though he was, Lippincott marched out of the library with his fingers twitching, ready himself to do everything that needed to be done.

That evening, the phone rang at Styles. The maid Anna found Archie at the dining table, his food before him uneaten, a tumbler of Scotch in one hand. His eyes, persistently, on the window. Dark now, only returning his own sad reflection.

'Colonel Christie,' Anna said, 'there's a police officer on the telephone. Says he's calling from Leeds.'

The Disappearance

Our Last Night
Monday, 13 December 1926

OVER THE YEARS, since our time in Yorkshire, Agatha and I have managed to steal a private moment or two, when our paths crossed – accidentally, in London, or at a family function. The funeral of Archie's mother, for example. Teddy's wedding. Times the blending of families past and present could not be avoided.

She and I agreed that although we'd spent not even a week in the Timeless Manor, in the dead of winter – bare branches and foggy windows – we remembered the house in every season. We could see the glorious canopy, dripping with moss and green, arching over the drive. The lawn where we played tennis soft with recent rain, so our feet left divots in the earth as we played. Birds making a racket when we woke, sun arriving too early and pouring through the curtains. The fields that rolled behind the house carpeted with dahlias, lily of the valley and primula. We remember Teddy running through the flowers, picking the brightest ones, hem of her skirt stained with mud and grass, though truly she was never there at all.

'To call it amnesia never quite feels like a lie,' she once told me. 'Because it all still seems a marvellous dream. The kind you create to take the place of something terrible.'

We should steal away together, I suggested at least once. *We should go back*.

Agatha admitted she'd thought of finding the owner and buying the house. But she never did, and neither of us returned there, not together or apart. The house lived on only as a place we visited in conversation and memory, no more visible to the outside world than we had been, inhabiting it, undetected.

Sometimes at night I have a marvellous dream of my own: a party. The manor's not dusty or spare of furnishings, but bright and fully appointed. Genevieve, and my little Rosie, and my sister Louisa's children, and even Colleen's: they sit in the upstairs hallway peering down through the banisters long after they were sent to bed. Finbarr is there, and Chilton, and my parents. Fiona and her son, the raspberry birthmark faded. Bess and Donny and Ronan – plus the three girls they'd go on to have. All three of my sisters. The Mahoneys and Uncle Jack and Aunt Rosie. Seamus, grown to a man, laughing as though he never knew a moment's sickness. Alby, black and white fur gleaming, a perfect gentleman, exactly at Finbarr's side. Sparkling lights, and trays of brimming champagne flutes, and the most cheerful music – not scratchy from an old Victrola, but a live orchestra. It's the happiest moment in the world. It's everything I've ever wished for, finally bestowed.

The four of us slept most of the day before adjourning again to the great room, settling with food and wine before a crackling fire. We'd exhausted the supply of fresh food, and Finbarr hadn't ventured out, so it was back to tins of tongue and kippers, laid out on a large linen tablecloth going yellow at the edges.

Once wine had been poured, Finbarr said to me: 'It's time to come out with it, Nan. They think you've done murder.'

People can seem especially beautiful by firelight. Agatha sat cross-legged, looking like a lady explorer in her man's clothes, hair vivid and tumbled, cheeks rosy. Chilton looked younger than I supposed he had in years, lying on his side, downright insouciant. Finbarr reached out and clasped my hand. I kissed his cheek.

'Do they?' is all I said.

Agatha held out a plate to me but I waved it away, not a bit hungry. 'Would you like to hear a story,' I said, 'about a time I could have done murder?'

It was a good night for ghost stories. Some wind outside. Nothing but the firelight. The four of us, close and safe and strangely delighted. I told them about my escape from the convent, and my hands around Sister Mary Clare's throat.

'And that was Mrs Marston,' Chilton said.

I didn't agree, but told them another ghost story, about a priest and a pregnant girl. Iron bars, plus laws of God and man, imprisoned us all inside a rambling stone convent. The priest had licence to do what he would. Inside the convent there was forgiveness for his sins, but not those of the girls he abused.

I didn't provide every piece of the story. Not Kitty and Carmichael (Chilton, as it turned out, was no Hercule Poirot – he had forgotten all about hearing their Irish accents), or Bess's real name, or where she lived.

'I've never done murder,' I said. 'I've only made my own justice.'

From upstairs a door creaked on its hinges, the wind rattling it open. Agatha's eyes moved to the ceiling, alert to anything that could indicate her discovery. I didn't want her thinking about that. I wanted her to realize and admit. When she had taken that baby into her home she'd accepted something stolen.

'Tell the truth,' I said to her.

'Yes,' Finbarr urged. 'Tell her. Put an end to it once and for all.'

The joy had snapped out of the room. Agatha said, 'I thought you knew without a doubt. Both of you.'

'I do know,' I said. 'But I want to hear you say it. I've confessed. Now it's your turn.'

'Very well, then. It's all true.'

Finbarr got to his feet. He rolled up his sleeves, almost as if he would hit her. Chilton tensed and sat up, ready to stand between them.

'Which,' Finbarr said. 'Which part is true?'

'Nan's part.'

'That's not right,' Finbarr said. 'You know it's not.'

'I'm sorry, Finbarr. But that's what I've got to say. Nan's right. I couldn't have a baby of my own so Archie got one for me. And I didn't know, I didn't think. The cruelty of it was lost on me. I'm sorry.'

'Nan,' Finbarr said to me. 'Don't listen to that. She's said just the opposite to me all along. I don't know why she's changing her story now.' He fell to his knees and gathered up Agatha's hands. Looked at her with his melting, convincing eyes. Convincing for just the right reason. Not because he was scheming, or had any ulterior motive. But because he was true to his core in every word he ever spoke.

'I'm sorry, Finbarr,' Agatha said. 'I truly am.'

He let go of her hands and stood. 'I don't know why you're doing this. I'll never know.'

But I knew. Everybody stared at me. Perhaps I was beautiful in the firelight, too.

It could be Agatha admitted Teddy was mine because she didn't want Archie anymore, and knew her pronouncement would make me go back to him. Or else she knew it was inevitable, that her marriage was over, and now she'd ensured that no matter what happened next, I'd always look out for her daughter as if she were my own. Perhaps she felt terrible for all I'd been through, and wanted to let me believe Teddy was mine, because my real child was lost to me forever, and with this kind lie she could return her to me, if only in deception.

Or perhaps the solution was simpler. Occam's razor. Perhaps she told me Teddy was Genevieve for one reason and one reason only:

Because it was the truth.

Upstairs Finbarr sat on the bed. I stood in front of him, his knees bracing either side of me. He tucked a strand of hair behind my ear. 'Remember when you used to wear it long?'

He'd never seen it cropped far shorter than this, up above my ears. 'I remember everything.'

'Will you remember this?'

'Always.'

If not for the fire, the room would have stood completely dark. As it was, our faces were obscured enough to look like they had our first summer – open to and untouched by the future. I could almost pretend I didn't know: we'd never be together like this again.

The room glowed with the fire's warmth. Smoke from the manor's chimneys should have given us away – four love-struck outlaws. The flames made the windows glow. This night in particular: when I picture the Timeless Manor, I picture the view from outside, every last window thrumming and glowing like a place possessed.

The Disappearance

Day of Discovery
Tuesday, 14 December 1926

I WOKE LONG BEFORE dawn and put more wood on the fire. At any moment the owners of the house could return, from wherever their primary residence was, or else the new owners, if this were a time of transition. Or, more likely, servants sent ahead to prepare. Whoever walked through the door next would find clues we'd been here. Ashes left in the fireplaces. Tins of food gone missing. Empty bottles slid back into place on the cellar's wine rack. And perhaps the remnants of happiness infusing the rooms, swirling like dust mites.

I kissed Finbarr's sleeping head and stole out of the room to walk the country roads in the low mist, not afraid of a thing: not of dogs barking from their fields, or the frigid air, or even the form of a man, who walked by me as a shadow and tipped his hat. If I'd walked right off the road into another world, it wouldn't have surprised me. But no matter how lovely the other world turned out to be, I'd do anything I could to claw my way back into this one, because my child still lived here, and I must never be far from her, not in this lifetime.

I crept up the stairs at the Bellefort and crawled into bed, where I slept for hours, until I woke to the sound of a familiar voice, loud enough to reach me from the lobby, searching – but not for me.

Chilton woke early too. He sat up in bed beside a sleeping Agatha. Last night they'd decided to move to one of the grander bedrooms on the first floor. He hadn't questioned Agatha's assertion about her daughter (did it contradict what she'd told him previously?), nor the assumption all three of them made, that he would protect me. Two people dead. And Chilton expected to just let it go.

He stroked Agatha's hair, softly, so as not to wake her. Somewhere in what passed between them a tacit agreement had been made, never to say the words. But now that she was safely, deeply asleep – her lips parted, her face flushed with that childlike fever dreams can induce – he let himself whisper it: 'I love you, Agatha.' Beneath their lids her eyes moved. A slight smile curled across her lips. Why shouldn't they expect him to do the wrong thing, where Nan was concerned? He'd done the wrong thing for Agatha.

For want of a nail the kingdom was lost. How many crimes were being neglected, throughout England, because of the manpower devoted to the discovery of the woman who lay beside him now, safe and sound and intoxicating, her warm breath across his face all he wanted of life from this day forward? He crept out of bed and walked to the window. He always did his best thinking while contemplating a landscape. From behind him he heard the rustle of Agatha waking. She rose and glided to him. Still he didn't turn towards her. She pressed herself against his back, wrapped her arms around his waist, rested her pointed chin on his shoulder to share the view with him, the further-reaching hills obscured by a stand of fir trees.

'I suppose you're thinking about Nan,' she said.

'I am.'

'Do you know the artist Claude Monet?'

'Lilies and blurs?'

'That's the one. He died earlier this month. I read in a notice about his death that he once said, "To see, we must forget the name of the thing we are looking at."'

'And that means what, precisely?'

'This is your case. You're the one looking at it. By grand good luck, you're the one who's been charged to solve it. So can't the solution, the name, be anything you like?'

'I suppose it can be.'

'Good.' She stepped away from him as though the matter were settled.

'And then what? We can't stay here forever.'

She sat on the edge of the bed.

'There can be no more days,' Chilton said. He kneeled in front of her and took up her hands. 'Or there can be all the days. If we leave, you and I. Together. Today. Let the disappearance last a lifetime. Why not?'

'Why not?' she repeated.

He didn't want to interrupt the joy bursting forth within him by muddying her agreement with details. They could work that out later. A car, a train, a destination.

'I'll go back to the Bellefort,' he said. 'And collect my things. Then we can work out a plan.'

'I'll go with you,' she said. 'I could do with some air.'

'But darling, you can't be seen with me.'

'That will make our life together rather difficult, won't it?'

She laughed and put on his hat, pulled it down over her fore-head. 'Nobody will recognize me. They might even take me for your brother.'

Perhaps Chilton was unnerved by the word 'brother' and that's why he didn't protest. Perhaps Agatha – in her heart, more than she was able to admit – wanted to be found after all. Or perhaps, as far as they knew, all the chances they'd taken so far had netted no danger. So why not take one more? Plain sight had proved as good a place to hide as anywhere.

Archie and Lippincott arrived at the Bellefort Hotel while Agatha was upstairs in Chilton's room, helping him gather his things. Mrs Leech ushered them into the library. She brought out the guest ledger for the two of them to look over.

Archie's eyes immediately landed on my last name. O'Dea. 'This,' he said, pointing. 'This is my wife's handwriting.' As if he'd forgotten me entirely, my name as well as my hand. A sleight of mind, confusing the two of us. One of his women's penmanship, what did it matter which? To give him credit, the mistake was likely borne of hope. He wanted his wife before his eyes, whole and alive. If he erased my existence by assigning my name and handwriting to her, he could make everything right. He could conjure her finally, safe and well.

Never knowing that I hadn't been erased. I was just upstairs. My feet directly above his head, gliding over the floorboards, my heart dropped into my bowels, as I pressed my face against the door.

Mrs Leech was adamant: the lady in room 206, Mrs Genevieve O'Dea, was not the missing novelist.

334

'Why, Sam,' she said to Lippincott, 'Mrs O'Dea has been with us more than a week. I know her face perfectly well. She's a smaller lady. Younger. Dark hair.'

'Hard to determine hair colour by a photograph,' Lippincott told her. 'I've seen photographs of my own mother I'd swear weren't her. Devilish art form, if you ask me.'

'Well, I know my own mother in photographs. And I know Mrs O'Dea and this isn't her.'

Mr Leech bustled into the room. He greeted his cousin with a heartily fond handshake, then squinted at the picture obligingly. 'I think this Mrs O'Dea could very well be this woman,' he announced.

'Good gracious, Simon. You've scarcely glanced at her,' said Mrs Leech. He wasn't even wearing his spectacles. She huffed off without a goodbye or backwards glance.

'I say.' Mr Leech smiled at Lippincott. 'It'll be marvellous publicity, won't it, Sam? The Bellefort Hotel splashed over every newspaper in the country. Good enough for Agatha Christie.' He'd never heard of Agatha Christie until this moment but if her name was in the papers over a few days unaccounted for, she had to be enormously famous.

Lippincott, Leech and Archie formulated a plan. They agreed Archie should not confront his wife by going to her room, or standing at the bottom of the stairs waiting for her to come down to breakfast. Instead, they situated him in the drawing room, an open newspaper obfuscating his identity, while Lippincott waited in the lobby to intercept.

'Isabelle assures me Mrs O'Dea is in her room,' Mr Leech told his cousin. 'And while she's been in and out a good bit, she usually does take a meal upon rising.'

His words had barely left his mouth when Chilton and

Agatha came down the stairs. They were engrossed in each other, heads close together. She had forgotten to wear his hat, as if she believed herself no longer visible to the outside world, but could move through it undetected, in any situation. Chilton did not have his arm around her waist, luckily, but his hand fluttered as he talked, cupping the air by her elbow in a manner that appeared intimate. Lippincott's jaw dropped. Partly at the audacity of it. Partly at the change that had come over Chilton in the mere days since last he'd seen him. He looked taller. His hair was neatly in place. And he seemed terribly light-hearted, not only for himself, but for someone who'd been investigating a missing person and a possible double murder.

But it was the woman who surprised him most. Looking younger than her photographs, and also light, happy – incandescent, even. Dressed as if she'd just walked in from ploughing a field, wholly inappropriate. He'd expected, if it were indeed her, to find a ghostly shell. The woman who stood before him – blind to surroundings apart from her companion – was quite the opposite.

'Mrs Christie,' said Lippincott. And just like that, the bubble burst.

Agatha and Chilton snapped their gazes to the foot of the stairs. Their hands came down to their sides. Lippincott was a kindly man on the whole but his tone in this moment – the four abrupt and indignant syllables, distinctly chastising with additional phrases implied. *Mrs Christie. How dare you. Mrs Christie. What on earth do you think you're doing?* A tone used freely by all kinds of men, meant to return a person to reality, meaning proper behaviour, befitting whomever it was they'd proclaimed her to be. Her imperviousness vanished. The shame whose absence she had marvelled at descended, a bucket of water, a shroud.

'Well, Mr Chilton,' Lippincott said, his voice changing entirely, aghast but with a whiff of admiration. 'I see you've found her.'

Archie, listening from behind his newspaper in the drawing room just off the main hall, could bear it no longer. He had to see if it was really her. He imagined two scenarios. One, feasting his eyes upon his wife, upon Agatha, seeing her alive and whole and well, knowing this entire nightmare had finally ended. And two, seeing a stranger, someone wholly irrelevant, this trip another dead end, a needless waste of time like dredging the Silent Pool or engaging spirit mediums, his life forevermore this circus of public scrutiny and unanswered questions.

Stepping into the front hall, he drew in his breath. There Agatha stood. Wearing trousers and a jumper. Hair grips holding back the wisps off her forehead like a girl. If he had registered Chilton and his proximity to her, he might have sprung at him. But Chilton was not the sort of man Archie registered unless he needed something. If he had walked into a room and seen Chilton close by, he might have wordlessly handed him his coat and hat.

Relief flooded Archie's body, as if it had been administered by syringe. He had pictured his wife's lifeless body in so many places: at the bottom of a lake, in a ditch, in the bonnet of some maniac's car. All the ways Agatha herself had imagined bodies ending up dead – all the ways she would imagine them ending up dead – Archie had imagined hers. And he was not an imaginative man. Now he felt too overcome to recognize the dismay on her face. It didn't occur to him that she hadn't wanted to be found. He should have realized. At one glance he should have known: he'd lost her.

'Agatha.'

'Archie.' Unnaturally loud, in case I was in the hotel. To warn me. There was no need for both of us to be caught.

Archie pointed to the door of the library. His hand trembled before him like it belonged to a hundred-year-old man. That's what these eleven days had done to him, how much they'd aged him. But there were things to be said in private that might restore him yet.

Agatha stood frozen, like a misbehaved schoolgirl summoned by the headmaster. The newspaper headlines and all their readers. The manpower wasted on the search for her, and all the worry. Her child left at home without so much as a goodbye. Everything she'd been miraculously able to turn a blind eye to came rushing in with the force of a river when the dam is lifted.

She dared not look at Chilton. She stepped away from him, bowing her head, and descended the stairs. She walked into the library obediently and sat on the very edge of the worn sofa, as if worried she'd dirty it, suddenly aware of how she was presenting herself to the world, in these outrageously inappropriate clothes, no jewellery. Like she was an urchin caught playing in the streets.

But Archie – he did something wholly unexpected. Alone in a room with her, seeing her mortified face – dear, pinched, pretty, familiar face – he dropped to his knees. He laid his face in her lap, immune to any foreign smells, wrapping his arms around her.

'A.C.,' he said, his voice as close to weeping as she'd ever heard it. 'You're alive. Are you all right?'

'I am.' Her voice sounded frightfully weak. She knew she was supposed to say it back, A.C., but she couldn't bring herself to do so.

He grasped at her hand and kissed the bare spot where her wedding ring should have been, then pulled the sacred jewellery out of his pocket and slid it back on her finger. Forgiving her for running off and creating all this worry (forgiveness from her for everything he'd done apparently a foregone conclusion).

'Where were you?' Archie said, as if the question had been plaguing him so it needed to be asked, despite her just being found in the place she'd presumably been. 'Where did you go? What did you do?'

The first thing she thought to say was, *Here. I came here.*

But that didn't feel true. So she said the next thing she could think, that somehow felt less like a lie, because everything had become so strange and confusing. And, after all, she was not the only party with a story at stake. She had already decided to protect me and from that she would never waver for an instant.

'I can't remember,' she said. And so it would stand for the rest of her life.

The Disappearance

Day of Discovery
Tuesday, 14 December 1926

Upstairs, I PACKED as quickly as I could and dragged my suitcase across the hall to Cornelia Armstrong's room. You'd think with two unexplained deaths she might have locked her door but the same determined, trusting spirit that made her remain at the hotel and travel alone let her leave it open. When I walked in she was sitting at her vanity brushing out her hair. She turned towards me with a start. I hadn't knocked. I held my finger to my lips.

'Please,' I said, 'may I leave this suitcase with you? And will you promise not to tell anyone that it's here, or that I was here?'

Miss Armstrong paused for a moment, then stood, took my suitcase and slid it under her bed. 'I'll never say a word.'

'Dear brave girl.' I crossed my hands over my heart. 'If I never come back for it, everything inside is yours.'

'Don't be silly. Of course you'll come back.' At the same time she nodded. Not long afterwards I would catch news of her quite by chance, in an item in the *Daily Mirror*. Mere months after our time in Harrogate, Miss Armstrong took a trip to explore the ruins of the Memorial Theatre in Stratford upon Avon, which had recently burned to the ground. While marching directly into the rubble, she caught the eye of a fellow adventurer, a disobedient and exceptionally handsome young earl. They married within a fortnight and she moved with him to his estate in Derbyshire, the star-crossed romance and happy ending for which she'd longed. As I never was able to return for my belongings, I like to think she was wearing my cashmere cardigan and faux pearls when they met.

For now I clasped her hand to bid her goodbye then crept to the top of the stairs in my stockinged feet, carrying my shoes. When I peered down, I saw Archie follow his wife into the library. Once inside, Agatha might tell Archie how I'd targeted him, seduced him, for the sole reason that I believed their daughter to be mine. That I had, during this time apart, been locked in a romantic and carnal embrace the likes of which he and I had never approached. That I'd known nearly all along where his wife was and hadn't told him. That I'd committed one murder and abetted another. Which of these actions, I wondered, would he find most egregious?

And why should I ever worry for a moment about what *he* would forgive? When Archie left Sunday's Corner, driving away with that bundled baby he'd bought and paid for, taking her home like a diamond to bestow upon his wife. Did he ever for one second give a single thought to that child's mother?

I had to take this chance. I flew past poor, stunned Chilton, and the gaping Leeches, and the consternated Mr Lippincott, through the hotel door. Once outside I put on my shoes and slid behind the wheel of Chilton's borrowed police car. Whatever his next destination he would have to go on foot. I drove clumsily, determined to arrive back at the manor before time returned with its brutal roar.

Luckily, Simon Leech pulled Lippincott into the drawing room before the police chief could give Chilton the lambasting that was clearly brewing. Chilton seized upon the opportunity.

'Mrs Leech,' he said, as the proprietress marched from the dining room to the front desk, 'may I have a word?'

The mind is a remarkable thing, its exterior and interior layers. The way Chilton was able to conduct himself, speaking words he hardly heard, while his mind could only concentrate on the horror of it – that this husband, who oozed arrogance like a honeycomb oozed honey, would abscond with Agatha.

'You must help me,' he said to Mrs Leech. 'At least by withholding contradiction. Listen. Agatha Christie has been here at the Bellefort all this while, registered under the name Mrs Genevieve O'Dea. She has been taking curing baths and massages and keeping to herself.'

'Absolutely not. As a point of honour, Mr Chilton, I never lie.' Mrs Leech folded her arms, her voice sounding all the more musical. The words comforted Chilton. Anyone who says *I never lie* has by that very statement told at least one.

'Have I had a chance to tell you?' Chilton said. 'I've concluded my investigation. Of the Marston incident. And I'm determined there's no murderer at large.'

Leech and Lippincott emerged from the drawing room in time to hear this pronouncement. Mrs Leech blinked slowly, absorbing whether a bargain was being offered.

'No need for word to get out,' he went on, confirming her suspicions. 'As there's no danger to the public and never has been. Mrs Marston killed her husband and then herself.'

'There.' Mr Leech clapped, with an expression that couldn't have been jollier. 'Just as Sam thought all along, eh? We'll keep that unpleasantness nice and quiet. And the Christie woman stopping here, we'll keep nice and loud. Business will be booming, Isabelle, just you wait.'

Mrs Leech let out a stream of breath. As her husband turned to say something to his cousin, Chilton whispered, 'It will help Miss O'Dea and her young man a great deal.'

Finally, Mrs Leech nodded, acquiescing. She preferred the idea of lying to help Nan to lying to save her hotel's reputation. 'I knew she was a Miss and not a Mrs,' she whispered back. 'I have a sixth sense for that sort of thing. I do hope she'll marry that sad, handsome fellow. I love a happy ending, Mr Chilton.'

'So do we all,' Chilton said. 'So do we all.'

The library door opened, and Archie and Agatha emerged. Chilton had never wanted anything so badly as to catch her eye in that moment, but she kept her gaze steadily to the floor, like a child who'd been properly chastised.

'Mrs Christie,' Chilton said, trying to regulate his voice into an official capacity. 'Perhaps you'd better return to your room, so we can conduct an interview.'

'She'll do no such thing,' Archie said. 'This case is solved. There's been no crime. Only a misunderstanding. There's no need for any more police, we've had quite enough of that to last our lifetime.'

Chilton wondered if he himself had ever spoken with such certainty. It pained him to note that when Archie turned to his wife he spoke much more softly.

'Agatha, darling. Go collect your things. We need to be on our way before the newspapers get wind of your discovery. I'm afraid you'll have rather a to-doing with them in the next weeks.'

Still without a look at Chilton, Agatha climbed the stairs to my room. Chilton took a step, as if to follow her, but Lippincott caught him by the sleeve.

Upstairs in my hotel room, Agatha looked around, as if the place where our identities overlapped could betray anything about me, or herself, that she didn't already know. Her eyes landed on a flash of lilac, a shawl thrown across the chair by the table. She picked it up sat down. The paper and pen I'd bought sat on the desk, unused. Agatha took up both, printing words so that her hand would not be recognizable, then folded the piece of paper in half and wrote 'Inspector Chilton' in large block letters. She didn't worry someone else might find and read it. She knew he'd be here searching for clues the moment she left the hotel.

Agatha wrapped my shawl around her shoulders, as if it could transform her mannish outfit into something more respectable. She glided out of the room and down the stairs to her husband, who stood waiting for her, his face open and relieved all over again, every bit of love and hope she'd longed to see when once it had gone missing.

'Where are your things?' Archie asked, a tremor of fear in his voice, as if worried she'd decided to stay.

'There's nothing I need here.'

She walked past him, out of the hotel, into the waiting car, my new shawl pulled tightly around her. On the drive back to Sunningdale, Archie plied her with all the questions that had befuddled him to the point of madness.

'Why did you abandon your car so precipitously?'

'How did you manage to get to Yorkshire?'

'Why are you dressed like that?'

'Didn't you see the papers? Didn't you know how many

people were looking for you? I can't believe you would stay away if you knew about all that fuss.'

She didn't answer, but rolled down the window a touch, needing the cold air to revive her. Archie shivered. Two weeks prior she would have closed the window hastily. Now she decided he'd have to endure it. She remembered her pearl ring and necklace, left behind at the manor house. They would do nicely, to pay for her time there, and all the provisions they'd stolen. Already she was returning to lawful ways of thinking.

'Did you know, A.C.?' Archie pressed. 'How many people were looking for you?'

'I don't remember,' she said, watching the landscape roll by through the window. Again and again, when pressed for an explanation, that's what she said. *I don't remember.* Because to say anything remotely resembling the truth would not only damn me, but possibly land her where, until recently, she'd wanted so badly to be: with Archie, forever.

When they arrived home in Sunningdale to face the press, Archie – whose job it was to shield his wife and who had so little imagination of his own – told them the answer she'd given him.

She doesn't remember.

'The next year in my life is one I hate recalling,' she wrote in her autobiography.

Years later, reading that sentence, I found myself smiling, as I often did when I saw little bits of our time out of time in her book. She scattered pieces of it, little remembrances, I never knew where or when they'd show up.

'Must you read every one?' Archie would ask, when I brought her newest novel to bed.

'I'm sorry,' I always answered, 'they're just so diverting.'

Agatha may have hated recalling some of that year. But not all of it. Certainly, not all of it.

Chilton watched Archie drive away with Agatha, then went back inside the hotel. He was aware of eyes upon him. The Leeches and Lippincott. He knew it should be an effort to remain composed. But it wasn't. He didn't feel numb. He only felt the absence of feeling. Which, strangely, gave him hope.

'Chilton,' Lippincott said, sterner than he cared to be with his dear friend. 'I believe you have some explaining to do.'

'I was tasked with finding Agatha Christie,' Chilton said. 'And so I have.'

Before Lippincott could answer Chilton turned and walked up the steps, taking them two at a time. Miss O'Dea's door had been left ajar. He pushed and it swung inward with a sad creak. No doubt Leech would oil the hinge before the next guest arrived. He might already have been envisioning a plaque for the door, commemorating the author's stay.

There on the desk, a folded piece of notepaper, Chilton's name written across it in plain letters. He walked over and touched it. Brought it to his nose. If she had been living, these past ten days, in her own world, it would have smelled of Yardley Old English Lavender. But instead, from the brief interaction she'd had with the paper, the side of her wrist resting as she wrote, it smelled of woodsmoke and pine. The barest bit of sweat. Even a little like himself. He opened the paper carefully. He thought it might say, *I'm sorry*, or *I love you*. He most hoped it would contain instructions as to where they should meet, what their next course of action should be, how they would manage to be together.

Please see to my typewriter and most importantly my papers, her note read. *I must have my work returned discreetly and as soon as possible.*

He turned it over once, then twice. But that was all she'd written.

As for me:

When I was a girl, I fell in love with the sea. I fell in love with impossible green, and the long, cheeping syllables of sky-larks, and kind, gentle people. 'It's like a country full of Father Christmases,' I told Da, the first summer I returned from Ireland, and he laughed and said, 'You make me wonder why I ever left.' Neither of us could know what the future held for us, back when I loved him without reservation, so we hugged in solidarity.

When I was a girl, I fell in love with sheep roaming emerald hillsides and the dogs that chased them. Swooping gulls and plovers. The clattering of hooves and the dampness in the air, salty seafoam spraying the land. Seals lolling on rocks. The lilting sound of the brogue my mother teased me for acquiring, whenever I returned to London.

And I fell in love with a boy. The years took away my love for all but the last. Never an accomplice but my fellow victim, the only one on earth who could comprehend the barest thread of what I'd lost. And I knew if I saw him even one more time, my resolve would waver. Finbarr had never seen Genevieve, or held her. He'd never learned she existed until after she was already gone. And so he might persist in his attempts to lure me away, and if I saw him even one more time, I might very well succumb.

I thought of Cornelia Armstrong's Yue Lao. The invisible

thread. But not the one between Finbarr and me. The one that connected me, still and always, to Genevieve. I could feel it like a living, tactile object, stretching out from my heart to hers. Taking me not to the Timeless Manor, but to the train station. Chilton had agreed not to prosecute me for murder. I felt safe in assuming he'd overlook auto theft as well. After all, anything I could do to win Archie back was to his benefit.

If Agatha and Archie reunited, I'd never again have access to Teddy. I needed to see her at least one more time. I needed to tell her if she ever found herself in trouble, she could find me, and I would take care of her. Whatever it took. I don't know why I believed that would help. My mother had made me the same offer.

I love you. I sent the message telepathically, which was not something I believed was possible. But still I hoped and prayed Finbarr – however abandoned – would hear it and understand. Perhaps there was a part of me that hoped I'd return to London to find myself shut out of the Christies' world. The failure of the plan I'd worked on single-mindedly for three years was the only chance for Finbarr and me to be together. If I had to accept its failure, then so be it. But I would never be the one to let it go.

Meanwhile, Chilton had to go on foot to the manor house – no longer timeless – to collect what Agatha had asked of him. Her typewriter, and everything she'd written in the midst of this adventure. She would never think much, in later years, of the work she did while she was away. A short story or two, and the beginnings of her novel *The Mystery of the Blue Train*. She always said it was the least favourite of all her books. But she published it just the same. She published everything she wrote – even the short story 'The Edge', which ended with my doppelganger dead at the bottom of a mountain. It appeared the following year in *Pearson's Magazine*, with the ending changed so that my character was not pushed, but leaped.

Chilton had no plans to transport Agatha's typewriter and work to Sunningdale. He would take it with him back to Brixham, so that she'd have to find him there.

'But where's Nan?' Finbarr asked, when Chilton told him Agatha had been discovered.

Chilton placed a sympathetic hand on his shoulder. He had already given me the gift of freedom. He did not have the remaining generosity to wish for Finbarr's romance resolved in favour of his own.

'I'm sorry,' Chilton said. 'If Nan's not back by nightfall, I don't expect she ever will be.'

'She'll be back,' Finbarr said, but he didn't sound sure. As if to confirm this, he said, 'If you see her, tell her I'll be waiting in Ballycotton, ready to go anywhere in the world she likes. She can find me there when she comes to her senses.'

But alas. I never did.

A New Year

1928

Y OU DON'T NEED to guess. You already know. Agatha and Archie's reunion did not last. The urgency to continue her marriage had left Agatha. Instead, she mooned about Styles mourning the loss of the Timeless Manor. All I had to do was reappear before Archie – smiling and smiling. Agatha left, this time for good, taking Teddy with her.

But eventually she sent Teddy back to Styles. By then Archie and I were married – a diamond ring and wedding band replacing Finbarr's Claddagh. Teddy would stay with us a full year while Agatha went off on her own, adventuring, the first of many journeys she'd take aboard the Orient Express.

Honoria brought the child to us from London. I had planned to be downstairs with Archie to greet Teddy on her arrival. But when the car pulled into the drive, I found myself overcome with emotion I didn't want my husband to witness. I'd seen Teddy several times since returning to Archie but this would be our first extended stretch, together in a home we shared, with myself her official stepmother.

'Are you quite all right?' Archie asked, placing a hand at my waist. He had learned a bit about being solicitous since his first marriage.

'Yes, I'm fine. Just the tiniest bit light-headed. I believe I'll go upstairs and rest.'

As I crested the stairs I heard them – Honoria and Teddy, one dark and stern voice, one small and light. I walked through the hall of what was now my own home and went into the nursery, nobody here anymore to scold me for intruding. Honoria would be heading back to London. 'I'm happy to take care of her myself,' I'd said to Archie, when he asked me how we'd manage. 'In fact, I'd like to.'

And I would take care of her myself, many times, in the years that followed. I would rush to her when she woke up crying from a terrible dream. I would hold her hand, my arm round her shoulders, when the doctor put stitches in her wounded knee. When she married during the Second World War, a small and hasty ceremony without even Archie in attendance, Agatha made sure to send a telegram so that I could be there, too.

There on the windowsill stood the dog Finbarr had carved for her. Sonny. I picked it up. I could hear Teddy walking quickly and purposefully down the hall. Whoever coined the phrase 'the patter of little feet' might be the most brilliant person in history. How the sound filled the house, the music of a child living inside it. I drew in a breath, determined that my eyes would not be full of tears when I turned towards her.

'Nan,' Teddy said, coming through the door of the nursery to find me with the whittled dog still in my hands. 'I was looking for you.'

I returned Sonny to the windowsill and kneeled, putting one hand on either side of Teddy's face, bright blue eyes staring back at me. Then I gathered her up in my arms, almost believing her hair – grown darker since I'd seen her last – smelled of the Irish Sea.

'I was looking for you, too.'

Finbarr returned to Ballycotton, where he received word of my marriage to Archie. I sent him a letter with the news, along with a lock of Teddy's hair. In a few years he would marry an Irish girl. It pained me to think of it and at the same time, how I did wish him happiness. How I loved him enough to wish him all the dogs, all the books, all the everything, we had planned for ourselves. He fathered three sons, and I can imagine how much he loved and enjoyed them before he died young, from a slow-burning cancer in his lungs, one last gift from the mustard gas.

The rage that lingers, when one thinks of war.

But forget all that. As readers, our minds do reach towards the longed-for conclusions, despite what we know to be true. Pretend there is no Second World War come to bombard England again, what no one should have to endure once in a lifetime, let alone twice. This story belongs to me. I hold no allegiance to history, which has never done me a single favour. Still, I can't end my own story with Finbarr, even in my imagination, because any ending with him is an ending away from our child.

But Agatha's story – I can end that however I like.

Let's pause another moment and go back in time. One month after leaving the Bellefort Hotel with her husband and returning to Styles, Agatha charged Honoria with packing a bag for Teddy. After placing a letter to Archie on the table in the front hall, she went through the morning's post and found a small package sent by, of all people, Sir Arthur Conan Doyle. She opened it to find a pair of lovely leather gloves that she'd never seen before in her life, which made his note, *So glad to hear you are safely at home. Allow me to return these to their rightful owner,* all the more perplexing. Still, she couldn't refuse a gift from him of all people, and it was chilly out, so she pulled them onto her hands.

Before she left, she made sure to gather the small staff at Styles and announced to them clearly: 'I'm going to Ashfield. I'm taking Teddy with me. If anybody doubts my whereabouts, please send them round to Torquay. If I'm not at the house, I'll be walking by the shore.'

Agatha loaded Teddy and her dog into her dear old Morris Cowley and off she drove, passing all chalk pits and bodies of water without incident. The Silent Pool shimmered, reflecting the cold blue sky as if nobody had ever been pulled, lifeless, from its silty depths. She drove past the length of stream where Annabelle Oliver had been found and pressed a hand to her chest, a kind of salute, a sad but grateful thanks.

Chilton had a place of his own by then, in Brixham, close enough to his mother's house for him to be able to check in on her daily. A cottage by the sea, they could be let for a song in those days. Although he'd quite given up on seeing Agatha again, he knew the moment he heard it, the knock on the door was hers. He opened the door to find her standing there in the chilly dusk, wearing a skirt and jumper under a fur coat, her hair a beautiful mess, her smile wide and liberated. Holding on to Teddy, who had fallen asleep in the car, the little girl's cheek flattened against Agatha's shoulder.

'I saved your work,' Chilton said. 'It's all here.'

'Thank you.'

He stepped aside so she could enter, then closed the door quietly behind her. A little dog wagged by her feet, regarding Chilton as if wanting to be properly introduced.

'Here,' Chilton said, gesturing with his good hand. Agatha followed him to the spare bedroom, and stood quietly while he hurried to put sheets on the narrow bed. Then she laid Teddy down – deaf to the world as only sleeping children can be – and pulled the quilt up to her chin. Kissed her forehead.

'She's a lovely little girl, isn't she?' Chilton said.

'Yes, she certainly is.'

The dog hopped onto the bed and curled up beside the child. Chilton and Agatha watched Teddy sleep a while, simple rise and fall of her chest. A child's breath has a different quality to an adult's. Deeper and more precious. They shut her door tightly and went together into the kitchen. The cottage was small and cosy, ceilings nestling close above their heads. 'Cup of tea?'

'No,' she said. 'No, thank you.'

And here came the embrace. It lasted a long while, Chilton feeling so happy, so grateful to be alive, he scarcely recognized himself. Oh, while we're at it, let's give him back the use of his left arm. It rose as if by magic, wrapping around her strongly enough to communicate that he had no interest in ever letting her go.

'It's a sweet cottage,' Agatha said, somewhere past midnight, the two of them tangled companionably in his bed. 'Wonderfully close to Ashfield. Teddy and I will settle there in the morning.'

'Yes,' he said. 'You want to be sure and be there when they come looking for you.'

The two of them laughed and laughed. The happiness

swirled through the small house. Teddy, in the other room, smiled in her sleep.

'You don't like love stories,' Chilton reminded her.

'Not as a rule. But I like this one.'

A mystery should end with a killer revealed, and so it has. A quest should end with a treasure restored. And so it has. A tragic love story must end with its lovers dead or parted. But a romance, that should end with lovers reunited.

Beyond the confines of these pages, life will go tumbling forward. But this is my story. I can make anything happen, not beholden to a future that has by now become the past. I can leave you with a single image, and we can pretend it lasts forever.

So, for this part of our story, at least, let's stop here. With Chilton and Agatha, walking together on the beach at Torquay. Her little dog hopping from one rock to another. Agatha's arm through Chilton's. Both of them smiling under a bright blue sky. Dwelling in the realms of day. Only for a time, like everything. No need to question or go forward, past this moment.

Indulge yourself instead and close this book on a happy ending.

Acknowledgements

I<small>N</small> F<small>EBRUARY</small> <small>OF</small> 2015, my agent, Peter Steinberg, sent me an email whose subject line read, 'What about writing a novel about this?' Attached was an article from *The Lineup* by Matthew Thompson: 'Lady Vanishes: The Mysterious Agatha Christie Disappearance.' Five years and much gentle encouragement followed as I worked on this book. I'm grateful every day for Peter's championship and his friendship.

Nan's theories of lucid living couldn't have conjured a more perfect editor for this project than Jennifer Enderlin, who knows how to ask all the right questions. I am immeasurably grateful for her brilliant insights, her unfailing catches, her warmth, her support and her kindness.

I'm thankful to everyone at St Martin's, including but not limited to Lisa Senz (author of the best email I've ever read), Sallie Lotz and Steven Boldt.

Thanks also to Yona Levin, Maria Rejt, Alice Gray, Marian Reid, Samantha Fletcher and Sabine Schultz. And to everyone at The Gotham Group, especially Rich Green, who is such a bright light I wish I could bring him with me everywhere I go.

My dear old pal Scott Rittinger knows everything about antique cars and is quick to answer out-of-the-blue texts. Celia

ACKNOWLEDGEMENTS

Brooks shared her knowledge of London geography. Thanks to my friends, colleagues and students in the Creative Writing Department at the University of North Carolina Wilmington, especially Philip Gerard, who advocated for time I needed away from the classroom, and Rebecca Lee, who's the most fun to share books with. My brother, Alex, helped with proofreading galleys. My parents have forever provided unfailing love and support. Melody Moezzi dreamed a crucial, prophetic dream; telling her and Matthew Lenard that it came true was one of my all-time favourite nights.

Danae Woodward is always my first and best reader.

This story is an imaginative history of sorts; I'm indebted to many books, documentaries, articles and papers for grounding it in actual events. Even if *The Christie Affair* had never come to fruition, I would be enormously glad to have read *The Adoption Machine* by Paul Jude Redmond. It's a beautifully researched, gorgeously written, hauntingly personal book and I encourage anyone moved by Nan's story to read it. Other books that were invaluable to me include: *The Light in the Window* by June Goulding; *Ireland's Magdalene Laundries and the Nation's Architecture of Containment* by James M. Smith (Dr Smith was generous with responses to my questions, recommended June Goulding's memoir and put me in touch with his equally generous colleague Claire McGettrick); *The Great Influenza* by John M. Barry; *Agatha Christie and the Eleven Missing Days* by Jared Cade; *An Autobiography* by Dame Agatha Christie herself (if you've never read it, you have a great treat awaiting you); and, of course, my stack of Christie's detective novels, in particular *Death on the Nile*, *Murder on the Orient Express*, *And Then There Were None*, *The ABC Murders*, *Death in the Clouds*, *Peril at End House*, *Crooked House* and *Endless Night*, as well as her short story 'The

ACKNOWLEDGEMENTS

Edge'. For various period details and anecdotes I was helped by too many articles and academic papers to list, chief among them: 'When the World's Most Famous Mystery Writer Vanished' by Tina Jordan (*New York Times*); 'The Mysterious Disappearance of Agatha Christie' by Giles Milton (*HistoryExtra.com*); 'Unmarried Mothers in Ireland, 1880–1973' by Maria Luddy; 'Unmarried Mothers and Their Children: Gathering the Data' by Dr Maeve O'Rourke, Claire McGettrick, Rod Baker and Raymond Hill; and the aforementioned 'The Lady Vanishes' by Matthew Thompson (*The Lineup*).

The stories from Peter Jackson's documentary *They Shall Not Grow Old* helped me imagine Finbarr and Chilton. And I will forever stand in awe of the brave women in Steve Humphries' arresting documentary *Sex in a Cold Climate*. My thanks, love and admiration to Brigid Young, Phyllis Valentine, Martha Cooney and especially Christina Mulcahy.

And thanks most of all to David and Hadley. I would spend a hundred years looking, and go everywhere in the world, to find you.